C000292244

To

Val and Michael,

with the author's best wishes.

Les Retallick

LESLIE RETALLICK WRITES

I was born in Hornchurch, Essex, one of the London suburbs that had spread out like a rash from the capital. When I was six my family moved to Rugby in Warwickshire, where I was educated. During my school days I developed a total lack of interest in all forms of sport through spending hours in the freezing cold on the school playing fields, but I did develop a passion for history by taking part in an archaeological excavation at the nearby Roman site of Tripontium. Our family moved again when I was seventeen to Torquay, where my parents bought a corner shop. Several years later, having tired of delivering boxes of groceries to the local hotels, I took a summer seasonal job at Torre Abbey, an historic house and art gallery in Torquay, which led to a full-time senior post during a thirty-six-year association with that building. There I expanded my interest in local history and have had a number of books and articles published on that subject. Later I became a full-time carer for my by then elderly and very frail parents until they both passed away, after which I used the caring skills I had acquired in those five years to become a primary carer for a seriously disabled local lady, to whom this book is dedicated. I am an avid photographer, a keen railway modeller, and passionate about local history, my knowledge of which underpins this novel.

OTHER BOOKS BY LESLIE RETALLICK

Torquay in Old Picture Postcards (Baarn: European Library, 1982)
Torre Abbey – An Illustrated Guide (Torquay: Torbay Council, 1983)
Torre Abbey – A Souvenir Guide (Torquay: Torbay Council, 1989)
Pictorial Torquay (Exeter: Obelisk Publications, 1994)
Torquay of Yesteryear (Exeter: Obelisk Publications, 2002)
Torquay through Time (Stroud: Amberley Publishing, 2009)
Torquay Revealed (Stroud: Amberley Publishing, 2013)

OTHER WORKS OF FICTION FROM COLENSO BOOKS

The life and death of Hangman Thomas (2016),
Corfiot tales (2017), *What price honour? – The convict* (2020),
all by Konstantinos Theotokis, translated from Greek by J. M. Q. Davies

The placebo by Lawrence Durrell (2018, in conjunction
with The Durrell Library of Corfu)

This spinning world: 43 stories from far and wide by Jim Potts (2019)

Stay with me by Louisa AdjoaParker (2020, short stories)

Kalamas and Acheron: Rivers of Hades by Christophoros Milionis (2021,
short stories), translated from the Greek by Marjorie Chambers

Life Tern by Mark Allen (2021, a novel)

Before The Fire

A NOVEL

BY

LESLIE RETALLICK

COLENSO BOOKS
2021

First published 30 November 2021
by
Colenso Books
68 Palatine Road, London N16 8ST, UK
colensobooks@gmail.com

ISBN 978-1-912788-18-7

The image on the front cover and the images on pages 44, 362 and 376
were created by the author; those on pages ix, x, 80, 266 (upper),
416, 445 and 446 (both) are from photographs taken by the author.

The images on pages 31, 118, 161, 183, 265, 333 and 382
are from unattributed items on the Internet
presumed to be in the public domain.

The remaining twenty-five images are all from the author's collection
of old photographs and postcards of Torquay.

CONTENTS

Acknowledgements   vii

Dedication   ix

Chapter

1	A fire in the night	1
2	Echoes from the past	17
3	Two-way mirror	33
4	Belmont	45
5	Burning proof	55
6	The past can't be changed	69
7	The boy with the notebook	81
8	Questions without answers	91
9	Meeting Daniel	107
10	The music room	119
11	A night vigil	143
12	A secret in the vault	151
13	Nightmares and choices	163
14	Among the primroses	185
15	A day at the beach	209
16	Answers from an unlikely source	227
17	Attempting a warning	243
18	Proof in the vault	251
19	Taking photographs	267
20	Moving in	275
21	A violent encounter	289
22	Maria and Connor	309
23	To savour every last moment	321
24	Asking for help	333
25	Accepting a dare	349
26	Precautions	363
27	Faces at the window	377
28	Forty-five minutes earlier	383
29	Partings	401
30	Picking up the pieces	417
31	Past and present	425

Afterword   447

ACKNOWLEDGEMENTS

To the staff at Torquay Reference Library, for their
patience and unfailing help

To Jane Palmer, for proof reading, suggestions on
improving the plot and for a totally ruthless
eradication of unnecessary commas

To the late Wendy Smith, for guidance on etiquette
and manners in the late nineteenth century

To Diana Manessis, for reading the original
manuscript, passing it around her reading club in
Corfu, and recommending it to Anthony Hirst

To Anthony Hirst of Colenso Books, for having the
faith to publish this book

Leslie Retallick
Torquay
December 2020

Colenso Books is grateful to Diana Manessis
for her generous contribution towards the initial
production costs of this book.

For my dearest Sarah, with all my love
and in gratitude for an amazing journey shared
and never to be forgotten

SARAH MARIE KNIGHT

1942–2020

When you live in the hearts of those you love,
remember then, you never die.

(Gitanjali Ghei, 'Farewell my friends')

Matt's house stood in the same spot as Belmont . . . the view was naturally familiar to him, but he hadn't realised that, where there was a plain sloping lawn in his own time, there had once been a series of terraces, with fountains, pools and intricately designed flower beds . . . The formal gardens also extended much further down the hillside, running right down to where they bordered the narrow lane at the bottom of the hill. Beyond lay the valley of the Aller Brook. There were a lot more trees in 1898 than in his own day, but the thing that really startled him about the view was the clarity. He could see the tower of Coffinswell Church clearly in the distance, and the high tors of Dartmoor on the horizon . . .

CHAPTER ONE

A fire in the night

Barney saved them. Not consciously of course, for that would have required a certain amount of logical thought, and the collie was notoriously lacking in that department. Even six-year-old Ben, always his most loyal supporter, would have been forced to agree that the dog was a disgrace to his breed, which was, on the whole, renowned for its intelligence. Ben had once heard his mother mention that it was probably a foggy night when Barney was conceived, something that she felt might explain his somewhat erratic behaviour. Ben had no idea what she was talking about, but then he often felt the same about all the members of his family. That night, however, Barney transcended his possibly muddled background and became a hero, even though no one realised it at first, as he let out a series of frenzied barks in the early hours of the morning. Ben tried his best to get him to calm down as shouts and yells from the rest of the family for the dog to put the proverbial sock in it (or, in Steve's case, something very much worse) went unheeded. Eventually Ben had left the warmth of his bed and sleepily tottered to the bedroom door, where the collie was frantically clawing at the paintwork. Opening the door, he wondered for a moment why he couldn't see very much. Then he coughed as smoke billowed in his direction. His eyes opened wide in fear and he let out a high-pitched cry.

Marion was out of bed in seconds. By the time she'd reached the bedroom door the smoke was getting thicker, a menacing glow could be seen hovering around the edges of the airing cupboard door along the corridor, and an acrid smell of burning material hung in the air. Raising four children, or five if you counted Steve as a child, which she invariably did with all men, had taught her not to panic when crisis threatened; and after taking a few seconds to get her fears under control, she was ready to confront this latest

test of her strength. An urgent shout of "Steve, we've got a fire, move yourself" was all she allowed herself before running to get the children to safety. The youngest first, sweeping two-year-old Kerry into her arms, then ushering the terrified Ben ahead of her to the next room, ignoring his screams of fright. By now the fire could be seen as an ominous red pulse at the heart of the smoke, which had thickened alarmingly. Ten-year-old Paula was already at her bedroom door, her scared face a pale oval in the smoke-filled corridor.

"Downstairs, now!" Marion ordered.

Matt last, but the sixteen-year-old was already busy, grabbing Barney's collar and lead in one hand and slamming the bedroom doors shut with the other. Pausing only long enough to put the collar on the still barking collie, he hauled the dog downstairs, out of the house and into the frosty chill of an early April night. Smoke was rapidly filling the whole house and the family emerged coughing and spluttering.

"Matt's called 999 on his mobile," Marion shouted to her husband, struggling to make herself heard above Barney's barking. "The fire brigade are on their way."

"I hope to God they're quick, it's spreading so fast."

A loud explosion reinforced his fears as one of the first-floor corridor windows blew out with the heat, showering the lawn with broken glass. Smoke and flames belched from the hole, as the greedy fire sucked in great gusts of fresh air. Paula screamed and Ben burst into tears.

"Steve, hold Kerry for me, will you?" Marion yelled above the roar of the flames. "I've only got one pair of hands and I can't see to all the kids!"

"We need to do something," he shouted back, taking the struggling infant from her. "We can't just stand here and watch the place burn!"

Without warning, he dumped a startled Kerry on the grass and ran around the side of the house. He was back in a few seconds with a fire extinguisher.

"It's from the garage; I'm going to see what I can do."

With that, Steve was gone into the cloud of poisonous smoke billowing from the open front door. Marion tried to shout at him to stop, but it was too late. The sound died in her throat as the front door closed behind him. Instead, she bent and picked up Kerry, who until then had been too startled at being unceremoniously dumped on the lawn to complain. The infant was rapidly recovering her senses and her voice, and several loud wails cut through the night. As she tried to comfort the frightened child, Marion prayed harder than she could ever remember doing before. Seconds later, her husband re-appeared at the front door, coughing, spluttering and staggering blindly across the gravel. He collapsed to his knees, loud racking coughs shaking his body. She ran to him, Kerry bouncing in her arms.

"I'm OK," Steve gasped, as he sensed Marion looming over him. "Just the smoke got to me a bit. Might have held the fire up for a few minutes. Don't know. Couldn't see much in there."

He coughed again and black-flecked phlegm dribbled down his chin.

"You stupid great fool, what on earth possessed you?" she almost screamed at him. Before she could remonstrate any further, two fire engines arrived in a flurry of sirens and flashing lights. By then the fire had spread alarmingly. Flames were still roaring from the blown-out window and could now be seen licking at the skylight in the attic. After quickly checking that everyone was out of the house the firemen struggled into the smoke-filled and burning building, their hoses writhing behind them like fat grey pythons. Marion felt that the scene in front of her resembled someone's deranged idea of hell. The smoke and the flames were bad enough, but the noise that the fire was now generating was frankly terrifying, as if a hundred of the banshees her Irish grandmother had told her about as a child had suddenly come to haunt her in a waking nightmare. She felt hysteria rising within her but forced it down again. No matter their house was in danger of burning to the ground, or that her husband was on his knees in front of her, coughing and retching up large gobbets of black filth. No matter that she and the children were outside on a cold night in only their nightwear. She had to remain calm for the children's sake. Thinking of them, she forced herself into action and looked round to see where they were. She was relieved to find that Matt had taken charge of Ben and Paula and had moved them a safe distance away from the house, to avoid the smoke now billowing across the front drive. Steve, slowly recovering from his coughing fits, was sitting on the ground beside her, his arms clasped around his knees, staring at the flames as if hypnotised.

"Steve," she shouted, trying to make herself heard above the noise of the fire, "the children have only got their night things on. We've got to get them something to wear."

There was no response.

"STEVE!"

His eyes gradually focused on her.

"Sorry," he muttered, "I was out of it for a minute."

"I said the children need clothes. They're in their night stuff and it's cold out here. Matt's only got his boxer shorts on."

"I'll get the car," he told her. "If I leave the engine running, they can get inside with the heater on. It'll be better than nothing."

"Have you got the keys?"

"No," he admitted, a look of irritation crossing his face, "they're on the bedside table."

Matt padded over to them, wincing as his bare feet found the sharp gravel that covered the front drive. He was holding his phone in his hand. Marion thought it was typical of him that the only thing he'd grabbed to save from his room was his phone. "Never mind you've only got your underwear on, save the phone," she muttered under her breath.

"Sorry?" Matt enquired. She shook her head, implying that it didn't matter. "I've called Uncle Conn," he told her. "He's on his way over. I was going to phone granddad as well, but then I thought that he and grandma would only get into a total flap, so I thought I'd better not."

In spite of his obsession with gadgets, he was, she thought to herself, always the practical one. A few minutes later Connor's elderly green Peugeot spluttered to a stop in the lane. It was over three miles from Connor's house to theirs and he told them later that he'd broken every traffic regulation in the book to get there so quickly.

"Into the car, you two," Connor told Paula and Ben, after a quick glance at the flames still belching from the first-floor window. "I've put a load of blankets in there, so cover yourselves up and keep warm."

"Here," Marion called after them, "take Kerry as well. And don't worry, everything's going to be fine."

"Is it?" Connor asked her, his eyes returning to the flames now leaping through the skylight.

"I've no idea, but we need to keep the children calm."

Matt led his younger siblings over to the car and helped them to burrow under the blankets. As an afterthought, Matt shoved the frightened collie in after them.

"Look after the dog," he told them, "I'm going to see if there's anything I can do to help."

He joined his parents as they were staring mesmerised at the fire, noting that his father was still sitting on the cold ground.

"Dad? You OK?"

"No, he isn't," Marion spluttered, with considerable asperity. "The stupid great clunkhead decided to be a hero and try to save the house with a fire extinguisher. He's been coughing his guts out ever since."

Connor hunkered down next to his brother.

"You need a doctor," he told Steve.

"No, I don't. I need a pint. Preferably three."

Connor laughed, and straightened himself up again.

"He'll live," he said to Marion, "but he should still see a doctor, just to check his lungs out."

Connor turned his attention to Matt.

"Nip to the car, will you? There's a large sports bag in the boot — can you fetch it?"

"Sure," Matt replied as he started to wince his way across the gravel.

"Hold it," Connor yelled after him. "Sorry, didn't realise you were barefoot. Stay there, I'll get it."

He was back in seconds with the bag, the contents of which he spilled onto the ground. "I've nothing very glamorous for you three to wear, but I've thrown some warm things in," he said, indicating the heap of clothing in front of them. "There's some thick sweaters, a couple of pairs of jogging bottoms and a pair of jeans that should fit Matt."

Even before he'd finished speaking Marion was rifling through the clothes and yanking on a pair of thick jogging bottoms.

"You've got great legs, you know," Connor told her, casting an appreciative glance in her direction.

In spite of herself, she burst out laughing.

"You pick the most inopportune moments to dish out the compliments," she said.

"One should never miss a chance to compliment a beautiful lady."

"Tell Steve — he never compliments me. Sometimes I think I might have married the wrong brother!"

Steve looked up from the ground.

"What on earth have you two found to laugh about?"

"Don't ask," Marion told him. "Connor's brought some things to wear, so get yourself into these," she instructed, throwing the other pair of jogging bottoms at him, while Matt hauled on the jeans and a sweater.

"No footwear. Sorry, didn't think about it," Connor explained.

"Doesn't matter," Matt told him. "The others have all got slippers on. It's only me who didn't think about them."

"I see you remembered your phone though."

"Of course — this is the latest model. Cost me a fortune!"

Connor and Marion exchanged eye-rolls. Steve struggled to his feet, his coughing fits subsiding to a few hacking coughs every couple of minutes. The four of them huddled together and watched and waited. It was all they could do.

◆

The house was quite remote, standing on the very edge of

Torquay in the Kingskerswell Road. Only a holiday park across the road kept it company and in early April very few of the chalets were let. Behind the house, the land sloped steeply down into the Daccombe valley and beyond were fields and open countryside. Nevertheless, an excited crowd had assembled in the lane, all gaping wide-eyed at the flames and the firemen rushing about. A press photographer appeared, seemingly out of nowhere, and was busily snapping away before anyone realised he was there. When Steve saw him he informed the photographer, between coughs, that if he came anywhere near a member of his family with a camera it would be used for a purpose that its makers had never imagined. The photographer took the hint and left with an "only doing my job, mate, no need to get nasty" hanging in the air after him.

Matt, who had grabbed one of the blankets from the car and draped it around him, noticed the crowd with some surprise.

"Where did all these people come from?" he asked his mother.

"No idea. And as for that photographer, well, words fail me."

"That'll be a first."

"Just because you're taller than me doesn't mean you can get lippy. Go and see if Ben and Paula need anything."

"I've just seen them. They're fine."

"Well, go and see again!"

"OK, OK, no need to get heavy."

◆

Half an hour later, the fire officer was able to tell them that the blaze was out. "You've been very lucky. Another few minutes and the fire would have spread through the whole roof and we wouldn't have been able to contain it."

"Just how bad is it?" Steve asked.

"Mainly smoke and water damage. The airing cupboard is completely burnt out, and you've got a hole in the roof above it. There are some windows gone but beyond that it's mainly muck and mess everywhere. It'll take you a while to get straight, but it could have been very much worse than it is. I gather you went back in with a fire extinguisher?"

"Yes."

"Not something we'd recommend, but I admit it probably held the fire back just long enough for us to get here. That and the fact that someone had shut all the upstairs doors."

"Is it fit for us to go back in?"

"No, not at present. The fire burned through the power cables, so there's no electricity, and no heating. There's also smoke everywhere and a lot of broken glass where a couple of windows blew out in the heat. The smoke will have cleared by the morning, but there's still too much in the air to sleep safely here tonight. We'll help you make it secure for the night. Have you somewhere you can all go?"

"We've friends nearby," Marion told him. "We'll be alright."

Even as the words came out, she wondered if she was correct. They did have friends in the area but phoning them up in the middle of the night with a request for accommodation might be stretching that friendship a bit far.

Matt was ahead of her again. He walked over, pulling a confused collie with him. "Barney needed a tree," he explained, in reply to his mother's raised eyebrows. "Much longer without one and Uncle Conn's car would have stunk for a week. He's fine now. Anyway, I've phoned the Westons," he continued. "They heard the fire engines go past but didn't realise it was our house that was on fire. They've said that we can spend the night at their place."

"But we can't lumber them with all of us," Marion protested. "Their house is a lot smaller than ours. Plus there's Barney to think about."

"Try telling Mrs Weston that. She's already got the kettle on, making sandwiches and sorting out bedding. Says it reminds her of when she was in the WRVS, whatever that is. Anyway, it won't be all of us. Paula says she wants to stay with Katy, and I'll go back with Uncle Conn for the night."

"But you can't wake Katy's parents at this hour of the night."

"Paula already has. She nicked my phone when I wasn't looking. Katy's mum is on her way up to collect her. Says that

Katy's dead jealous that our house has caught fire and not theirs."

"OK, fine. But what about Connor? You can't just dump yourself on him."

"Sure I can. He won't mind. Besides, his main computer's a lot more powerful than mine and he bought me a huge screen to use with it. It's much better playing my games there than it is here."

"I give up."

Matt grinned at her, as Connor joined them.

"This pain in the neck says he's staying the rest of the night with you. Is that going to be OK?"

"Don't see why not if he wants to. The bed's already made up in the spare room. What about the rest of you? There's not a lot of room in the cottage but you're all welcome to squash in if you want."

"Thanks, but we're fine. Hannah and Eric Weston have said we can stay with them. It's only just along the road."

"If you're sure. But Matt wants to come back with me?"

"Yes. He says that your computer's better than his."

"It's nice to know I'm appreciated," Connor laughed. "Besides, he uses it far more than I do. I've no idea how most of the stuff works."

"He may not have any of his own gear left," she winced, looking up at the smoke blackened first-floor windows.

Hot tears pricked her eyes, but she blinked them away before turning back to Connor.

"I don't know how much stuff we've lost up there," she said.

"I've got thick shoes on," he replied. "I'll go and ask if I can have a look. I don't think that they'll let you go back inside with only slippers on."

A short argument convinced the fire officer that the family needed to know how bad things really were inside the house.

"It's against every regulation I can think of, but I'll get one of the lads to go with you. You'll need breathing gear and a torch and you're to do exactly as my officer tells you."

Connor followed a fireman into the gloom of the interior. The light from the torches seemed to intensify the darkness rather than illuminate it as they struggled upstairs, past the runs of hoses that were still laid out. Reaching the landing, Connor thought the damage had been understated. It was a total mess and at the end was a tangled heap of charred wood, twisted metal and burnt clothes and linen. He thought that it was lucky that Marion couldn't see it. It was going to be bad enough in daylight, but in the darkness it looked, and smelled, appalling. He opened the nearest door. The beam of light from his torch showed him that the room was intact, although a thin fog of smoke hung in the air. The same with the next two doors he tried.

The fireman put his head close to Connor's and shouted to him.

"It's lucky someone managed to shut all the doors up here, otherwise it would be a lot worse than it is. It's really only the landing and the cupboard at the end that have copped it, plus some stuff that was in the attic."

Connor nodded. "I've seen enough," he shouted back.

As he trailed downstairs after the fireman, he heard music coming from somewhere, and thought that a radio had been left on. He was about to turn back to investigate when he remembered that the power was off throughout the house, so he assumed the music must be coming from outside. The tune was nagging at him, as he felt he ought to know it. He strained to hear more, but the sound had faded before his mind could latch onto the title. By the time they'd reached the front door he'd forgotten all about it.

◆

Marion and Steve were waiting anxiously for Connor's report.

"As the officer said, it could have been a lot worse. It looks a mess at first sight, but apart from smoke, the bedrooms themselves are mainly all right."

"I want the truth, Connor," Marion said, "how bad is it really? No soft soap."

"OK. The landing's a total mess, and the airing cupboard and whatever was in it, including the central heating boiler, isn't there anymore. I think you'll need new floorboards at one end, plus some slates to repair the hole in the roof. You'll also have to wash just about everything to get rid of the muck and the smell. But that's about it."

"Honest?"

"Honest."

"Thank God for that. I think we should get the children down to the Westons as soon as possible. Katy's mother has already collected Paula. There's not much more we can do here at the moment, other than make the place secure for the night. Steve wants to hang around for a bit longer, but I want the children to get out of the cold."

"I'll run you down to the Westons, then I'll come back for Steve."

"No need to come back for me," Steve interrupted. "The fire officer says he'll drop me down there when we've finished here. If you can take Marion and the kids down, you and Matt can then go on home."

"Sure? I don't mind coming back to help."

"No, it's fine. There's not a lot more we can do tonight anyway."

"Alright. Once I've dropped everyone off, I'll carry on home. I'll make sure we're back as early as we can in the morning and I'll load the car with cleaning stuff."

"Conn?" Marion said, catching his arm.

"Yes?"

"Thanks."

"No need."

"Thanks anyway."

◆

"You alright?" Connor asked Matt as they were driving away after dropping Marion and the others at the Westons.

"I'm fine," Matt replied, clutching his blanket more tightly around him. "Apart from the smoke it doesn't seem as if there was too much damage. We'll soon get it sorted tomorrow."

"I think the words 'soon' and 'sorted' don't necessarily go

together at times like this. It'll take a long time and a lot of hard work to clean that mess up."

"I heard you telling Mum that it wasn't too bad. Were you telling porkies?"

"No, not really, but it looked worse than I said. I just didn't want your parents to be more worried than they already are. In the dark and with water dripping everywhere, it looked horrible. It's not going to look great in the morning, but at least it won't seem so bad in the daylight."

There was silence for a little while before Matt spoke again.

"Uncle Conn?"

"Yes?"

"How long have you known mum?"

"Only as long as Steve has. Why?"

"It's just something mum said the other day," Matt replied. "She said that she went out with you for a while before she started going out with dad."

"Didn't you know that?"

"No. Neither mum or dad have said anything about it before."

"Well, your dad and I have lived in this area all our lives, but your mum only moved here when she was in her late teens. She and I went out together a few times, but the first time I brought her home with me Steve was there. Your mum and Steve took one look at each other and that was that. They hit it off right from the start."

"But dad's younger than you, isn't he?"

"Only by just over a year. I'd just turned twenty-one and Steve was nineteen when we met Marion."

"But weren't you upset, having your girlfriend nicked by your kid brother?"

"Not really," Connor laughed. "It hadn't got as far as being anything serious between your mum and me. Besides, only a few months later I met Laura. Marion and Laura got on really well so the four of us used to go out together. We'd even talked about a double wedding, but it didn't quite work out. Still, it meant that I could be best man at your parents' wedding and Steve could be best man at mine and Laura's."

"I never knew that."

"What, about us being each other's best man?"

"No, I mean about the four of you going out together before you were married."

"Oh yes. And you wouldn't want to know some of the things we got up to."

"Yes, I would!"

"Well, you're not going to. Or at least not from me. Ask your mother sometime."

"Don't suppose she'll tell me either," Matt grumbled.

"Just as well. Why the questions anyway? You've never asked before."

"No real reason. It's just that I heard you telling mum that she'd got great legs, so it sort of set me thinking about things."

Before Connor could say anything sensible in reply, they'd arrived at his home, a small cottage close to Torquay seafront. Matt jumped out of the car to open the garage doors, forgetting for a moment his bare feet. He swore as they found a sharp stone on the pavement.

"You'd have been toast if your mum had heard that remark," Connor observed.

"She uses worse when she's in a temper."

After he'd parked the car, Connor let them into the cottage.

"That's new," Matt said, indicating an oil portrait of a young woman over the fireplace.

"Not really. It's been in the attic for years. I just decided that it was about time I hung it somewhere."

Matt looked at the painting closely, suddenly realising he knew who it was.

"It's a painting of Laura, isn't it? You've shown me photos of her. Where did you get it from?"

"Always had it. It was Laura's present to me the first Christmas we were married. After she died, I couldn't bear to see it, so I stuck it away. I brought it out a few weeks ago."

Matt stared at the portrait. Laura's fair hair was falling in waves down the sides of her finely chiselled features. A pair of startling blue eyes gazed serenely out at the world. This was a beautiful and confident young woman for whom life was full of promise. Matt glanced across at his uncle and saw the pain in his eyes as he looked at the portrait.

"I wish I'd known her," Matt said.

"I wish you had. She was as delighted as I was when Steve asked us to be your godparents. She was so happy at the christening, even though she was miffed that it was me you giggled at and not her. She said it was probably wind."

"Perhaps it was."

"No way! I know a giggle when I hear one."

"You loved her very much?" Matt asked, returning his gaze to the painting.

"More than my own life."

"How long did it take you to get over it?"

"I never got over it, not really."

"Never?"

"You don't stop loving someone just because they're not around anymore, Matt. It's not something that can be turned off like a tap. If you have a really bad cold or something like that, you feel really rotten, but when the cold's gone you're back to where you were before. You've got over it and everything's as it was. Losing someone isn't like that, because nothing is ever the same again, it can't be. There's this great gaping hole in your life and it can't be filled. What you do, what you *have* to do, is come to terms with it. Accept it, adjust to it, and get on with your life as best you can. When Laura became ill, she made me promise not to give up, but to carry on with my life. She said I would have to live for the two of us. For the first few months after she died, I didn't know if I could keep that promise. If we'd had children, then I'd probably have been kept busy looking after them, but as it was there was nothing. The nights were the worst. Still are for that matter. Sometimes they can seem endless, with no-one there to talk to, to share things with."

"I'm really sorry, I never realised."

Connor said nothing, but busied himself getting the spare room ready for Matt. There was something that he'd never told anyone, not Matt, not his own parents, not even Steve and Marion. A secret he'd kept buried deep inside himself for almost fifteen years. Laura had been pregnant when she died and the illness that had taken her from him had also stolen his unborn child. She'd been excited beyond measure when she found out for certain that she was pregnant and they'd made plans and even discussed names. Laura's parents were away on holiday, so they'd decided to wait until they returned a week later to break the news to family and friends.

Then the hospital had phoned. The tests that Laura had been given when she believed that she was pregnant had produced something unexpected. An "anomaly" they'd said. Could she go back for more tests? They went to the hospital the same day, and by the afternoon the "anomaly" had turned into something else, something dark and terrible. The doctors were sympathetic but could offer no comfort. The disease was widespread and beyond treatment. Connor had argued with them, they'd both argued. Laura had never felt better — she was full of life and energy. The hospital had obviously made a mistake. She couldn't possibly be ill. There were sympathetic mutterings but the doctors were adamant. The disease never showed outward signs until it was too late.

"What about the baby?" Laura had eventually asked. "Will the child inherit the condition?" Even the doctors' professional calm had wavered at that point and they'd looked at each other, none of them wanting to be the one to tell the distraught young couple the blunt fact. There wouldn't be a baby. Laura had at most two months to live and the child would not be developed enough to survive.

They'd returned home in total silence, neither knowing what to say, what to do. That night they'd clung to each other in shock, looking for comfort and finding there was none to be had. They'd both agreed that they wouldn't tell anyone that she was pregnant, so Connor had carried the knowledge imprisoned within him.

Laura had fought tooth and nail to cling onto life long enough to give their child a chance to survive. The eight weeks the doctors had given her became nine, then ten. Even at the end, when it was obvious her last minutes were ticking away, she still defied death with all her being, but in the end it was all for nothing. She had died just short of eleven weeks after they had learned of the disease. The doctors had tried to save the child, a boy, but he was too young, too weak and unformed to survive after Laura had died. Connor had never revealed the truth to anyone. He'd come close once or twice but had backed off at the last minute. He often found himself looking at Matt and wondering what his own son would have looked like had he lived.

There had been times when he'd thought about giving up and joining Laura. On the fifth anniversary of her death he'd almost done it. He'd been ferreting about at the back of a drawer looking for something and had found a handkerchief, one of Laura's. It still had a faint echo on it of the perfume that she habitually wore. A black fog of grief had descended on him and he'd stumbled blindly into the bathroom. The pills were there, the ones the doctor had given him when the nightmares had become too much for him. He'd stared at the bottle, even got as far as taking the cap off and pouring the little pink tablets into his hand. The ringing of the phone had slowly penetrated his brain. He hadn't intended to answer, but habit sent him into the bedroom and he'd picked up the receiver.

"Hi, Uncle Conn," a small, excited voice had piped up. "Guess what! I got a part in the school play. Mummy's got to make my costume 'cos I's going to be a pirate! Can you come and watch me?"

He'd said that of course he would, he wouldn't miss it for anything. The tablets had gone back in the bottle and a month later he'd tipped them down the toilet and flushed them away. Watching Matt as he'd grown from a child into a boy, and now into a young man, had given some meaning to his life and a reason to carry on.

CHAPTER TWO

Echoes from the past

Connor stuck his head round the door of the spare room the next morning to find, as he expected, that Matt was still fast asleep.

"Wassertime?" came the sleepy answer, after Connor had managed to get his nephew into a state approaching being awake.

"Just gone eight."

"Twirly," was the rather plaintive response.

"Agreed, but twirly or not, you need to get up."

"But I *never* get up before ten when I stay with you."

"You never get up before eleven when you stay with me, but that's beside the point. I promised we'd be back at yours as soon as we could, so get yourself up and sorted. Speaking of which, you're going to need clothes. The ones you had on last night stink of smoke. You'll have to borrow some more of my gear."

Connor opened a couple of drawers and started to pull items out. He threw a pair of undershorts at Matt, who was still showing reluctance to leave the warmth of his bed.

"Get those on, then come and choose what you want to wear."

Matt crawled out from under the duvet and dragged the shorts on, then tottered over to the drawers and rifled through the contents.

"You're not going to a fashion parade," Connor told him after a while, "just pick something that'll keep you warm."

"Haven't you got any decent gear? Most of your clobber looks like it's been around for years."

"Most of it has. If it hasn't got holes in it, then I keep wearing it."

"Looks like it," Matt grumbled, eventually choosing a black sweatshirt and a pair of jeans. "I'm going to have to take you clothes-shopping one day soon. Get you to buy yourself something decent."

"We'll see," Connor laughed. "Now go and grab a shower. And don't be all morning about it, we've got to get going."

◆

They arrived outside Matt's home by nine o'clock.

"Odd," Connor said as they got out of the car. "There doesn't seem to be anyone about. I thought that your parents would have been here at the crack of dawn. You know what your mum's like when something needs doing."

"Do I ever."

They walked up the drive towards the house, Connor looking around him in amazement.

"Someone's been very busy here," he observed. "The mess has all been tidied up and the window's been replaced upstairs. Your parents must have managed to get some workmen out in the night."

Finding the front door unlocked, Matt pushed it open and entered, Connor a few steps behind.

"Did you hear something?" Connor asked.

"Like what?"

"Not sure. I thought I heard someone singing."

Matt shook his head.

"No, didn't hear anything. It must be your age. Your hearing's starting to go funny."

"Thanks."

"You're welcome. Mum! Dad!" Matt shouted as they entered the living room.

The house was silent. Connor was looking round him, at first with astonishment, then in puzzlement. Lines of worry started to crease his forehead.

"This just isn't right," he eventually said.

"What isn't? Everything looks fine. It looks just like it did yesterday morning."

"That's just the point. There's no mess, no smoke damage — nothing. There's not even any *smell* of smoke. It just isn't right."

He started up the stairs, Matt following close behind.

"Look," Connor told him, as they reached the landing. "Nothing here either."

"So the fire didn't do as much damage as we thought, what's so bad about that?"

"Matt, I was up here last night. I *saw* it. The airing cupboard was burnt out, there was plaster off the walls and muck and smoke everywhere. There's not a trace of anything here, nothing."

"So what are you suggesting?"

"I'm not suggesting anything, just saying that last night the whole of this part of the house was a mess, with a hole in the roof. Now it isn't."

"It must be what you said outside, mum and dad managed to get a builder in last night to sort it out."

"And clean it and decorate it as well?"

"Can't think of anything else. It would explain why mum and dad aren't here either. They probably stayed up all night, so they're still in bed now. Which *I* would have been if some mean-minded person hadn't dragged me out of mine at the crack of dawn."

Connor was inspecting the paintwork around the airing cupboard door.

"Didn't you get grounded a few years ago for carving your name in the paint on this door?"

"You know I did. Anyone would think that I'd wrecked the joint. Mum went totally ape. Why?"

"Your name. It's still here in the paintwork."

"So?"

Connor took a deep breath to prevent himself losing his temper.

"Because, dimwit, if the door's been replaced, how come your name's still in the paint?"

"So obviously they haven't replaced the door."

"Give me strength! The old one was just a heap of burnt wood last night."

Matt frowned as he looked carefully around.

"Well," he conceded doubtfully, "perhaps I'd better phone the Westons to see what mum and dad say about it all."

"At last — a good idea!"

Fishing his phone out of his pocket, Matt tapped the screen to call the number. He frowned and tapped several more times.

"Problem?" asked Connor.

"No, not really. It's just that all the numbers I call regularly should be in the memory, but there's nothing there, they've all been wiped."

"How come?"

"No idea. Perhaps some of the equipment the fire brigade were using last night jiggered it. I'll have to look the number up in the book."

They went back downstairs and Matt looked through his mother's telephone book to find the number for the Westons' house, and keyed it in.

"Hi, Mrs Weston, it's Matt. Can I speak to mum or dad please?"

He frowned at the reply.

"You mean they've already left? What about Ben and Kerry?"

More frowns.

"But we brought them down to you last night, after the fire . . . The fire here of course . . . No, I mean the fire here at our house . . . The one that took out part of the first floor."

Even deeper frowns.

"I'll get back to you later."

He ended the call.

"She doesn't know what I'm talking about. Says no one spent the night with them, she knows nothing about a fire here or anywhere else and thinks I'm playing some sort of practical joke on her. What the hell's going on?"

"I think we should get down there and find out."

"Too right. This is getting really weird."

They made their way towards the front door, but before they reached it Connor stopped and listened carefully.

"Can you hear something?" he asked.

"You said that to me before. No, I can't hear any . . ."

His voice tailed off, and he looked round him in surprise.

"Yes, I *can* hear something. Someone's singing. Sounds like it's coming from upstairs."

"Perhaps someone left a radio on or something."

"I'll go check."

"Considering what sort of morning we're having I think we should *both* go check."

On the landing, it sounded as if the singing was coming from Matt's room. Pushing open the door, the singing became louder and clearer. It was the voice of a young girl. Matt checked all the equipment in his room. Everything was off, yet still the singing continued. They looked at each other, neither knowing what to do. Connor investigated the rooms to either side, but it was loudest in Matt's room. Suddenly, without warning, it stopped. It didn't fade away, nor did the song finish. It just stopped abruptly, in the middle of a bar.

"I've heard it before," Connor said, after a pause.

"You said you heard something when we first got here."

"Yes, but I meant I've heard it before then. I heard it last night, when the fireman was showing me round. I didn't pay much attention then, and afterwards, what with one thing and another, I forgot all about it. Until now. Same song, same singer."

"Who is it?"

"No idea."

"You just said you knew who it was."

"No, I didn't. I said it was the same singer as last night. But I don't know who she is. I know the song though."

"I couldn't understand it."

"That's because you gave up French in your second year. It's an old French folk song. We had it played to us at school to improve our pronunciation. Didn't help in the slightest, but I remember the song. Not sure of the exact title, but it's something like 'Petite Rosette'."

"Whatever it is, how come we could hear it in my room?"

"I wish I knew, Matt, I really do. Perhaps it just sounded as if it was coming from inside. Perhaps someone outside had their radio on very loud."

He walked to the window and looked out.

"Who's that?" Connor asked.

Matt glanced out of the window to where a girl was standing in the front garden. She was staring up at the house windows.

"Not a clue. Never seen her before."

"Then we'd better go and find out what she wants. Come on."

◆

The girl was young, perhaps ten or eleven. Large brown eyes were looking at Matt and Connor intently from a face that held more than a hint of future beauty.

"Who are you?" she asked.

Connor sensed that Matt was about to answer her, probably with a rude comment, so he forestalled him.

"My name is Connor and this is Matthew," he told her.

"Your clothes look strange," she said.

Connor decided to let that pass for the time being.

"And what is *your* name?" he asked.

"Mary-Anne Debbon."

"And where does Mary-Anne Debbon live?"

"Here, of course. What a silly question."

"What's she talking about," Matt hissed in his ear. "I've never seen her before. And what does she mean about our clothes. Hers look like something from a fancy dress shop."

Connor ignored him, but continued talking to the girl.

"How long have you lived here?" he asked.

"All the time. You do ask a lot of questions."

"Are your parents here?"

"Mama is inside. I don't have a father. He died."

"I'm sorry. Could we have a word with your mother, please?"

"You talk strangely as well. I'll go and see if Mama will receive you, but I know she is tired today as there were some callers very late last night."

"Thank you."

The girl ran off towards the house, but instead of entering through the front door, she seemed to head off around the side

22

of the house.

"Curiouser and curiouser," Connor muttered.

"Huh?"

"Quotation from *Alice in Wonderland*."

"She was right about one thing," Matt said, "you *do* talk strangely. Where'd she go, anyway?"

"Inside, I assume."

"But she didn't go through the front door, and the other doors are locked. I checked. Besides, what's she doing wandering around our house?"

"How should I know? We'd better go and find out."

They checked in every room, but the search proved fruitless. The girl was nowhere to be found.

"I really think," Connor said after a while, "that we ought to find out where Steve and Marion, and the others for that matter, have got to."

"Too right. Then perhaps I can find out what on earth Mrs Weston was talking about."

◆

"I thought you left the car out in the lane," Matt said as they walked along the drive.

"I did. Why?"

"Because it's not there now."

"What? You're kidding me."

"No, I'm not. See for yourself."

The lane was empty.

"You sure you locked it?" Matt asked.

"Absolutely certain. Besides, who in their right mind would want to steal that heap of junk?"

"Someone obviously has. Either that or you left the handbrake off and it's rolled down the hill."

They ran down the lane, but there was no sign of the car.

"This day just gets better and better," grumbled Connor, as they toiled back up the hill to the house. "Makes me wonder what's going to happen next."

"No need to wonder," Matt told him. "It just has. Look."

He pointed ahead of them. There, in the lane, just where they'd left it, was the car.

"Is someone playing games?" Matt asked.

"If they are, then it's a very clever one. Look at the house."

Together they stared at the house. Its upper floor was now blackened by smoke, there was broken glass everywhere, and a heap of charred wood and fabric. A builders' van was parked in the drive, ladders were leaning against the side of the house, and Steve and Marion were busily directing operations. Connor and Matt looked at each other, and then back at the house. Neither of them had any idea at all what to say.

◆

"*There* you are," called Marion as she caught sight of them. "I wondered where you'd got to. I saw the car in the lane, but there was no sign of either of you. Where did you get to?"

"Where'd *we* get to?" spluttered Matt. "Don't you mean where did *you* get to?"

"What are you talking about? Your dad and I have been here since seven. Ben and Kerry are staying at the Westons for the day, and Paula's still at Katy's. There didn't seem any point dragging them back here. There wouldn't be anything they could do and it would only upset them."

"But when we got here this morning you weren't here, there hadn't been a fire, and Mrs Weston didn't know what I was talking about and . . ."

He tailed off into a miserable silence. Marion looked at Connor for an explanation.

"I can only think that we've both been hallucinating. It was a terrible shock, what happened last night. When we got here this morning, we both thought that the house looked as though there hadn't been a fire. There was other stuff as well, but, as I said, we must have imagined it."

"Do you think you should both see a doctor?"

"No," he smiled at her, "we're both fine. Mind you, I did get him out of bed at just after eight this morning, which was another shock to his system."

"Eight? That explains a lot."

"Well, we're here now. Where do you want us to start?"

"At the moment we're still clearing the debris out of the way. The builders don't seem to think it's too bad at all. The insurers are coming later this morning, so all we can do before then is just a general clear-up."

"Fine with me. I've got an old pair of overalls in the car. I'll go and get them. Come on Matt, you can give me a hand with all the cleaning stuff I put in the car."

◆

"Were we hallucinating?" Matt asked as they unloaded the car.

"Didn't look like it to me. And whoever heard of two people having the same hallucination at the same time?"

"So what could it have been?"

"Don't know. Maybe some sort of delayed shock?"

"But why would we both see the same things?"

"How should I know?"

"Well, what happens now?"

"Nothing, I hope."

They staggered back to the house laden down with buckets, mops, and cleaning materials.

◆

By early afternoon the worst of the debris had been cleared from the house. The insurance assessor arrived and authorised the builders to continue and electricians to be brought in to get the supply working again.

"Do they know yet what caused it?" Connor asked Steve as they were waiting for the electricians to arrive.

"Central heating boiler. It must have had some sort of fault and just flared up. They don't know what the fault was, and probably never will now. It was quite old though, as the previous owners had it installed."

"You're going to be chilly in the evenings until they can get a new one installed."

"It won't be too bad. We've got a fair number of electric fires left over from our old house, so we can drag them out and get them working."

"Get them checked first. After all, you wouldn't want to cause a fire, would you," Connor said, grinning at him.

"No, I wouldn't. There have been enough fires round here as it is."

"Why, have you had more? I don't remember another one."

"Not us, no, but there was another house here before this one was built that burned down. That was in Victorian times — I don't remember the exact date. The previous owners told us. After the fire the house had to be pulled down, and the site was derelict for a long time. Most of the land was sold to a farmer to extend his grazing land. Just one much smaller plot was left and this house was built on it in the 1920s."

"I didn't know that."

"Forgotten all about it myself until now. This sort of jogged my memory. I can't remember much about what the Mitchells, that's the previous owners, told me, but I do remember that they thought several people died in the fire, including a little girl, I think."

Connor felt a cold wind blow across the back of his neck, and he shivered involuntarily.

"Conn? Are you alright?"

"Yes, sorry. Just a shiver, that's all. The little girl who died in the fire, you don't know her name by any chance, do you?"

"No, 'fraid not. The Mitchells probably told me, but I can't remember it now. Interested?"

"I'm always interested in local history. I'll have to look it up sometime."

◆

By early evening, with the power back on and some warmth from the electric fires permeating the building, the house was looking more like a home than a bombsite. Connor found it difficult to concentrate though, his mind turning over the story of the fire at the old house on the site and the death of several people, including a young girl. He offered to go and pick up the other children to bring them home, an offer quickly accepted.

"Matt," he shouted as he was getting ready to drive off, "want to come for the ride?"

"No, it's fine, Uncle Conn — I've still got a load of sorting out to do. Everything in my room stinks of smoke!"

"Come with me anyway."

"Why, feeling lonely?"

"No, but I've something I need to talk to you about."

"OK, I'm coming."

◆

"Well?" Matt asked as they were driving off. "What's so important that it couldn't wait ten minutes?"

"Your Dad told me something earlier that was a bit unsettling. I thought you ought to know."

Briefly he recounted the story that he'd heard about the fire in an earlier house.

"So what are you saying?" asked Matt, after Connor had finished.

"Nothing really, or at least nothing for certain. It's just odd that a little girl died in a fire on the site, and we saw a little girl in very strange circumstances this morning, a little girl who promptly vanished as if into nowhere."

"Coincidence?"

"Don't believe in them. It's Saturday tomorrow. Do you reckon you could come down to the reference library with me and look through some old papers?"

"Why the library? Why not just go online?"

"The reference library will have full copies of all the local papers going back over a hundred years. You can't get that sort of detail online. Want to come with me?"

"Don't see why not. Because I missed college today I haven't got any homework set for the weekend."

"You could always phone one of your mates and find out what the homework is."

"Do you want to be thumped?"

"No, not really."

"Then zip it."

"It was only a suggestion."

◆

Connor picked Matt up late the next morning.

"The problem is," Connor admitted, once they were settled in the reference library, "that we don't know the date we're looking for. It could be anytime over a twenty- or thirty-year period. They've got complete sets of *The Torquay Directory* and *The Torquay Times*, but I don't know where to start looking."

"What were they?"

"The local papers of the time. They both came out once a week, but I'm not sure on which days. I'll go and ask someone."

The reference librarian turned out to be a fund of local knowledge.

"Yes, I know the fire you're talking about," he told him. "Caused quite a stir at the time according to all the reports. It was in 1898, I think."

"You don't know the time of year?"

"Round about this time. Not sure of the exact date, but I could find it for you."

"No need. That's enough for me to go on. Thanks very much."

He returned to where Matt was busily scrolling through digitised newspapers. He'd started with *The Torquay Times*, which came out on Fridays.

"There doesn't seem to be anything here," he grumbled. "It's all adverts for boarding houses, cigars and other odds and ends. No news at all."

"The front page was nearly always reserved for adverts. Sometimes an important news item would make the front page, but mostly they're inside. Anyway, I've got the date of the fire, more or less, so it shouldn't take too long."

It took under ten minutes to find what they were looking for. One of the issues carried a brief notice near the bottom of the front page:

> LOCAL TRAGEDY. Mother and children die in house fire.
> FULL REPORT PAGE 4

Quickly scrolling through to the right page they read the report in silence.

> Belmont, a noted local landmark and one of the finest houses in the district, was burned to the ground last Friday night. The residents, Mrs Maria Debbon, her son Charles and her two daughters, Helen and Mary-Anne, tragically perished in the flames. Despite the valiant efforts of the local fire brigade and a number of staff and passers-by, there was nothing that could be done to save them. Witnesses stated that they could see Mrs Debbon and her children screaming for help from behind an upstairs window, but they could not be reached because of the intense heat. Due to the steepness of the hill where Belmont stood, the team of horses had difficulty pulling the heavy fire engine up the slope. By the time they arrived, Belmont was beyond saving. When the flames had finally been brought under control, little remained of the house except the outer walls. It is believed that these will have to be demolished.
>
> There were several unusual features of the fire that are giving rise to speculation that it was not accidental. A number of the servants stated that many of the doors and windows had been locked and bolted shut and could not be opened, including the door to the servants' wing, thereby leaving the occupants no means of escape. Also the speed with which the fire spread has prompted suggestions that it was started deliberately and in several places at once. Local people have talked of seeing mysterious visitors to the house in recent weeks.
>
> It is believed that all the resident staff escaped unhurt

from the separate servants' wing. A number of people were hurt trying to gain access to the house to rescue the family. Notable among them were Daniel Hardwick, aged sixteen and Master William Stone, aged just eleven. Both suffered injuries during their fruitless attempt to enter the blazing mansion. Master Hardwick had to be restrained by others from trying yet again to reach the family.

Mrs Debbon and her late husband leased Belmont twelve years ago. They entertained on a grand scale until Mr Debbon's early death, since when his widow has taken little part in the local social scene, although she has made a number of generous donations to local causes. Their children, Helen, aged sixteen, Mary-Anne, aged eleven, and Charles, aged ten, were being educated privately, though they were well known in the local area. It is not known for certain from where the family originated, although it is believed that the late Mr Debbon had connections with France.

Connor and Matt looked at each without speaking after reading the report.

"Mary-Anne Debbon," Connor eventually said. "So it was the same girl that we saw."

"Really saw or just thought we saw?"

"I wish I could answer that. She seemed as real as you and me."

"I know. It just seems so, so . . . " Matt tailed off, not knowing what to say.

"There's something else," Connor said. "Look at the date of the paper."

"Friday May the 6th, 1898," Matt read.

"That means the fire was on Friday April 29th," said Connor. "Mary-Anne must have been about eleven when we saw her. Judging by what we saw, it was the same time of year as now."

"So?"

"So in about three weeks' time from when we saw her, she and her mother, sister and brother are going to die a terrible death."

"But there's nothing we can do about it."

Connor said nothing.

"Is there?" Matt continued.

"I don't know. I don't believe the past can be changed, but I do think we saw Mary-Anne for a reason. I don't know what that reason is, or what we're supposed to do about it, but there's a purpose behind all this."

"You can be really spooky at times, Uncle Conn."

"I know," he said. "It's my age," he added quickly, before Matt could say it for him.

They scrolled through the next two issues. There were more reports of several suspicious aspects to the fire but none of them really added anything to their knowledge. And then, three weeks later, there was a report that a memorial service had been held, but after that — nothing.

"No mention of any funerals, just a memorial service," Matt stated.

"If the fire was as intense as the reports indicate, then I doubt there'd have been anything left to bury."

"That sounds pretty gruesome."

"I know, but probably accurate," Connor replied. "Come on, let's get home."

◆

Little was said on the drive home, Connor and Matt each busy with their own thoughts. They parked in the lane as usual, but before they could enter the garden, Matt came to a sudden stop.

"What's up?" Connor asked, almost bumping into him.

"Look!"

Mary-Anne Debbon was standing at the garden gate staring at them.

CHAPTER THREE

Two-way mirror

"Hello," Mary-Anne said. "I asked Mama if she would receive you yesterday, but when I came back you had gone."

"I'm sorry, we were called away," replied a bewildered Connor.

"It doesn't matter. Mama said she was too tired to receive callers anyway."

Matt elbowed him in the ribs.

"Look behind you," he hissed. "The car's gone again."

Connor swung round to find that not only had his car disappeared, but so had the streetlights in the lane. He returned his gaze to the serious little girl in front of them.

"Would your mother be able to receive us this morning, do you think?" Connor asked.

"I'm sorry, but Mama and Helen have gone to Exeter today. They were going to ask Edward to take them in the carriage, but Mama decided the train would be more convenient. I wanted to go as well because I haven't been on a train yet, but Mama said Charles and I had to stay here."

"Charles is your brother?"

"Yes. He's ten."

"The two of you are alone then?"

"Oh no, the servants are all still here."

"I see. Perhaps we can call again on another day?"

"Certainly. I told Mama that you spoke strangely and she said I mustn't say that. It isn't polite."

"It doesn't matter."

"Mama says that manners are important. As a lady, I'm expected to show an example to others."

"Your mother is very wise."

"Thank you. Are you Egyptians?"

"No, we're not Egyptians," snorted Matt. "Do we look like Egyptians?"

"Well, your clothes are rather odd. We had some Egyptians call a little while ago. Mama gave them some of our old clothes, but Hannah said that Mama was unwise to trust them."

"Hannah?" asked Connor.

"She's our cook. She tells funny stories sometimes. I have to go in now," she told them. "Will you be calling again?"

"I don't know," Connor told her.

"I hope you do. I told Helen and Charles about you, but I don't think they believed me."

She ran off towards the house, but again went out of sight around the side of the building.

"What the hell's going on?" Matt demanded. "Are we seeing ghosts or what?"

"I've no idea. She can obviously see us, and we must look very strange to her dressed like this."

"Dressed like what? There's nothing odd about our clothes."

"There would be to someone from Victorian times. There's something else as well."

"What?"

"Your house. It's gone back to looking like it did before the fire again."

"This is freaky," Matt groaned, glancing towards the undamaged house. "Has anything like this ever happened to you before?"

"Not even remotely. I don't know what . . . ," he said, suddenly stopping in mid-sentence.

"What?"

"Listen. Someone's singing again."

They both listened intently. The singing didn't seem to be coming from anywhere in particular, just to be in the air all around them.

"That's the same song that we heard before, isn't it?" Matt asked.

"Yes, but it doesn't sound like the same singer. It sounds like

34

an older voice. It's richer and deeper than a little girl's."

"Can you translate the words?"

"My French is no better than yours. I did it for five years, but that was at school, and that was a long time ago."

"A *very* long time ago."

"Thanks."

"You're welcome. Any idea as to . . . what the hell's that noise?"

A high-pitched whine had suddenly started up. It grew louder and louder, until they were both forced to cover their ears. It went as quickly as it had come.

"Well, that was nasty, whatever it was," Connor said.

"It sure was. I don't . . . oh hell!"

"What now?"

"Look at the house."

It was back to its fire blackened appearance.

"*There* you are. That's twice you've managed to park up without us seeing you. You must be practising."

Marion and Steve were standing in the doorway staring at them.

"It's odd. I looked out only a few seconds ago, and I could have sworn that you weren't here then," Steve said.

Connor and Matt looked around them. The noise of the builders at work came from the house.

"Anyway, did you find what you wanted at the library?"

"Yes," Connor said, once he'd recovered his senses. "There was a newspaper report about the fire, and it gave the names and ages of the people who died."

He went on to tell his brother and sister-in-law the gist of what the newspaper report contained.

"Speaking of newspapers," Steve told him, "we've made the papers as well. That photographer must have managed to get a couple of pictures before I saw him."

He showed them the morning paper, the front page of which bore a photo of the fire and the headline 'Family saved by pet dog'.

"They've been on the phone several times wanting interviews."

"Are you giving any?" Connor asked.

"Not a chance," Steve replied. "I just want to forget all about it as soon as possible. Which probably won't be until the builders have stopped making so much noise."

"The kitchen's been cleaned up though, so I can cook again," Marion said. "Come over for lunch tomorrow."

"Thanks. The nearest I get to Sunday lunch is a frozen dinner for one from the supermarket," Connor admitted. "Anyway, I'd better get off and out of your way. You'll still have a lot of sorting out to do."

"I'll walk you to the car," Matt said.

◆

"Do you think it'll happen again?" Matt asked, as they walked along the drive.

"I've no idea, none at all. And I've no idea what actually happened anyway."

"Maybe we just looked into the past. But that wouldn't explain why that girl could see us and talk to us, would it?"

"No. But one thing I'm sure of. It's not possible to physically go back in time. The past is fixed. It's permanent. No changes possible."

"But you can't be sure of that. Maybe there are rifts in time and sometimes it's possible to just sort of slip through one of them. Wouldn't that be neat — being able to go back in time and change things if you wanted to?"

"No. It's not possible," Connor said forcibly. "I want to forget all about this. As far as I'm concerned, it hasn't happened."

"Alright, if that's what you want," Matt said, looking at his uncle in puzzlement.

"It is. Anyway, as your mother's invited me for dinner, I'll see you tomorrow."

"OK, see you tomorrow. Bye!"

"Bye, Matt."

Matt walked slowly back to the house, pondering why his uncle had refused to even consider the idea that altering the past might be possible.

◆

Connor arrived mid-morning the following day, having slept only fitfully the previous night. He was deeply unsettled by the experiences of the past few days but couldn't quite pinpoint why. He took the coffee that Marion had given him and went to sit in the lounge, assuming Matt would be still sound asleep in bed. He was rather startled to find him sprawled on the sofa.

"You're up and about early for a weekend," Connor said, as he flopped into the nearest chair.

"Couldn't sleep. I keep going over seeing that girl and what it might mean. If anything. How about you?"

"Much the same. I try to put it out of my mind, but it keeps on worming its way back in again. Hopefully it'll just fade away. By the way, there's a fantastic aroma coming from the kitchen. What's Marion cooking?"

"It's not mum, it's Paula. She's baking cinnamon cookies."

"I hope they taste as good as they smell."

"They do," Matt answered gloomily.

"What's up with you? I thought cinnamon cookies were your favourites?"

"They are."

"So why the glum face? You must be in Paula's good books if she's baking your favourite cookies."

"No, I'm not. She wanted help with her homework yesterday but I said I was too busy sorting my room out. This is her way of getting back at me."

"She's mad with you, so she makes you your favourite cookies. Doesn't make a lot of sense."

"Yes, it does. She bakes a batch, gets my taste buds working overtime and then won't let me have any. Everyone else will get some, but not me."

"Clever girl. She'll go far," Connor told him, laughing at Matt's sour expression.

"It's not funny!"

"I think it is."

"You're not the one missing out on the cookies."

◆

Over dinner, Steve asked if Connor had learned any more about the previous fire.

"No. I looked through several local histories last night. They all mention it, but don't give any more details. One of them had a description of Belmont. It must have been quite a house."

"Do you know whereabouts it actually stood, Uncle Conn?" Paula asked.

"Not for sure, but it must have been somewhere close by," he replied, rather reluctantly Matt thought.

"I know where it was," Matt said. "It was right where our house stands."

"How do you know that?" his father asked him in some surprise.

"Because it's in the deeds. You showed them to me, after you collected them from the building society when you'd paid off the last chunk of the mortgage."

"So I did. I don't remember anything in there about the previous house though."

"I do. There was a sort of plan showing where Belmont stood and where this house stands. They're both in the same place, only this house is much smaller of course."

"Well, you remember more than I do. I do recall that there were plans to build several more on the site, but the builders ran out of money. I suppose that if we're actually on the site of Belmont itself, perhaps the foundations are part of the cellars of the original house."

"I don't think we've ever looked under the floorboards, have we?" Marion asked.

"No," Steve said. "Perhaps we should. There might be traces of the old house down there."

"If there are, they can wait. There's been enough disruption already, without taking up any more floorboards."

"I think it would be great looking under the floor," said Paula excitedly. "Perhaps there are whole rooms down there. Maybe even the bones of the people who died in the fire."

"That's quite enough of that, thank you," her mother said sharply.

"Do you think there are really bones down there?" asked Ben, his eyes wide.

"Now see what you've done," Marion told Paula.

"I don't think there'd be any bones," Matt said. "Uncle Conn says that the fire would have been so intense it would have burnt everything, including the bones. He thinks that's why there wasn't a burial service after the fire, just a memorial service. There was nothing left to bury."

Steve glanced over at his brother, who hadn't said much since the conversation had turned to Belmont and the fire. He decided to try to change the subject.

"This is a very morbid conversation for Sunday lunchtime," he said. "We must talk about something that's more fun. How do you reckon we should liven things up? Conn? Any ideas?"

Connor, heartily relieved that the talk had turned away from the fire, looked up from his dinner.

"We could discuss Matt's progress at college," he suggested, grinning at his nephew.

"You are in serious danger of having this fork shoved somewhere painful," Matt told him.

"Matt! Connor may well let you get away with talking to him like that, but I won't," his mother warned him.

"Sorry, Uncle Conn," Matt said, trying hard to look guilty, but failing.

"Have you noticed that young people today have no respect for their elders and betters?" Connor observed to no-one in particular, winking at Matt at the same time.

"Elder, maybe, but whoever said you were better than me?" Matt retorted.

"I think you're better than him," Paula said, sticking her tongue out at her brother. "He wouldn't help me with my homework when I asked him to."

"Anyone's better than him," Ben added. "He nicked the last of the cornflakes this morning before I could get at them."

"Did not!"

"Did too!"

"Could we *please* have just one meal during the course of the week where we can all behave like civilised people?" Marion asked plaintively.

◆

After dinner, Marion insisted that they weren't going to do any more work that day. The rest of the cleaning up could wait.

"Suits me," Matt said with relief. "I'm not sure I could look another bucket of hot, soapy water in the face at the moment."

"What are you going to do instead?" his mother asked.

"Think I'll go for a walk to get some of that dinner down."

"Mind if I tag along?" Connor asked.

"No, of course not."

"How about me?" Paula piped up.

"You can stay here and keep me company," Marion said, having seen the look of dismay that crossed Matt's face. "There are some cartoons on this afternoon, we can watch them together."

"Alright, but I want Uncle Conn to try my cookies first," she said, smiling sweetly at Matt.

"Thank you, I'd love to try one."

Paula dashed to the kitchen, returning with a plateful of still warm cookies, which she handed round, ostentatiously missing her older brother out of the invitations.

"These are gorgeous," Conn told her, trying hard not to laugh out loud at his nephew's expression.

"Take some with you on your walk," she suggested brightly. "There are plenty to go round."

"Thank you, princess — that would be great."

◆

Connor and Matt left the house and strolled to the gate.

"Do you really want to go for a walk, or was that just an excuse to get out of the house?" Connor asked.

"I wouldn't mind a bit of a walk."

"These cookies are really very good," Connor told him, nibbling at another one.

"Shut it."

"Ask me nicely and I may be persuaded to part with one."

"One? You've got a pocketful!"

"Ah, but I was given them to sustain me on the walk."

"Are you going to hand one over, or what?"

"Your sister has got your measure, without a doubt," Connor laughed, passing his nephew a handful of cookies. "But don't you dare tell her I gave you some. I'd never hear the end of it."

"You think I've got a death wish?"

He opened the gate and they started along the lane in the direction of Barton Hall, a large Victorian mansion long since converted into a holiday park, keeping a watchful eye out for the traffic that tended to use the narrow lane as a rat run. They hadn't got very far before Matt looked behind him and groaned with dismay.

"What's up now?" Connor asked him. "You've got most of the cookies."

"See for yourself."

Connor turned and saw that the lane had narrowed even more behind them and the streetlamps had disappeared.

"It's doing it again," Matt complained. "What do we do now? Walk back and see what's happened to the house? "

"Suppose so," Connor agreed, without much enthusiasm.

They retraced their steps along the lane and stopped at the gate to Matt's house.

"No fire damage," Matt said. "We've flipped back again."

"What do you mean, we've flipped back?"

"I don't know what else to call it."

"If you're trying to tell me we've gone back in time then forget it. We haven't."

"But we *must* have. Things have changed. The lane's narrower, there are no streetlamps, and the house hasn't had a fire. They widened the lane and put streetlights in about two years ago, so we must have flipped back at least a couple of years."

"No, we haven't. We're still in our own time. This is all imagination."

Matt glanced worriedly at his uncle.

"But you're the one who has all those science-fiction books at home. You're always buying them. And you've got one called *The Time Machine*. I know you have, I've seen it."

"I know what's on my bookshelf, Matt. And yes, I've got a copy of H. G. Wells' novel about time travel. But that's the whole point — it's a novel. Science *fiction*, not science *fact*."

"But supposing it isn't fiction. Supposing it's really possible to flip from one time to another. Wouldn't you just love to do that, to see what places looked like years ago."

"But it isn't possible. This is just imagination."

"Well, I'm not imagining that I'm getting cold. There's a fog coming in from somewhere. I can't see the house as well as I could two minutes ago."

Connor didn't answer him, staring as the fog swirled around them. It was damp and cold and seemed to seep through their clothes until they were both shivering. For his part, Matt couldn't understand why his uncle was so dead against the idea that they may have travelled back in time. He wasn't too keen on science fiction himself, but he'd gone with his uncle to the cinema sometimes when Connor wanted to watch the latest science-fiction epic that had burst onto the screen. They'd usually discussed things afterwards and Connor had always seemed almost exhilarated at the idea of space travel, of other dimensions and of travelling to alternative universes. But now that he was thinking about it, not once had they ever discussed time travel. He found that rather odd, but decided that as his uncle was so vehement in his denial he'd better steer clear of the subject.

"Well," Matt said eventually, "I suppose it could be a sort of two-way mirror. We can see and hear people in the past and they can see and hear us."

"Exactly. A two-way mirror. That would explain everything," Connor told him.

No, it wouldn't, Matt thought to himself. Not by a long way it wouldn't. He said nothing, though, and tried to peer through the grey mist that was gradually growing thicker and thicker. Living in a coastal town had made him used to sea fogs — dank and dripping cocoons that rolled in from the sea, often reaching several miles inland. They could blow in at any time of year, but this strange, freezing cold mist that swirled around them now didn't seem to resemble any fog that he'd ever seen before. It didn't even *smell* the same. He was about to comment on it when it started to blow away. Or that was the effect it was having, even though Matt was fully aware that there wasn't even a hint of a breeze. The fog cleared and he stared open-mouthed at the sight that was revealed. His house had vanished altogether and in its place was a vast, rambling grey stone mansion.

"What the . . . ?" Matt asked, turning to where Connor was equally dumbfounded.

"No idea at all," was the reply.

Neither of them could find anything sensible to say for some time, until Matt suddenly realised what they were looking at.

"I know what it is," he said.

"You know what *what* is?"

"The house, I know what it is. It's the house that stood on the site of our house, the one that was burned down. I saw a photograph of it once." He turned to look at his uncle, his face pale. "It's Belmont."

CHAPTER FOUR

Belmont

They stared at the huge grey stone house, with its elaborate, fanciful chimneys, great windows and high-pitched roofs. Immaculate formal gardens bordered the drive, with two ornamental fountains. A gardener was weeding one of the flowerbeds. He looked up from his task, saw Connor and Matt staring at the house and touched his cap to them before resuming his job.

"He can see us," Matt gasped. "So what should we do now?"

"I don't know. But there's someone else who can see us as well as the gardener. Look," Connor said, pointing to the side of the house. Mary-Anne Debbon waved to them before running along the drive to the gate.

"Should we leave?" Matt asked.

"Too late. She might follow us to see where we go."

The girl arrived at the gate and stopped to look at them.

"Hello," she said.

"Good afternoon, young lady," Connor replied.

"You do keep arriving at odd times. I looked out of the window a minute ago and you weren't there, but the next time I looked you were."

"It's a nice walk along this lane," Connor explained, saying the first thing that came into his head, "so we stroll this way quite often."

"Where do you live?" asked Mary-Anne.

"Warwickshire," Connor told her.

"Here," Matt said at the same time.

"He means that we live in Warwickshire, but we're staying in Torquay for a while," Connor said, kicking Matt on the ankle and earning a glare from his nephew in return.

"I don't know where Warwickshire is," the girl admitted. "Is it a long way from here?"

"About two hundred miles," Connor replied.

"Is it nice there?"

"It can be," he said.

Matt nudged Connor in the ribs and nodded towards the house. Following his glance Connor saw movement behind one of the first-floor windows. Seeing his look, Mary-Anne also turned to look at the house.

"Mama is looking to see who I'm talking to. She worries about me," she said.

"Would it be convenient to see your Mama this afternoon?" Connor asked.

"I'm not certain. I'll go and ask."

She started to walk back to the house, then changed her mind and turned back to them.

"You will be here when I get back, won't you?"

"I think so, but sometimes I get called away at very short notice," Connor said.

"Perhaps you could come with me as far as the door?" she suggested.

"What do you think?" Matt asked his uncle.

"Wouldn't do any harm, I suppose."

Mary-Anne opened a small gate to the side of the main entrance, and together the three of them walked up the carefully raked gravel drive towards the house. Instead of taking them to the main front door, Mary-Anne led them around the side of the house to a smaller door.

"I don't use the front door very often," she explained. "This door's much more convenient. I won't be long."

She entered the house and closed the door behind her.

"This explains why she seemed to vanish around the corner when we've seen her before," Matt said. "She must have been heading for this door."

Connor agreed with him, but before he could say anything else the door reopened to reveal Mary-Anne with a tall, formally dressed young man.

"This is James, our butler," Mary-Anne explained.

"I understand that you wish to see Mrs Debbon?" he said.

"That is correct."

"Mrs Debbon regrets that she is not 'at home' this afternoon. Perhaps you could call again in the morning?"

"What does he mean, she's not at home?" Matt hissed at Connor. "We've just seen her at the window."

Connor nudged him to keep quiet.

"Our apologies for disturbing you. We will see if we can call tomorrow, but it depends on my work."

"I will give Madam your message," he said, inclining his head slightly towards them before re-entering the house.

"I'm sorry," Mary-Anne said, "but Mama usually rests in the afternoon."

"It's no problem, young lady. Perhaps we'll be able to call again at a more convenient time."

"Could you come in the morning? Helen and Charles are getting very jealous that I know someone that they don't."

"I don't know. If we walk this way tomorrow then we may very well call in, but I cannot give any promises."

She walked with them back to the gate and waved as they walked down the lane and around the corner out of sight.

"What was all that nonsense about not being at home? You saw her as well as I did," Matt asked.

"It's an old expression. It doesn't mean that she's not in, it's just that she's not receiving visitors this afternoon."

"Stupid idea. Anyway, we've got a bigger problem at the moment than someone who's at home and not at home at the same time."

"Such as?"

"Such as how we get back to *our* home. I don't want to be stuck here."

"I thought we'd agreed on that one. We're not really here, are we? We're just looking through that mirror that you mentioned."

"Fine. So how do we stop looking through the mirror, then?"

"How should I know? Last couple of times it just sort of

happened."

"Well, I wish it would hurry up and get on with it. The others will wonder where we've got to if we're too long."

As he finished speaking the high-pitched whine that they had heard before started up again, making them both cover their ears with their hands. It stopped as suddenly as it has started, but was replaced with the loud imperious blast of a car horn as a large black BMW swerved to avoid them. The driver mouthed something, but perhaps fortunately they couldn't hear what he said.

"I think we're back again," Matt said.

"So it would seem," Connor agreed.

◆

They found Steve and Marion dozing in front of the fire, while Paula and Ben were watching cartoons. Kerry was playing with some building blocks.

"How about us doing some research to try to find out more about Belmont?" Matt asked.

"If you want," was the less than enthusiastic response.

"I thought you were mad keen about local history."

"I am, usually. Alright, let's go for it."

Matt started trawling through various websites, most of them to do with local history. One concentrated on buildings of historic and architectural importance, with a section devoted to Belmont and its owners, including several photographs of the building.

"It says here that Belmont was built in 1864 for a Mr Davenport," Matt said. "It also says that it was constructed of solid granite transported from quarries on Dartmoor. That must have cost him something."

"Does it say who Mr Davenport was?"

"Yes. Seems he was a retired banker with an irrational fear of burglars and the means to do something about it. Look at this — it says that all the doors were solid oak, at least three inches thick. The outer doors were five inches. What's that in metric?"

"Getting on for eight centimetres for the inner doors and

thirteen for the outer ones. Those are some solid doors."

"It carries on to say that all the doors, internal and external, were fitted with heavy locks and bolts. The windows were metal framed and, though large, were made up of a great quantity of small panes, each only inches across. They were also triple glazed, an idea copied from Robert Dykes when he'd built Kilmorie some years earlier. What's Kilmorie when it's at home?"

"A big house that used to stand on the hillside overlooking Meadfoot Beach," Connor told him. "It's been replaced by a block of flats."

"I didn't know they had double glazing back then, let alone triple glazing."

"I don't think you'll find it was what we'd call double or triple glazing today. It's most likely to have been three separate windows, one behind the other, with the metal parts welded together. That would have made them incredibly strong. Also explains why they couldn't break them to get in or out."

"Oh. It seems that there were very few opening windows and they were all on the first floor. Even so each of them was fitted with a lock, so once all the doors and windows were secured, Belmont became a fortress that none could enter without its owner's permission, it says."

"Enter or leave," added Connor.

"He didn't enjoy the place for long though. It says that a couple of local thieves heard that the house contained a lot of valuable antiques and paintings and thought they'd try their luck. They never got further than breaking a single small pane of glass in a ground-floor window before being caught, but the episode so unnerved Mr Davenport that he went to live in a hotel in the south of France for the rest of his life."

"Did he sell the house?"

"No. He decided to keep it, but let it out on lease."

"Is there a list of tenants?" Connor asked.

"Yes . . . It was let first to a local family called Pellew. They had it from 1865 to 1875, then it was leased to Sir Edward Atherton until 1882, then Mr and Mrs Debbon leased it."

"Any details about them?"

"Not much more than we already know. Mr Debbon died in 1889, but it doesn't say what he died of, then it goes on to say that Mrs Debbon took over the lease and she and her children lived there until the house was destroyed by fire."

"Nothing about the fire itself?"

"Not really. Only what it said in the paper, that the fire was 'suspicious' because it seemed to spread so quickly and that all the doors and windows seemed to be locked and bolted."

"Anything else?"

"No, that's it. Any idea why this is happening to us?"

"Why what's happening?"

"This flipping back and forth. Sorry," Matt said quickly, noting the expression on his uncle's face, "I mean this looking through a mirror business?"

"No idea. Maybe it's like a window that opened for a while so that we could look back, like seeing an old photograph. Perhaps the fire just sort of triggered it off."

"But why us? I mean I could maybe sort of understand it if it was just you, as you're the one who came inside the night of the fire. You said that you heard singing that time. But why me? Why not mum and dad? Or why not the firemen? They were in here for a lot longer than you were."

"You're asking questions I can't possibly answer. Why you and I can see into the past, and a very specific part of the past at that, I've no idea at all. Nor do I know why the others can't. Or at least I assume they can't. Have Paula or Ben said anything about seeing strange sights or having odd dreams?"

"No, nothing at all. It's just you and me. Do you think it will happen again?"

"Hopefully not. I wouldn't want to still be looking back when the house goes up in flames."

"Nor would I," Matt agreed, "but what if it does happen again, tomorrow for example. I've got to go back to college tomorrow, but I don't fancy walking into college in the morning then suddenly finding that everything looks as though it's 1898."

"No more than I relish the idea of walking into work and finding the two-way mirror makes it seem as if I'm at the end of the nineteenth century either."

"I'll text or call you each morning and each evening. If you don't hear from me, then can you drive up here and see what's happened?"

"Sure, although what I'm supposed to do if I can't find you, I've no idea."

They agreed to leave it at that, and after Connor had returned home that evening, Matt called him as promised.

"No sign of anything yet," he said.

"OK, Matt, give me a call in the morning. Maybe it's all over with now."

"Maybe. 'Night."

"'Night, Matt."

◆

Connor's phone startled him awake early next morning. He groggily answered it to hear Matt on the other end.

"Couldn't sleep, so I got up early," he said, in response to Connor's enquiry as to what he was doing awake at such an ungodly hour. "Nothing's happened yet, but I thought I heard that singing."

"Anything else?"

"No, not really."

"You don't sound certain. Was there anything else, anything at all?"

"Well, it was probably nothing, but when I heard the singing, or thought I heard the singing, I got out of bed and looked out of the window. It wasn't clear at all, but it almost looked as if there were two people in the garden."

"What sort of people?"

"Not sure. They didn't look real — it was as if they were photographs."

"You're not making much sense, Matt."

"I know, but I don't know how else to explain it. They just

didn't seem solid. I looked away for a moment to look at the clock and when I looked back, they'd gone. I also felt very dizzy for a few minutes."

"I would have said you were seeing things, but with everything that's happened, I'm not so sure. Anyway, the main thing is that mirror hasn't started its work again. Get yourself off to college and phone me this evening, or text whenever you feel like it, if it comes to that. I assume that you're taking your phone to college with you?"

"Don't ask stupid questions."

"Catch you later, Matt."

"You too. Bye."

◆

The phone calls and texts continued but Matt became more and more convinced that something was building up around him, though he didn't know what. By Wednesday lunchtime he'd had enough and called Connor at work.

"Sorry, but can you think of an excuse to come up this evening?"

"I don't need an excuse, I'll just call in. Problem?"

"Not exactly. I haven't really seen anything so far this week, but from when I get home after college each day to when I leave for college in the morning, I've got this strange feeling. It's as if something's tugging at me all the time. I keep thinking I can see people in the garden, even though they don't seem solid. I'm sure I saw Mary-Anne once as well. I keep getting dizzy spells and this morning it was so bad I thought I was going to be sick, but it passed off."

"Perhaps you *are* sick, Matt. You may have caught a chill or something."

"Don't think so. Anyway, can you come up?"

"Of course. I doubt I'll be there much before eight though. Will that be alright?"

"Fine with me. I'll see you then."

"OK, but if you get any other strange feelings, call me and I'll come straight up."

◆

At just after eight, Connor parked his car in the lane outside Matt's house. Matt was waiting for him at the gate.

"Hi, Matt. How are you feeling now?"

"Not too bad, but . . . whoa, what was that!"

They both staggered a little as if the ground had moved briefly beneath them.

"Well, if weren't in Torquay I'd say it was an earthquake, but as it is, I've no idea," Connor said. "Let's get inside — it's getting chilly out here in the dark."

Matt stood aside to let Connor open the gate but as he did so a swirling fog quickly blew in and obscured their view of the house and within seconds they could see little beyond each other. Connor tried to peer into the grey nothingness that surrounded them but without any success.

"Just like last time," Matt said.

"Yes," Connor answered — rather grimly, Matt thought.

Before he could say anything else the mist blew away as quickly as it had come, to reveal the grey walls and tall chimneys of Belmont. Most of the ground-floor windows showed lights burning brightly within, as did some of the windows on the upper floor. Gas torches flamed along the length of the drive, illuminating the way to the front door.

"What do we do now?" Matt asked, but before he got an answer there was a shout from Belmont's front door, which neither of them had noticed opening. Mary-Anne was there, beckoning to them.

CHAPTER FIVE

Burning proof

"Hello," she said, as they drew close.

"Good evening, Mary-Anne," Connor replied.

"The window in the nursery was open and I heard someone walking on the gravel, so I looked out to see who it was. Have you come to see Mama?"

"Have we?" Connor asked Matt in a low voice so that Mary-Anne couldn't hear him.

"I suppose we'd better, now we're here," he whispered back.

"Yes," Connor told the girl. "Is she at home?"

"She nearly always is in the evenings, but you'd better ring the bell so that James can go and ask her. Mama says that things should be done properly or not at all."

"Sounds a right old dragon," Matt said under his breath.

Connor said nothing but walked up to the front door and pulled on the bell rope. The same formally dressed young man they had spoken to before opened the door to them.

"I will go and ask Madam if she will receive you," he said, in answer to Connor's request.

He returned within a few minutes with the answer that Mrs Debbon would be pleased to receive them both.

"Please follow me," he said, leading them into the house.

The entrance hall was a vast, ornate room, reaching the full height of the house. A gallery ran around at first-floor level, supported by a series of carved wooden columns, and above was an intricately carved roof. In daylight the hall would be lit from the large glass lantern in the centre of the roof, but as it was dusk a series of gaslights projecting from the walls flooded the hall with light. The room was panelled in light oak and adorned with paintings and statuary. Directly in front of them, a wide, carpeted staircase rose to the gallery level.

"This is some room," Matt said, looking around him in surprise.

"It certainly is," Connor agreed. "I never knew that any house in Torquay was quite this grand."

They followed James across the hall to one of the internal doors, which he opened, ushering them into the room beyond.

"Please wait here. Mrs Debbon will not be long," he said, leaving the room and closing the door behind him.

They found themselves in an elegant drawing room. It was not as large as the entrance hall but even more sumptuously appointed, with a luxurious gold and white deep-pile carpet covering the floor, and matching floor to ceiling drapes across the windows. A huge gaslit chandelier glittered in the centre of the room, its light reflected in the polish on the antique furniture. A fire blazed in the marble fireplace, above which was a portrait of a lady in a flowing white dress. Connor walked over to study the painting more closely.

"I could be wrong, but I'm pretty sure this is by Reynolds," he told Matt in some amazement.

"Who's he?"

"Your education has been woefully neglected. Sir Joshua Reynolds was one of the greatest-ever English artists."

"Valuable?"

"In our own time, extremely valuable. It's not the value though; it's the sheer artistry in the painting. It's magnificent."

He was still staring at the painting when the door opened and James re-entered the room.

"Mrs Debbon," he announced, standing aside to let her pass.

"Good evening, gentlemen," she said, as James left the room. "I'm so pleased that we have finally met, as my daughter has talked of little else since she first saw you."

Connor realised there was no doubt from whom Mary-Anne had inherited her looks. She was a quite astounding beauty with that rare bone structure that ensured she would carry her beauty with her into old age. Dressed in a deep red evening gown, she crossed the room to meet them. Looking at her, Connor had to fight the strong feeling that he ought to bow, so regal was her bearing. No stooping would ever be permitted to bend her ramrod straight back, nor, he suspected, would so much as a single strand of hair ever have the nerve to fight free from her elegant coiffure.

"A dragon?" Connor murmured to Matt.

Matt didn't bother replying.

As she reached them she extended her gloved hand to Connor who bent and lightly kissed the proffered hand.

"Good evening, Mrs Debbon. Thank you very much for receiving us without an appointment. My name is Connor Harvey and this is my nephew, Matthew."

"Charmed," she said, offering her hand to Matt, who copied his uncle's actions as best he could. "Please sit down and tell me about yourselves. Mary-Anne tells me that you are here on holiday from Warwickshire?"

Connor wished that he'd had the time or the forethought to think of a story in advance, but instead he had to make something up as he went along and hope that he sounded convincing. He also hoped that Matt would back him up. They settled themselves on a trio of chairs by the fireside.

"Not on holiday, Mrs Debbon," Connor said. "History is a hobby of mine and I've been commissioned to write a short history of British seaside resorts, concentrating on the architecture and art treasures of the towns. As we had to come to Torquay it seemed a good idea to try and work up a chapter on the town. Belmont is one of Torquay's most interesting buildings, so I'm hoping to be able to do some research on the house and its owners and tenants."

"How fascinating. Have you discovered anything so far?"

He briefly related what they had already researched.

"You seem to have already found out all there is to know," she said. "Belmont is not particularly old and doesn't have the history that some of the other buildings in the area possess."

"It's not just the history," Connor said, trying hard to think as he went along. "It's the architecture and the contents. I was given to understand that the house contained a wonderful art collection and even in the short time we've been here I've seen some superb paintings, such as the Reynolds over the fireplace."

"You recognise it as a Reynolds? It isn't labelled."

"His style is unmistakable. I suppose it could be by someone copying his style, but I don't think so. I'm as certain as I can be that it's genuine."

"You have a good eye, Mr Harvey," she replied. "Yes, it's a Reynolds. It's not mine, it was here when we leased the house, but it was languishing in one of the upper rooms. I had it brought down here where it can be seen. There are two others by him in the house, but they are not as fine as this one."

"Do you know the sitter?"

"No, I regret not. She was, however, a very beautiful lady, don't you think?"

"She was indeed," he replied.

"And what is your opinion, Master Harvey? She would have been a number of years older than you, so I would value an opinion as to whether someone as young as you would still find her beautiful?"

"She certainly is," Matt said. "But not as beautiful as you are, Mrs Debbon," he added.

Two pairs of eyes turned to stare at him. Connor was about to apologise for him, but Mrs Debbon managed to speak first.

"Why Master Harvey, how very gallant of you. Thank you very much; I'm quite overwhelmed!"

"You're welcome," Matt said, wondering what on earth had possessed him to say such a thing in the first place.

Connor heaved a quiet sigh of relief.

"Would it be possible to arrange to call and study the works in the house?" he asked.

"I see no reason why not," she replied. "I don't believe there has ever been a proper appraisal of the artworks here at Belmont. There is an inventory of course, but it is little more than a list of contents. My late husband always intended to arrange for an art historian to make a thorough catalogue, but he passed away before it could be arranged."

"I'm so sorry. Was this recently?"

"No, it was almost ten years ago. He died of a heart attack. He was only thirty-seven. I have thought every so often of trying to arrange to have a catalogue produced myself, but somehow I never seem to find the time. However, when would you like to call to view the collections?"

"Would Saturday be convenient, Mrs Debbon?"

"Certainly. At what time should we expect you?"

"We will try to be here at ten o'clock, but it is dependent on my work."

"I thought that writing the book that you spoke of was your work. Did you not say it was a commission?"

"That is correct, but it is not my actual work. It is more of a hobby. I'm not being paid for it. My paid employment is with the Great Western Railway. I have to travel extensively wherever the company sends me."

"How interesting. And what sort of work do you have to do?"

He tried desperately to think of something that would explain why he and Matt often disappeared and couldn't guarantee keeping appointments but floundered. He'd mentioned a job with the railway as explaining why they were in Torquay when they were supposed to live in the Midlands, but couldn't for the life of him get any further.

"Uncle Conn has to investigate accusations of fraud in the company," Matt explained. "He very often has to just drop everything and go when he gets a call."

"That's right," said a much relieved Connor. "I often make appointments, and then find that I'm called away and can't keep them."

"I understand, Mr Harvey. Do not trouble yourself. If you find that you are unable to be here on Saturday, it's of no consequence. Another date can always be arranged."

"Thank you. You are very kind. I would ask though that you keep your knowledge of my work a secret. If word got around that an investigator was working in the area, then anyone engaged in unlawful actions would have time to cover things up before I could make the necessary checks."

"Your secret is safe, Mr Harvey, have no fear. Now, I'm afraid that I've been a most inhospitable host and not offered you any refreshment. Would you and your nephew care for a glass of wine?"

"Thank you. I'm sure that Matt would appreciate one, but I'm afraid that I have little taste for wine myself."

"Some port perhaps?"

"Uncle Conn doesn't drink alcohol," Matt told her. "He can be very boring at times."

"You've signed the pledge, Mr Harvey?"

"Only in a manner of speaking, Mrs Debbon. I regret that it's not a high moral sense or anything. I just don't like the taste."

She laughed gently.

"You are two most unusual people," she said. "Mary-Anne was quite right. Would a cup of tea be more to your taste?"

"That would be perfect, thank you very much."

She rose and pulled one of the number of cords hanging by the fireplace.

"Susan," she said, when a maid had answered the summons, "please ask James or Mrs Gregson to arrange for a tray of tea to be brought in, will you? And ask Helen, Mary-Anne and Charles if they could join us as well. Tell them we have guests."

"Yes, Madam."

"Master Harvey, perhaps you would care to help yourself to a glass of wine from the decanter on the small table," she said.

"Thank you," he replied, getting to his feet and crossing the room to the table that she had indicated.

"I do not wish to appear rude, Mr Harvey, but Mary-Anne did mention your unusual clothes. I explained to her that it was most improper to do so, but I must admit that I myself have never seen such garments. Are they some form of uniform, perhaps?"

Connor had forgotten what he and Matt must look like to someone from 1898.

"No, not really," he said. "Matt and I were in South Wales before I was called here to Torquay, so we bought these clothes there to try to blend in."

"They wear clothes like that in South Wales?"

"Yes."

"But when I was in Cardiff a few years ago I'm sure I saw nothing like that."

"That's in the city, Mrs Debbon," Connor said, wondering how he'd got himself into this situation. "The clothes in Cardiff would be very little different to the clothes here, or anywhere else. We were right out in the country. They wear these to keep warm. It can be very chilly in the country, even at this time of year. When I got the call to come here, there wasn't time to get any normal clothes."

"You become more fascinating by the minute, Mr Harvey. No wonder Mary-Anne was so taken with you."

It seemed that the invitation to join them was not unexpected as it was only a matter of minutes before the drawing room door was opened to admit Mary-Anne, closely followed by a young lady.

"You already know Mary-Anne of course, but allow me to introduce my elder daughter, Helen," Mrs Debbon told them. "Helen, these gentlemen are studying local architecture and works of art and are interested in this house. This is Mr Harvey and his nephew, Matthew."

What was a promise of things to come in Mary-Anne was a promise fulfilled in Helen. The prettiness of a child was replaced with the flawless beauty of a young woman. Had she been born into a later age, her features would without doubt have graced the covers of fashion and society magazines the world over. Connor nudged Matt with his elbow.

"Close your mouth," he whispered.

Matt managed to shut the offending part of him, but it was a difficult task made none the easier by the fact that his throat had dried up and he felt he couldn't breathe properly.

"Good evening," Helen said. "My sister told me about you, but I'm ashamed to say that I wasn't sure whether to believe her or not. She tends to make up a lot of stories and I suspected that you were one of them. I'm delighted to meet you both."

Although she used the word "both", her eyes were centred on Matt, who was still having trouble controlling his breathing. Looking at her, he saw a slim and very elegant young lady, dressed in a deep blue gown that matched the colour of her eyes. He tried to decide in his mind what colour her hair was. To say it was blonde would be like saying that emeralds were green. Both statements would be factually correct, but neither would give the slightest hint as to their true appearance. The light from the gas lamps seemed to reflect in her hair and made it sparkle with a life of its own. Matt gave up the unequal challenge and just gazed at her. Connor, glancing sideways at his nephew, saw the effect that Helen was having on him, and groaned inwardly. Since he turned fourteen, Matt had gone out with a long succession of girlfriends, all of whom were presented by him as being "the real one". None of them lasted more than three months; one had lasted less than two days. Connor had sometimes put his foot in it by enquiring how Matt's latest girlfriend was, only to find that a new one had replaced her while he wasn't looking. He recognized the expression on Matt's face.

Helen and Mary-Anne settled themselves on chairs next to Matt. Helen turned to look at him.

"You are interested in art, Matthew?" she asked.

"Uncle Conn is," he said, hoping that his voice didn't betray how nervous he was. "I'm not too interested myself, but I often go with him on his trips."

"So what are you interested in?"

"I like sports," he said, "and music."

"I'm very fond of music myself," she said. "Which composers do you like the best? I have a certain liking for the choral works of Sir Arthur Sullivan, but Mama considers him to be rather vulgar, don't you Mama?"

"I do indeed. He would have been much better off if he hadn't written those dreadful so-called comic operas with Mr Gilbert. I cannot imagine what he was thinking of."

"Do you like the old masters, or do you prefer the modern

movement, Matthew?"

Matt swallowed hard and tried to think of a composer that he'd heard of, but couldn't find one other than Beethoven, but he was fairly sure that mentioning him would lead to even more problems. He could hardly mention the singers and groups of his own time that he regularly tested his parents' patience with.

"Matt likes a wide variety of music," Connor said, noticing the trouble that Matt was getting into. "His current passion is for the works of Claude Debussy."

"Really? Mama met him once. Where was it, Mama?"

"In Paris, my dear, three years ago. A most gifted young man, is he not, Master Harvey?"

"He certainly is," Matt said, hoping that the subject would soon be changed from composers that he was supposed to like but had never heard of. He fervently prayed that Helen wouldn't ask him which his favourite piece of music was.

"And which of his pieces is your favourite?" Helen asked him.

Matt was beginning to wish the ground would open up and swallow him, but the door opening and the maid entering the room holding a young boy by the hand saved him.

"I'm sorry for the delay, Madam," she said, "but Nurse said that Master Charles needed his hair combing and he didn't take too kindly to it."

"He never does. Thank you, Susan."

The maid left the room as Mrs Debbon introduced the boy to them.

"This is my son, Charles. Charles, say 'good evening' to our visitors."

"Good evening," he said. "Are you the Egyptians that Mary-Anne told us about?"

"Charles!" gasped a horrified Mrs Debbon.

"Yes, Mama?"

"You were told not to say that, it's not polite."

"Sorry, Mama," he said, looking anything but sorry.

"Yes," Connor said, "we are the ones that your sister mistook for Egyptians. She hadn't seen clothes like these before."

"Nor have I," he replied. "Where are they from?"

"They're from Wales," Mrs Debbon told him. "Now *please* try to show our guests that you can behave yourself when necessary."

"Yes, Mama."

The maid re-entered the room with a tea trolley. An hour passed in pleasant conversation before Connor realised that it was getting late. They had been there for over two hours, much longer than previous times.

"Would you like another cup of tea, Mr Harvey?" Mrs Debbon asked him.

"It's very kind of you," he said, "but Matt and I really must be going. It's a long walk back to our hotel."

"There is no need to walk, Mr Harvey. I will get Edward to drive you down in the carriage. It will not take him long to harness the horses."

Connor mentally kicked himself for not realising in time that Mrs Debbon was bound to offer them transport back to their non-existent accommodation.

"Thank you, Mrs Debbon, that's most kind of you, but the walk will do us both good."

"You're certain? It will be no trouble."

"Quite certain. Come on, Matt, we must be going."

"So soon, Mr Harvey?" asked Helen, without taking her eyes off Matt.

"I'm afraid so," he said. "We will, however, be back on Saturday. Your mother has kindly given me permission to study the works of art in the house."

"And will you be coming as well, Matthew?" Helen asked.

"Yes, I think so," he replied.

"Good," she said, "that will be nice. I will look forward to it."

"So will I," Matt replied fervently.

"Thank you for your hospitality, Mrs Debbon," Connor said. "You've been very kind. We shall see you on Saturday, work permitting."

"I understand, Mr Harvey," she replied. "Good night to you both. I'll ring for James to show you out."

"Don't trouble to ring for the butler, Mama, I'll show our guests out," Helen told her.

"As you wish, my dear."

◆

After handshakes all round, they were escorted to the front door by Helen, the two younger children being dragged protesting off to bed the minute they left the drawing room. The door closed behind them as Connor and Matt walked back along the gravel drive.

"Why did we have to leave? I was having a great time," Matt asked.

"So I could see. But we've been looking back into the past for a couple of hours or more now — that's longer than before and Steve and Marion will be wondering where we've got to."

"Oh, rats. I'd almost forgotten about that. Why do you think it was longer this time?"

Connor didn't answer, but walked a short distance along the gravel drive to where one of the gas torches was hissing and spluttering. He stared hard at the flames for some time before evidently coming to a decision. Matt followed him and stood by his side.

"You OK?"

"I'll let you know in a minute."

To Matt's horror, Connor placed his hand on the metal lamp, just below the flame.

"Uncle Conn!" Matt shouted, as Connor snatched his hand away with a grunt of pain, looking at his hand where it was reddening with the effect of the hot metal. "What on earth did you do that for? Have you burned your hand?"

"Yes, but not badly. I only touched the metal. Don't worry, Matt, I'm fine."

"But why do it in the first place?"

There was no answer as Connor just seemed to stare into space.

"Uncle, please!"

"Sorry, Matt, I didn't mean to worry you. I just needed to prove something to myself."

"And that meant burning your hand?"

"Yes."

Looking at him, Matt had the feeling that his uncle was hovering on the verge of tears, but he didn't think it was from the pain in his hand.

"What's the matter? What's wrong?"

There was silence for a while until Connor eventually answered him.

"If we're looking through a mirror into the past, then I'm perfectly able to accept that we can see and hear people, talk to them and even interact with them. Even drinking tea could just about be explained. But there's no way that you'd be able to really *feel* anything from looking in or through a mirror. And I certainly felt that hot metal," Connor said, glancing down at his hand.

"So . . . ?"

"So I've got to accept that we're really here, Matt. We've really . . . Sorry, I've forgotten the word again."

"Flipped," Matt reminded him.

"Yes. Flipped. We've really gone back in time and we're standing in the grounds of Belmont. It's taken touching that lamp to convince me. But you've never doubted it though, have you?"

"No," Matt told him. "It just seemed so obvious."

"To you maybe, not to me."

"But now you believe that we really have flipped? Gone back in time to . . . That's a point," Matt said, looking around him. "To when, exactly. What date is it? And what year for that matter?"

"Yes, I believe it. Totally against my will, but I believe it. And as to the date, I don't really know but I can make an educated guess."

"So what's your best guess?"

"I'd say 1898 — the year of the fire. And as to the actual date, I'd guess same as in our own time — April thirteenth."

"What makes you think that?"

"The time of year is the same as ours, you can tell that from the leaves starting to sprout on the trees and what time it goes dark. As to the year, it's a guess based on how old Mary-Anne, Charles and Helen appear to be."

"Sounds reasonable. But why didn't you want to accept it — that we've flipped back in time?"

Before he could answer, the high-pitched whine that they'd heard on the two previous occasions started up, even louder this time. They both winced in pain and were forced to cover their ears with their hands. When the noise finally stopped, they realised that the streetlights had suddenly reappeared in the lane.

"I wish I knew what that noise was."

"So do I. It's getting louder all the time, and more painful. Now let's get inside before your parents send out a search party."

CHAPTER SIX

The past can't be changed

They managed to explain to a worried Steve and Marion that Matt had wanted some fresh air, had gone for a walk and had met Connor by chance in the lane. Marion seemed unconvinced by this, but let it pass.

"There's something I want to show you," Matt said, after Connor had said that he ought to be going.

Once in his room, Matt sprawled full length on the bed, while Connor parked himself in a chair.

"Have you got something to show me, or was that just an excuse?"

"Just an excuse. I wanted to talk. Why do you think we flipped so quickly this time? You'd only just got here and then whoosh, off we went."

"I think maybe that this explains the strange things you've been seeing all week and your dizzy spells," Connor said. "Something's been trying to flip you back in time, but you can't do it by yourself. The two of us have to be together for it to work. And before you ask, I've no idea why."

"But why so quick?"

"Making up for lost time, I suppose. If whatever it is that makes us flip has been trying all week then it's probably in a bit of a rush by now."

"That makes no sense at all. Why would it, whatever it is, be in a hurry?"

"How on earth should I know? I'm as much in the dark as you are about all this."

They were both silent for some time, each busy with his own thoughts, each trying to come to terms with what was happening to them and what it might mean. Matt thought back over the evening's events: entering Belmont for the first time and meeting the Debbon family. Especially Helen. He looked over to where Connor was still deep in thought in the armchair. He was about to ask him why he'd been so reluctant to accept that they had really flipped back to 1898, but something told him that it wasn't the right moment and he changed what he was about to say.

"Helen's absolutely fantastic, isn't she?"

"Yes, she is," Connor said, looking up from his thoughts. "She and her mother. And as Mary-Anne would no doubt have been."

"Would have been?"

"She died in the fire, Matt. They all did. She didn't live to grow up."

Matt was silent for a while as he let the implications of his uncle's words sink in.

"So we've got to warn them," he said eventually. "Next time we flip back, we tell them."

"Tell them what? That we've travelled there from the future? That we know they're all about to die in a fire? We'd be locked up."

"But we have to do something!"

"I think we need to sleep on it, Matt. I'm tired and I need time to try to work out what this is all about. Why we keep flipping back and forth, why it's you and me and not anyone else, whether it will happen again and what the purpose behind it is. I can't think straight at the moment. I might be able to make more sense of it all tomorrow."

"Fine. You coming up here tomorrow evening after work?"

"That depends on whether you want to flip back or not."

"Huh?"

"It seems that neither of us can flip on our own, so if I stay home tomorrow then you stay home as well. No shooting back to 1898. There's no certainty we'd flip tomorrow, but the time between flips is getting shorter and the time we're there is getting longer."

"Come up as soon as you can. If we flip, we flip. I want to see what this all means. And it would mean I'd see Helen again."

In spite of his worries Connor couldn't help but grin at the expression on his nephew's face.

"By the way," Matt added, "what was all that about Egyptians? Mary-Anne said it the other day and Charles mentioned it today. Neither of us looks anything like Egyptians."

"I'm not so sure about that. Those are very tatty jeans you've got on."

"What's that got to do with anything?"

"Egyptians. It's where the word 'gypsy' comes from. People used to think that Roma and other travellers came from Egypt, so they were always called Egyptians. It's been shortened over the years to gypsy."

"She thought we were gypsies?"

"Evidently."

"Bloody cheek!"

"We keep shifting back and forth in time and all you're worried about is that a young girl mistook you for a gypsy?"

"These jeans cost me a packet!"

Connor stared at him briefly, then burst out laughing. Matt looked at him sourly for a few seconds before joining in.

"OK, I've got to go, otherwise I'm going to fall asleep in this chair. I'll see you tomorrow, Matt. Any problems in the meantime, get in touch."

◆

"Dad?" Matt asked at breakfast the next morning.

"Uh-huh?"

"If you were able to go back in time, say to any time you wanted, where would you go?"

"What brought that on?"

"It's for a project for college. We've got to study what we think could be the possible outcome of time travel," he said, thinking quickly.

"Well," Steve mused, "I've had a sort of general interest in Roman history ever since we had that day out in Bath last year. I think maybe I'd like to go back to see what Bath really looked like when it was a Roman city."

"Alright. Now suppose you could go back in time to change something in your own past. What would that be?"

"I'd get him to get rid of his bike way before he actually did," Marion interrupted. "That would have saved everyone a lot of trouble."

"Ignore your mother," Steve told him. "She was always jealous of my motorbike."

"I didn't know you'd had one," Matt said in some surprise.

"He hasn't, not since he crashed it on the ring road years ago and nearly broke his neck. It was the last straw. He always drove it way faster than he should have and was always falling off it."

"Is that really what you'd change, dad?"

"I suppose it would be a good idea," his father conceded. "I'd have to think about it, though. I loved that bike."

"I sometimes thought he loved that bike more than me," Marion said drily.

"Tough call," Steve replied, grinning at his wife.

"What about you, mum? What would you go back to change in your own life?"

"I'm not really sure I'd change anything."

"How about something from when you were young?"

"Oh, really," she said. "Meaning that I'm now old?"

"Try engaging your brain before opening your mouth, son, it'll save you an awful lot of grief over the years," Steve told him, smiling at the look on his wife's face.

"I didn't mean it like that," Matt protested.

"And just how did you mean it?"

"I just meant, well, I meant that . . . I think I'll shut up," Matt said lamely.

"Now there's a good idea," his mother told him.

"But . . ." Matt started up again.

"But what?" Marion said, a warning note in her voice.

"But what about Uncle Conn? What do you think he'd like to change if he could?"

His parents glanced at each other before Marion answered him.

"I don't think it would be a good idea to ask him that."

"Why not?"

"He'd find it hard to talk to you about it."

"No, he wouldn't. He and I talk about anything and everything. He's always answered every question I've ever asked him, no matter what it was."

"I didn't say he wouldn't answer it, Matt," Marion said gently, "but I think you'd find that it would upset him greatly."

Matt looked at them, more questions hovering on his lips. He was certain he was being warned off but couldn't for the life of him figure out why. Eventually his father spoke again.

"Many years ago, your mum, Connor and I went to the cinema to see a remake of *The Time Machine*, based, rather feebly as it happens, on the novel by H. G. Wells."

"I know it," Matt said, "or at least I know the book. Uncle Conn's got a copy on his bookshelf."

"Yes, he has, which is why we went to see the film. Anyway, we had a meal afterwards and were chatting about it and the possibility, or otherwise, of time travel. We decided that although time travel itself was theoretically possible, changing things by travelling back in time wasn't. There'd be a paradox and it wouldn't work."

"I don't get it. If it was ever possible to go back in time, then surely it would be possible to change things, to make things better?"

"Look at it this way," Steve said. "What would you change in *your* life, if you could?"

"I wouldn't have carved my name in the door surround."

"Good choice. Not one of your better moments, I have to agree. So you go back in time and somehow prevent your younger self from making that carving in the door frame. Yes?"

"Yes."

"So the carving therefore never happened, yes?"

"Yes."

"So you don't get shouted at . . ."

"Screamed at," Matt interrupted.

"OK, screamed at," Steve agreed. "It doesn't happen. No screaming. No grounding, no withdrawal of pocket money and so forth. None of it happened because you didn't do it."

"Yes, but why . . ." Matt said, suddenly halting in mid-sentence. He was silent for a while, thinking things through. "But if it didn't happen, then I wouldn't have any memory of it happening. So when, years later, the time came for me to decide what I wanted to change in my past, I wouldn't choose that, as it had never happened. But if I *didn't* choose it, then I wouldn't go back to stop myself, in which case I *would* carve my name after all. That's what you meant by a paradox?"

"Exactly," Steve said. "The past can't be changed. I'm not saying that time travel, either by a machine yet to be invented or by some other means as yet unknown, isn't possible in itself, although I seriously doubt it. I'm saying that *changing* the past isn't possible, even if it were possible to travel back in time."

"But why would that be so upsetting for Uncle Conn?"

"You've spent a lot of time with my brother over the years, Matt. Have you really no idea what Connor would change if he could?"

Matt was about to say no, when a picture flashed into his mind. A picture of a young woman with laughing eyes gazing out of a painted portrait. And a man with desperately sad eyes looking back at it.

"Oh, dear God. Of course. He'd want to go back to try and save Laura's life."

"I don't think you realise quite how much he loved her, Matt. He absolutely worshipped her, and her dying like that almost broke him. In some ways he's never been the same since. There's always a deep sadness in him. And if ever there was a means to travel back in time, then I dread to think of the effect on him."

"Why so?"

"Because he'd know as well as I do, like we've agreed, that changing the past, changing what's already happened, isn't possible. But in Connor's case, even though he'd know it was totally futile, he'd never stop trying. Not for a single second. He'd go back in time over and over again, trying to alter the past and he'd fail. Laura would die anyway every time, no matter what he did. It would eventually kill him, I think."

"That's terrible," Matt said, trying to hold back the hot tears that he could feel pricking his eyes.

"Yes, it is," Steve agreed. "So even though it's only an innocent question, I suggest that you don't ask him about it. It would open up too many wounds, too many bad memories."

"I understand," Matt told him, realising at last why his uncle had fought so hard to avoid accepting that the two of them had flipped back in time. What emotional turmoil it was causing his uncle he dreaded to think.

◆

Connor arrived early that evening, having been invited by Marion for an evening meal. Afterwards, he joined Matt in his room on the pretext of doing some research for Matt's homework.

"Had any bright ideas?" Matt asked him when they were alone. "About what we can do about flipping back and forth, I mean."

"I don't think there's anything we *can* do. We just flip as and when."

"I know, but that's not quite what I meant. I mean, do you think there's a reason for it? Do you think that we're there to do something?"

"I think there has to be a purpose. I don't believe it's purely random, but I don't know what the purpose is. And as such I can't say if we're there to do anything or not."

Matt steeled himself for what he needed to say next.

"Uncle Conn?"

"Yes?"

"I'm really sorry. I've been such a total dork."

"Why? What have you done this time?"

"It's not what I've done — it's what I've said."

"I don't remember you saying anything particularly out of order. What's up?"

"It's about me banging on and on about us really going back

in time and then pestering you as to why you didn't want to accept it," he explained, going on to tell Connor about the talk that he'd had with his parents that morning. "I understand why you found it so hard to accept. I'm really sorry."

"There's no need to be sorry, Matt. You weren't to know."

"But I should have realised. I'm sixteen, not a snot-nosed kid. I should have figured it out, particularly after I saw the way you looked at that portrait of Laura the other day."

"Sixteen is hardly old, Matt."

"Doesn't matter. I'm not a child anymore, I should have understood how much it would hurt, knowing that it's possible to flip back in time, but knowing that you can't change anything when you do."

Connor glanced up at his nephew's worried face, making Matt even more concerned as he saw the glint of tears in his uncle's eyes.

"I've never seen you cry before. Is there anything I can do? Anything at all?"

After a while Connor looked at him directly, making no attempt to hide the tears coursing down his face.

"I cry quite often, Matt. Usually late at night when I reach out for Laura and find she's not there."

"It must have been a terrible time when you found out she was ill. I can't even imagine how you must have felt. How did you cope?"

Connor paused before replying, trying to put his memories into some sort of order.

"Laura coped far better than I did. We both had a belief, a faith I suppose you'd call it, in a higher power. Neither of us felt that church attendance as such was a necessary part of what we believed in, even though we would go when we felt like it. Afterwards, after she died, I mean, I just about lost my faith, my belief. I shouted at God, screamed at Him in fact, blaming Him for taking Laura away from me. I just couldn't believe that an all-powerful, all-loving God could be so cruel as to rob me of someone that I loved more than my own life, someone who *was* my life. But then something happened."

"What?"

"I'm not really sure what to call it or how to explain it. It was a few weeks after Laura died. I was in the car, just driving aimlessly about, not really going anywhere. I just wanted to be out of the house, away from the memories for a while. I saw a sign for a woodland nature reserve and parked up and went for a walk in the wood. It was very peaceful and no-one else about. A fallen tree trunk had been made into a bench and I sat there for ages, just letting the peace and quiet wash over me. And then I heard her."

"Heard her? Who?"

"Laura. It was her voice as clear as if she was sitting next to me. She told me she loved me and was waiting for me. And when I eventually joined her, then we would have eternity together."

"You're sure it was her?"

"Oh yes. I know the human mind is immensely powerful. It can conjure up almost anything it wants to. It can play tricks and make you see and hear things that you want to, even when they're not really there. But I'm absolutely certain that she came to me that day to tell me that things would be alright, that one day we'd be together again."

"And you still think that?"

"Yes."

"Can I ask you something else? You don't have to answer if you don't want to."

"I've told you before, Matt, you can ask me anything you want. As you well know from some of the questions you've asked over the years."

"This might be different."

"Go ahead anyway."

"Well, it's just that . . . I mean I'm not sure how best to put it. What I'm trying to say is — you're not just waiting to die, are you? So that you can be with Laura?"

"No, not anymore. At the start I was. I just wanted to go to sleep and never wake up again. It was always the waking up that was the most difficult part, coming out of sleep, reaching out for

Laura and then it hitting me that she'd gone."

"So did you ever, you know, try to make it happen?"

"Take my own life? I thought about it often. I kept on working out the best way to do it and came very close more than once. But eventually I came to understand that Laura wouldn't have wanted it that way. She'd have wanted me to have a full life before I join her again."

Matt felt the hot tears running down his own face. He went over and hugged his uncle tightly.

"You haven't done that for years, Matt," Connor said in some surprise, hugging his nephew back. "Not since you decided you were too old for hugs."

"Well, I should have done. In fact, I should have done a lot of things. Been a lot more understanding for one. All the times you've been there for me when things have gone wrong, but I've never really given much thought to how you must be feeling."

"No need to get upset, Matt. Everything's fine. Anyway . . . we need to try to sort out about the flipping — try to figure out why it's happening and if there's anything we should be doing."

"But if there's no possibility of changing what's happened then I don't see what we can do."

"I've been thinking about it and I'm sure there's a reason for all this. A purpose if you like. Mrs Debbon and her children are due to die in a fire in a couple of weeks' time. I've no idea whether we can do anything about it, but I really think that we ought to try."

The thought of Helen burning to death was not something that Matt wanted to dwell on.

"So what do you think we should do?"

"So far, each time we've gone back, it's been for a longer period than the one before," Connor said, marshalling his thoughts. "We were there for over two hours last time. That would seem to suggest that we'll be there even longer next time. By the way, that's why I suggested Saturday. That way it won't seem unusual if you're not around during the day. Anyway, I suggest that next time we flip back, we try to find out more about the family. Where they come from, for example."

"Why?"

"The paper and the websites all hinted at arson, that the fire was deliberate. Putting it bluntly, the family was murdered. If that's the case, then they've got enemies. If we're to stand any chance of helping, we need to know everything we can."

"That makes sense. Sort of. Just one thing about Saturday though. How do you know that Saturday's a Saturday?"

"Huh?"

"I mean, just because it's Saturday in our own time doesn't mean it's Saturday in 1898. Saturday now might be Wednesday back then."

"I hadn't even thought about that. We need to find out, or we'll flip back on Saturday to find we've arrived on the wrong day. Anyway, go online and see if you can find an 1898 calendar on there somewhere that'll tell us which day is which."

A quick search showed that the calendars coincided.

"That's lucky," Matt said. "It means that we can go back on Saturday and it'll be the same day there."

"I'm beginning to think that luck has nothing to do with it. I don't believe in coincidences. I think that the fact the both the day and the date are the same in both years is another reason why all this is happening."

"We only seem to flip back when we're both together," Matt said, "and so far it's only been from here, but do you think we'd flip back wherever we were?"

"You mean if we're in town or something?"

He got a nod in response.

"No idea. We could test it out if you want."

"How?" Matt asked.

"If you come and sleep over at my place tomorrow, we'll see what happens. If nothing happens, we'll come back up here on Saturday morning. We can tell Steve and Marion that you're spending the weekend with me. That way we can flip back for even longer and no-one will worry about it. "

"Fine with me."

"OK. If anything happens between now and then, just call or text me. I don't know yet what time I can pick you up, so I'll call in the early evening to let you know. Will you want feeding tomorrow evening?"

"You do ask stupid questions."

Kingskerswell Road

The boy with the notebook

There was no message before, so Connor duly phoned Matt early the next evening. Matt usually answered his phone within a couple of seconds, but this time it rang for quite some time before a cheerful "Hi, Uncle Conn" came on the line.

"That took you long enough," Connor said. "What were you doing?"

"Drying my hands. I didn't want to get the phone wet."

"Oh. Anyway, I've been doing some research to see if anything really important happened in 1898."

"Have you found out anything?"

"Yes and no. Quite a lot of things happened in or around April and May of 1898, but I'm certain that they're nearly all irrelevant."

"Nearly all?"

"Yes. There's just one that could have a bearing, but I'm not sure. The newspaper report about the fire mentioned that the late Mr Debbon had connections in France. There were elections in France in May of that year. The political situation was, to say the least, complicated. The left-wing parties, for the first time, had a landslide victory, which apparently shook up the French political system as a whole. It's too complicated to explain over the phone, but the changes were quite radical."

"And you think that the Debbons are tied up with that in some way?"

"I don't know. I can't think how they could be, but it's the only thing that I could find that just may have some connection with all this. On the other hand, it may well be a complete red herring."

Their conversation was interrupted by a loud splashing noise at Matt's end of the phone.

"What on earth was that?" Connor asked.

"Sorry, nearly dropped the phone."

"What was the splashing sound?"

"Me, sloshing the bathwater everywhere. I'll have to get it mopped up before Mum sees it or she'll go ballistic."

"You're in the bath?"

"Yes."

"I thought you hated having a bath."

"I do, but the shower's not working at the moment. Dad thinks the fire may have warped some of the pipes. So I'm stuck with having to have a bath for a couple of days until the plumber can get here."

"But you've still got your phone with you?"

"Of course."

"I think your Mum's right — you *are* permanently attached to it. Is there anywhere you go without the phone? On second thoughts, don't answer that. I was thinking of picking you up in about an hour. Is that OK?"

There were more splashing noises before Matt replied.

"That'll be fine. Gotta go now. I'm out of the bath and it's cold standing here with nothing on."

"That's a horrible thought. Bye, Matt, see you shortly."

◆

An hour later Connor was driving up Barton Hill Road, but as he slowed to take the turn off into Kingskerswell Road he saw Matt standing by the side of the road with his backpack.

"Hi," Matt said as he clambered into the car.

"Hi yourself. How come you're here and not at the house?"

"I was getting that tugging feeling again, so I thought that if I waited at the house then we'd flip back as soon as you got there. I wanted to see if it would happen here."

"Obviously it hasn't," Connor said, glancing around him.

"I don't think it will. The tugging feeling stopped as I got to the end of the road."

"Which makes me think that nothing's going to happen at my place either."

"Guess so."

"Oh well, we'll soon find out. So do you want to call in somewhere for a meal, or do you want to pick up fish and chips to take home?"

"Make that burger and chips and you're on."

◆

After an uneventful night, Connor hauled a protesting Matt out of bed at nine the next morning.

"That's twice in succession you've got me up early. I'm thinking of having you reported for cruelty."

"Think yourself lucky I left you until nine o'clock. Come on sleepy head, get your clothes on, we've got an appointment to keep with Mrs Debbon."

Muttering under his breath that some uncles were getting to be no fun at all, Matt did as he was asked, and they were soon on their way.

"I'd better park up before we get to your house, Matt. I don't particularly want your Mum and Dad to see us. They'll wonder why we're back, and there's always the chance that they'll see us flip. How we'd explain that I wouldn't have a clue."

"So what do we do?"

"Just walk along the lane, I suppose. If you were getting that tugging feeling yesterday I assume it means that we'll go quite quickly."

They did as he suggested and walked towards Matt's house.

"You got that feeling yet?" Connor asked.

"No, not yet, but it went as soon as I was out of sight of the house yesterday."

As they walked round the bend in the road and the corner of the house came in sight, Matt suddenly stopped.

"The feeling's back again. Can you sense it as well?"

"No, I can't feel anything."

"Perhaps it's just me then. It's a weird sensation, as if half a dozen people are pulling me in different directions all at the same time."

"Painful?"

"No, just odd. It's not as if they're pulling hard or anything like that."

As they reached the garden gate they both felt the same juddering sensation they'd experienced before and the scene in front of them grew misty and insubstantial, until a thick fog obscured it. When it cleared, they were rewarded with the sight of Belmont in all its glory standing before them. They opened the small gate at the side of the main entrance and started to walk along the drive, stopping before they reached the house to admire the formal gardens that bordered the immaculately raked gravel drive. As they did so, Connor caught a glimpse of something bright blue off to one side. He didn't say anything, but indicated to Matt that they should leave the drive and walk across the lawn a little way.

"Where are we going," Matt asked.

"You'll see in a minute."

They crossed the lawn and stood by the side of a dense shrubbery.

"If you're so interested in us, you'd see us a whole lot better if you'd come out from behind that bush," Connor said, addressing the nearest shrub.

The leaves parted to reveal a small boy of perhaps ten or eleven.

" 'Oo are you?" the boy asked.

"We're friends of Mrs Debbon and her family," Connor told him.

"Never seen yer before," came the suspicious reply.

"You know all the family's friends?"

"Yeah. I looks out fer the fam'ly, I does. Since they ain't got no man abaht the place, I keeps me eye on 'em, sees they don' get inter no trouble."

"Rather a small bodyguard, aren't you?" Matt asked.

"You wan' a thick lip?"

"Belligerent with it."

Connor nudged him to keep quiet.

"And does the family bodyguard have a name"

"Course I gots a name. Name's Bill, Bill Stone."

"Well, Master Stone, I'm very pleased to meet you. My name is Connor Harvey, and this is Matthew Harvey, although he doesn't like the name Matthew and prefers to be called Matt."

"Yer means yer likes to be called a carpet?" asked Bill, staring at Matt in some surprise.

"No, I'm just not particularly keen on the name Matthew, that's all."

"But a mat's a carpet, ain't it?"

"Yes, but it's not spelt the same. The kind of mat that means a carpet has only got one T, the name has got two Ts, and how did we get into this conversation?"

Bill ignored him and turned to Connor.

"I likes words, so I's always innerested in new uns, or ones wot are spelt diff'rent."

"It's unusual for someone of your age to like words. Have you always liked them?"

"Yeah. I's got this notebook, see, and when I sees or 'ears a word wot I ain't 'eard afore, I writes it dahn, plus what it means, or what I finks it means. That ways, when I gets back ter London, I'll be eddicated proper."

"May I look at the book?" Connor asked.

"Yer ain't gonna nick it?"

"No, I'm just interested."

Bill grudgingly handed the book over. It was full of surprisingly neat handwriting, and a long list of words with, for the most part, very accurate descriptions of the meanings.

"This is very good," Connor told him as he handed back the book. "When did you start using it?"

"'Bout a year ago. I's got pages for words wot are *fings* — them's nouns — and I's got pages for words wot describe fings — them's ad-jec-tives," he explained, saying the last word very carefully. "We're doin' 'em at school now."

"You go to school?"

"Course I go's to school," came the indignant reply, "you fink I'm common or summat?"

"I apologise, young man. What were you saying about going back to London?"

"Me old man, he brung Ma, me sister an' me dahn 'ere when I were little. When I's older, I's goin' ter go back ter London and make meself a lot of money. Then, when I's rich, I's goin' ter come back so's Mary-Anne and me can get married."

"You've got it all well planned," Connor said, trying hard to avoid laughing at the serious face looking up at him.

"Mary-Anne's a lady. I's got to be rich so's I can look after 'er proper."

"Does Mary-Anne know about this."

"Course she do. We talked abaht it. She's gonna wait for me."

"I admire someone who knows exactly what he wants and goes about getting it. Other young men that I know," Connor said, giving his nephew a sidelong glance, "have absolutely no idea what they want to do in life."

"Bollocks."

Bill stared at Matt for a few seconds before diving into his pocket for his notebook.

"Should I puts that under words wot mean sumfink, or words wot describes sumfink?" he asked Matt, who looked at Connor for help.

"Don't look at me, you dug this hole yourself."

"Well, I suppose it's a word that means something," Matt eventually said.

"So wot's it mean?"

"It's another word for a part of the body."

"Oh. So's I puts it dahn as a part of the body then?"

"Yes," said Matt, heaving a sigh of relief.

There was a long pause.

"So wot part of the body do it mean?"

◆

They left Bill writing in his book and walked back across the lawn to the drive.

"You could have helped me out there," Matt grumbled as they

neared the house.

"Just because you got yourself into a mess doesn't mean that I've got to get you out of it. Besides, the boy had a right to know exactly what the word meant."

"So why didn't you tell him?"

"Because you're the one who used it. By the way, we've come across him before."

"We have?"

"Yes. It was in the newspaper report about the fire. It said that there was a William Stone who was hurt trying to get into the house on the night of the fire to rescue the family. There was another name as well, of someone a bit older, but I can't remember it off-hand."

"I can. It was Daniel Hardwick. I remember because he's the same age as me."

"So he was. Well, we've now met William Stone, who obviously likes to be called Bill. Perhaps we'll meet Daniel Hardwick as well at some stage."

They reached the door and rang the bell. Mary-Anne, who had evidently been looking out for them, opened it.

"Mama told me that you were supposed to be calling today, but that your work might mean that you weren't able to come. We've been taking it in turns to look out for you. I only took over from Charles about five minutes ago, so he's going to be very cross that it was me here and not him. Mama's in the drawing room, so I'll take you through to her."

She proceeded to lead them through the entrance hall to the same room that they had been in before. This time, though, it was flooded with morning sunshine, and through the tall windows they could see the formal gardens at the rear of the house, plus a stunning view across the Daccombe valley. Mrs Debbon rose to greet them.

"Mr Harvey, Master Harvey. I'm delighted that you were able to be here. The children were all worried when I told them that your work might prevent it."

"Luckily, nothing of any importance cropped up. It's a

pleasure to be here."

"How would you care to proceed, Mr Harvey? Would you like to wander around the house at your leisure, or would you prefer one of the servants to escort you? I would have been delighted to show you myself, but I am due to attend a charity bazaar this morning."

"I think that it would be nice if someone could show me around the house to begin with, otherwise I'm likely to get lost."

"I'll show him, Mama," Mary-Anne piped up. "There's no need to bother anyone else."

"I hardly think that Mr Harvey would want you getting in his way, Mary-Anne."

Connor assured her that he couldn't think of a better guide, earning him a beaming smile from the girl.

"And you, Master Harvey, will you be accompanying your uncle on his tour, or would you prefer to do something else?"

As she was asking him, the door opened and Helen entered the room.

"I thought Matthew and I might go for a walk as it's such a lovely day," she said, having heard her mother's question. "That is unless you want to look round the house with your uncle, of course."

In spite of the sunlight streaming in through the windows, Matt couldn't help but get the feeling that the room had brightened considerably when Helen had walked in. As on the previous occasion, he was having trouble breathing, but managed to catch his breath long enough to be able to reply.

"I'd like to go for a walk, thank you. It would be great," he said.

"Good. Then that's settled. Would you like to go now, or would you like to wait for a while first?"

"Now would be fine, unless there's anything you want me to do, Uncle Conn?"

"Not that I can think of," he replied.

Connor walked with Matt and Helen to the door, pulling Matt to one side just before he left. He lowered his voice so that only

Matt could hear him.

"Matt, be careful. Social customs are very different here than they are in our own time. Don't come on too strong."

"I won't, don't worry. We're only going for a walk. Besides, you said you wanted to find out about the family, and this is a good chance to do that."

"I suppose it is. OK, you pump Helen for info about the family's background, and I'll do the same here. Don't be too long, because we don't know how long we've got here."

"We won't. Bye."

◆

Connor returned to the drawing room, to find that Charles had joined his sister and mother.

"Hello, Mr Harvey."

"Hello, Charles."

"You're still wearing those strange clothes. Haven't you got any proper ones?"

"Charles!" his mother exclaimed. "If you're going to be uncivil you can go back to the nursery and stay there for the morning. I've warned you about this before."

"It's all right, Mrs Debbon. Both Matt and I must look very odd to him. I regret, young man," he said, turning his attention to the boy, "that we came to Torquay so quickly that we didn't have time to pack anything other than the clothes we were wearing in Wales. No doubt we will get some others in due course."

"Don't listen to him, Mr Harvey. I think they look just fine," said Mary-Anne.

"Thank you, young lady. Now, I believe you volunteered to escort me around the house."

"Why can't I show him? I'm the man of the house," asked Charles.

"Because I offered first," Mary-Anne stated indignantly.

"Why don't you both show me," Connor suggested.

"Are you sure that you will be all right, Mr Harvey?" asked Mrs Debbon. "It will be no trouble to get one of the servants to escort you."

"Please, Mrs Debbon, it's no problem. It will be fun having two enthusiastic guides."

"Well, if you're certain," she said. "I must go now, as Edward will have brought the carriage round to the front of the house and will be waiting for me. I will not be gone for very long, two hours at most. You will still be here when I get back?"

"I see no reason why not."

"Then I will see you later, Mr Harvey. And I trust that you two," she said sternly, addressing Mary-Anne and Charles, "will not cause too much trouble whilst I'm away."

"No, Mama," they answered in chorus.

Once Mrs Debbon had left, the two children each took one of Connor's hands and started to show him around the great house. They were both constantly plying him with questions, with 'Mr Harvey' this and 'Mr Harvey' that, so much so that Connor was feeling tired before they'd even looked round the ground floor.

"I think," he said, after another series of questions, "that it would be a lot simpler if you were both to call me 'Uncle Connor'."

They both giggled and asked him even more questions than before. At least, he thought to himself, he was able to pick up a few bits of information about the family from what they were saying. He wondered if Matt was having such a trying time.

CHAPTER EIGHT

Questions without answers

Matt was having a wonderful time.

"What a beautiful morning," Helen said, as they halted by an old gate. "It's the sort of morning I wish I could put in a bottle, so that I could open it whenever I want, especially in the winter, when it's cold and dark. I especially like the view from here, don't you?"

They gazed across the rich landscape, the bright green of early spring dappling the fields and the hedgerows. There was a valley in front of them, and as they looked over it, a plume of smoke moved slowly along the valley floor. It took Matt a few moments to realise that it was a steam train travelling along the railway line towards Newton Abbot.

"Uncle Conn would have loved to have seen that," he said. "He's into steam engines and things."

"Really? I would have thought your uncle was the sort of person who would be more into antiques than modern-day things."

"He is. That's why he likes steam trains. I'm more into cars myself."

"Cars?" was the disapproving response. "I don't think I like them very much. Very dirty, smelly things, and not at all reliable."

"Not yet, but I believe they will be one day."

"They'll never replace horses. You can rely on a horse."

Matt decided to change the subject. He knew he ought to be trying to get some information about Helen's family, something that might help them make sense of why he and Connor kept on flipping back to 1898. He tried to think of something.

"Do you ever go away on holiday?" he eventually asked.

"Mama has friends in the south of France, so we usually spend part of each summer with them."

"How much of the summer?"

"Oh, not very long really. Sometimes as little as five weeks, but usually six or seven weeks."

"Six or seven weeks?" Matt said, in some surprise.

"Yes. I know it's not long, but it's not easy getting away for a real holiday. How about you?"

"The most I managed last year was a week on Tenerife."

"Tenerife? I don't believe I've heard of it."

"It's one of the Canary Islands."

"I don't believe I've heard of them either. Where are they?"

"They're in the Atlantic Ocean, about a hundred miles from the African coast."

"Africa! How wonderfully exotic. I wish we could go somewhere really exciting. Mama's friends are very nice, but terribly dull."

"I don't think Tenerife is particularly exotic."

"But it sounds so exciting, being so close to Africa. You say you went just for one week."

"Yes."

"But how did you get there? Surely it would have taken nearly a week each way?"

"No, nowhere near. We flew there, of course."

The smile disappeared from Helen's face.

"Really, Mr Harvey, I do not appreciate being the object of sarcasm."

"No, I'm sorry Helen, I'm not making fun of you, honest," Matt replied, mentally kicking himself. "When I said we flew, I meant the ship we went on was so fast it seemed like flying."

A weak smile returned.

"But I still don't see how you could get there and back within a week and still have time to stay there."

"We didn't. I meant we had a week actually there. It took four days each way, sailing from Plymouth, but I wasn't counting the days we were on the boat, or the time it took us to get to Plymouth."

The smile returned in full force.

"I'm sorry. I can be very stupid sometimes. Mama says I must take after Papa at times like this. I want to know what sort of things you did on holiday and where you went. Tell me all about it, I want to know everything."

Get yourself out of this one, Matt thought. He could hardly tell her about aquaparks, crazy golf, cable cars, bars and nightclubs. He took a deep breath and managed to answer Helen's question without making a complete fool of himself.

"Has your mother known these friends in France for long?" he asked, after eventually satisfying Helen's thirst for knowledge about the Canary Islands.

"Oh yes, many years. They were actually friends of Papa's first, but after he and Mama married they became friends of both of them. Then, after Papa died, Mama carried on seeing them. We used to see other people in France as well. They were also Papa's friends, but Mama didn't like them very much, so she stopped seeing them after he died. I think there was some trouble with them, and Mama got very upset."

"Trouble?" asked Matt. "What sort of trouble?"

"I'm not sure. But we don't want to talk about that on such a lovely morning, do we Matthew?"

Yes, we do, he thought.

"No," he said, "of course not."

"Good. Let's walk a little further along the path. There's another view at the end across the valley that I'd like you to see."

◆

When Mrs Debbon returned to Belmont, she found that Connor was still being shown around by the two children, each of whom seemed to be competing for his attention.

"Charles, Mary-Anne, leave Mr Harvey alone now. I'm sure he's had more than enough of you both."

"But Mama . . . ." they both started up.

"No buts, if you please. Now both of you go and find Mrs Gregson and ask her to find out from Cook what she intends serving us for luncheon."

"Are you staying for luncheon, Uncle Connor?" asked Mary-Anne.

"I'm not sure."

"You are most welcome to stay, Mr Harvey. It is usually a very informal affair. I prefer to reserve the formalities until the evening."

"Then I accept with pleasure on behalf of Matt and myself. Assuming, that is, that he and Helen return from their walk in time."

"Helen will make sure that they are back in good time. She knows how vexed I get if people are late for meals. It isn't fair on the servants to keep them hanging around."

"It must take a large number of staff to maintain a property like this in such good order," Connor said.

"Yes, it does, but I have had to cut the numbers in recent times. As a widow with a young family to support, I find that I cannot maintain the size of establishment that we once did. We are now down to sixteen servants in total. When my husband was alive we used to have a staff of twenty-seven."

"You just have sixteen servants?"

"Yes. Not counting the gardeners or the stable staff, of course."

"Of course," he replied, trying to work out what the annual cost of maintaining a staff of sixteen plus gardeners, grooms, stable lads and, presumably, general handymen would be. "Do they live in?"

"Nine of them do, the others, mostly the kitchen staff, live locally. Most have been with us for years."

Connor would have liked to ask for more details of the staff, to see if there was anything there that could account for the forthcoming murders, but decided that it wouldn't be prudent just yet.

"When I was being shown around the first floor, I didn't notice any stairs leading up to the attic floor."

"There is no attic floor here, Mr Harvey. The main house has just the ground and first floor, plus a basement with the kitchens and storerooms."

"And the servants' quarters?"

"Mr Davenport, the original owner of the house, was afraid of just about everybody, as I believe you know. Therefore, he would not allow any servant to remain in the house once he had retired for the night. The servants were, and still are, accommodated in a separate wing connected to the house by a short corridor. The connecting door would be locked from the inside at night."

"So he would then be all alone in the house?"

"Yes. He was, by all accounts, a very strange man."

"And you and the children are therefore alone at night?"

"Yes, but the door is now never locked, so if I or the children require anything at night, we can summon a member of staff and they can be here in moments."

Except, Connor thought to himself, when the door *is* locked, as we know it was on the night of the fire from the newspaper report. Otherwise the servants would have been able to reach the family. His thoughts were interrupted by the arrival of Matt and Helen, back from their walk.

"Hello, you two. Enjoy your walk?" he asked.

"Sure, it was great," Matt said.

"It was really most pleasurable," Helen added. "I must go and change, if you will excuse me."

"And I will arrange for luncheon to be served shortly," Mrs Debbon said, moving towards the fireplace to pull the cord to summon the maid, but stopping halfway. "On second thoughts, I will go and make the arrangements myself. I expect that the children will have ignored my request to ask Mrs Gregson to contact Cook and have instead gone down to the kitchens themselves. I need to make sure that they are not hampering Cook too much. I think they spend more time in the kitchen than they do anywhere else."

Mrs Debbon and Helen left the room, leaving Connor and Matt alone together.

"You look like the cat that got the cream," Connor told him. "What's put the smile on your face?"

"Don't know what you mean."

"Oh really? That innocent look of yours might be able to fool everyone else, but not me, so give."

"Honest, it's nothing. We just walked down the lane, across a couple of fields and then along a footpath. You'd have liked the view because you can see the trains on the railway line in the valley and of course they're still steam trains in this time. Then we walked further along the path because Helen said there was another view she wanted to show me. There's a big house on the hill the other side of the railway line. Helen said it's called Hengive or something like that."

"Hengrave?"

"Yeah, that's right, Hengrave. You know it?"

"I know *of* it. It's still there but completely dwarfed by surrounding buildings."

"I thought I hadn't seen it before."

"You may not have seen the house but you've been very close to it enough times."

"Have I?"

"You have. It's part of Torbay Hospital which was built in the grounds of Hengrave. I think the original house is now used as offices or something. And you've been in the hospital enough times over the years."

"Don't remind me. If there's a bone that I haven't broken, I haven't found it yet."

"Well, if you insist on playing contact sports you must expect these things."

"But why me? No-one else seems to get injured."

"No-one else is daft enough to get so involved. Anyway, did you manage to find anything out about the family? Anything that would give a clue as to what's going to happen, or rather why?"

"Not really. Helen did mention some friends in France, or rather ex-friends. They were friends of her father, but her mother didn't care for them, so after he died they more or less lost contact."

"You don't know why she didn't like them?"

"No. I got the impression it's a sore subject, because Helen didn't want to talk about it and sort of clammed up on me. How about you, any luck?"

"Not much. I didn't get anything from Mrs Debbon, other than the fact that she feels a bit hard done by having to manage with only sixteen members of staff as opposed to the twenty-seven that they had when Mr Debbon was around. And that isn't counting the gardeners or those that look after the stables and the horses. I managed a bit better with Charles and Mary-Anne. It seems that there are sometimes callers at the house late at night, after everyone except Mrs Debbon has gone to bed. Mary-Anne says that they're not supposed to know about it, but their nurse insists that they have to have a window open in the nursery at night and Charles gets woken up by the sound of people walking across the gravel."

"Does he know who they are?"

"No, but he said that he heard angry voices a couple of times, and his mother shouting at someone. This, I gather, is such a rare occurrence as to be memorable. Apparently, Mrs Debbon *never* shouts at anyone."

"I wouldn't think she needs to. Would you argue with her?"

"I wouldn't dare."

"Exactly."

"Next job, then, is to find out who annoyed her so much that she felt the need to shout at them."

"How do we do that?" Matt asked.

"Don't know. It's hardly the sort of thing we can bring up at the lunch table."

"We're staying for lunch?"

"We've been invited, but I gather lunch is very informal. I'm worried about how long we've been here, though. We don't want to be sitting having lunch and then just vanish into thin air."

"Perhaps we should leave now."

"It would seem rude, and if we're going to discover any more then we don't want to get anyone's back up. I'm hoping we'll get some sort of warning that we're going to flip — enough warning to be able to make our excuses and leave anyway."

They were interrupted by the return of Mrs Debbon.

"Now that I have removed Charles and Mary-Anne from the kitchen, it seems we can have luncheon in about twenty minutes. I will get Mrs Gregson to show you upstairs."

"Mrs Gregson?" Connor asked.

"The housekeeper," she told him.

Connor had the distinct impression that Mrs Gregson wasn't Mrs Debbon's favourite employee but decided not to enquire further. The maid was summoned and asked to fetch the housekeeper.

If Connor had been asked to paint a mental picture of a late-middle-aged, severe, dissatisfied, permanently disapproving spinster, then he'd have painted Mrs Gregson. Tall and thin to the point of being gaunt, she was dressed from head to toe in black. Her dark hair was scraped back and tied with a small black bow, something that did nothing to enhance her pale complexion. Connor knew only too well that appearances could be deceiving, that one should never judge a person from their looks, but in Mrs Gregson's case he felt reasonably confident that his first impression was probably correct.

"Mrs Gregson, could you please show our guests upstairs?"

"Yes, Madam. The . . . gentlemen are staying for luncheon?"

Connor noted with wry amusement the short pause before her use of the word 'gentlemen'. Obviously she didn't approve of Connor and Matt.

"Yes, Mrs Gregson, Mr Harvey and his nephew will be joining us."

"As you wish, Madam. If you would care to follow me, gentlemen."

She led them upstairs and along one of the corridors, stopping at one of the doors.

"I think you will find everything you require in here, but if you need anything else, just pull on the rope by the door and one of the footmen will fetch whatever you need."

"Thank you," Connor said. "Have you worked for Mrs

Debbon for long?"

"I have been with the family for many years."

"You knew Mr Debbon then?"

"I was Mr Debbon's housekeeper before he married. Now, if you will excuse me, gentlemen, I have duties to attend to."

They entered a large, well-appointed bathroom.

"I wouldn't like to meet her on a dark night," Matt said. "What waxworks did they find her in?"

"Don't be nasty. She may well be a very nice person. You can't tell just by looking at someone what they're like," Connor said, only too aware that he'd been doing exactly the same thing himself moments before.

"I can't see her being the life and soul of the staff Christmas party. Anyway, why have we been shown to a bathroom?" Matt asked.

"Because it wasn't done for a lady to ask a gentleman if he needed to use the loo. She would also expect us to have a quick wash."

"The loo I can understand, but why the wash? I thought she said lunch was informal."

"Depends what you mean by informal."

"Informal means having a sandwich in the kitchen."

"I don't think you'll find it does here."

◆

A loud gong sounded a few minutes later, its echoes reverberating around the house.

"What on earth was that?" Matt asked.

"Lunch, I assume. We'd better go down before they send someone to find us."

They walked down the grand staircase to find Helen waiting for them.

"Mama asked me to wait and show you into the dining room."

"Thank you," Connor said, "but it's the door over there, isn't it? I remember from my tour with Charles and Mary-Anne this morning."

"Yes, it is. Anyway, we'd better go in; Mama is a stickler for time keeping."

"So I understand."

They entered the dining room to find the rest of the family already seated at the table. The dining room was a much more formal room than the drawing room, lined with rich mahogany panelling and with solid, heavy looking furniture. The table was covered with a clean, white damask cloth on which a silver service gleamed in the sunlight pouring through the windows.

"Please be seated, gentlemen," Mrs Debbon said, indicating the two empty seats.

If this was informal, Matt thought, as they were served with piping hot soup, freshly made bread rolls and a beef salad, then he wasn't sure if he wanted to see a formal meal. As it was, there were four servants in the room, all busy seeing that the family and its guests had everything they wanted. He wondered if it was the done thing to talk during the meal, but didn't like to be the one to start a conversation, in case it was frowned upon. Mrs Debbon solved the problem for him.

"So, Master Harvey, Helen tells me that you and she enjoyed your walk this morning?"

"Yes, Mrs Debbon, we certainly did. It was fun."

"I'm not sure what there is in a walk to be called fun, but if you enjoyed it then I am happy for you."

"We enjoyed our walk around the house this morning, didn't we, Uncle Connor," Charles piped up.

"I'm pleased," said Mrs Debbon, "but I'm not sure I approve of you calling Mr Harvey 'Uncle Connor'. It's rather familiar."

"Don't scold him, Mrs Debbon, it was my idea. They were asking so many questions this morning that I thought it would make things simpler for all of us."

"Well, if you're sure that you don't mind?"

"Quite sure, Mrs Debbon. It reminds me of when Matt was their age, he was always asking questions."

"Then I have no objection."

"Incidentally, we met the family bodyguard this morning."

"I beg your pardon? Our bodyguard?"

"Yes. A very small one who goes by the name of Bill."

"Oh, I see. Young Master Stone. I take it he was in the garden?"

"Yes. He seems to have taken on the role of the family protector."

"He has indeed. He and his family live in a small cottage in Barton. His elder sister Martha works here as a kitchen assistant. Ever since we took her on about two years ago, young William seems to have been under the impression that we need protecting. Mary-Anne, did you know that William was in the garden this morning?"

"No, Mama," she replied.

"I did," Charles said. "I saw him in the garden when I was watching out for Uncle Connor and Master Harvey to arrive."

"Oh dear. Is he still there?"

"I don't know, Mama."

"Geoffrey," Mrs Debbon said, beckoning one of the servants over to her. "Would you be kind enough to see if young William Stone is still in the garden and if he is, then tell him to go to the kitchen. Then please ask Cook if she will kindly see that he is given a meal."

"Certainly, Madam."

"I'll go, Mama," Mary-Anne interrupted. "He's probably hiding somewhere and I'll know where to look."

"Oh, very well, but kindly do not be too long. I do not wish luncheon to be disturbed any more than is necessary. Remember we have guests."

"Yes, Mama."

She left the room and shortly after they could see her through the windows running across the lawn and disappearing out of sight into the shrubbery. She reappeared in a couple of minutes with Bill in tow and not much later she re-entered the dining room.

"I sent him down to the kitchens, Mama, and I asked Hannah to feed him as you asked."

"Thank you," she said, and then turned to Connor. "I have given up trying to stop that boy from keeping guard on us. At least I have managed to see that he is receiving an education. I thought perhaps that he would object to being sent to school, but he seems to be coping remarkably well."

Connor kept quiet about knowing that the only reason that Bill was going to school was so that he could make his fortune and then marry Mary-Anne.

"I like Bill," Charles said. "He's funny."

"I'm sure he is. Now kindly eat your meal."

◆

Lunch passed pleasantly for all concerned. Matt was looking forward to spending more time with Helen in the afternoon, but almost as soon as the meal was finished he thought he could hear, even though faintly, the high-pitched whine that he and Connor had heard each time they'd been dragged back to their own time. He looked over at Connor, who returned his gaze with a slight nod. He could evidently hear it as well.

"Thank you very much for a delicious meal, Mrs Debbon. I regret that Matt and I must take our leave of you now."

"Oh, but Mr Harvey, I had hoped to show Matthew around the garden this afternoon. Can you not stay a little longer?" asked Helen.

The noise was getting louder and Connor realised that they didn't have much time left.

"I'm sorry, but I have an engagement this afternoon that I must keep and unfortunately Matthew has to come with me. Come on Matt, or we'll be late."

"We will see you again, Mr Harvey?" Mrs Debbon asked as she escorted them to the door.

"I am certain you will. I would very much like to have a further look at the works of art in the house. Perhaps I could repay your hospitality by making a more detailed catalogue than the list that you have at present?"

"Certainly, but we can discuss it on your next visit. Do you know when that is likely to be?"

I wish I did, he thought to himself.

"I'm sorry, but my work means that I cannot make plans very far in advance. It may be possible to call tomorrow, if that is convenient to you."

"It would be a pleasure. The children and I attend church in the morning, but if you would care to call in the afternoon, that would be excellent."

"Thank you. We may see you then. Good-bye, and thank you again."

"Good-bye to you both."

She closed the door quietly behind them. As soon as it was shut, they ran as fast as they could along the drive and into the lane, the high-pitched noise now louder and more intense. The noise seemed to penetrate directly into their skulls, almost as if it was coming from inside their heads. They both cried out in pain, and then, abruptly, it stopped. Matt recovered first, and looked around him.

"We've flipped, Uncle Conn. We're outside my house again. Whatever that noise is, it's getting louder every time."

"And a lot more painful. I hope it doesn't get any worse."

"Still no idea what it is?"

"No. We'll find out eventually, no doubt."

"Probably just before our eardrums burst and we're both deafened for life."

"Cheerful soul, aren't you?"

"It's all this dodging back and forth in time, it's unsettling me."

"It's unsettling both of us."

They stood still for a while to recover their breath.

"Hello. We weren't expecting you back until tomorrow evening," said a voice.

Looking up, they saw that Marion was in the garden weeding.

"Hi, Mum," Matt said. "I needed a textbook for my homework, so Uncle Conn ran me up here to get it."

"Where's the car?" she asked, staring down the lane.

"It was making a funny spluttering noise so I didn't want to drive further up the hill in case it stalled. I can always coast back down if I can't get it to start," Connor said, thinking quickly.

"Want me to get Steve to have a look at it for you? He's only inside reading the paper."

"No, it's probably all right now. Bit of muck in the petrol feed, I expect."

"Well, if you're sure. Anyway, while Matt's getting his book I'll make you a coffee."

◆

Half an hour later they were on their way back to Connor's house.

"Where do we go from here?" Matt asked as they were driving down the hill.

"Come back up tomorrow and see what happens, I suppose. At least you're off college tomorrow, so there's no problem there. It's what happens after the weekend that's bothering me. If we keep flipping back for longer and longer then someone at your college is going to notice your absence and phone up to find out where you are. What we do then I've no idea."

"We could try telling the truth."

"Do you really think anyone would believe us?"

"Probably not."

"Even if they did, your Mum and Dad would probably try to stop you going."

"How would they do that? It just happens."

"I know that, and you know that. Trying to convince anyone else might prove impossible. Up to you, though. If you think it's worth a go, then I'll back you up."

Matt thought about it as they drove down to Connor's cottage. He came to a conclusion as they were getting out of the car.

"No, I don't think we should say anything. It would only make more problems and we've got enough already."

"So what we're going to have to do is find some means of explaining your absence from college. Any bright ideas?"

"I could manage a couple of days by pretending to be ill, but then Mum would want to make sure I was all right so she'd be checking on me every few minutes and if I wasn't in bed or resting on the couch then she'd wonder where I'd got to."

"Well, we've got until tomorrow evening to think of something. We'll have to get it sorted by the time I drop you home — assuming of course that we're here and not in 1898."

"What about *you*?"

"What *about* me?"

"About your work. You can't just disappear either."

"Not a problem. I've still got most of my holiday entitlement due. The fire is due to happen in about two weeks from now, or from now in 1898 that is, so I'll book a fortnight's leave starting on Monday."

"Don't you need to give more notice than that?"

"Yes, but·I'll make out that I've got a family crisis to sort out. There won't be a problem. It's just you that we've got to work something out for, especially as you've got exams coming up at the end of May."

"Don't remind me," Matt said, as he followed Connor into the house.

◆

"Clothes," Connor announced a little later.

"Huh?"

"Clothes. If we're going to keep flipping back we need clothes. We can't keep on appearing in modern dress. We need period clothes. There's a top-flight film and theatrical costume provider in Torquay. We just need to hire the right clothes from them."

An hour or so later there was a small heap of clothes on the back seat of the car as they headed back to Connor's house.

"At least we won't stick out like sore thumbs next time," Connor said. "I'm not sure the clothes will pass muster at close quarters, but they won't be as obviously wrong as the ones we've been wearing."

◆

"I look a total dork," Matt fumed that evening, as he stood in front of a mirror wearing his hired suit. "And this collar is throttling me."

"Think yourself lucky that the clothes are made of modern material. At least they're soft and stretchy. The real thing would be a lot coarser and rougher. If we go back for any length of time, we may well end up having to buy some genuine clothes."

"These are bad enough, thank you very much."

"Anyway, I think you look very smart."

He was rewarded with a glowering look as Matt stomped off to change back into his ordinary clothes.

CHAPTER NINE

Meeting Daniel

The strangers watch from the darkness, concealing themselves in the cover of the trees at the end of the garden. There is no need for this. It is a moonless night, but they feel safer this way. The darkness is their friend, the more of it the better. They watch and they wait. They have seen the arrival of the man and the youth earlier in the day, and consider whether or not this is a threat. Their instructions were explicit. Nothing must go wrong; nothing must stand in the way. If the unknown man and youth are perceived to be a threat, they will be removed. Quietly, but permanently. The girls are unimportant, the mother only slightly less so. Only the boy matters. He is vital to their plan. If others must be sacrificed, then so be it. They are dispensable. There will be no questioning the morality, no self-doubt, and no mercy.

They consult each other and weigh the arrival of the couple in the balance. They decide that, for the moment anyway, they will wait. Wait and watch. It will not be long before the time comes to act, for time is something they do not have much of. They must act within the next two weeks. Others of their calling have been applying pressure on the mother for many months, but she will not, so far, yield. The boy would be easier to manipulate if the mother would go with them. In the end though, if she does not agree, they will have to take the boy on his own. It will make the task much more difficult for she is not without friends and the boy could prove obstinate. They may have no choice. Nothing matters but the boy. They settle themselves back into the darkness to watch and to wait.

◆

"If anyone sees me wearing these things, I'm never going to live it down," Matt grumbled as he and Connor walked along the Kingskerswell Road the following afternoon.

"Doesn't bother me if anyone sees us," Connor told him.

"That's because you never wear anything decent in the first place. How do we explain the clothes if we get to my place and find that we don't flip?"

"I'll leave that to you. You'll think of something."

"You're no help at all."

Fog obscured them as they walked along the lane, blowing away to reveal the now familiar grey outline of Belmont. Their arrival had evidently been anticipated and the front door was opened before they reached it by Charles, whose turn it was to keep watch for them.

"Hello Uncle Connor, hello Master Harvey," he said.

"Hello to you as well," Connor said.

"You're not wearing those strange clothes again," he said, sounding disappointed.

"No, we were able to buy these yesterday afternoon."

"I liked the other clothes better," he stated.

"So did I," Matt agreed, with considerable feeling.

"They looked very comfortable, Master Harvey."

"They are, or rather they were. And there's no need to call me Master Harvey," Matt told him. "My name's Matthew, or just Matt if you like."

"Thank you. I'll go and tell the others that you're here."

He raced off, leaving them in the entrance hall. Because of his walk with Helen the previous day, Matt hadn't yet seen much of the house nor had time to study the hall in any detail. Whilst they waited for Mrs Debbon, he let his eyes wander over the intricate carving of the columns and brackets that supported the first-floor gallery, and of the beams that held up the roof high above them. He wasn't as passionate about old buildings as his uncle or his father were, but had seen a fair number over the years, enough to recognise that the workmanship at Belmont was of the very highest quality. Mr Davenport may have been a very strange man and scared of just about everybody, but he evidently hadn't lacked taste. There was something very satisfying about the entrance hall. Large as it was, it didn't seem overpowering. Part of that was due to the light oak with which it was panelled, but it was also down to the delicacy of the carvings and the clever way that daylight was refracted by the glass in the lantern that rose above the roofline, causing spears of sunlight to dapple the panelling and make the dust motes gleam in the air as the light caught them. He looked at the series of doors that opened onto the gallery and idly wondered which one of them was the door to Helen's room. He decided that maybe he hadn't better let his train of thought follow that route. Perhaps fortunately Mrs Debbon chose that moment to enter the hall.

"Gentlemen, how pleasant to see you again. My apologies that you've been left waiting in the hall. Charles was supposed to have shown you into the drawing room, but I regret that his excitement caused him to forget his manners."

"It's of no importance, Mrs Debbon. We were admiring the workmanship of the hall."

"It's extremely fine, is it not?" she said. "My late husband considered it the finest example of its type in Torquay, much better than the reception rooms in even the best hotels in the town."

She escorted them into the drawing room and invited them to be seated.

"I have been considering your offer to catalogue the collection, Mr Harvey, and I would like to accept. How would you wish to proceed from here?"

"I would prefer to put in as much time as I can, depending of course on developments in my employment. If I am contacted by my superiors on the Great Western Railway then I will have to leave at a moment's notice."

"I understand. There is also the matter of the book that you are working on?"

"There's no problem there. There's no deadline to meet, so it really doesn't matter if it takes six weeks, six months or even six years to write. I can always continue with it after I have finished the task here. Besides, making a proper catalogue of the works in the collection could almost be described as part of the job anyway."

"If you are certain that it is no problem to you, then you may start when you wish, and also come and go as you wish. What about you, Master Harvey? I would imagine that staying here all the time would soon bore you. Perhaps you would prefer to stay in your hotel, or perhaps take a few local excursions whilst you are in the area? There are several companies offering charabanc trips to places along the coast and even one or two onto Dartmoor, although why anyone in their right senses would want to visit such a remote and desolate area, I have no idea."

"Thanks, Mrs Debbon, but I'd just as soon come up here with Uncle Conn whenever he comes."

"In that case you will be most welcome. I know that Helen in particular will be pleased. She has spent much of the past hour trying on dresses. I believe she wishes to create an impression."

She already has, Matt thought.

"Now, as I believe you are aware, I usually rest in the afternoon, so I shall retire now for a while. Helen will be down shortly, but I have instructed Charles and Mary-Anne not to disturb you until later. That way you may get the chance to view the house at a somewhat more leisurely pace than yesterday. I trust that will be agreeable to you?"

"Very agreeable, thank you," Connor said.

"In which case I will see you in a few hours. If you need anything then just pull one of the cords and ask to see James or Mrs Gregson. They will fetch you whatever you require."

Almost as soon as the door had closed behind her it reopened to admit Helen.

"Mr Harvey, how nice to see you again. And you too, of course, Matthew."

"You're looking especially attractive this afternoon," Connor said. "That dress brings out the colour of your eyes."

"Why thank you, Mr Harvey, but this is only an old thing that has been hanging about for a while. I don't really know why I decided to wear it today."

Connor decided not to let on that her mother had already told them how long it had taken her to get ready. Besides, he knew who the effort was directed at and it certainly wasn't him. He glanced at Matt to see if the dress was having the desired effect. It was.

"Hello, Helen," Matt eventually managed, his voice sounding somewhat unsteady.

"Mama tells me that you are going to catalogue the paintings and other items in the house, Mr Harvey. Won't you find that terribly dull?"

"Not in the least," he said. "It will be most interesting."

"Uncle Conn's always liked old things. That's why he keeps on looking in mirrors."

"Thanks, brat, I love you too. Anyway, whilst this old man is busy cataloguing, what are you going to do?"

"I don't know. How about you and me going for another walk?" Matt asked Helen.

"That will be most pleasant. I'll go and fetch a coat, this dress is rather thin."

"Matt," Connor said after she'd left the room, "whilst you're on your walk, see if you can get any more information about those ex-friends in France, plus anything else you can find out. That fire's going to happen in less than two weeks. If we're going to do something about it we've got to get a move on."

"Why don't we just tell Mrs Debbon what we know?"

"Oh sure. 'Excuse us, Mrs Debbon, we're actually time travellers from the future and we know that you and your family are about to be murdered.' She'd have us locked up."

"Sorry, dumb idea. OK, I'll try and find out more. How about you?"

"When Mary-Anne and Charles are let out again I'll try to find out something from them. I don't want to ask any of the staff in case they get suspicious and tell Mrs Debbon that they're being pumped for information."

"Fine."

"Any idea where you're going to go on your walk?"

"Not really. I suppose we could walk along the lanes to Daccombe. That's still rural in our time, so I don't suppose it's changed that much from now."

"Don't forget that we're supposed to be visitors. Helen won't expect you to know any of the lanes around here."

"I'll leave it to her."

Helen returned a few minutes later, and she suggested that they could take a stroll down to Barton village.

"I want to take a few things down for Martha and William's mother," she said.

"Martha and William?"

"Yes. Martha's one of Cook's assistants and William you met yesterday, in the garden."

"Oh, of course, you mean Bill."

"Yes, only Mama doesn't approve of shortening people's names. Mama says that a person's name is part of them and should never be shortened."

"I suppose that means that she won't call me Matt if I ask her to?"

"No. However, she would call you Matthew if you would prefer it to Master Harvey."

"I would."

"Then I will tell her later on. Your uncle calls you Matt, does he not?"

"Yes, he always has. Everyone does, except my grandparents, who insist on calling me Matthew."

"Would you be offended if I did likewise?"

"Of course not, I'd be delighted, but won't your mother object?"

"Probably."

"I wouldn't want you to get into trouble just for calling me Matt. Perhaps you'd better call me Matthew when your mother's around."

"There won't be any trouble. Now that I'm sixteen, Mama considers that I'm old enough to make my own decisions, even if they're ones that she really doesn't approve of very much."

"Well, if you're sure."

"It will be fine. Anyway, I was thinking that on the way down to the village we could call in and see if Daniel would care to come as well. He lives a little way down the road. You'll like him. His father owns a small fleet of coastal steamers. They've just started supplying the new electricity works at Beacon Quay with coal. Daniel says that electricity is the way forward, and that it will soon replace gas for lighting and heating."

Matt was very put out by the idea of someone else muscling in on their walk but wisely decided not to say anything until the memory of the newspaper article came to him.

"This Daniel," he said. "Would that be Daniel Hardwick?"

"Yes," said Helen in surprise, "it would. How on earth did you know that?"

"Er, it was when we were down by the harbour," he replied, wishing he could learn to keep his mouth shut. "There was a steamship moored against Beacon Quay with the name 'Hardwick' on it as the owner. I just guessed because you said that his father owned some ships."

"How very clever of you," she said. "I think you and Daniel will get on very well. He's sixteen and we've known each other since we were ten. Incidentally, how old are you, if you don't mind me asking?"

"I don't mind. I'm sixteen as well."

"Wonderful! Then we'll all get on famously. You're sure that you won't get bored here by yourself, Mr Harvey?" Helen asked, turning towards him. "You could always come with us if you wanted to?"

"No, thank you. I'll be just fine here. You two go and enjoy yourselves."

As they left the house, Matt found himself thinking that he'd enjoy it a whole lot more if they didn't have to call in for Daniel.

◆

To Matt's regret, Daniel was at home when they called and readily agreed to accompany them. He was a cheerful young man, who looked at Matt a little oddly, but shook his hand readily enough when Helen introduced them to each other.

"We're just going down to Barton," Helen told Daniel. "I asked Hannah to make up a basket of food for Martha and

William's family. I have to be careful though. Mr Stone has been out of work for a long time since he had an accident, and he's a very proud man. He won't accept what he sees as charity."

"Where are you from, Matthew?" Daniel asked, as they strolled down the narrow and leafy lane.

"Warwickshire," Matt told him, going through the story that he and Connor had made up. Luckily, Daniel had no more idea where Warwickshire was than Helen had.

"Matt saw one of your father's ships in the harbour," Helen told Daniel. "He guessed what your surname was by seeing it on it. Wasn't that clever?"

"I didn't know one of Father's ships was here," he replied in some surprise. "I thought they were all still at sea. When was this?"

"Er, I'm not exactly sure," Matt said. "A couple of days ago, I think."

"Odd. Father never told me."

"Perhaps they just called in for supplies or something," Matt said, trying desperately to get himself out of a hole that seemed to be getting deeper by the minute.

"Perhaps. I must remember to ask Father next time I see him."

In Matt's time, Barton was an urban sprawl, with only a few old cottages dotted here and there as a reminder that it had once been a separate settlement, albeit a small one. In 1898 it was still a rural community with a life of its own. As they walked into the heart of the village, Matt couldn't help but think that if it had managed to survive intact instead of being drowned by developments in the 1920s and '30s, then it would have become a major tourist attraction. He also knew that the thatched cottages, occupied by some of the poorest people, would fetch astounding sums of money in the twenty-first century. They stopped outside one such cottage. The thatch on the roof needed major repair, but the tiny garden was neatly kept, and the short path to the door was swept free of leaves and debris. Helen knocked at the door and it was opened by a plump, rosy-faced lady who beamed widely on seeing her.

"Why, it's Miss Helen. Come in, my dear, and your friends,

come in."

She ushered them into the low, dark room, which, though poorly furnished, was spotlessly clean.

"Jem, see here, it's Miss Helen come to visit, from the big house."

This was addressed to the occupant of the chair by the fireside, a thin wizened man, with a grey pinched look.

"'Ow do," he said. "You'll excuse me if I don' get up, only me bloomin' back's givin' me jip."

"Of course, Mr Stone. There's no improvement then?"

"Nah. Them doctors don' know nuthin," he said. "They gives me stuff but it don' do no good."

"I'm sorry. I wish there was something I could do," Helen said.

"You do enough for us as it is," Mrs Stone said. "We'll always be grateful to you for suggesting that our Martha could work at Belmont."

"When I went down to the kitchen this morning, I found that Cook had ordered too much meat this week. It will only go bad if it isn't eaten, so I thought perhaps that you might do me a favour and take it for me? There's some pork and a large piece of mutton. I don't like to see good food go to waste. I also brought some vegetables from the store as they're starting to get a bit stale. I do hope you don't mind?"

"Mind? Of course we don't mind, do we Jem? It's very kind of you to think of us."

"Them taters don' look stale ter me. We don' need no charity, yer know. We can manage on us own."

"Of course you can, Mr Stone. If you think you can't use them, then please just dispose of them. As I said, they would only be thrown away."

Jem was quiet for a while, his mistrust of anything even remotely resembling what he thought was charity fighting against the sight of enough fresh meat and vegetables to feed the family for a week or more. Eventually common sense won.

"Well, I suppose we could take 'em off yer 'ands, if yer sure yer don' need 'em."

"Quite sure, Mr Stone."

There was the sound of an argument from outside the house and a small whirlwind rolled through the front door and into the room. When it had subsided, it proved to be Bill and another boy of about the same age and size.

"Yes, yer did!"

"No, I didn'."

"Bleedin' did!"

"Bleedin' didn'!"

"Boys! We've got company, control yourselves," Mrs Stone told them sternly.

"Sorry, ma," Bill answered, "but Joshua an' me were playin' an' 'e cheated."

"Didn'!"

"Did!"

"Boys! I don't care who did what. Now Miss Helen's come to call with some friends, and I'd take it kindly if the two of you could behave."

"Hello Miss Helen, hello Daniel," Bill said, after giving his friend a sly kick on the ankle when his mother wasn't looking.

"Hello William," Helen said.

"I've seen yer before, ain't I?" Bill asked, looking at Matt. "You was at the 'ouse. You's the one wiv a name like a carpet."

"Yes," Matt said, deciding not to get involved in that discussion again.

"Yer didn't 'ave proper clothes then," Bill added.

"No, we didn't. We've bought some new ones since then."

"You bought them?" he asked, peering closely at Matt's hired suit. "You was done. They don' fit proper."

"Bill!" his mother remonstrated.

In spite of feeling awkward at having his badly fitting clothes pointed out to Helen and Daniel, Matt couldn't help but grin at Bill, who seemed completely unaware of what it was he was supposed to have done wrong.

"It's alright," he said. "He's correct, they don't fit very well. My uncle's going to buy us some new ones as soon as he can.

These were all we could get at the time."

◆

They left the cottage with Mrs Stone's thanks ringing in their ears and strolled a little way back along the lane.

"I wouldn't worry about what William said about your suit," Helen said. "It doesn't look too bad."

"Yes, it does," Matt said. "It only fits where it touches."

Daniel reached over and felt the material of the jacket sleeve.

"What's it made of? I don't recognise the cloth."

"I don't know, but the man in the shop said it was something new," Matt said, hoping that the subject would soon change from his clothes onto something less controversial. His prayer was answered by a loud roaring noise approaching from behind them. When they looked round, they saw a huge cloud of dust approaching up the narrow lane. As it drew closer they could see that at the heart of the dust storm was a gleaming motor car lurching towards them at what seemed a very dangerous speed given the state of the road they were on, which was little more than a cart track. With a loud braying from its horn and enough dust to keep an army of cleaners busy for a fortnight, the vehicle stopped as it drew level with them.

"Good afternoon Helen, good afternoon gentlemen," boomed a voice. "Glorious day, is it not?"

"It certainly is, Mr Brown," Helen replied, looking at the spluttering and hissing car rather nervously and wishing it would go away.

"Only got her yesterday, brand new, this year's model. Daimler-Cannstatt, isn't she a beauty?"

"Rather!" Daniel agreed enthusiastically. "What sort of speed can she do?"

"No idea, lad, haven't found a road straight enough to try her out on yet. She pulls ten horsepower though, and I got her up to nearly fifteen miles an hour yesterday afternoon."

"Wow, ten horsepower? That's some engine you've got there." Matt was looking at the car in amazement. He'd seen something like it in a museum, but to see one out on the road and evidently brand new, was something else again. The white paint, the maroon leather seats and above all the gleaming brass work, gave an extraordinarily rich impression.

"You said you like cars, didn't you, Matt?" asked Helen.

"Yes, I do, but I've never seen anything like this before."

"It must be a male thing," she muttered to herself, seeing both Matt and Daniel staring at the car as if in a trance.

"Just on my way back to Barton Hall. Sorry I don't have room for the three of you, but I can offer you a lift home," he shouted to Helen.

"Go on Helen, you take the ride, we can walk up," Daniel told her.

"It's very kind of you I'm sure, but I prefer to walk," she said, privately deciding that she wouldn't go in that thing if her life depended on it.

"Then how about you two young gentlemen. It'll be a bit of a squash, but if you don't mind that, then just hop up."

"Rather!" said Daniel. "Come on Matt, we won't get another chance," he added, clambering up into the car.

"Is it all right with you?" Matt asked Helen.

"Of course. Go ahead."

Matt needed no further urging. He climbed up by the side of Daniel, the clutch was let in, the brakes released, and in a flurry of dust and exhaust fumes they coughed and spluttered up the lane. Helen, left alone with only the birdsong for company, watched the car as it disappeared round a sharp bend.

"Men!" she grumbled, kicking a completely inoffensive stone from out of her way, before starting the long haul up the steep hill back to Belmont.

CHAPTER TEN

The music room

Connor, busily jotting down notes as he worked his way round the paintings in the dining room, heard the spluttering of the car and looked out of the window, to where the vehicle was coasting to a halt outside the front door. He saw Matt clamber down from the passenger seat, shake hands with the driver and walk towards the door, before the car, with a couple of loud explosions from the exhaust, growled off down the drive. A few moments later a very excited Matt arrived in the dining room and quickly told him what had happened, concentrating mostly on telling him about the car ride.

"It was fantastic. No wonder people were so excited by these early cars. It's nothing like driving in our time."

"Well, you certainly seem to have enjoyed yourself. What about the other young man — Daniel?"

"Mr Brown let him off outside his house. It's down the hill from here towards Barton."

"And Helen?"

"She's walking back."

"You left her on her own to walk all the way up the hill while you rode up in a car?"

"Well, she said it was OK by her," Matt answered, sounding rather defensive. "She said she preferred to walk, and when I asked her, she said that she didn't mind at all about being left."

"Matt, what a young lady says and what a young lady actually means often bear little resemblance to each other. By the time she gets back here you'll be lucky if she's speaking to you."

"Oh."

"Oh, indeed. Now I suggest that you walk back down the hill to meet her, and with a bit of luck she may just have forgiven you by the time the two of you get back. And don't forget that you're supposed to be pumping her for information. You can hardly do that if you're in one place and she's in another."

"All right, all right, you don't have to labour the point. I'll go and find her."

"Good idea," Connor said, returning to his task.

Matt let himself out and walked back the way he'd come. He met Helen plodding up the hill about twenty minutes later.

"Matthew? Is something wrong?" she asked. "I thought Mr Brown was giving you a ride home."

"He did, but I didn't like the idea of you walking back alone so I came to meet you."

"Are you under the impression that I am incapable of finding my way home, Mr Harvey?"

"No, of course not, I didn't mean that at all," he said, noting the use of his surname.

Helen was about to find something else cutting to say, but relented when she saw the expression on Matt's face. He looked so miserable that she decided not to pursue the matter any further. Whenever she was in a mood with Daniel, she usually spent hours trying to find new ways of making him know that she was annoyed with him, without it degenerating into a row, which was something that no well brought up young lady should ever consider having. The trouble was that Daniel never took the slightest notice of her moods or her carefully thought out cutting phrases. He just carried on grinning at her until she gave up. Matt was evidently different. She would have to be much more careful with him. She was, she admitted to herself, very attracted to him, although she didn't really know why. Perhaps it was the intriguing air of mystery that he carried with him. Somehow he just didn't seem to fit in. She decided to change the subject.

"Oh, it's all right Matt, I was only joking. I'm delighted that you've come to walk me home."

His face lightened and she was relieved to see a smile reappear.

"I've been meaning to ask, if you don't think it forward of me," she said, "about your hair."

"My hair?"

"Yes. The way it's cut. It's very unusual."

"Oh, that. I like it very short; it means I don't have to worry about finding a comb in the mornings."

"I see," she said, laughing. "But doesn't it make it, well, rather coarse?"

"No, I don't think so."

She lightly ran her hand over his head, feeling the soft hair. She was rather surprised, in part because his hair wasn't rough and coarse as she'd expected, but mainly at how brazen she'd been about it. This simply won't do, she told herself. She must show more self-restraint in future. Luckily, he didn't seem to think that she'd done anything odd and just carried on walking.

The spring sunshine was warming, but it didn't explain why Matt was feeling so hot. He fumbled with the tight collar of his shirt to try to cool himself, but to no avail. He knew the reason anyway, and it was nothing to do with his collar. He fought the desire to put his arm around Helen, but lost the battle almost before it was begun. She didn't complain, just smiled at him as she felt the pressure of his arm around her waist.

"Matt?"

"Yes?"

"Back home, where you live I mean, in Warwickshire, do you have anyone special?"

"Special? You mean, like a girlfriend?"

"I suppose that's what I mean. A lady friend anyway."

Matt thought of the long list of girlfriends, including his latest, Karen, a classmate of his at college, whom he had introduced to the family only the previous week.

"No," he said, without even a twinge of conscience.

"Oh," she responded with a smile. "Good."

They walked in companionable silence for a time until Matt realised with a start that he still hadn't found out anything about her, anything that would help explain why this beautiful young lady and all her family were going to be burned to death in less than two weeks. He searched for an opening.

"I remember your mother saying that she'd met that composer

that I like in Paris a few years ago," he said.

"Yes, that's right. Monsieur Debussy was staying at the same hotel as Mama."

"Were you with her?"

"No. Mama didn't think I was old enough for Paris at the time."

"Have you been since then?"

"Yes. I sulked so much that Mama finally agreed to take me two years ago. It was wonderful, so different to the south of France, which is where Mama's friends live. Have you been to Paris, Matthew?"

"Yes, last summer, but only for a few days. I went with my parents, whilst my grandparents came down to look after Ben, Paula and Kerry."

"And they are?"

"Oh, sorry. They're my brother and my two sisters."

"I see. And did you like it? Paris, I mean."

"Yes, I thought it was great, especially the view from the top of the Eiffel Tower."

"Don't let Mama hear you say that," she told him with a laugh. "Mama is of the opinion that Monsieur Eiffel should be publicly flogged for disfiguring the city with that great monstrosity. Luckily, it's due to be pulled down in a few years' time, so she won't have to worry about it for too much longer."

Matt kept quiet on the subject, as he could hardly tell her that the tower was still going strong well over a century later.

"Where else did you like?" she asked.

"Napoleon's tomb in the Church of the Dome at Les Invalides," he said. "That was really impressive."

"I think perhaps it would be best if you didn't mention to Mama that you've been to Paris," she said, laughing again. "I fear she may take an extremely dim view of your taste in Paris highlights."

"Why?"

"Mama usually purses her lips when the subject of Napoleon comes up. I don't really know why. There was a picture of

Napoleon hanging in the library at Belmont when we first moved in, but Mama had it taken down. I think it's in one of the stores."

"I didn't know there was a library."

"That's because you haven't seen over the house yet. I will show you around when we get back if you would like that."

"I'd like it very much. Is there anything else in Paris that your mother doesn't like?"

"She says that it's being ruined by too many motor cars. The fumes are going to poison everyone eventually, she says."

Matt decided that he'd better keep quiet on the subject of cars as well as Paris, so he tried another tack.

"The friends of yours who live in the south of France. You'll be going to visit them again later this year?"

"I expect so," she said, without much enthusiasm. "It's possible that we may not be able to go. I think Mama may have some money worries."

"What makes you think that?"

"There have been callers late in the evening when most of us have retired for the night. Charles can hear them because the nursery is at the front of the house and his bed is close to the window. Mama has never said anything to us about the visits, so I assume that we're not supposed to know. I suspect they may be creditors. I think that they're French."

"Why?"

"Because of their accents. Mama can speak French fluently of course, as we all can, but Mama says it's very bad form to speak a foreign language when one is in England. French should be reserved for France. When we're on holiday there we're not allowed to speak English. Likewise, except in lessons, we're not allowed to speak French here. Mama is a stickler for that sort of thing. I opened my door a little one night and heard one of the visitors speaking French. Mama refused to answer him until he spoke in English. I couldn't really hear what they were saying. Papa had business connections in France, so I think these people might have been associates of his."

Matt decided not to press the matter any further for the

moment, in case Helen should wonder why he was so interested. They had arrived back at Belmont by then, so he asked her if he could have a tour of the house.

"Of course, but as it's so nice at the moment, why don't I show you around the gardens first."

"Fine with me."

She rested her arm lightly on his, and together they walked around the side of the house and into the main formal garden. As Matt's house stood in the same spot as Belmont, even though many years in the future, the view was naturally familiar to him, but he hadn't realised that, where there was a plain sloping lawn in his own time, there had once been a series of terraces, with fountains, pools and intricately designed flower beds. Elegant stone balustrades bordered each of the terraces, and they were joined by broad flights of stone steps. The formal gardens also extended much further down the hillside, running right down to where they bordered the narrow lane at the bottom of the hill. Beyond lay the valley of the Aller Brook. There were a lot more trees in 1898 than in his own day, but the thing that really startled him about the view was the clarity. He could see the tower of Coffinswell Church clearly in the distance, and the high tors of Dartmoor on the horizon seemed so close that he felt he could almost reach out and touch them.

"The view really is splendid, isn't it?" Helen said.

"It's magnificent," he replied, wondering why it seemed so much better than the view that he knew at home. He decided eventually that it was because of the lack of pollution. There were no fumes or gases building up in the atmosphere, so the air was crystal clear. He took in a deep breath. It even tasted cleaner. They strolled around the large formal garden, two of the gardeners doffing their caps to Helen as they passed and being rewarded with a radiant smile each time. After Helen had pointed out all the various highlights in the garden, they retraced their steps, and entered the house through the garden door. A gong was sounding as they did so, which Helen said meant that afternoon tea was being served in the drawing room. They found the others were already all in the room, with Mrs Debbon, her afternoon rest completed, presiding over a tea trolley groaning under the weight of thinly cut sandwiches, muffins, cakes and shortbread.

"Hi," Matt said to Connor as he and Helen entered the room.

"Hi yourself. How was your walk?"

"Brilliant, thanks," Matt said, as Helen went to talk to her mother.

"Are you in Helen's bad books for abandoning her earlier?" Connor asked him, once he was sure Mrs Debbon was out of earshot.

"No, but I would have been if I hadn't gone back to meet her. How about you, did you get much work done?"

"Yes. Luckily the list of contents is more thorough than I was expecting, so the basics are already there. It's just a question of adding detail to them, plus giving a guess as to the artist when the list says 'artist unknown'. Did you manage," he continued, checking that neither Mrs Debbon nor Helen could overhear him, "to get any information?"

"Some, but not very much."

"OK. When tea's over, we'll have a talk and exchange notes. I got a little more out of Mary-Anne earlier, but I don't think she knows too much."

"Master Harvey," Mrs Debbon said, walking over to them, "Helen tells me that you would prefer it if I were to call you Matthew. Is that correct?"

"Yes, Mrs Debbon, I would."

"Then I will do so from now on. Would you care for some sandwiches, Matthew, or perhaps you would prefer a muffin?"

"Thank you, a sandwich would be nice."

A small and obviously very expensive china plate found its way into his hand and he was told to help himself to whatever he wanted. Taking a selection from the trolley, he hoped that he wouldn't make some terrible breach of manners by doing something wrong. Just how *did* you eat a sandwich in 1898? As he glanced around he was relieved to see that his uncle seemed equally ill at ease with a plate in one hand and a cup and saucer in the other. One of Matt's sandwiches decided that it wanted a closer acquaintance with the drawing room carpet and slid off his plate. He retrieved it, but had no idea whether he ought to put it back on his plate or dispose of it. He wanted to go home. Luckily the rest of afternoon tea passed without any more problems, although Connor did nearly drop his plate and only rescued it with a clatter that made everyone in the room turn and look at him. Afterwards, Charles and Mary-Anne escaped into the garden and Mrs Debbon left to speak to the housekeeper about the menu for dinner. Helen took Matt by the hand and firmly guided him to the door.

"I'm going to give Matthew a tour of the house," she said as they passed Connor. "Would you care to come with us, Mr Harvey?"

"No, thank you. I'm beginning to find my way about by myself, so if you two are going off for a tour, I'll put in a bit more time on the cataloguing."

"Very well, if you're sure. Come along Matthew, I want to show you the library."

As they walked to the door, Matt managed to tell Connor that they'd have to talk later. Connor nodded in return and went to retrieve his notes.

To Matt, the house seemed huge. The library, which Helen showed him first, was a dignified, solemn affair, with dark panelling like the dining room, but with the addition of large wooden columns designed to look like something from a Greek temple. Helen told him that she took her lessons with her tutor in the room. Charles and Mary-Anne had their lessons in the nursery. His tour continued with the morning room, the billiard room and others that he didn't grasp the names of. He'd lost all sense of direction by the time they returned to the entrance hall to climb the stairs to the first floor. The upper floor was even more confusing. Although the rooms were, on the whole, smaller than the main rooms on the ground floor, there were more of them, and corridors seemed to lead off in all directions. Many of the rooms were unused, Helen told him, except when they had guests to stay, which wasn't very often.

"There are really only two rooms on this floor that are of any real importance. That door over there leads to Mama's boudoir. I can't show you in there unless Mama gives permission. The best room up here though is this one."

She opened a door to reveal a large room with a curved bay window. It was the ceiling that grabbed Matt's attention, as it was covered with intricate plasterwork, picked out in gold. The carpet, also in cream and gold, matched the ceiling pattern to create a dazzling effect. It took Matt some time to realise that the room was full of musical instruments. A grand piano dominated the centre of the room, but there was also a harp, another smaller piano and a cello on a stand in the corner of the room.

"We often all come up here for musical evenings," Helen told him. "Can you sing, Matt?"

"I'm in the college choir," he told her, "but I can't sight-read music."

"Nor can I," she said, seating herself at the smaller of the two pianos. "This is what Mary-Anne and I are learning at the moment. It's an old French folk song. It was one of Papa's favourites, so Mama says it would be nice for us to learn it."

She concentrated for a moment, and then began to play. After several bars, she started to sing, her voice a much deeper and richer tone than Matt would have imagined. He also knew he'd heard it before, when he and his uncle had first gone back to the house after the fire. He found it very eerie to be hearing it again. He had to admit that Helen had a wonderful voice. She ran through a couple of verses and then stopped.

"Why don't you join in, Matt?" she asked.

"I can't speak French," he said.

"You don't need to. Come over here."

He went and stood at her side.

"This is the English translation," she told him, handing him a few sheets of paper. "Now listen to the tune. It's fairly simple, but I'll play it through twice, then we can try it out."

She played it through and he realised that the tune itself was indeed very simple.

"All set?" she asked.

"Yes."

She started the song again, and Matt joined in, reading from the sheet in his hand. He admitted to himself that he was having a wonderful time.

"There," Helen said, as the song finished. "That was excellent. You have a fine voice, Matt. I must tell Mama so that we can have a musical evening sometime soon."

Matt wasn't at all sure that was a good idea, but just nodded in agreement.

"Now," she said, "let's carry on with the tour."

They left the music room and continued to the gallery running around the entrance hall.

"This is my room," she said, indicating one of the doors along the gallery. Opening the door, she revealed a light, airy room with large windows that looked over the rear gardens and the view beyond.

"It's not really the done thing to invite a young gentleman into a lady's bedroom, but I don't suppose it will matter for a few moments. I must leave the door open though, in case Mama happens to walk by. She most certainly would not approve if we were inside with the door closed."

As he looked around the room, he wasn't sure if being there was a good idea or not. Now that he'd seen inside, he knew that his imagination would be working overtime later on. He felt himself sweating again.

"Matthew? Are you feeling unwell? You look very flushed." Helen asked with concern.

"I'm fine," he answered, "it's just a little warm in here. This jacket is rather thick."

"Perhaps we should go downstairs and I'll get you a glass of lemonade."

"Thank you, that sounds great."

They descended the stairs and Helen ushered him into the drawing room, summoning the maid at the same time, whom she sent to get the lemonade from the kitchens.

"Please sit down, Matt, and if you're feeling unwell, then feel free to take your jacket off."

Matthew did as he was told, even though he knew full well it wasn't the jacket making him hot. The lemonade arrived swiftly and he drank the cold liquid gratefully.

"Are you feeling better?" Helen asked, sitting down beside him and taking his hand in hers, which made his temperature shoot back up again to somewhere approaching that of the Sahara Desert at midday.

"Yes," he said, lying through his teeth, "much better, thanks."

"Good," she said, patting his hand gently.

He closed his eyes and tried to think about something else, anything to take his mind off how near Helen was to him. He could feel the warmth of her next to him. If he'd been back in his own time he wouldn't be having these problems. He knew the rules, what you could do, how far you could go. But in 1898? He'd no idea. His thoughts were interrupted by a whining noise in his ear. At first he took it to be a fly buzzing somewhere nearby, but then realised it was the sound that foretold that he and Connor were about to flip back to their own time. He heard a noise and opened his eyes to see Connor entering the room, evidently having also heard the tell-tale sound.

"We ought to be going, Matt. Don't forget we've got an appointment this evening, and we'll need to get changed."

"Sure," Matt replied. "I'd almost forgotten."

"You have to leave?" Helen asked. "I hoped that you might be staying for dinner."

"I'm sorry," Matt said, "but we've really got to go."

"Will you be here tomorrow?"

"I'm not sure. It depends on my uncle's work."

"Mr Harvey?" she asked, turning towards him.

"I'm sorry, I really don't know, not for certain. It may be tomorrow, but if my work keeps me away then it may be a little longer."

"I will go and find Mama and tell her that you're leaving. She will want to see you before you go."

"I've already seen her," Connor told her. "She knows that we can't guarantee when we'll be able to return."

"But you will be back?" Helen asked anxiously.

"Of course."

Helen walked them to the door, her hand laid rather possessively, Connor noticed, on Matt's arm.

◆

By the time they'd said their good-byes to Helen and walked the length of the drive the noise in their heads was becoming more and more painful.

"Quick," Connor said, holding his hands to his ears. "We need to get out of sight of the house before we flip, just in case anyone's watching."

They ran as fast as they could along the lane until they were sure that Belmont was well out of sight. By this time the pain was intense. When Matt tried later to recall what it felt like, he could only say that it sounded as if there was a loudspeaker inside his head that had very bad acoustic feedback. The pitch, though, wasn't level. The tone of the noise rose and fell, but always there was a searing pain that got worse and worse, and then stopped. No fading, no gradual lessening, just a complete stop. Matt was the first to recover. Connor was sitting on the grass verge, holding his head in his hands.

"Are you going to be OK?" Matt asked.

"Give me a few minutes and I will be."

"Do you think it means something, that noise?"

"Don't know. It may just be part of flipping, but I'd have thought we should have it both ways if that was the case. Plus, it's getting much, much worse each time."

"Have you noticed that the noise isn't constant?"

"No, not really. I've been too busy trying to block it out to pay much attention."

"It's as if there's more than one noise there, but they're all jumbled together and played back at full volume. I think it may be important."

"I'll have to take your word for it, Matt."

Even though his head was still throbbing painfully, Connor managed to look around him to confirm that they were home again.

"What time is it?" he asked, after trying, and failing, to focus his eyes on his own watch, after dragging it out of his pocket where he'd put it to keep it out of sight.

"Just after eight. I heard the church clock in Coffinswell striking as we arrived back."

"By the time we get to my place, change out of these things and grab something to eat, it's going to be time to get you back home again. And . . . what's that noise?"

"My phone. No doubt a load of text messages and missed calls coming through."

"You had your phone with you? Why?"

"I know I can't use it back in 1898 but I don't feel dressed without it. I need it in my pocket."

"So, don't you need to answer some of the messages?"

"No," was the terse answer.

"With the number of beeps that thing was giving out it sounds as if there was a whole telephone book of calls and messages."

"I'll sort it later."

"Hmm. By your manner I'd guess that most of those messages and missed calls are from the same person?"

"Perhaps," was the rather flat response.

"And I'd guess that the person would be Karen, wanting to know where you are and what you're doing?"

"Maybe," Matt replied — rather evasively Connor thought.

"Look Matt, this is none of my business, but if you've lost interest then you really should tell the poor girl. It's not fair on her otherwise."

"Who says I've lost interest?"

"I do. Anyway, we've got a more urgent matter to sort first. We've got to think of a reason why you need time off college next week."

"Rats. I'd forgotten. Any ideas?"

"None at all. As you said, even if you fake being ill, Marion will want to keep popping into your room to keep an eye on you. You really can't just disappear, or at least not for hours on end."

"How about if I were to come and stay with you for the next couple of weeks?"

"Maybe, but then your college would phone your house to find out where you were, then your Mum would try to phone me, and when she got no answer she and your Dad would be down to find out what was going on. Besides, in order to flip it seems we have to be at your place."

"This whole thing's a mess."

"Understatement of the year."

"Why us?"

"Not a clue. Perhaps because I was the first one in the house after the fire, and you just happened to be there when we saw Mary-Anne."

"So why not one of the firemen? They were the first."

"I really don't know, Matt. Anyway, I'm tired, so let's get home."

◆

Showered, changed and fed, they arrived back at Matt's house at a little after nine o'clock, to find Steve and Marion in a flurry of activity, pulling clothes out of drawers and piling them in suitcases. Marion glanced up from trying to stuff a large jumper into a case that was already overfull.

"At last!" she said. "Where on earth have you two been? I've been trying to get you since lunchtime."

"Sorry. We've been out for the day. Problem?"

"No, not really a problem. What about your phone, Matt? I've been ringing and ringing, as well as leaving messages, but no answer."

"The battery's flat and I forgot to take the charger."

"That's got to be a first, you without your phone. I thought you were glued to it."

"So why've you been trying to get us, and why all the packing?"

"Because we're going away for a couple of weeks, all of us. My Uncle David, you know, the one in Sussex? Well, I phoned him to tell him about the fire, and he said that we probably needed a break so he's invited us to go and stay with him and Aunt Jenny. We had a chat and decided that we do need a break and there's no time like the present. The repairs are all finished, but I'd like to get away from the smell of new paint for a while, so we're going first thing in the morning."

Connor and Matt exchanged worried glances.

"But I can't mitch off college, not even for a few days, let alone a couple of weeks. I've got exams coming up, and I've got to revise."

"Credit us with some sense, Matt. Of *course* you can't take all that time off college, not at the moment anyway. We were wondering if Connor could have you for the time we're away, if that's not imposing on you too much?"

"It wouldn't be an imposition in the least," Connor said, "but all Matt's books and equipment are here. How about if I move in here instead while you're away."

"Could you do that?"

"Don't see why not. It'll be a break for me and Matt will still have all his gear. It's not far, so I can always pop down home every so often to make sure everything's OK."

"What about work?"

"I was thinking about taking a break anyway, so this will be a good opportunity. I can bring my laptop up here, so while Matt's at college I can still get on with some work as well if I want to. What about Barney?"

"Barney's coming with us, the kids wouldn't hear of us leaving the dog behind."

"No problem then. I'll move in first thing in the morning."

◆

Early the next day, Connor arrived at Matt's house with his computer, a bag of clothes and a heap of books. Matt met him at the door and helped him carry his stuff inside.

"Are you still dragging that cumbersome old thing with you?" Matt asked, noticing his uncle's laptop case. "What happened to the latest pad I got you to buy?"

"I'm still figuring out how to use it," Connor said.

"I showed you weeks ago how to use it."

"You showed me how to turn it on, not how to use it," was the rather tetchy response.

"Honestly, Uncle Conn, you can be slow at times. I have to show you how to use every electronic gadget you buy!"

"Don't get cocky with me — I had to teach *you* how to use a spoon!"

There didn't seem to be a sensible answer to that so Matt contented himself with a quick roll of the eyeballs.

◆

"You're having my room, Uncle Conn," an excited Ben told him as Connor struggled to get a heap of books up the stairs. "Paula wanted you to have hers, but it's full of girl's stuff so I knew you wouldn't want that one."

"Thank you, Ben," Connor said, following Ben upstairs and into his room, and then dumping his books on the desk in the corner.

A flurry of farewells and a few last-minute dashes back into the house to collect suddenly remembered things, and then they were off, leaving Matt and Connor waving to them as they drove away.

"Well," Connor said, once the car was out of sight.

"Well, what?"

"Nothing really. It's odd that just when we've got to have a couple of weeks when we can come and go as and when we need, the rest of the family choose that couple of weeks to take themselves off to Sussex. Quite a coincidence."

"And as you've said before, you don't believe in coincidences."

"Exactly."

"So, if it's not a coincidence, then what is it?"

"Not a clue. Perhaps this is all part of the same story. Perhaps this was all meant to happen."

"You're being creepy again."

"Maybe. Anyway, let's get inside and try to sort out what we do next. Are you going to college today, by the way?"

"Do you think I should, or should I stay here?"

"I suppose you really ought to go to college. What you said to your Mum about having exams coming up was true. You can't afford to take too much time off, not at the moment."

"What happens if I get back this afternoon and you've flipped?"

"We'll worry about it if it happens, but I don't think it will. I think we have to be together for it to work."

"I hope it doesn't happen as soon as I arrive back. I'll still have my college clothes on if that happens and I'll look even more stupid than I do wearing that suit that you hired for me."

"I'll bring a change of clothes for you with me when I pick you up after college. If it looks likely that we're going to flip you can change in the car."

"Could do, I suppose. Fine, I'll go to college, but contact me if there's a problem. I'll leave my phone switched on to silent. Can you run me down to the main road to catch the college bus?"

"Of course, but I can run you right to college if you want. What time do you want to leave?"

"In about half an hour or so if that's OK, and just to the bus stop will be fine. I want to talk to some of my mates before we get to college."

"And Karen? Are you going to tell her?"

"Tell her what?"

"You *know* what."

"Suppose so," he answered gloomily. "As if I don't have enough problems at the moment."

"Just time for breakfast, then. Go and get your gear together and I'll sort out some food."

◆

The day passed without incident, and Connor picked Matt up from the college bus drop-off point.

"I didn't see or feel anything unusual today at all," Connor said as they drove up the lane. "It's odd because I'd have thought that there would have been something. Evidently this flipping business isn't regular. I thought perhaps that it might run to some sort of formula, so that we could work out when we're likely to go, but it seems not. How about you, what sort of day have you had?"

"A really crappy one. I've got a load of coursework to do and Mrs Hindes was in a right old strop. None of us could do anything right and she loaded us all up with a ton of work. I think that she was burnt at the stake in a previous life. And to make the day complete, Karen's dumped me."

"She has? Why?"

"Seems she was peed off with me for not answering her text messages, so she's started going out with Scotty instead."

"You don't sound very happy about it."

"Of course I'm not happy. Would you be?"

"But it's worked out, hasn't it? You said you were going to tell her it was over."

"Yes, but I'm not used to being the one who's dumped. It's always been the other way round before."

"Ah. Welcome to the real world."

◆

Half an hour later, Matt was stretched out full length on the living room sofa. He was trying to make some sense of what was happening, but without much success. He turned his head to look at his uncle, sprawled out in an armchair staring into space. He was obviously having the same problem. He returned his gaze to the ceiling, but it just stared blankly back at him, as it always did.

"We need to do some shopping," Connor said, breaking into Matt's train of thought. Not that it was difficult, as that particular train had been stuck at the signals for quite some time.

"What for?" he asked, once he'd got the train moving again.

"It seems that on each occasion we've flipped we've stayed for a longer period. Last time it was for a whole afternoon and part of the evening. If that carries on, then next time we may be there overnight. I suspect that sooner or later we're going to go back to round about the time of the fire and then we may be there for several days, if not longer. That means we're going to need money."

"Money? Why?"

"To buy food if nothing else. We're going to have to eat, and that probably means going into a restaurant, assuming there were some in Torquay at that time. We can't use today's money, so we need to get some of the period. If we're stuck overnight, then we'll need somewhere to stay. We'll need clothes as well. We stick out like sore thumbs in this kit and the ones we hired just aren't good enough."

"I know that. Even Bill thought I looked like a sack tied in the middle. So where do we get money from?"

"Stamp dealers usually deal in old coins and notes. There are a couple in the town."

"Won't they be expensive?"

"Yes, but even if I have to pay thirty pounds for a five pound note from 1898, that five pound note will keep us both for some time. You could get a reasonable meal for a few coppers provided you kept out of anywhere fashionable."

"I don't suppose there'll be a McDonald's back then?"

"No, 'fraid not. You'll have to make do with whatever we can get."

"I'll bet it'll be something with spinach in it," he grumbled.

"Spinach is very good for you, it's full of iron."

"So why don't *you* eat it then?"

"Because it tastes revolting, of course."

"If I wasn't too tired to move off this sofa you'd get thumped."

"That's the trouble with the world today, far too much violence."

Matt ignored him and went back to studying the ceiling.

"So, when are you going to try and get this 1898 money?" he asked after a while.

"Now, I think," Connor said, hauling himself out of his chair. "I should be able to get into town before the shops shut. Seeing as how we've no idea when we're going we'd best be ready. Do you want to come, or will you be all right here on your own?"

"Now that I know that I'm not going to suddenly flip back to 1898 on my own, I'll be fine here. I'll get on with my coursework. How long will you be?"

"An hour or so. I'll be as quick as I can."

◆

He was back in less than an hour, having bought all the Victorian money that he could find in Torquay.

"I managed to get about thirty pounds in total, in notes and coins. I hope it's enough to keep us going for a while," Connor said when he got back. "I've no idea what hotel rooms cost back then, so we'll just have to be careful with it."

"So, what now?"

"Hanged if I know. What do you fancy for dinner?"

"I'll get it. Sausage and chips all right?"

"Sure, but I don't mind getting it."

"No worries. It'll give me something to do other than college work."

By the time dinner had been eaten dusk was starting to fall, and there'd still been no sign of them flipping back. Matt was just drawing the curtains in the living room when he glanced outside.

"I think we're about to go again," he said.

"Why, have you got that tugging feeling you mentioned?"

"No, but I saw young Bill in the garden for a few seconds. He's gone now, but he was definitely there."

"That means not much sleep for us tonight then. What do you reckon, should we go in these clothes or put the hired gear back on?"

"I suppose we'd better put the suits on," Matt said, without much enthusiasm. "Now that we've said we've bought them we'd better stick with the story."

"If we're still there in the morning we can go and buy some

proper stuff."

"Where from?"

"How should I know? There are bound to be clothes shops in the town, even at that date. We'd best get changed. It's going to be cold," he added, "so we should take something warm with us as well as these suits. I've got an overcoat that won't look too much out of place. How about you?"

"There's that full-length thick coat that Mum and Dad bought me for Christmas. Would that do?"

"Ideal, I should think. How about a scarf and gloves as well?"

"I've got them somewhere, but it's not going to be that cold, is it?

"It will be if we're out in the open all night. It'll be a long walk down into the town if we need to find somewhere to stay, and that's assuming that we can find somewhere that will take us in the middle of the night."

"OK, I'll find them. Anything else?"

"Yes, phone your Mum and Dad. You don't want them phoning here to see if you're all right, then getting no reply."

"I'll give them a buzz while I'm finding the scarf and gloves."

◆

Once they'd changed into their hired clothes, with Matt complaining bitterly about his appearance again, they went downstairs and out into the garden, Matt locking the door behind them, before they walked along the drive and out into the lane.

"Now what?" he asked.

"I've no idea. Suppose we go as far as Barton Hall and back and see what happens?"

"No need."

"Huh?"

"Look behind you."

A fog bank had blown across the road, only to blow away as quickly as it had come, revealing the outline of Belmont, silhouetted against the night sky. Lights could be seen in several of the downstairs rooms, as well as one or two of the first-floor rooms.

"Should we go and knock at the door?" Matt asked.

"I don't think so. It'll seem very odd, us just turning up unannounced at this time in the evening."

"But I call round at mates' houses in the evening without letting them know I'm coming."

"Different times, different customs. To call on a family like the Debbons in the evening without an appointment would be considered very bad form. If we're going to try to gain their confidence, we don't want to make a bad impression."

"So, what do we do?"

"Not certain. What time is it?"

"Just gone nine o'clock," Matt told him, "I checked the time just before we left."

"I don't know whether to stay here for a bit and keep watch, to see if any of these mysterious night-time visitors turn up, or whether to trek down into Torquay and see if we can find somewhere to stay for the night. What do you think?"

"What time do these night visitors turn up?"

"I'm not really certain. Charles said it was very late, but then I expect he goes to bed early, so his idea of very late and our idea of very late may be two different things."

"Helen said it was always after she'd gone to bed as well."

"I don't suppose she goes to bed early, so it's probably getting on for midnight when these people call. If we don't hang about too much, we could walk down, find somewhere to stay, and then get a cab back up here again to keep watch for a bit. How do you feel about that?"

"Fine with me. Any idea where we could stay?"

"I'm trying to remember which hotels were operating in 1898. I know the Imperial was going strong, but we'll never afford that, not with the money we've got."

"So where?"

"Perhaps it might be best to stay somewhere really cheap to start with, even if it's only for a couple of nights. I know that there were several hotels in the town centre that catered for commercial travellers and the like. They'll be much cheaper than the sea front hotels and it won't seem odd us turning up in the evening with no luggage, as they'll be used to people arriving at odd times."

" 'Ello," said a voice, startling both of them. "Wotcher doin'?"

"I could ask you the same question," Connor said, as Bill emerged from the shelter of the shrubbery. "You told me you'd seen him in the garden," this to Matt, "but I didn't really take it in."

"I forgot as well," Matt said.

"Well, what *are* yer doin'?" Bill insisted.

"We were going to call on the family, but now realise that we've left it too late," Connor said.

"Sounds funny ter me."

"My work means that we have to come and go at odd times," Connor told him, trying not to grin at the very suspicious expression on the boy's face. "Isn't it late for you to be out as well?"

"I told yer. I keeps me eye out fer 'em, sees they don' 'ave any bovver."

"I'm sure they're very grateful. Anyway, Matt and I have to go now. How long will you be here for?"

"I gots ter go 'ome soon. Ma gets a stew on if I ain't in by ten."

"How do you know what time it is?" Matt asked.

"Church bells o' course. You stupid or summat?"

"Why do I bother to ask?" Matt said. "Come on Uncle Conn, if we're going to walk down to Union Street we'd better go. It's a long way down from here and we'll be knackered as it is by the time we get there."

Bill made a dive for his pocket, and produced his notebook and pencil.

"Wot were that word?" he asked.

"Which word?" Matt asked, somewhat mystified.

"The one what sounds like where they gets rid of old 'orses."

"He means 'knackered'," Connor told him, and told Bill how to spell it. "It means 'very tired'. Now before you learn any more new words, we'd better go."

He grabbed Matt's arm and pulled out into the lane, leaving Bill still laboriously writing in his book.

"I *wish* you wouldn't do that," Connor grumbled as they started their long walk into the town. "At this rate you are going to be single-handedly responsible for introducing some of the more regrettable examples of the English language into everyday use. You *know* he writes everything down."

"I can't help it, they just sort of come out before I've time to think."

Entrance to the
Union Hotel

A night vigil

It took them over an hour to reach central Torquay.

"What on earth is that smell?" Matt asked with disgust, holding his hand to his nose as they walked down Union Street.

"A mixture of drains, horse droppings and butchers' shops, I would think."

"How on earth do people put up with it?"

"If you were born into this era I don't suppose you'd even notice it."

"It stinks."

"Agreed, but there's not a lot we can do about it. Anyway, we need somewhere to stay. There used to be a place at the bottom of the street called the Union Hotel. I've got an old postcard that shows it. We could try that first, and then if it's full or we don't like it, we'll have to head on down to the harbour area and find somewhere there."

The Union Hotel was a substantial affair with a large portico that extended out over the pavement. Three burly looking men were busily unloading barrels from a horse and cart outside and rolling them in through the doors. Connor and Matt narrowly avoided being mown down by the barrels, as the men seemed to pay them no attention whatsoever, being far more concerned with getting their task done in the shortest possible time. The entrance hall of the hotel was dimly lit, and the thick haze of tobacco smoke didn't add much to the hotel's charms. A small, terminally bored man was seated behind the reception desk reading a newspaper.

"Can I help you?" he asked, in a voice that suggested he'd much rather be somewhere else.

"We'd like a room for a few nights, please," Connor told him. "How much would that be per night?"

"Front or rear?"

"I'm not sure. How much would the rooms at the rear be?"

"Three and sixpence a night, but they're all taken."

"I see. Then in that case, how much would a room at the front cost?"

"Four shillings a night. In advance."

"May we see the room, please?"

He didn't reply, but rang a small bell, which was answered by the porter, a boy who couldn't have been more than ten years old at most.

"Show these people up to room 103," he said, handing the boy a key from the board behind him before returning to his paper.

The room that the boy showed them turned out to be a reasonable size, overlooking Union Street, and cleaner than they might have expected.

"Not as bad as it could have been," Connor said. "OK with you for now, Matt?"

"Sure."

"In that case I'll go down and pay old misery-guts for three nights, then we'll see how things go."

The boy who'd showed them the room sniggered behind his hand at the reference to the receptionist.

" 'E is an old misery, ain't 'e?" the boy agreed.

"He certainly seems to be. Is he always like that?"

"Never known him no diff'rent. Mind, if he ever smiled it'd prob'ly frighten people."

On the way downstairs Connor asked him if the hotel dining room was still open, but was told that it closed at eight o'clock.

"Is there anywhere else we could get a decent meal without it costing too much?"

"There's a good spot down near the 'arbour in Abbey Place," the boy replied. "They do a really tasty steak pie. If you go there, tell 'em Joe sent yer. That way they'll see yer right and won't overcharge like they does with the nobs."

"Thank you, Joe. I think we'll do that."

He gave the boy a few coppers, which seemed to delight him, and then went on to pay the receptionist, who examined the coins that he was given as if he thought they might be forgeries. When Connor returned to their room Matt was laying full length on one of the beds staring at the ceiling.

"When you need the toilet," Connor told him, "it's down the corridor on the left. I saw it on the way up. The bathroom is at the other end of the corridor, but at least the bath looks fairly clean."

"Don't they have showers in 1898?" grumbled Matt.

"They're about, but few and far between. Think yourself lucky there's a bathroom. But you couldn't have a bath now even if you wanted one."

"Why not?"

"Look at the sign over there. Baths are only permitted between half past six and half past eight in the morning, and between seven and nine in the evening. As it's now gone ten, you're out of luck."

"What about eating?"

"The dining room's shut as well, but the boy who showed us up says that there's a restaurant that stays open late down in Abbey Place. He says if we mention his name, they won't overcharge us like they do any 'nobs' that call in. We could go there before we head back up to Belmont."

"Nobs?"

"Wealthy visitors."

"They'd never mistake us for wealthy visitors, wearing this gear. Anyway, can we just relax for a bit first? I'm knackered."

"Join the club," Connor said, collapsing onto the other bed.

"Uncle Conn?" Matt asked after a while.

"Yes?"

"I've been trying to work things out, but it doesn't make any sense."

"What doesn't?"

"Us being here, trying to change things. I don't see how we can. It's that paradox business dad was on about. If we change the past, won't that change the future as well?"

"Perhaps."

"So, all of this may be for nothing. I mean, suppose we stop the fire from happening, then Belmont won't burn down. But that would mean that our house won't get built, which means that we won't be living there in the future. When I get home, home may not be there, or at least not the home I remember. But if we don't live there, then we won't learn about the fire, so we won't go back and stop it. It's all so complicated."

"I don't know whether we can change anything or not, Matt, but we're here and we ought to at least try. We shouldn't let four people burn to death just because we're afraid of what might happen in our own time."

"I know that. It's not that I'm afraid of what might happen. Well, I am I suppose, but that's not the point. I'm afraid of what might *not* happen. Perhaps it's as both you and dad have said. The past can't be changed. Perhaps everything is going to happen whatever we might do to try to stop it."

"I don't believe it's possible to make major changes in history," Connor said. "What happens, happens. Alter, or try to alter, a major event and the whole future alters. For example, suppose someone found a way to go back in time as and when he or she wished. Then suppose that person, with the very best of intentions, decided it would be a great idea to stop World War II from happening. So, without doing anything too dramatic, he stops Mr and Mrs Hitler from meeting. Hence, no little Adolf, hence no world war. But then, countless millions of people would never have been born. People whose parents met during the war perhaps. National frontiers would change, entire regions would be in different countries, huge advances in science and medicine wouldn't take place and so on. So much would be changed from one very small event. Perhaps the person who went back in time to change things would never have been born if they had. No, big changes aren't possible, I'm certain of that."

"So, we're wasting our time?"

"I didn't say that. I said I don't believe we can make major changes, changes that would have a dramatic effect on the future. I think the fire will happen whatever we do. What we may be able to do is stop four innocent people from dying in it."

"And to think a few weeks ago all I had to worry about was whether my coursework was going to get handed in at college on time. Now I'm living before I was even born and trying to change something that probably can't be changed anyway."

"Maybe. Come on, if we're going to eat before we go and keep an eye on Belmont, we'd best get moving."

◆

The restaurant that Joe had told them about proved to be very good, and his recommendation of the steak pie was also accurate. From there they walked up to the top of the town and hired a cab to drive them to Belmont. The driver was a morose individual with a permanent sniff that got on both of their nerves as the horse clopped its way up the long hill. He hadn't been too pleased about taking them in the first place, as the prospect of picking up a fare to come back was remote. In the end Connor had to agree to pay him for the return trip as well, even though they wouldn't be using him. As they drew near to Belmont, Connor rapped on the cab roof to get the driver's attention.

"Here will do fine, thanks," he told him, as they neared the top of Barton Hill.

"Thought you wanted to go to Belmont," he grunted.

"We do, but we prefer to walk the last part, thank you."

"Seems a funny time of night to go calling," the cabbie grumbled as he took the fare, before turning his horse and heading back down towards the town.

"I think he must be a relation of the hotel receptionist," Matt said.

"You could be right," Connor laughed. "Anyway, at least it saved the long walk up the hill."

"What do we do now?"

"No idea, not really. I suppose we just find somewhere to park ourselves for a couple of hours or so and see what, if anything, happens."

"Supposing there *is* someone who calls late at night. What do we do about it?"

"Just play it by ear, I guess. We're bound to be seen if we try to get close enough to the house to hear anything that might be said, so the best we can hope for is to get some clues about who they are or what they want."

"I suppose so," Matt said, without much enthusiasm. "How about over there?"

He pointed to a small stand of trees and shrubs almost opposite the main gates of Belmont.

"As good as anywhere," Connor said.

◆

By the time an hour had passed they were cold and miserable. Matt in particular was getting more than fed up and was saying so.

"It's cold, I'm tired, I'm hungry, my back aches and my butt aches from sitting on this rock!" he complained.

"Is that all?"

"It'll do for now. I'll think of some more later," he said, with some heat.

"You'll have to save them up then — look over there."

He pointed down the lane, where the lights of a horse-drawn carriage could just be seen coming up the hill. A few minutes later, the coach rattled to a halt just yards from where they were concealed. There was a faded coat of arms painted on the side of the coach door. Two men descended, their hats and full-length cloaks concealing most of their features.

"Turn the coach here and wait a little way down the lane. We will not be long," one of them told the driver.

The driver did as he was ordered, and the carriage rattled back along the lane a short way. The two men looked at each other, and then went up to the gates of Belmont.

"I believe we are wasting our time," one of them said. "I have told the Marquis that she will not agree, but he insists that we try again."

"I agree, but he will not give up. Is there anyone about?"

They looked intently around them, including the undergrowth where Connor and Matt were trying not to breathe.

"No, we are alone. Go and tell the Marquis that he can leave the carriage."

The other nodded and walked back to where the carriage was standing and evidently said something to the occupant, for another man then descended and walked back with him. The third man was obviously of some importance, as the other two men treated him with great deference, even though he didn't seem to acknowledge that they were there. One of the men opened the small side gate and bowed slightly as the third man swept through it with a flourish of his cloak and walked along the drive. Connor and Matt watched him approach the front door and ring the bell. His arrival was not unexpected as the door opened almost immediately. He entered and the door was closed behind him.

"He'll have no more luck this time," one of the remaining men said.

"Of course not."

"How long will he wait before he realises that his great scheme is not going to work?"

"Not long now, I would have thought. If they are to get the boy to Paris in time, they will have to leave within the next two weeks."

"So if she refuses?"

"Then the others will act."

"I do not care for this."

"Nor I. However, we will not have to do anything. The others will see to it. We are just hired help, of no account to the Marquis or his friends."

Connor and Matt glanced at each other in the darkness and tried to make sense of the conversation. Connor wished he could see or hear what was going on in the house.

Abbey Place

Union Street

150

CHAPTER TWELVE

A secret in the vault

Mrs Debbon stood in the entrance hall face to face with her visitor.

"Could you not invite me into the drawing room?" he asked. "It would be easier to talk there."

"No," she said, shortly. "We have nothing to say to each other. I thought I had made myself understood on this matter at our last meeting."

"I hoped that after a period for reflection you would change your mind, and see that this is what your husband wanted."

"My late husband was a dreamer and a romantic. He was also easy prey to scoundrels like you who used him for your own ends."

"But do you not see that by refusing to follow his dream, you are, in effect, desecrating his memory?"

Her hand moved quicker than his eye could follow, and she struck him a stinging blow on the cheek. The force, and the action, took him completely by surprise and he staggered back, his hand pressed tight against his reddening cheek. She glared at him with eyes colder than the polar ice caps.

"My husband was a good man and a doting father. He should be here now, caring for his children and loving them and me. But no, you and your friends used him, manipulated him and would have ultimately destroyed him with your wild scheme. His death robbed you of your mad dream, me of my husband and the children of their father. Leave this house and do not presume to come here again. You will not be admitted."

He tried to muster some dignity, to leave the house with a flourish, but failed. In the end he left looking like a deflated balloon. After he had gone, Mrs Debbon remained motionless for several minutes. She was shocked by her own violence and needed to regain her composure. Once she was sure she could speak calmly, she rang for her maid.

"Sarah," she said, when the girl appeared. "You need not wait up any longer. I think I will take a short stroll in the garden to get some air before retiring."

"It is very late, Madam. Would you like me to accompany you?"

"No, but thank you for the offer. I will only be a short while."

"As you wish, Madam. Are you sure that you would not like me to attend you later?"

"Quite sure, thank you."

"Very well. Good night, Madam."

"Good night, Sarah."

Mrs Debbon retrieved two keys from a cabinet in her boudoir and then let herself out into the garden, but instead of taking a short stroll along the upper terrace, she descended the broad steps down to the middle terrace and walked purposefully to a small green door that was let into the retaining wall. She unlocked the door and took an oil lantern that was hanging just inside. Lighting it using a tinderbox on an adjacent shelf, she held the lantern aloft and walked a short way along a narrow, brick-lined passage, stopping by another door in the right-hand wall. She opened the unlocked door and let herself into the tiny vault that lay beyond, then turned to her left and removed several loose bricks from the wall to reveal a space occupied by a large tin box. She reached in, and with an effort, for the box was heavier than it appeared, lifted it out of the compartment. She inserted the second key into the lock on the box and opened the lid. Holding the lamp high above her, she gazed at the contents for a long time in total silence.

"Such trouble you have caused down the centuries," she said to herself eventually. "Far too much trouble. People, good people, have died because of you, and to what end? No, I will not permit those times to return."

She closed the box, locked it and restored it to its hiding place. After carefully replacing the bricks she retraced her steps, emerging into the moonlit garden. She took several deep breaths before locking the passage door, then made her way back into the house.

Meanwhile, her visitor had stalked angrily along the drive, holding his hand to his still smarting cheek. He lifted his other hand, which he then brought down in a savage chopping motion. He would show her. How dare she try to stand in the way of what was so obviously their destiny? She would pay. He swept furiously through the gate without speaking to either of the two men waiting there. They looked at each other and followed him along the lane and into the coach, which then sped off down the hill.

◆

"Well, he'd got a right cob on, whoever he was," Matt said, once the carriage was out of sight.

"Yes. You heard what the others were saying?"

"About getting the boy to Paris?"

"Yes. I presume they mean Charles. But what could be so important about him? And why would they need to take him to Paris? I also didn't like the sound of that business about the others acting if she refuses, and by 'she' I assume they mean Mrs Debbon."

"You think they're the ones that started the fire?"

"Not those two, no. They seemed to be referring to some others who would act. They didn't want to and were glad that they wouldn't be doing it."

"That Marquis fellow obviously didn't get anything out of his visit. By the look of him he was ready to murder someone."

"Yes. And we already know who."

"What have we got ourselves into, Uncle Conn?"

"I don't know, Matt, but I'm beginning to think it's something much bigger than we thought."

"Something too big for us to cope with?"

"Maybe. Anyway, I don't think anything else will happen tonight, so I suggest we go back to the hotel and get some sleep."

"Fine with me, but I think we should try to avoid being seen."

"Who's to see us?" Connor asked him. "There's nobody here."

"The Marquis. When he was walking along the drive, didn't you see him lift his arm and then drop it?"

"Yes."

"I think he was signalling to someone. I reckon the house is being watched."

"I never even thought of that. You could be right. Let's see if we can work our way back to Barton Road by cutting across the field behind us."

They crossed the field as Connor had suggested, but only at the cost of several scratches from unseen brambles and a number of bruises from falling over the lumps and bumps in the field.

"Next time we flip, I'll make sure I bring a torch with me, it's darker than a cow's gut out here," Matt griped, as they finally emerged into Barton Road.

"A torch wouldn't be a bad idea, but where on earth did you pick that expression up from?" Connor asked.

"What expression?"

"That bit about a cow's gut."

"No idea," Matt said, shrugging his shoulders.

"OK, come on, we've still got a fair way to walk."

"Don't I know it."

◆

Almost an hour later, and tired out, they arrived back at the Union Hotel. Misery-guts was still on duty and gave them a strange look, evidently wondering what they'd been doing wandering about at a time when all decent people should be in bed. He decided that it was none of his business and said nothing as he handed them the key. When they reached their room, Matt flung himself on his bed. When Connor returned from the bathroom a few minutes later he found his nephew fast asleep.

"What trouble have I got you into, Matt?" he said softly, taking the teenager's shoes off and covering him with a blanket.

He kicked his own shoes off and lay down on his own bed. He was asleep in seconds.

◆

Matt groaned loudly and sat up on the bed. Or at least he tried to sit up, but he found that he was stiff and sore, and it took some time before he could actually move. He looked over at his uncle, still fast asleep on his bed.

"Looks like we were both knackered last night," he said to himself, noticing that neither of them had bothered to undress. He realised that there was a lot of noise from outside in the street, so he stood up and staggered to the window, pushed the curtains back and peered out.

In his own time, Union Street was the main shopping street of Torquay and often crowded, but it wasn't a patch on the noise and bustle that greeted him that morning. The street was packed tight with vehicles of every description, mostly, but not all, horse-drawn. Two brewers' drays were making slow headway with their heavy loads of beer barrels. A dozen or so horses and traps were each striving to get through to wherever they were going: one of the drivers, a large, florid man with beetroot-coloured cheeks shouting obscenities at the owner of a hand-drawn cart who was blocking his way. A loud hissing noise came from a steam-powered lorry, sparks belching from its chimney, the sight of which was sending several of the horses, and not a few of their owners, into a panic. One of the horses, evidently deeply put out by all the noise, decided to relieve himself, soaking the dress of a middle-aged lady who had chosen that moment to walk across the road behind the horse. On the pavement below the window a young lad was selling newspapers, trying to make himself heard above the din.

There seemed to be just as many shops as in his own time, ranging from boot-and-shoe makers to photographers and butchers. These last, he noticed, had carcasses of pigs hanging in their open windows, the dust and grime from the street blowing over them. A health inspector would have a field day with this lot, he thought to himself. Even though the day itself was dull, with a leaden grey sky, the street was like a great colourful, bustling fair, with everyday people the entertainers. There was a sound from behind him and he turned to see Connor struggling to get off his bed.

"You've got to see this, it's really great. There's so much going on."

"I'll take your word for it. I've got enough problems getting off this bed. All my joints ache, including some I didn't know I'd got."

"You're getting old, that's your trouble."

"Thanks, brat. I'll remember that next time you're due a birthday or Christmas present."

"You're my godfather as well as my uncle. That means you're supposed to buy me presents."

"The promise was to love, cherish, protect and guide. There was nothing in there about buying presents — I'd have remembered."

"Comes under the heading of cherishing."

"You wish. What time is it?"

"Twenty past eight."

"So how come you're up at this time? You usually grumble if you're up before ten."

"Too much going on."

"Oh. What time did you say?"

"Twenty past eight. Is your hearing going as well?"

"No. It's just that I need a bath and I've only got ten minutes to get one according to the sign."

"You'll need to beat me to it, then," Matt said, making a dive for where the towels were neatly folded on the washstand.

"No problem. I've already got my towel," Connor said, quickly opening the door before Matt could get to it.

"No way, you're not getting in before me."

"Watch me," Connor said, managing to get through the door and shutting it in Matt's face. Matt wrenched the door open but by then Connor was already at the bathroom door.

"Tough luck. Age and treachery will always win over youth and ability. Better luck next time," he called, closing and locking the bathroom door.

"You'd better leave me some hot water," Matt shouted

through the door.

He returned to their room and flopped down on the bed. He'd more or less come to terms with flipping back and forth, but admitted to himself that it had more to do with Helen than anything else. He'd never met anyone like her before, and that wasn't just because she lived in late Victorian times. It was everything about her, her beauty, her freshness, her laugh. Everything. He wondered what she was doing, and if she was thinking about him.

His thoughts were interrupted by Connor returning from the bathroom, a towel draped round him and carrying his clothes.

"Go to it, Matt. If you're quick you'll get a bath in before time's up. There doesn't seem to be any shortage of hot water, but watch out for it. It's almost scalding hot, so don't burn yourself. And hurry up, we need to go shopping."

"You," Matt said, grabbing a towel and heading for the bathroom, "are fast becoming a pain."

He was back in less than ten minutes.

"That's got to be a record," Connor observed, as Matt entered the room. "Anyway, get your clothes on, we've got shopping to do."

"So you said, but what's the hurry?"

"Do you really want to wear the same suit when we go up to Belmont? Not to mention the rest of your gear."

"No, I don't. The others have already noticed that this one doesn't fit right."

"Exactly. We need clothes, so as soon as you're ready and we've had breakfast, then we try to find a gents' outfitters."

"Any idea where there is one?"

"No. Hopefully old misery-guts will have gone off duty, so if his replacement is more helpful perhaps we could ask at the desk. If not, we'll just have to walk up the road and see what we can find."

Breakfast that day was kippers and eggs, which didn't go down very well with either of them. Luckily, the day receptionist was a lot more cheerful than his predecessor and told them where to find a good, reasonably priced gents' outfitters towards the top of Union Street. After the expenditure of some fourteen pounds — almost half the money that Connor had left — they were properly kitted out with clothes and a large canvas holdall and they returned to the hotel to change.

"These things are going to be very scratchy," Matt complained as they were sorting out their purchases.

"Don't be so picky. Anyway, put some clean things on so that we can get up to Belmont. At least the tailor was able to tell us that the 'in' thing at the moment is a collarless shirt, not those awful stand-up things that we hired. These should be a lot more comfortable."

Still grumbling to himself, Matt sorted out a set of clean clothes.

"What on earth are these?" he asked, holding up what looked like baggy, knee-length, thin white trousers."

"Those are the 1898 equivalent of your boxer shorts."

"You're kidding!"

"No, I'm not."

"No way, I'm not wearing these. I'll stick to my shorts, thanks very much. I'd look a right dork in these."

"Who's going to see them?"

"So if no-one can see them it won't matter if I stick with what I've got, will it?"

"And how many pairs of shorts did you bring?"

"Just the ones I've got on of course. We didn't exactly have time to pack, did we?"

"My point exactly. Seeing as you insist on a clean pair at least once a day, more if you've been sweating, it's a case of either these, or keeping the same pair of shorts on until we flip back again. Which, I have to admit, is not a pleasant thought. It's those, or nothing."

"Rat farts. Next time I'll make sure I bring a heap of shorts with me," he complained, starting to get changed and hauling the offending underwear on.

"You're not the only one with problems. I can't shave because

I haven't got a razor, so by midday I'm going to be sporting some very untidy stubble."

"You could start a fashion for stubble."

"It's fine for you, you only have to shave every other day at the moment."

He started to put the rest of the clothes, plus their hired suits, into the canvas holdall.

"Why do we need to take everything with us? Why not just leave it all here. We've got the room for three nights."

"I know we have, but I don't know how long we'll be here this time. It's possible we'll flip back unexpectedly. Then if we don't get back within the next couple of days, all our stuff will no doubt get chucked out. At least if we carry it we'll be able to take it with us. Anyway, if you're ready, let's get going."

They walked up the road and hired another cab to take them to Belmont.

"Uncle Conn?" Matt said, once the cab was moving. "That coat of arms, the one on the coach last night. I think I know what it is, or at least part of it."

"You do?"

"Yes. Part of it had those gold three-pronged things on — you know, like the Scouts have?"

"Fleur-de-lys?"

"Whatever. Anyway, that was the coat of arms of the French Royal Family. We covered the French Revolution at college last year. I'm sure that's the same design that was in my history book."

"But you say it was only on part of the design? I couldn't see it properly."

"Yes. It was in the top left-hand quarter. The three other quarters all had a different design."

"Could you see what they were?"

"Not properly. I just noticed those gold things and remembered what they were. The others were more complicated, as if there were several designs in one."

"Sounds like the coat of arms of a very old family with close connection with the French Royal Family."

"I guess so."

"But the dates don't fit, Matt. It's 1898. Even in this era the French Revolution was a hundred years ago. When the monarchy was restored after the fall of Napoleon it didn't last very long. France is a Republic even in this year and has been for some time."

"I know. I didn't say it made sense. I just said that's what the coat of arms is."

"Anything else you remember about it?"

"I wish now I'd paid more attention instead of staring out of the window in history lessons. I don't think we covered much beyond the Revolution itself. We stopped when Napoleon took over. What about you, do you know anything about it?"

"No, not really."

"I thought you were into history."

"British history, not continental. I don't suppose I know any more than you do about French history, certainly not in this period. When we get back I could go and look it up. It could well be important. Why would a carriage bearing a coat of arms that hasn't been in use for a very long time arrive outside a house in an English seaside resort?"

"Especially when it seems to come and go only after dark."

"We know that Mr Debbon had connections with France. Have you spoken with Helen about it?"

"Only in a roundabout sort of way. She was very young when he died, and her mother doesn't like to talk about him. She gets upset apparently."

"Perhaps that's our next job. To find out just what his connection with France was."

"So how do we do that?"

"See if you can get Helen to find out. It'll be better coming from her. After all, it's only natural that she should be interested in what her father was like, and what he did for a living, so if you can get her interested, then she might ask her mother."

"OK. We'll probably go for another walk later, so I'll ask her then."

"You and Helen seem to be getting on very well together."

"She's great, she really is. I've never met anyone like her."

"Matt?"

"Yes?"

"Be careful. Don't go getting too attached. We're only visitors here. I think that in a couple of weeks' time, after the fire, we're going to be back in our own time for good."

"Don't worry, it's nothing like that. We're friends, that's all."

"I don't want to see you hurt."

"You worry too much. Everything's cool, don't fuss."

CHAPTER THIRTEEN

Nightmares and choices

Twenty minutes later they were at the gates of Belmont. The sky was still heavy and a cold wind was blowing across the hilltop.

"Not a good day for a walk," Connor said as they crunched their way along the drive. "You might need to think of some other way of chatting to Helen in private so that you can ask her about her father."

"I'll think of something."

They were expecting either Mary-Anne or Charles to answer the door, but instead it was opened by the butler, James.

"Good morning, gentlemen," he said. "Please come in. Madam asked me to say that she apologises for her absence, but she has an appointment in Exeter this morning."

"I'm sorry," Connor said. "Should we call again later?"

"Not at all," he said. "Madam has given instructions that you are free to come and go as it suits you, and that you are to be made welcome. May I take your coats for you?"

"Are the others here?" Matt asked.

"Miss Helen is in the library with her tutor, and Master Charles and Miss Mary-Anne are in the nursery with theirs. Madam insisted that lessons were to continue, even though they wanted to be here to see if you arrived."

"I hope that our coming and going doesn't inconvenience anyone too much," Connor said, as James showed them into the drawing room.

"Not in the least. I believe Madam looks forward to your visits."

"How long do the lessons last?" Matt asked.

"Usually for the morning, but I would anticipate that Miss Helen will persuade her tutor that her lessons should be curtailed today. Quite dramatically curtailed, I think. She has a way of getting what she wants. Master Charles and Miss Mary-Anne will not, I believe, be quite so fortunate."

"I see," Connor said with a laugh. "Will it be in order for us to wander around by ourselves, or will you or one of the other staff need to come with us?"

"I will accompany you with pleasure if you wish, but you are quite at liberty to go wherever you want by yourselves. Those were Madam's instructions."

"We wouldn't want to put you to any trouble."

"It is no trouble. It is why I am here," he said, smiling. "However, if you are happy to look after yourselves, then I do have other duties to attend to. If you need me for anything, then use one of the bell pulls wherever you happen to be, and either I or Mrs Gregson will attend you. Would you care for some refreshment now, or would you prefer to wait?"

"I think we'll wait," Connor said. "I'll sort out my notes, then get on with the catalogue."

"Very well," James answered, and left them alone in the room.

"I've been thinking," Matt said, "and don't look at me like that because I do sometimes think. Anyway, I've remembered something that Helen told me. I didn't pay much attention at the time, but I've just thought that it might have some connection. I was telling Helen about when I went to Paris and she asked what I'd liked best. I mentioned Napoleon's tomb, and she said I'd better not talk about that in front of her mother. She said that there was a picture of Napoleon hanging here when they moved in but Mrs Debbon had removed it and put away somewhere."

"Did Helen say why?"

"Not that I can remember, but I gather her mother doesn't approve of Napoleon at all. Mind you, she doesn't approve of the Eiffel Tower either, so perhaps it's not important."

"Perhaps. Still, we'll keep it in mind. Any idea what you're going to do while I'm cataloguing?"

"None at all. I hadn't realised that Helen would be having lessons."

"How about giving me a hand until she escapes from her

tutor?"

"I don't know anything about art."

"I know that, but you can measure the paintings and sculptures for me while I'm jotting things down. I haven't done the works in this room yet, so we might as well start here. I have to say it's all a bit dispiriting though, knowing that everything here is going to go up in flames in a week or so."

"Four people are going to burn to death and you're worrying about some paintings?"

"Sorry, wrong priorities. You're right, of course."

They were busy measuring and recording when the door opened to admit a somewhat out of breath Helen.

"Good morning," she said. "I'm so sorry I wasn't able to get away earlier, but Miss Fossett was being rather irksome. Usually she's very amenable, but today she was particularly difficult when I told her that I would like a shorter lesson than usual. I believe Mama must have had a word with her."

"What time do your lessons normally finish?" Connor asked.

"At half past twelve."

"It's now only half past eleven," Connor said, glancing at a clock on the wall, "so she's let you off a bit early."

"Yes, but not as early as I wanted. She insisted that I finish my needlework task first."

"Did you finish it?"

"Yes. However, I believe Miss Fossett may be a little vexed with the quality when she has a look at it. I did rather hurry it."

"No wonder you and Matt get on so well. He always hurries through his chores if there's something else he wants to do instead. Ouch! What was that for?"

"Sorry, my foot slipped. I didn't hurt you, did I?"

"Not as much as I'll hurt you if you come any closer. Anyway, I suppose you're going to abandon me now that this young lady has arrived?"

"Of course."

"Thought so. What are you two going to do for the rest of the morning? It's a bit cold and gloomy outside."

"I thought we could walk down and visit Daniel," Helen said. "I know he's at home this morning, and I do so want us all to be friends. Is that all right with you, Matt?"

It was very far from all right with Matt, but he didn't dare say so, and he agreed to her suggestion.

"Excellent. In that case I can collect my coat as we go. Come along Matt, or we will not have time to get there and back before luncheon. You will be all right on your own, won't you Mr Harvey?"

He assured her that he would manage perfectly well by himself, and so she and a very reluctant Matt left him alone in the drawing room. This is all very well, he thought to himself, but it isn't getting us very far in finding anything out. He wondered if the two younger children would be out from their lessons any time soon. Although they were doubtless too young to know much in the way of family secrets, it was always possible that he could pick up the odd piece of information. He was starting to get very worried that they weren't going to find anything useful before it was too late. He decided on another course of action and rang the bell pull.

The summons was answered within a couple of minutes by Mrs Gregson, causing Connor to immediately regret having pulled the cord.

"Good morning, sir," she said. "Can I help you?"

"Good morning, Mrs Gregson. Yes, please. It mentions a picture of Napoleon on my list, but I don't seem to have seen it. Would you know where it's hanging?"

"I believe that the one you're referring to is the one that Madam instructed should be removed when the family first moved in, sir. I believe it's in a cupboard somewhere."

"Oh," Connor said, trying not to let slip that he already knew full well that the picture had been taken down. "Do you know why that was?"

"Madam has never liked the subject being mentioned."

"I seem to remember you telling me that you were Mr Debbon's housekeeper before he married?"

"Yes, sir. My family has been in service to the Debbon family for three generations. It was a tragedy when he died. We were all heartbroken."

"I understand it was a heart attack?"

"Yes, sir."

"He was very young to have suffered from a heart attack."

"Yes, sir. I believe that all the people who kept calling to see him got him too worked up. Madam tried to restrict their visits but Mr Debbon seemed to be almost obsessed with whatever ideas they had."

"Do you know who the callers were?"

"No, sir, although Madam did refer to them once as dinosaurs who couldn't accept that what's passed is past."

"I see. And the picture of Napoleon, do you think it's possible to find it?"

"I'll ask James, sir. He's sure to know where it is."

"Thank you, I'd appreciate that."

She left to find James, leaving Connor pondering on whom Mrs Debbon could have referred to as dinosaurs. He felt he was skirting round the edge of something without ever being able to break inside and find out anything that would help him and Matt in whatever they were supposed to be doing. Even assuming that there was anything that *could* be done. He was getting a headache.

James arrived shortly afterwards and told him that the picture he was looking for was in store in one of the unused rooms, along with other items that the family either had no present use for or had decided were not suitable for display.

"I have the key to the room, sir, if you would like to follow me?"

"Thank you, James. I understand that Mrs Debbon doesn't like this particular picture, but I ought to see it if my catalogue is going to be complete."

"Of course, sir, I quite understand. Please come this way."

They climbed up to the first floor and along one of the corridors almost to its end. James unlocked the last door to reveal a room piled high with trunks, old boxes and, leaning against the wall, some half dozen framed pictures.

"The painting you want to see is this one, I believe," James told him, struggling with one of the pictures.

With Connor's help he eventually managed to turn the picture round so that Connor could see it. It was larger than he'd been expecting, and was an oil painting of Napoleon on horseback, striking a heroic pose in the act of leading his troops to victory in one or other of his many battles.

"It's a fine picture," Connor said, in some surprise. "The inventory didn't really make it clear what it was and I was more than half expecting an engraving. This is really very good. Do you know why Mrs Debbon took such a dislike to it?"

"Not really, sir, but I believe that it was originally hanging on the main stairs when the family first leased the property. I think it was Mr Debbon rather than Mrs Debbon who took such a dislike to it, and she had it taken down in order to please him."

"Would it be in order for me just to make a few notes while I'm here? I wouldn't want to inconvenience you at all."

"It is not often that what a servant wants, or doesn't want, is ever considered," James said with a smile. "It is no trouble to me at all, sir. Take as long as you wish. Can I help you with anything?"

"Yes, you can help me to measure it."

About twenty minutes later Connor had all he needed, having found two other paintings in the storeroom that needed to be recorded, although neither as fine as the oil of Napoleon. As they walked back along the corridor, Connor tried again to get some information about the family.

"Helen has been telling my nephew about her visits to France. Does the entire household go?"

"About half, sir. The others stay here to make sure that Belmont is well maintained."

"Do you go with them?"

"Yes, sir."

"I suppose it means a lot of extra work."

"It most certainly does."

They were interrupted by the sound of children laughing and the noise of running feet.

"I believe this means that Master Charles and Miss Mary-Anne have finished their lessons for the day. If you will excuse me, sir, I must go and ensure that everything is as it should be for when Mrs Debbon returns home shortly."

"Of course."

Connor walked slowly down the stairs and back to the drawing room. A picture of Napoleon removed because it disturbed Mr Debbon. People described as dinosaurs because they wouldn't change their views. Late night callers in a coach bearing a coat of arms that hadn't been in use for a very long time. A family murdered by being burnt to death. It made no sense; no sense at all. His headache was getting worse.

"Hello, Uncle Connor!" came two voices in unison, which didn't help his headache one bit.

"Hello, Charles, hello Mary-Anne. Finished lessons, I see."

"Yes," Charles said. "I've been doing adding up. This is my book."

He held up a thin exercise book for him to look at. Connor couldn't help noticing that Bill's writing skills were more advanced than Charles's, whose scrawl he could only just decipher. He didn't comment though, as the child was obviously very proud of his efforts.

"Very good, Charles," he said, riffling through the pages.

He was about to hand it back when something at the very start of the book caught his attention. Charles had written his name at the top of the first page, but instead of Charles Debbon, he'd written L. Charles Debbon.

"Charles?" he asked. "Your name in the book. You've put an 'L' in front of Charles."

"That's because his first name begins with 'L', Uncle Connor," Mary-Anne butted in.

"He asked me, not you," Charles complained, annoyed that his sister had interrupted him.

"But," she continued as if Charles wasn't there, "everyone uses his second name."

"I thought your mother didn't approve of shortening people's names."

"Yes, but this isn't shortening. His first name is Lewis. Papa's first name was Lewis, and so was Grandpapa's."

"Mama says it's a tradition," Charles said, determined to try and wrestle the conversation back from his sister. "All the eldest boys are named Lewis, so to stop everyone getting confused they all used their second name instead. Papa was called Robert."

"And Grandpapa was called Hubert," Mary-Anne added, equally adamant that she was going to be in charge.

"So your correct full name would be Lewis Charles Debbon?"

"Yes," the boy replied, sticking his tongue out at his sister.

Before Connor had a chance to ask any more there was a positive flurry of activity from the servants as Mrs Debbon returned home from her appointment.

"Mr Harvey," she said when she caught sight of him, "how pleasant to see you. I hoped that you would be able to visit today. The servants have been looking after you, I trust?"

He assured her that they had.

"And young Matthew? Is he not here today?"

"He was, but Helen kidnapped him. They've gone for another walk."

"Hardly a good day for a stroll, I think," she said. "The wind is positively chill today."

"I don't think they have gone very far. Helen said that they were going to call in to see Daniel. I gather Matt and he were introduced the other day."

"Ah, yes, young Master Hardwick. He is a fine young man, but I think perhaps my daughter is a little naive. She firmly believes that because she is friends with someone, then everyone she knows will be friends as well. I regret that she still has much to learn."

"You don't think that Matt and Daniel will be able to get along?"

"If left alone I am sure they would. Unfortunately the presence of Helen tends to make young men somewhat competitive. As I am sure you will have noticed, she is a very attractive young lady."

"She is indeed. She takes after her mother."

"You have been taking lessons from your nephew, I see," she said, laughing. "However, young people have to work things out for themselves. As for you, Mr Harvey, how have you been getting on?"

"Very well indeed, thank you. I asked James if he could find a painting on the inventory that I couldn't locate, and he showed me to a small storeroom on the first floor."

"I assume you are referring to the painting of Bonaparte?"

"Yes. It's very fine, but I gather that you don't care for it."

"As a work of art, it is exceptional. It is the subject matter that I do not care for. Nor did my late husband. We both considered that Bonaparte did France a great disservice."

"Yet he is now buried in Paris, is he not?"

"Yes," she said. "As an act of reconciliation, it was not perhaps, a bad idea, but to bury him in the church that Louis XIV, the Sun King himself, built as a memorial to the royal dynasty is, I feel, insensitive in the extreme."

Connor decided that the subject of Napoleon was not Mrs Debbon's favourite topic and decided to change the subject before he lost favour.

"I believe that there are several works of art in your boudoir, Mrs Debbon. Although I was told that I could go wherever I wished, I didn't feel I could trespass there without your presence. It wouldn't be right. Would it be possible for you to show me the room at some time convenient to yourself?"

"With pleasure. Now if you wish. Luncheon will not be for another half-an-hour or so yet."

Together they walked up the stairs and around the gallery to a door in the corner. She showed him into a light, bright, room decorated in yellow and white, with a view over the front garden.

"A beautiful room, Mrs Debbon," Connor told her.

"Yes, it is. After Robert died I decided to move my bedroom to this part of the house, and as this room is adjoining it seemed the logical thing to do to make it into my boudoir."

"So you had another room prior to this one?"

"Yes. You will not have seen that one either as it is usually kept locked. There are, however, a couple of items in there that would repay cataloguing. As soon as you are finished here I will show you."

Cataloguing the items in the boudoir took only a few minutes, and then Mrs Debbon led him along one of the corridors and paused in front of one of the doors.

"The room itself is of no great interest," she said, once she had unlocked the door, "but the view from here is the finest in the house, and the main reason that Robert and I chose it to be ours," she told him. "Even on such an inclement day as today, it seems that you can see forever."

Connor agreed that the view was indeed very fine. The light green of early spring leaves was dappling the trees in the valley, and the blackthorn was in full flower, creating great sweeps of white among the greenery. There were even some patches of blue, where early bluebells were showing their heads under the trees to the side of the house. Staring at the view, Connor found himself wondering how people could be so cruel and full of hate and bitterness when surrounded by so much beauty.

"The workmanship of this is remarkable, don't you think?" Mrs Debbon said, breaking into his thoughts as she indicated a small bronze figure of Venus that stood on a table.

"It certainly is," he said, once he'd regained his senses. He consulted his papers and started to make notes. He wondered how Matt was getting on.

◆

Matt wasn't getting on too well at all. He and Daniel were not yet at a point where open warfare had broken out, but they were not exactly the best of friends either. As Mrs Debbon had predicted, the subject of Helen had come between them, as each vied for her attention. Helen herself was extremely vexed. She had decided that the three of them were going to be friends, and so far, it wasn't working out at all. She was not used to her wishes being thwarted, but she was at a loss how to repair the damage that was being done. Things had started off not too badly at all. Daniel had been pleased to see them both and had invited them into his house. It was nowhere near the size of Belmont, but a substantial building all the same, as befitted the owner of a small fleet of steamships. There were several scale models of the ships in the house, and Daniel had willingly told a very interested Matt all about them, and showed him a working scale model of the new engine that the latest ship in the fleet, under construction in Bristol, was going to have. If things had been allowed to proceed from there everything would, perhaps, have turned out as Helen would have wished. Unfortunately, she was bored with the subject, and let it be known she would prefer a walk around the garden instead, in spite of the dull weather. They both made to take her arm, which is when things started to go downhill. The quiet walk around the garden turned into a competition to see who could hang onto Helen's arm for the longest, and the battle lines were being drawn up.

By the time they left Daniel's house to walk back to Belmont for lunch the two young men had been reduced to glowering at each other. Helen herself said very little as they walked up the hill and Matt sensed that he wasn't in her good books. He was, however, unsure what to do about it. He decided to give it a try anyway.

"Helen?"

"Yes?"

"I'm sorry that the morning didn't go very well."

"I'm sure I don't know what you're talking about."

"I mean Daniel and me. I know you wanted us to be friends, but I don't think that he and I got on too well."

"Really? I hadn't noticed."

Matt gave up and they walked on in silence. By the time they reached Belmont, Matt was in a turmoil of emotions. He liked Helen, more than liked her. He wanted to be with her, to be near her, to hold her hand, to watch her as the sun caught the gold in her hair. He wanted to hear her laugh; yet here he was, walking with her side by side, neither of them saying a word. He was beginning to wish he was somewhere else.

◆

"You'll stay for luncheon, of course?" Mrs Debbon asked Connor, although the tone of her voice made it quite clear that it was a statement of fact rather than a question.

"It's very kind of you, thank you very much."

"Now where has that daughter of mine got to," she said as she glanced at the clock. "She knows better than to be late."

"My nephew has little respect for mealtimes, I'm afraid. If they're late, I've no doubt it will be his fault."

"Nevertheless, I still . . . Ah, I believe I can hear them."

The door opened, and Helen and Matt entered. Connor could tell straight away that all was not well between them, and hoped that it was only a temporary tiff and not something that would hinder their investigations. He decided not to ask if they'd enjoyed themselves.

"We've been invited for lunch, Matt," he said. "It won't be very long, so you and I should go and sort ourselves out. Come on."

Matt trailed after him without a word, and still hadn't spoken by the time they reached the first-floor guest bathroom.

"You're normally only this quiet when you have to get up early. Something happened between you and Helen?"

"No, not really."

"Had a row?"

"I don't want to talk about it."

"Matt, this isn't our own time. We're in 1898 and everyone here is going to die shortly. It's not like at home where you can fall out with your girlfriend and either make up the next day or find yourself another one. If there's a problem, tell me."

"It's not really a problem," Matt sighed. "It's more like I don't know what to do. I don't know the rules, what I can say, what I can't say. Helen wants me and Daniel to be friends. He's all right I suppose, but he's obviously been going out with Helen for a time, and now I turn up and start going for walks with her. He thinks I'm a rival."

"Are you?"

"How can I be? You said yourself we're only visitors."

"That's the brain talking, not the heart. I know you like her, Matt, it's obvious. Besides, who wouldn't? But you mustn't get involved, you can't. We're not going to be here for long. Try to explain to Daniel that you and she are friends, no more, and that even if you wanted there to be more between you, it isn't going to happen."

"I'm not sure I'll get the chance. She's giving me the cold shoulder and if Daniel sees me he'll probably smack me in the mouth."

"You do get yourself into some scrapes, don't you? Don't worry — we'll sort something out. I don't suppose that you managed to find out anything, under the circumstances?"

"No, didn't get the chance. You?"

"Yes, a little. The subject of Napoleon is definitely off the menu: Mrs Debbon is clearly of the opinion that he was the devil incarnate. She also thinks that burying him in the Church of the Dome at Les Invalides is something close to sacrilege."

"Does that help?"

"I wish I could say it did but I've no idea what it means. I've also found out that Charles's first name is actually Lewis, as it was of his father and his grandfather."

"So, does *that* help?"

"No," he said heavily. "I'm sure that it's very important. I can feel it, but I don't know what it is."

The loud beating of the lunch gong interrupted their conversation.

"Come on, Matt, we're on."

"I could get to dislike that gong if I really thought about it."

◆

By the time lunch was over, relations between Matt and Helen had started to thaw a little. Once or twice she smiled at him, and things would probably have worked out if Matt hadn't heard the now familiar sound of a fly buzzing in his ear just they were finishing the meal. He didn't need to be told what to do. He joined Connor who was already giving his apologies to Mrs Debbon and grabbing his bag with their stuff in it.

"I realise that it is difficult for you to say when you will be back, but I trust that it will not be too long?"

"I hope not," Connor said, thinking to himself that if they didn't get some sort of breakthrough soon then they might as well not bother. "Come on, Matt, we've got to go."

◆

By the time that they'd reached the lane the noise in their heads was becoming more than just painful. Connor had the feeling that his skull was about to explode and he felt physically sick. They managed to get out of sight of Belmont before he collapsed by the side of the road and passed out. Matt wasn't much better. He managed to remain conscious, but only just. By the time the noise stopped he was on the ground, his hands clamped tightly to his head. Five minutes later a white-faced and very badly shaken Matt struggled to crawl over to where Connor was slowly regaining consciousness.

"That noise, Uncle Conn, I know what it is," he gasped, when he saw that Connor was awake enough to listen.

"What?"

"It's people screaming — screaming in terror and pain. It's Helen and her family, they're screaming as the fire reaches them! We can't save them, they're all going to die!"

He curled up on the ground and buried his face in his hands.

◆

Connor's sleep that night was troubled and restless. Black shapes bore down on him out of the darkness and images of burning buildings and children screaming for help invaded his dreams. Twice he woke, sweating in the darkness. He woke a third time because he'd imagined he'd heard a shout, but it came again and he realised that this time it wasn't a dream. Matt was shouting from his room, and Connor swung himself out of bed and ran along the corridor to Matt's room. He was writhing in his bed, shouting "No!" again and again.

"Matt, wake up."

"No! Can't do it! No!"

"MATT!"

The shouting stopped and slowly the thrashing about calmed. Matt opened his eyes and gradually focused on his uncle's worried face.

"Uncle Conn?"

"It's OK, Matt, you've had a nightmare," Connor said, putting his hand on Matt's forehead. It was hot and flushed and he was dripping with sweat.

"It was horrible. Helen was trapped in the fire and I couldn't get to her. I don't think I can do this. I don't think I can cope with it," he sobbed, the tears running down his cheeks.

"I know, Matt, I know."

"If I thought we could change anything it would be easier, but I don't think we can. Do you really think we can change things? Please, be honest with me, I need to know."

Connor tried hard to think of an answer that would save Matt from what he believed to be the brutal truth, that no matter what they did, the past was fixed and unalterable. He couldn't.

"No, Matt. I don't think we can change anything."

"Then I can't do it anymore. If I thought there was a chance, I'd take it. I'd go back gladly and even if things turned out wrong, at least I'd know I tried. But to know that everyone's going to die, that I'm going for long walks and holding hands with someone who's going to burn to death in a week or so's time, it's more than I can bear."

"If that's really how you feel," Connor said, sitting on the side of the bed, "there's a way we can avoid this."

"There is? How?"

"You phone your Mum and Dad and tell them that I've had to go back to work, so you're moving down to stay with me. They won't mind, because that was their first suggestion anyway, until

I offered to stay here. I can still run you to college each weekday."

"But how would that help?"

"Because we have to be *here* to flip. As soon as you're away from the house, you don't get that tugging feeling you told me about. If you're not here, nothing happens."

"But as soon as I come home it will."

"Not if you don't come back until after the fire. You sit out the next week or so with me, until after the 28th. Then you come home. The fire will have happened and we both get on with our lives."

Matt turned troubled eyes towards him.

"I'm scared. This whole business scares the hell out of me."

"Me too."

"You as well?"

"I'm not the hero type, Matt, I'm plain Mr Average. I'm not the one who'll tackle a gang of thugs who are trashing someone's car. I'm the one who'll go and phone the police and hope that someone else will sort it out. I've had nightmares as well. I wish that none of this was happening, or at least that it was happening to somebody else. I don't want to keep flipping back to 1898; I don't want the responsibility of trying to save four people from something that I believe is inevitable. I want to crawl into a corner and hide until it's all over."

"But that's just how I feel."

"I know. That's why I won't be the one to make speeches about it being our duty to try to save these people, I won't be the one to shout coward and I won't be the one to try to change your mind. I feel just the same as you."

"But if we just sit back and do nothing, how will we feel afterwards?"

"You know the answer to that. We'll feel bloody awful. But I'm tired, Matt, this whole business is knocking me out. I'm not even sure I'm physically capable of going through that noise again."

They were both silent for a while, not knowing what to say.

"You're soaking wet with sweat, Matt, and so are the

bedclothes," Connor eventually told him. "Go and grab a shower and I'll put clean sheets on your bed while you're doing it. When you come back from the shower we'll decide what we're doing."

Matt nodded and slipped out of bed and padded along to the bathroom, Connor getting fresh sheets out of the rebuilt airing cupboard and making up the bed. Matt was back in a few minutes.

"I've decided," he said. "I want to go home with you, and I want to go as soon as possible. Can we go now before I get that tugging feeling again?"

"Yes, if you're sure that's what you want."

"Yes, it is. And it's what you want as well?"

"Yes."

"How much stuff do I need to pack?"

"Only enough for tomorrow and what you need for college. I don't get those tugging feelings that you get, so I can always come up here by myself and get whatever you need. You get yourself dressed and I'll go and pack a few odds and ends that I'll need. I'll leave most of my gear here for tonight and come and fetch it tomorrow."

"OK," Matt said, giving his uncle a smile that was too weak to reach his eyes.

◆

They were on their way within half an hour. Once in Connor's home they fell into their beds and were asleep in seconds and there were no more nightmares for either of them that night. Morning found both of them unusually quiet.

"We *are* doing the right thing, aren't we?" Matt asked anxiously over breakfast.

"I'm not sure we should linger on that question for too long," Connor told him. "We might not like the answer. We'd be best trying to forget about it for the duration. You've got your college work, and once I've picked up my gear from your place later this morning, I'll get on with some work. By the way, phone your Mum and Dad and tell them what we're doing."

◆

An hour later, Connor dropped Matt at the college bus pick-up point and then drove up to collect his computer, some more of Matt's clothes and their 1898 gear. He didn't want Steve and Marion to arrive home unexpectedly and find him there. The house seemed eerily quiet, and he loaded up his car as quickly as he could. He was about to drive off when he remembered that Matt had asked him to pick up his football, and he went back to get it. Football in hand he was just leaving Matt's room when he heard the singing. He knew who it was. Mary-Anne, singing the same old French folk song that he'd first heard on the night of the fire. He went to the window and glanced out. She was in the front garden singing to herself, or at least he thought it was to herself until he realised that Mrs Debbon was sitting on a garden bench listening to her.

"I'm sorry," he whispered, "I'm so sorry. I can't help you."

The tears were running down his cheeks as he drove away from the house.

◆

He said nothing to Matt about his experience when he picked him up from the bus stop that afternoon, and the subject of Belmont wasn't mentioned at all for the rest of the day. They talked about college, about a forthcoming football match, about Matt's prospects at the following month's swimming championships; in fact, about everything but what they both really needed to talk about. They ate the meals that Connor prepared, they watched television, Matt phoned his parents then did his homework, and they went to bed. All without mentioning the Debbon family.

Next morning, Connor again saw Matt off to college, and then tried to do some work, but gave up. He couldn't concentrate, and other thoughts came unbidden. Napoleon. Carriages with coats of arms. An unknown Marquis. Lewis Charles Debbon. Especially this last. Lewis Charles Debbon. The name ran round and round inside his head, trying to open doors but managing only to rattle the handles. There was something about that name, if he could only latch onto it. He turned his computer on and did a search for

Lewis Charles Debbon, but without learning anything. There was someone with that name in the States who owned a pilchard cannery, and someone else in Canada who was trying to research the history of the Hudson Bay Company. He turned the machine off. Lewis Charles Debbon, he thought, who the hell are you, and why are you so damned important?

◆

Matt was playing in a football match after the end of classes that afternoon, so Connor drove over to the college to pick him up and save him having to wait for a bus. The name Lewis Charles Debbon was still doing lazy circles in his mind when Matt opened the passenger door and clambered in.

"Thanks for driving over," he said.

"No problem. Who won the match?"

"They did, but only because Dillon managed to get himself sent off. You look like crap, Uncle Conn, are you OK?"

"Thanks, I really needed to know that. Yes, I'm fine I suppose, just been thinking a lot today. Couldn't concentrate on work at all."

"What were you thinking about?"

Connor started the car, and then turned to look at him before driving off.

"You know what I was thinking about. The same thing that both of us are thinking about but neither of us will talk about it."

No more was said on the subject until they arrived home and Connor was busy getting the dinner.

"Uncle Conn, can we have a serious talk?"

"Of course," he said, placing their meals on two trays and carrying them into the living room. "What about?"

"The fire, flipping back, Helen — everything."

"I thought you didn't want to."

"I didn't, or at least I thought I didn't. Now I'm not sure what I want. I'm not sure I, or rather we, made the right choice."

"Are you saying you want to go back?"

"Do you?"

"We're skirting round it again. I've been thinking about very little else. I wasn't going to tell you this, but when I went back to your place to get your gear, I heard Mary-Anne singing and saw her and her mother on the front lawn."

"What did you do?"

"Nothing. Just crept away and slunk back here with my tail between my legs."

"But we've agreed that there's nothing we can do. We can't change anything. All we'll do is give ourselves loads of grief for nothing, you said so yourself."

"That's not exactly what I said. I said I don't believe that it's possible to go back in time and make changes. The past is fixed."

"But that's the same thing."

"Not quite. Just suppose that we're *meant* to go back. That us going back to 1898 is part of what's already happened."

"You mean that by us *not* going back, then they die, because we're not there to save them?"

"Maybe. We need to decide what we're doing, Matt. Once and for all."

They were both quiet for a long time, both busy with their own thoughts.

"I think," Connor said eventually, "that both of us are afraid to say what we really think, in case it upsets the other. We both want to pass the buck, to let the other decide for us. I'll find some paper."

"Paper? Why?"

"You'll see in a minute."

He fumbled in his pockets, eventually finding two old till receipts. He handed one to Matt.

"Write on the back of that what you want to do, and I'll do the same."

"How do you mean?"

"Just write one word. If you want to go back home, which will mean that we'll no doubt flip as soon as we get there — and you're willing to try to cope with everything that going back to 1898 will mean — then write 'go'. If you want to stay here and ride this out until it's all over, because you believe that there's nothing we can do anyway, then write 'stay'.

"What about you?"

"I'll do the same."

"What if each of us writes something different?"

"I don't know. Let's worry about that afterwards. Have you got a pen?"

Matt nodded.

"Then make your choice."

Matt unwillingly took the scrap of paper and stared at it. It was a receipt for a couple of magazines from the local paper shop. He recognised the titles. They were car magazines that Connor had bought for him the last time he'd stayed over. He stared at the smudged print for inspiration, not knowing what to do. Then he realised that wasn't true, took a deep breath and wrote on the back of the paper.

"I've done mine," he said. "How about you?"

"Done. Put yours down on the table and I'll put mine down at the same time."

Both pieces of paper were placed side by side on the table. After what seemed an eternity, Connor looked up and smiled at his nephew.

"Well, it seems we're agreed. We're going back to 1898."

CHAPTER FOURTEEN

Among the primroses

Helen couldn't sleep. Matt hadn't turned up on either Wednesday or Thursday, and she was worried that she'd created such a bad feeling between them that he didn't want to see her again. She didn't know what to do. She should have known that Daniel and Matt were bound to see each other as rivals. She had wanted so much for the three of them to be friends that her customary good sense had deserted her. She had known Daniel for years and liked him. They had very little in common but they got along together just fine. There was an unspoken agreement between them that, although at the moment they were friends, one day soon that friendship would deepen into something more. She had never seriously looked at anyone else, including the long string of dull young men that had attended the receptions that she had been invited to at the various large houses and villas in Torquay. Then along had come Matt and she didn't know what to think anymore. She liked the way he looked, the way he talked, even the way that he somehow didn't fit in. But, she told herself, he was only a visitor, just travelling with his uncle for a few weeks. They would be going home soon, so why was she making trouble for herself with Daniel? She tried to go to sleep but it evaded her, so she was wide-awake when she heard voices in the entrance hall. She strained to hear who it was, but the thickness of the doors made that all but impossible. Moonlight shining through the window showed her the clock on the mantelpiece. Two in the morning. Who on earth would be calling at this time? She slipped out of bed, put her robe around her shoulders and went to her door. Easing it open slightly, she could now hear clearly. Her mother was talking to a man whose voice she didn't recognise. It wasn't the same man who had called on several previous occasions. That voice she had now got to know quite well. This one was different, but its owner's reception by her mother seemed to be just the same. He seemed to be alternately demanding and then pleading, but neither approach was doing him the slightest good. She decided to risk getting a little closer, and slowly opened her door and slipped out onto the gallery. Crouching down, she peered over the balustrade at the scene below.

"You must agree. You have no choice," he was saying.

"I have every choice, and do not try to threaten me. I have no fear of you or your kind."

"I have many friends."

"As do I, but my friends will not desert me. Yours, I fancy, will melt like snow in the spring when your time comes. You will not escape what is coming to you. I would have thought that your trial would have shown you that."

"I was cleared of all charges."

"By a corrupt court whose officials were only looking to save their own necks, as Monsieur Zola pointed out in his letter."

"Monsieur Zola! What good did his letter do? He has been accused of libel and will have to leave the country."

"He will be proved right in time," she replied calmly. "As you will be found guilty. Now I strongly advise you to leave, Major, and go back to France. I also advise that if you have any unfinished business there you get it sorted out as soon as possible, for I am certain that once the truth is made public you will have to leave. Good night to you, Major."

"You are a traitor to the cause, Madam," he stormed.

"The only cause you are interested in is one that will save your own neck. Good night, Major," came the calm reply. "Please close the door quietly, my children are all asleep. I would not want them woken."

Helen saw the unknown Major sweep furiously from the house, leaving the door wide open. Her mother walked to the door and gently closed it, and Helen slid back into her own room before her mother could turn and see her. She had assumed that the visitor was another creditor, but it didn't sound to her as if he wanted money. It was all very frustrating, and sleep only came to her just before dawn.

◆

Sleep was also hard to come by for Matt. He and Connor had agreed that it would be best, not to mention far more convenient, to wait until the morning to return to Matt's house, and therefore, by implication, to 1898. Even if they saw more visitors to the house late at night, it would not in itself tell them any more, and they would still need to find accommodation. The three nights that Connor had paid for at the Union Hotel had expired, so they would need to book again. Matt was in turns excited and apprehensive. He desperately wanted to see Helen again and was cheered by Connor's suggestion that going back was what they were meant to do, but he was also worried that, in the end, it would all turn out the same. He heard footsteps going down the stairs, and slipped out of bed. He found Connor in the kitchen making himself a coffee.

"Couldn't sleep?" he asked.

"No. Nor could you by the look of it. You want a coffee?"

"Please," he said. "Apart from the clothes, is there anything we ought to take with us?"

"Your shaver's battery powered, isn't it?"

"Yes."

"And fully charged?"

"As far as I know."

"Good. Bring it with you. The charge should last for a few days, so that I won't look too unkempt when we turn up at Belmont. Mrs Debbon didn't mention my stubble when we were last there, but I know she noticed it."

"OK, one shaver. I want to take some shower gel. That soap at the hotel was awful."

"Yes, it was, but I doubt very much that we'll find anywhere with a shower."

"Doesn't matter, it'll work just as well in a bath."

"Fine. I've thrown a few things into the bag with the clothes in it, but we can't take too much and we can't take anything that'll be too obvious. The shaver will be fine, because no one will see it apart from us, but we'll have to be careful. Anyway," he said, draining his coffee cup, "I'm off back to bed to see if I can get at least a few minutes' shut-eye before the morning."

"I think I'll stay here. There's no way I'll go to sleep."

"No problem with me. 'Night, Matt."

"'Night, Uncle Conn."

They still wait and watch, but they know time is now very short. The Marquis had no luck, nor did the Major earlier that night. They begin to accept that she will never agree and that the boy will have to be taken by force. They have been told that there will be one last attempt to persuade her and then they will act. Decisively and finally. They have watched with interest the coming and going of the man and the youth, and have learned that the man is only interested in the art treasures in the house and the youth is only interested in the daughter. They have not seen this for themselves, but they have been told that this is so, for they are not the only ones who watch the house and those who live and visit there. There is another.

Matt was woken by the smell of bacon and eggs frying, and raised his head from where he'd been slumped on the kitchen table.

"Morning, Matt. Breakfast in five minutes. I thought we'd better eat well this morning as we don't know what we're going to face when we get there."

"Brilliant," Matt said, yawning and stretching his arms and legs. "Must have nodded off in spite of myself. What time is it?"

"About nine. From what little I know of late Victorian etiquette it wasn't done to go visiting too early in the morning."

"I could get to like these late Victorians. They sound very sensible people on the subject of getting up in the morning."

"Don't forget to phone your parents. I'll phone your college in a bit and tell them you've got a stomach bug and are likely to be off for a few days. I've no idea how long we'll flip for this time, but I expect it'll be a good deal longer than before. I only hope

I've got enough money left to house and feed us for the duration. If not you'll have to go out singing on the streets."

"No problem, I'd soon have enough to build a mansion."

"You mean they'll pay you to go and sing somewhere else," Connor said, dishing out the bacon and eggs. "Eat up, go and get your 1898 clothes on, then we'll be off."

◆

Connor stopped the car some distance from Matt's house.

"Is there anything you want from your place before we go?"

"Can't think of anything."

"Then if you hop out here, I'll drive on to your house and park up and you follow along in a few minutes. I don't want to be driving up to the house when we flip."

"Sure. I won't be long."

Matt got out of the car, and counted to a hundred before starting to walk along the lane to his house. It was a cold and miserable morning, but he found himself getting excited at the prospect of seeing Helen again. He hoped that she was looking forward to seeing him as well, and hadn't given up on him altogether. He reached the gate and saw Connor had parked the car by the side of the house and was waiting for him halfway along the drive. He wondered if his uncle was as nervous as he felt himself.

"Hi," he said, as he joined his uncle.

"Hi yourself. We're going to look total idiots dressed like this if we don't flip. I'd have thought that we'd have gone as soon as you got here, but it doesn't seem like it."

"Perhaps we have to . . . whoa, what was that?" Matt asked, as they both staggered.

"That small earthquake feeling again. I think we just flipped."

"No fog this time though. Why do you think that is?"

"Wouldn't have a clue. You sure you're happy with this, Matt?"

"Yes. Now that I think there's a chance we can do something, or at least be of some use, I'm happy. It was just the idea that there was nothing at all to be done that was bugging me."

"And you're prepared for things not to work out?"

"Sure. As you said, it may be that we're meant to be here, that we're already part of this. But if it isn't, well, at least I'll be able to live with myself afterwards. How about you?"

"The same as you. On the assumption that you and Helen will be going off somewhere, try to find out anything you can, especially about her father and what his connection with France was."

"I'll see what I can do."

There was a shout from behind them and they turned to see Bill playing in the garden with Charles. The miserable, cold day of their own time had been replaced with blue skies, and the windows of Belmont reflected the warm spring sunshine.

"Hello, Uncle Connor," Charles said. "I didn't see you coming, even though we were looking for you. Why didn't you come yesterday or the day before?"

"Sorry, young man. I was called away urgently, but we're back now."

"Good."

"Where've yer been?" asked Bill.

"Tell him where we've been, Matt," Connor said.

"Er, we had to go back to Wales for a couple of days," he said, glaring at his uncle for dropping him in it.

"So we did. Yes, back to Wales."

"But yer ain't got those funny togs on," Bill said, "the ones wot yer wore when yer was 'ere first."

"No, we had time to change them. Shouldn't you be having lessons with your tutor this morning, Charles?" asked Connor.

"He's got a cold, so Mary-Anne and I have got the day off."

"What about you, Bill? No school today?"

"Nah, fort I'd skip it an' come up 'ere."

"Can you ask you mother if it will be in order for us to call today?" Connor asked Charles.

"Yes, but I know it will be. Mama said she was hoping that you would be back soon."

He ran off with Bill in tow to the house, reappearing a couple of minutes later followed by Helen. She walked over to them, looking, Matt noticed, rather worried.

"Mr Harvey, Matt, how nice to see you again. We were getting concerned about you, but didn't know where you were staying, so we weren't able to get in touch. Is everything well?"

"Everything's fine, thank you," Connor told her. "I had some work come up that needed attending to urgently, but it's now been settled."

"And you had to go with him?" she asked Matt.

"Yes, but everything's fine now."

"Please go straight in, Mr Harvey," Helen told him. "Mama knows you are here. She is in the drawing room."

"Thank you," he said, smiling to himself as he noticed that Helen had taken Matt by the arm and was leading him off in a different direction.

"Matt?" Helen asked, once they were alone. "Are you vexed with me?"

"No, of course not. Whatever makes you think that?"

"It's just that when you were last here, when we went to see Daniel, I know that the day wasn't as I had hoped it would be. I thought perhaps that you didn't want to see me again."

He assured her that nothing could be further from the truth, and she smiled warmly at him. He felt his resolve not to get too involved slipping. He wanted so badly to take her in his arms that the pain was almost too much.

"I've seen Daniel," she told him. "He says he's sorry that he wasn't a better host."

"It's not a problem, honest. Daniel's all right, I'm sure he and I can learn to get along."

"Wonderful," she said, her smile becoming positively radiant. "That's exactly what I want."

Matt wasn't at all sure if it was what *he* wanted, but if it pleased Helen then he'd go along with it. He wasn't sure that Daniel would, though, but he'd worry about that later.

"What shall we do this morning," she asked, taking it for granted that Matt wouldn't want to stay at the house. "I thought perhaps we could take a stroll into Daccombe. It's a small village not far away, and the lanes will be very pretty at this time of year."

Matt remembered just in time not to tell her that he knew Daccombe like the back of his hand, and instead told her that he'd enjoy that very much. She left him in the garden while she went inside to fetch a light coat, and then led him around the house, down through the terraced gardens, and out into the lane. It was a glorious day and as they strolled hand in hand between the high Devonshire banks, Matt knew that they'd made the right choice by coming back. He took his jacket off and slung it over his shoulder. He'd walked this way a thousand times before, but never in such company. He tried to find something to say, to tell her how he felt, but didn't know how to go about it. Just how did a boy talk to a girl in 1898, and what was he allowed to do and what was off limits? He had absolutely no idea at all. He supposed he'd just have to make it up as he went along and hope for the best.

"The primroses are coming into bloom," Helen said, breaking into his train of thought. "I love it when they do, it means that spring is really here and summer's not far behind."

"Yes, I suppose it does."

"There's usually a large patch of them in the middle of that field. Do you think we could go and see if they're in flower yet? Mama would love some to put in a vase."

"Sure, why not."

He helped her over a stile and they walked through the long grasses across the field. The primroses that Helen had mentioned were indeed starting to come into flower, so they gathered a few of the blooms to take home.

"I don't want to take too many," she told him, "or it will spoil the rest."

"Helen?"

"Yes?"

"I know that I'm not going to be here for very long, but I was wondering if, while I *am* here, do you think it would be all right, I mean, would you consider, er, walking out with me, if you'd like to, that is?"

"Walking out? My, what an old-fashioned thing you are."

Her lips found his before he had time to remember that he wasn't supposed to be getting involved. She pulled him down into the sweet scented grasses and opened her arms to him.

◆

Some considerable time later she sat up and brushed a few offending pieces of grass off her blouse. The forgotten primroses were strewn around and she started to collect them up again. After they'd been sorted to her satisfaction she let her hand run lightly over Matt's cheek and then leaned over to kiss him. He smiled at her, lifted his own hand and let it lazily trace a pattern over her cheeks and lips.

"Are you happy?" she asked.

"Never been happier," he told her truthfully.

"We should be getting back," she told him, "or we will be late for luncheon and Mama will not be pleased."

He stood and helped her to her feet, then picked up his jacket where he'd dropped it. He brushed pieces of grass and the odd crushed primrose off his clothes and they walked hand in hand back to the lane.

"Was your father such a stickler for punctuality at mealtimes?" Matt asked.

"I think so. I can only just remember him; he died when I was very young. Charles and Mary-Anne have no memory of him at all and I know that Mama is sometimes very sad about that. We have photographs of him, but as Mama says, it isn't the same."

"I think I heard your mother telling my uncle that he had a lot of connections with France. Is that why you had a lot of friends there?"

"I believe so, but I really don't know a lot. Some of the people that Papa knew were not to Mama's taste at all. Some of them have been among those calling at the house late at night. There was one last night, or rather early this morning. I don't think I'm supposed to know about it, but I couldn't sleep last night and heard him and Mama in the hall. I could tell from her voice that she really did not like him."

"Who was he?"

"I don't know his name. Mama called him 'Major', so I presume that is his title. She also mentioned a Monsieur Zola and a letter he has written, but I don't know to whom the letter was sent. Whoever it was must have been very annoyed about it, because Monsieur Zola was accused of libel. Just before the Major left he said that Mama was a traitor to the cause."

"What cause?"

"I don't know. It's all very distressing."

Matt decided not to press her any further. At least he'd found out something. He'd no idea if it was of any use or not.

◆

"And she doesn't know who this 'Major' is?" Connor asked him when they were in the guest bathroom, getting themselves cleaned up in time for lunch.

"No. Any ideas?"

"Yes and no. That 'traitor to the cause' bit sounds interesting. Monsieur Zola must be Emile Zola, a French author and playwright. He wrote a very famous open letter to the French Press in which he accused the government and the military of a cover-up in the Dreyfus affair."

"What's that when it's at home?"

"I don't know the details, Matt. I remember it had something to do with someone called Dreyfus being accused of spying, found guilty and sent to Devil's Island, a French penal colony. Later it was found that the whole thing had been a set-up, and there was a campaign to get him released, but the government dragged its heels because it didn't want to admit to being part of it. There was a huge scandal and it was years before Dreyfus was eventually pardoned."

"But you don't know any more?"

"No. I really only know that much because there have been several films made about it. It's the first bit of real information we've had, though. When, and if, we flip back to our own time, we'll have to do some research. Anyway, there's the gong, so let's go and get fed. I assume from the extremely irritating smile on your face that you and Helen have made it up?"

"Yes," he said, as they left the room. "We're fine now."

Lord help us all, Connor thought as he followed Matt down the stairs.

◆

Once the meal was over, Mrs Debbon announced that she would be retiring as usual for a while.

"Do you wish to continue with your catalogue this afternoon?" she asked. "I would not want to think that the task was becoming onerous."

"Not at all," Connor told her. "It's very enjoyable. I wonder, though, if I could beg a favour."

"Of course."

"Would it be possible for your coachman to take me into Torquay and back? I will need to sort out accommodation for Matt and myself. I only booked for three nights originally and that will have expired due to my being called back to Wales."

"With pleasure. Where were you staying?"

"At the Union Hotel. You know it?"

"Of course, but it is not one of the better hotels. It is more used by people spending just one or two nights than for a stay of any length."

"I know, but it has one very appealing feature."

"And that is?"

"It's cheap. I regret the Great Western Railway doesn't pay very well. It's all I can afford."

"My dear Mr Harvey, how very remiss of me. It never even crossed my mind to ask about the finances. I am so sorry. I will arrange something at once."

"Please, Mrs Debbon, there's no need. Everything is perfectly all right. The Union Hotel is clean and comfortable, that is all that Matt and I need."

"Nevertheless, we can do very much better. The Belgrave

Hotel is one of the more preferable hotels in the town. It is on the seafront, you may have seen it?"

"Yes. Matt and I saw it when we went for a walk one evening."

"It has very recently been purchased by a syndicate and they have appointed Monsieur Lerida as manager. He used to manage a hotel in Paris and I know him very well. I will send James in the carriage down to the hotel and tell Monsieur Lerida to arrange for rooms for you and Matthew."

"That's very kind of you, Mrs Debbon," Connor said with some agitation, "but I regret that I will not be able to . . ."

She raised her hand and stopped him in mid-sentence.

"I will tell him to send the account here for me to settle. I will also arrange for a sum to be paid to you by way of expenses. I have been extremely remiss in not sorting out these arrangements before. I hope you will forgive me?"

"But, Mrs Debbon, really, I can't accept . . . "

The hand came up again.

"The matter is settled. Now, as it is such a beautiful day, I think I will change my mind and forego my usual rest and take a turn in the garden instead. I hope that you will accompany me?"

"It will be a pleasure," he told her, recognising defeat when he saw it. No wonder these unknown people trying to persuade her to do something that she didn't want to do were having no success whatever. He, for one, would not like to be on the wrong side of her. He took her arm and escorted her into the garden. As they strolled slowly along the terraces he could see Matt and Helen sitting side by side on one of the ornamental seats. They were obviously having a great time, as they were both laughing loudly. Mrs Debbon sent a slightly disapproving look in their direction, but they were far too wrapped up in each other to notice. Connor hoped against hope that his nephew wasn't getting too deeply involved, but inwardly understood that he already was.

◆

The afternoon wore on and James returned from his visit to the Belgrave Hotel with the news that the accommodation for

Connor and Matt had been secured.

"Excellent," said Mrs Debbon when she heard. "The hotel also has something of a reputation for its cooking, but I would like you to dine with us this evening."

Connor knew that he wasn't expected to argue, but felt that he ought to mention something that he could see would no doubt prove embarrassing.

"That's very kind of you, and I'm sure that Matthew and I would be delighted, but I regret that neither of us has brought evening clothes with us. As you know, I was called here at short notice and evening wear wasn't needed in Wales. I wouldn't want to embarrass anyone by arriving for dinner dressed in these clothes."

"I understand," she said. "However, there is no problem. I still have a number of my late husband's clothes here. Ridiculous of me, I know, but I keep them hanging in his wardrobe. Looking at them I can sometimes imagine that he is still here. You and he would be much the same size. I would be greatly honoured if you would wear his dinner suit tonight."

She thought for a while, and then called for Helen to come over.

"I'd like you to do me a favour," she said, when Helen had arrived. "Would you take Matthew along to Barton Hall and ask Mr Brown if it would be possible for Matthew to borrow an evening suit, please. Mr Brown has several sons and I have no doubt that they will have something suitable. I have asked Mr Harvey and Matthew to dine with us this evening."

"Of course, Mama. That will be pleasant."

◆

It was only a short stroll along the lane to Barton Hall, and Mr Brown received them with delight.

"Of course, you may borrow whatever you wish," he exclaimed loudly, sending one of the servants running to sort something out. "I'll go and get the car out and give you a lift back."

"Really, Mr Brown, I assure you there's no need. It's such a short distance."

"Nonsense, young lady. It'll be a pleasure. Had a bit of a tinker with the engine since I last saw you — she goes much more sweetly now. You enjoyed the last trip, didn't you, young feller?"

"I certainly did," Matt replied. He was delighted at the prospect of another ride, even though he could tell Helen wasn't at all enamoured.

The servant arrived with a set of clothes for Matt, and Mr Brown got up at once and led them out of the house to the stables.

"Had some of them converted into a garage," he boomed, opening the doors to reveal the gleaming brass work of the Daimler-Cannstatt.

As he was busying himself getting the car ready, Helen dragged Matt to one side.

"I'm not at all sure I want to go in that thing," she hissed. "It's not safe."

"Of course it's safe," he said, reassuringly. "Besides, we're only going along the lane. We'll be there in two minutes."

"That's what I mean. Think of the speed we'll be going at. I have even heard that some cars can travel at nearly twenty miles an hour. Human beings were never meant to travel at that speed."

"But trains go faster than that," he told her.

"Yes, but one is safely enclosed in a carriage, not exposed to the elements!"

"Just give it a try, you might find you like it. Besides, he's hardly going to have the time to get the thing out of first gear before you're home again."

"Oh, very well, if you insist. I'm sure it has an effect on people's hearing, though. Have you noticed how Mr Brown keeps shouting? He never used to before he got that thing. Now he never does anything else. I think the noise has made him deaf."

By this time the car was coughing and barking its way out of the old stable block and it spluttered across to them.

"Come on then, hop up. You'll have to squash together as it's really only meant for two, but I don't suppose you'll mind that."

He's right there, Matt thought, as he helped a very nervous Helen clamber up and onto the seat. Once she was as settled as she was ever going to be, he climbed up beside her, conscious of her warmth as he eased himself onto the seat.

"Splendid," Mr Brown shouted, and they were off.

They chugged along the drive at a sedate pace, but when they got out into the lane, instead of turning right to head towards Belmont, Mr Brown turned left, in the direction of the village of Kingskerswell. Helen tapped him on the shoulder, and had to shout to make herself heard above the noise of the engine.

"Mr Brown, you're going the wrong way!"

"I know, my dear, but you won't see what she can do in that short distance. Thought I'd show you what the beauty's capable of, don't you know?"

With that he let the car gather speed, until they were literally rattling along, a cloud of dust billowing behind them. Helen let out a nervous gasp and grabbed Matt's arm, something that Matt didn't mind at all. She then shut her eyes. They reached the top of a long hill that led down into the village, and Mr Brown gave the engine all it was worth.

"I think, my dear," he shouted, "we're doing about twenty at the moment. Wonderful, isn't it?"

Helen opened her eyes and saw the fields and hedgerows flashing past. She stared at the road ahead and was suddenly and totally overtaken with excitement. It felt so alive. She hadn't realised it would be like this: why on earth had she ever been frightened? Cars were wonderful, marvellous creations and she decided, then and there, that she would persuade her mother to get one, no matter how long it took, and how many refusals she got. The car slowed as it entered the village and she felt almost cheated. Mr Brown turned the car, and started back up the hill, although now at a much more sedate pace.

"Are you all right?" Matt asked.

"I feel absolutely wonderful," she beamed at him.

◆

She was still talking about it several hours later when the family started dressing for dinner. Mrs Debbon had given Connor and Matt the use of one of the bedrooms to change in, to save having to use the guest bathroom. Connor changed into his suit and helped Matt with his bow tie. Once he'd arranged it to his satisfaction, he stood back to see the overall effect. The result both startled and upset him.

"Uncle Conn? What's the matter?"

"Sorry, Matt, it's nothing. Just that you look so grown up in that outfit. I'm used to seeing you in jeans and tops. I'd almost forgotten that you're growing up so fast."

"You sound just like my mother."

"Sorry. Anyway, come on, let's go down and see if we can get there before they sound the gong."

As he followed Matt out of the room and along the corridor, Connor felt a stab of sorrow so sharp that it was almost physically painful. The boy that became almost delirious with excitement whenever Connor bought him a new toy car or some other small gift had been replaced by a young man while he wasn't looking. It was perfectly natural of course, but it was damned difficult all the same.

They reached the dining room at the same time as Mrs Debbon. Her green silk evening dress was cut low on her shoulders and she looked absolutely stunning. Not for the first time, Connor wondered why on earth there wasn't a long line of men beating a path to her door. She was beautiful, intelligent and very wealthy. He could only assume that the men of 1898 were all blind.

"I omitted to mention," Mrs Debbon told Connor as she took his arm to enter the room, "that Charles and Mary-Anne will be dining with us. I know that it is not customary for ones so young to join the adults at dinner, but with only Helen and myself here, it can sometimes seem very lonely in the room. We have, therefore, become accustomed to dining together. I do hope that you don't mind?"

"Not in the least. Matt has a brother and two sisters at home, all younger than him, and the family has the same arrangement."

"Good," she said. "I regret that some of the families in the area see it as the first step to hell and damnation."

Connor heard a gasp from behind him and turned to see Matt staring at Helen who had just entered the room. Connor nudged him in the back and whispered that his mouth was open again. He wasn't surprised at Matt's reaction. Helen had obviously gone to great lengths to create an impression and she'd succeeded beyond even her own expectations. In a deep pink silk strapless gown that rustled in a most alluring fashion as she walked, she was every inch a lady. Her shoulders were bare and Matt found himself wondering how the dress stayed up. He also noticed that a most tantalising amount of cleavage was on show, in contrast to the high-necked blouses that she often wore during the day. He managed to pull himself together enough to hold her chair for her as she sat down and then took his place next to her. Trying hard not to stare at the amount of bare flesh that was sitting next to him, he was rescued by the arrival of the first course of dinner and turned his attention to trying to fathom out which particular spoon, out of the six or seven laid out, was used for the soup.

Somewhere between the third and fourth courses, Connor took the chance to try to discover something about the unknown Major who had called the night before.

"My work for the Great Western Railway means that I get to hear of new developments on continental railway systems," he began. "I have heard that, in France, the government is assisting with the building of new lines by purchasing the land required itself, then handing it over to a private company to actually build the line. This would seem a very sensible way of proceeding. I wondered, with your friends and contacts in France, if you knew anything more about it?"

"I regret not, Mr Harvey, but with the French government in its present turmoil I doubt that they are able to concern themselves with matters such as the building of railway lines."

"I recall reading something about there being political problems in France, but didn't quite understand what it was all about. The newspapers have referred several times to something called the 'Dreyfus Affair', but with travelling about so much I haven't been able to study it too closely. Do you know any more?"

A slight frown, no more than a fleeting shadow, crossed her face before she replied.

"Only what has been reported in the newspapers," she replied. "It would seem that several years ago, a French spy in the German Embassy in Paris discovered a handwritten note that listed a number of secret French documents, including several that purported to contain information about new weapons that the army was testing. The note had been delivered to the German military attaché at the embassy."

"So someone had sent them this letter?"

"Evidently. Suspicion fell on an officer in the French army, Captain Alfred Dreyfus. The evidence against him was questionable in the extreme, but nevertheless he was arrested, tried, found guilty and sent to the penal colony of Devil's Island. The whole trial was a mockery, with so-called evidence being fabricated and several experts being called who blatantly lied throughout the affair. All this, of course, was suppressed at the time and only a few knew the truth. Little by little, pieces of evidence came to light and it became more and more obvious that the whole thing was a fraud."

"But why would someone want to go to all that trouble? Did this Captain Dreyfus have enemies?"

"He was not, I gather, a very popular man, but that was beside the point. Several key elements in the army hierarchy were very nervous about the way French politics were developing. The right-wing parties and alliances had been losing ground steadily to those on the left. There were those in high places in the army who would stop at nothing to prevent this."

"But how would accusing someone of spying achieve anything?"

"The army had lost face several years ago when France was forced to concede territory to Germany at the end of the Franco-Prussian War. They needed to try to stir up public feeling behind them. If they could find that someone was spying for Germany, then there would be an outbreak of patriotic fervour, and the people would unite behind the army. Most of the higher-ranking officers in the armed forces are right-wing nationalists, so support for them would mean loss of support for those on the left. Captain Dreyfus was, as far as the army was concerned, just a means to an end. He would be sacrificed for the good of the army. The real culprit, the man who forged the letter and planted it in the embassy, was discovered earlier this year. He was named as Major Ferdinand Esterhazy."

Helen, seated on Connor's right, started when she heard the name mentioned, and glanced at her mother. For Mrs Debbon's part, another almost undetectable frown flitted across her face when she saw Helen's reaction, but she said nothing.

"So I assume, now people know the whole thing was a fraud, that Captain Dreyfus is to be released?" Connor asked.

"On the contrary. Major Esterhazy was court-martialled, but to find him guilty would have been to admit that the whole affair was a sham, so he was acquitted and poor Captain Dreyfus remains on Devil's Island."

"But surely something can be done?"

"As soon as the result of the court martial was made public, Emile Zola published an open letter in the press accusing the government of assisting in the cover-up. He is a man of great standing in France and his letter could not be ignored. However, the government is still trying to conceal all evidence of its guilt. Mr Zola was accused of libel and found guilty, but I am informed that he plans to flee here to England very soon. I feel it will not be long before the French government is forced to face up to its deeds. Major Esterhazy, in particular, will not escape justice for long, I think."

"The whole affair is quite incredible."

"It is indeed, Mr Harvey. It shows what lengths people will go to in order to cling on to power. The old order in France is dying out. There are elections in a few weeks' time and I think there will be great changes: changes that will see the end of much of what many of those currently in power stand for."

Mrs Debbon stared into space for some time and Connor was certain that she knew far more about the affair than had been printed in the newspapers. He suspected that the mystery visitor from the evening before was the Major Esterhazy that she had mentioned and it was evident that Helen thought so as well. He had no idea at all why the Major should have crossed the English Channel to see her, or for what end, but, not for the first time, he suspected that the stakes were far higher than he had at one time thought. He decided to change the subject, in case Mrs Debbon wondered why he was so interested, and steered the conversation towards the weather, always a safe topic at the dining table. By the time the vagaries of the British climate had been discussed, the atmosphere around the table was much lightened.

"Do you think that you will be able to call tomorrow?" Helen asked.

"Helen, my dear," Mrs Debbon gently chided her. "I'm sure that both Mr Harvey and Matthew have better things to do than to come up here every day."

"It would be a pleasure to come tomorrow," Connor said.

"But it would be most unfair to expect you to work on the catalogue all the time," Mrs Debbon told him.

"But, Mama," Helen said, "couldn't we perhaps go out somewhere tomorrow, all of us? The weather seems to be settled at present."

Mrs Debbon smiled softly at her elder daughter.

"Suppose I arrange for us all to go on a picnic tomorrow, if the weather is kind. Would that satisfy you?"

"Oh yes, Mama, what a wonderful idea. Where could we go?"

"I'll ask James to tell Edward to get the carriages ready for the morning. Then how about a drive out to Anstey's Cove?"

"Marvellous. We haven't been there in almost a year and it's such a pretty spot. Have you been there, Mr Harvey? How about you, Matt?"

Sensing that Matt was about to tell her that he'd been to Anstey's Cove more times than he could remember, Connor decided to get in first.

"No, we haven't been there, although I've heard that it's a most picturesque spot," he said.

"It is. If it weren't so difficult to reach we could go more often, but then if it were easy to get to it wouldn't be so exciting, would it?" Helen said, evidently relishing the prospect.

"No, I suppose it wouldn't."

"I'll go and see Cook and ask if she can make some of her special pies for the hamper."

"I'm not at all sure that I approve of you going down to the kitchens by yourself," her mother interrupted. "It would be much more proper to ask James to arrange it."

"But I want to make sure that Hannah knows exactly which sort of food to supply."

"Oh, very well, if you must. I'm sure it's setting a bad precedent, though."

"Thank you, Mama. Can you ask James to send Edward down to see if Daniel would like to join us as well? It will be so nice to have us all together."

"As you wish," she said, summoning the butler to receive his instructions.

Matt just about managed to avoid scowling when he heard that his rival was being invited, but only with considerable difficulty. Still, with any luck he'd manage to get some time alone with Helen. The memory of her kisses and warm embraces of that morning were still fresh in his mind, and he hoped that they'd be able to carry on from where they'd left off.

"What about Bill?" Mary-Anne interrupted.

"What about young Master Stone?" asked her mother.

"If everyone else is going I think Bill should come as well to keep me company."

"My dear, young William is a very personable child, but he's hardly suitable company for you."

"I like Bill as well," Charles said. "I want him to come, then he and I can play together."

"He's my friend, not yours," Mary-Anne told him.

"He's my friend as well!"

"Children, really! I will not have bickering at the dinner table. We have guests, so kindly remember your manners."

"Sorry, Mama," they both said together.

There was a short pause before Mary-Anne returned to her subject.

"So can Bill come with us, please?"

"I wish that you would remember that his name is William. You know perfectly well that I do not approve of altering names."

"So can William come with us, please?" she said, sticking steadfastly to her intention.

"Oh, very well. It seems that I will get no peace at all unless I say yes. What your father would have thought of all this I shudder to think."

James arrived in answer to Mrs Debbon's summons and she gave instructions for the carriages and horses to be prepared for the morning, and for invitations to be sent to Daniel and Bill to accompany them.

"If your coachman is going to take the invitations down to the others, perhaps he could take Matt and myself down to the hotel at the same time?" Connor suggested.

"Certainly," she said. "I will also send him to collect you both tomorrow morning. I think it would be more convenient to assemble here before we leave for Anstey's Cove. If the weather proves to be unkind, we can always cancel the arrangements."

◆

"Anstey's Cove? A long way? It's only three or four miles from here at most. What's all this difficult to get to business?" Matt asked, when he and Connor were in the coach on their way down to the hotel.

"You've got your future head on, not your 1898 head. An outing to somewhere like Anstey's Cove would have been quite an adventure in the late nineteenth century. Besides, we may not be going. It's only the middle of April, and if the weather's at all iffy, then no doubt it'll be called off."

"No, it won't. It's going to be warm and sunny."

"And how would you know that?"

"Helen told me."

"And how does she come to that conclusion? Weather forecasting is only in its infancy in 1898."

"She's got this big piece of seaweed hanging by the back door of Belmont. She says it never fails to predict the weather perfectly."

"And her seaweed says that it's going to be warm and sunny tomorrow?"

"Yes."

"And to think the weathermen in our own time spend millions on satellites and computer systems when all they have to do is hang a bit of seaweed outside the door."

"Not just any seaweed. Helen says it has to be just the right sort of seaweed or it won't work."

"And what is the right sort?"

"I don't know. We sort of got onto other subjects after that and I never found out."

"There are times when having a conversation with you is as confusing as a summer service train timetable."

"Thanks."

"You're welcome."

◆

They arrived at the Belgrave Hotel to find that Mrs Debbon had done them proud. Instead of one room for the two of them, they had a small suite, with a bedroom each, a sitting room between the two, and a private bathroom.

"This is really fine," Connor said, "and you've got a bedroom to yourself."

"Good. At least it means I don't have to listen to you snoring all night."

"I do not snore!"

"How would you know? You're asleep, so you don't have to listen to it."

"You," Connor replied, "are a pain."
"I know."

CHAPTER FIFTEEN

A day at the beach

The weather the next morning was, as Helen's seaweed had predicted, ideal with warm sunshine soon burning away the morning mist.

"I ought to get a piece of that seaweed that Helen told you about," Connor mentioned to Matt over breakfast. "I could make a fortune with it when we get home."

"When do you think that will be?"

"You mean, when do we next flip? I've no idea. I hope that it won't be when we arrive at Belmont this morning. That would be very difficult to explain, arriving in the carriage, and then suddenly disappearing. With a bit of luck, we might just get through the day, then if we flip later this evening it won't seem so bad. Tomorrow's Sunday, so we won't really be expected at Belmont. Or at least not until the afternoon at any rate."

"Have we learned any more that will help?"

"Yes and no. The Major who called the other night would seem to be this Major Ester-whatsit that Mrs Debbon was talking about. She quite obviously knows far more about the whole thing than she's letting on, but I've no idea why, or how it helps. Time's going by, and we're not much further forward."

"But you do still think that there's a chance, don't you? For us to change things, I mean."

"I don't think things can be changed, Matt, I honestly don't. The more I think about it, the more certain I am of that. But I also think," he added, in response to the bleak look that had come into Matt's eyes, "that we're here for a purpose, and I can only think that it's to ensure that the family survives. How we're supposed to achieve that, and at the same time make no change to history I've no idea, but that's what I believe."

"So there's still hope?"

"There's always that."

♦

The carriage arrived for them and they rattled their way up the long hill to Belmont to find a flurry of activity, with servants busily loading hampers and other gear into the second carriage with a third carriage standing empty by its side. Daniel and Bill had already arrived: Daniel, Matt noticed with a touch of jealousy, already in deep conversation with Helen. She smiled at Matt as she saw him climbing out of the carriage, and walked over to greet him.

"Isn't it a lovely day?" she said. "I knew it would be — my seaweed is never wrong. Come and say hello to Daniel."

The two young men greeted each other warily, each trying not to upset Helen by appearing to dislike the other.

"Helen says that you haven't been to Anstey's Cove before," Daniel said eventually, when the silence between them was becoming embarrassing.

"No, but Helen says it's very nice there. You've been before, I expect?"

"Yes. We all had a picnic there last summer."

Another long silence followed, but luckily it was broken by Bill chasing after a hoop that he and Charles had been playing with. The hoop careered across the lawn and hit Matt on the leg.

"Sorry," Bill said, when he caught up with the errant hoop. "I fink young Charlie don' know 'ow ter play this game."

"No problem, Bill," Matt said, rubbing his leg where the heavy wooden hoop had caught it.

The incident had, however, broken the ice, and the atmosphere was somewhat easier as the final preparations for the excursion were being made. Mrs Debbon called Matt over to her.

"Do you think that you will want to bathe when we get to the cove, Matthew?"

"I don't know. I hadn't really thought about it."

"Which means that you won't have a costume, I assume?"

"No, I haven't."

"And Mr Harvey?"

"No, he hasn't got one either, but I don't think he'll want to bathe."

"A sensible man. However, in case you decide that you would like to, I'll ask Geoffrey, one of the footmen, to lend you his. He will not be accompanying us today and I understand from James that he bathes regularly."

She summoned James and gave instructions for the suit to be obtained. It arrived in a large canvas bag a few minutes later, together with several towels. By then the carriages had been loaded to Mrs Debbon's satisfaction and everyone was asked to board.

"Perhaps you and I should go in the first carriage, Mr Harvey, with Helen and Matthew, and then Daniel, Mary-Anne, Charles and William can go in the second carriage. The servants will go in the third carriage. I hope that Daniel will be able to control my two youngest. I fear that I have not been diligent enough with their upbringing since their father died."

"I'm sure that he would be proud of them, all of them. And of you," he said.

She didn't answer, but smiled at him, a reward in itself. Daniel was obviously very unhappy about being relegated to the second carriage, so Connor arranged to change places with him, explaining to Mrs Debbon that he might be able to keep an eye on the other three children better than Daniel. This move earned him another smile from Mrs Debbon and a very black look from his nephew.

◆

As the carriages rumbled along the lanes between the tall Devon banks, Connor found it hard to concentrate on the endless chatter of the children. Feelings that he had ruthlessly suppressed for almost fifteen years began to surface. Since Laura had died, he hadn't so much as considered another relationship, feeling that to do so would have been somehow disloyal. He found that he was very attracted to Mrs Debbon. A fine thing, he thought to himself.

Here I am telling Matt not to get involved, and yet I'm doing the same thing. He also thought that his feelings were returned, as he'd sometimes caught her glancing at him when she thought he wasn't looking. This whole thing is ridiculous, he told himself. I'm a middle-aged widower, not a lovestruck teenager. He was still struggling with his thoughts when the carriages slowed and finally stopped. Glancing out of the window, he saw that they had drawn up in a field and guessed that this was as close to the cove as the carriages could get. There were more carriages drawn up as well, so other families must also have decided that it was a good day for a picnic. The carriage door opened, and one of the servants was there to help him out.

They made a fairly long line as they walked down the narrow path to the cove. Matt had started off first before suddenly realising he wasn't supposed to know the way down.

"You'd best go first," he told Helen. "You know the way."

She smiled as she brushed past him to take the lead. Matt followed as close behind as he dared, leaving a rather grumpy-looking Daniel trailing behind them. The three younger children were next, followed by Mrs Debbon and Connor, then four or five servants struggling with the hampers and other things that the family had obviously decided were necessities for a day out.

Anstey's Cove, when they reached it, was both familiar and strange to Connor at the same time. The outline of the cove and its surrounding rocks was just as he knew it, but other things were very different. What was a modern-style beach bar in his day was a small wooden hut in 1898. A sign indicated that teas could be obtained, although with the amount of food the servants were bringing down Connor doubted they would need its services. Fishing tackle and various other items that the proprietors felt their customers might need were also available, and there was an offer to arrange swimming lessons. There were also some tables dotted here and there for the convenience of those having a picnic, and down by the water's edge were three bathing machines. Connor had only seen them in museums before. To his left as he looked out to sea was a mass of tumbled rocks that guarded the way round into the next, and much larger, cove. Several chairs arrived with the servants and Mrs Debbon settled herself into one, indicating that Connor should sit next to her.

"For once," she told him, "my daughter appears to have had a sensible idea. It really is very pleasant here today, don't you think?"

"It certainly is," he agreed, and meant it. What little breeze there had been up at Belmont had vanished down at sea level, or at least they were sheltered from it. The sun shone down from a cloudless sky and it was a truly glorious spring day. Without in the least thinking what he was doing, he took her hand in his. She smiled at him and did not object.

Meanwhile, Matt was having his own problems. The younger children had dragged Daniel off for something, leaving Matt alone with Helen for the first time that day. Now he *was* on his own with her, he found he didn't know what to say.

"Do you fancy a swim?" he asked eventually. "It'll probably be freezing cold, but I'm game if you are."

"Why Matthew, how very modern of you," she replied, managing to look slightly shocked and rather amused at the same time. "I don't think Mama would approve though."

"She wouldn't?" said a totally mystified Matt.

"Certainly not. Even when we're in France, and they're so much more relaxed about it than we are here, she still doesn't think it's proper. Anyway, as you say, it will be chill at this time of year. Daniel will probably go in though, he swims regularly. Mama considers it to be a failing on his part, but thinks he'll grow out of it."

"I see," said Matt, who didn't see at all.

"Daniel?" she called, to where he was talking to Charles, "Matt wants to go swimming. Can you show him the gentlemen's bathing area for me?"

"Of course," he replied, in a tone of voice that suggested he'd rather eat glass.

"Take Charles and William with you as well, would you?" called Mrs Debbon. "They'll only become difficult if they're left out."

"How about you?" Helen asked, turning to Connor. "Would you care to go with them?"

"No thank you, young lady. I've more respect for my aches and pains than to subject them to sea water at this time of year. I'll stay here."

Daniel reluctantly led the group over the rocks and around the headland to the larger cove next door.

"This is the men's bathing place," he said to Matt, "but before we go for a swim there are one or two things that you and I should get sorted out."

"Come over 'ere, Charlie," Bill called, "these two are abaht to 'ave it aht. Come an' watch."

"They are?" asked Charles, intrigued at the prospect.

"Sure they are. Come on."

With that he and Charles sat on the beach close by, Bill looking at them with a wide and expectant grin on his face.

"Are we about to have it out?" asked Matt.

"Not like Bill means. I just want to know what your intentions are towards Helen."

"My intentions?"

"You know what I mean. Me and Helen, we've been friends, well, more than friends for some time. Then you come along and all she talks about is you. So, are you and she going to be stepping out together, or what?"

"I don't know, I really don't," Matt said, after a while. "I like her, I like her a lot, but I'm only a visitor, and I'll be gone in a week or so's time. If I lived here, or was going to be staying here for a long time, I could give you a proper answer, or at least see how things worked out. I know that you and she have a sort of understanding, she told me so."

"She did?"

"Yes. She also said that you were pissed off with me being around."

Bill's notebook came out and there was more scribbling. Matt was very glad that Connor hadn't heard him use the expression.

Bill didn't say anything, so Matt assumed that he guessed what was meant.

"It's true that I was getting heartily sick of hearing your name mentioned every few minutes, especially as she and I have been going out for a long time now."

"I don't know what to say to you, Daniel. I've already said I'll be going home soon, so no matter what my feelings are for Helen, or hers for me, there can't be anything permanent between us."

So his new rival wasn't going to be around for long. In that case, Daniel decided, he could afford to be generous. He was, by nature, a patient young man. Time was on his side, he could afford to wait.

"Suppose we call a truce and see how things work out?" he suggested.

"Fine by me."

"Shake on it?"

"Sure," Matt replied, taking the hand that was offered him.

"So, do you still want that swim?"

"I suppose so, although the water's going to be freezing."

"Of course it will be, but you get used to it after a bit."

"It's the getting used to it that worries me."

Bill seemed very disappointed when he realised that Matt and Daniel weren't going to fight.

"I fink the two of yer should 'ave sorted it aht wiv yer fists."

"Sorry Bill, we've shaken hands on it and that's an end to the matter."

"Oh well, it'll 'ave to be anuvver time then. Come on then, let's get in the water."

Matt reached into his bag and extracted his costume, causing the others to collapse with mirth.

"What on earth is that?" Daniel asked him.

"Helen's mother borrowed it from one of the servants for me when I said I didn't have a costume. Why, what's wrong with it?"

"Nothing, if you're forty years old."

"But I haven't got anything else."

"Obviously," Daniel said.

"So what do I wear?"

"The same as the rest of us, of course — nothing."

"You're not serious."

"Of course. This is 1898, not 1848. Besides, there's nobody else here. Don't be such an old woman."

Matt wished he'd never suggested going for a swim as he took his jacket off and started to undo his shirt.

◆

"I do hope Matthew isn't going to be embarrassed, Mr Harvey," Mrs Debbon said as she watched the group climbing around the corner to Redgate beach. "I fear that Daniel is a little piqued that Helen is paying so much attention to him and may try to belittle him."

"How might he do that?"

"Daniel is the Torquay Regatta swimming champion in his age group. I think he may well challenge Matthew to a race, especially as he has indicated that he would like to go for a swim."

"Matt's old enough to look after himself," he assured her.

"I do hope you are right. I would not like any unpleasantness to spoil the day."

◆

After they had been in the water for a while, Daniel did indeed do as Mrs Debbon had predicted.

"Matthew?"

"Yes?"

"Race you to that rock over there?"

"No thanks."

"Why, afraid you'd lose?"

"No, just not in the mood, that's all."

"I think you're afraid."

"Oh, please yourself. Which rock did you say?"

"The big one out there, with the waves lapping over it."

"Fine. Do you want to start in the water, or by diving in?"

"By diving in. There's a flattish rock over there where we can both dive from."

"And what stroke do you want to use?"

"Stroke?"

"Crawl, back, butterfly, breast. You know, which stroke?"

"Don't know what you mean. I only know front and back."

"So any stroke?"

"Suppose so."

"Get Bill to start us off then."

Daniel called for Bill to come over to the rocks so that he could shout for them to go. Bill waited for the two youths to settle themselves, and then gave them the off. They both dived in, and Daniel at once settled himself into the rhythm that had won him every race in his year group at the annual regatta for the last five years. He was a strong, natural swimmer, and was supremely confident in his ability to show that there was something that a local was better at than an upstart visitor from nowhere. His confidence was misplaced. Matt cruised past him with lean, powerful strokes, cleaving through the water with a minimum of fuss and no wasted effort, a style that had won him the Southwest of England Open Championship for the last three years. He reached the rock comfortably ahead of Daniel and trod water waiting for his rival to catch him up. Daniel said nothing when he finally arrived at the rock.

"Want to race back?" Matt asked.

"Yes," said Daniel, not at all sure whether he did or not.

"Backstroke?"

"All right."

"You shout the off then."

Matt won the return race even more easily and trod water again, waiting for Daniel to catch up. When he'd done so, Daniel glared at him for a moment, and then burst out laughing.

"Well, that certainly put me in my place. I made a right fool of myself there. Where did you learn to swim like that?"

"Er, back home. I've been taking part in swimming contests for years."

"And winning them, I assume?"

"Some. Not all."

"But enough to make you a lot better than me. That'll teach me to try to get myself one up on you. It's as well Helen couldn't see us — I'd never live it down."

◆

Helen had long ago decided quite calmly that she was a biological freak. She had the head, body and arms of an eminently respectable young lady, and the legs and feet of someone else entirely. Her reasoning for this state of affairs was quite simple. Her legs and feet very often simply refused to obey the orders that her brain gave them. They had, over the years, taken her into places that no well brought up young lady should even consider visiting. Her brain had issued streams of frantic commands, but her legs had taken not the slightest notice and carried on walking to where they wished to go. They had conveyed her into rather dubious bookshops, one or two theatrical shows of a somewhat risqué nature, and once into a public house that was reputed to be the haunt of "ladies of the night". This last was a profound disappointment. She had expected to find a number of glamorous young ladies draping themselves languidly over various pieces of furniture. Instead, she found three not so young, rather seedy looking ladies staring into space with looks of terminal boredom. The publican, once he noticed her, was scandalised, and ushered her out of the door as soon as he could. She tried to explain about her legs to him, but he was too shocked that a "respectable young lady" should have found her way into his premises.

On the day of the picnic, she found that her legs were up to their old tricks. She had told her mother that she was going to go for a stroll inland but her legs had decided otherwise, and were even now carrying her above the small headland that separated Anstey's Cove from Redgate Beach. They took her into the woods above the beach and to a place where she could look down unseen onto the gentlemen's bathing place, somewhere that she manifestly shouldn't be. It didn't really surprise her, as they had brought her here before, in fact on the last occasion that they had all picnicked here and Daniel had gone for a swim. She stared down into the crystal-clear water, to where the green-white shapes of Matt and Daniel's bodies were gliding through the water.

◆

Unaware that he was the object of such close scrutiny, Matt hauled himself out of the water and onto one of the rocks that surrounded the cove. He grabbed a towel, dried himself vigorously to restore the circulation and lay down full length on a flat rock to warm himself in the sunshine, draping the towel around him. Daniel did the same, the two of them blissfully unaware that Helen had seen the entire race and had been enraptured by the sight of them as they knifed through the water. She was interested in their swimming ability. The fact that they were naked didn't, she lied to herself, make any difference at all. She decided that it was time to go back to Anstey's Cove before her mother started to wonder where she was, but her legs wouldn't let her. Not until the two young men were dressing did her feet allow her to make her way back. She managed to arrive back before the others, but only just.

"That was a long walk, my dear," her mother said. "I was beginning to get concerned."

"Sorry, Mama, but it's so beautiful here in the spring, I just forgot the time."

"No matter, you're here now. Ask James to arrange for luncheon to be served, will you?"

The meal wasn't quite as formal an affair as it would have been at Belmont, but it wasn't far off. The servants still bustled about and there was more food than either Connor or Matt would have thought possible on a picnic. Tea from the wooden hut also arrived, piping hot, together with a heap of fresh scones, jam and cream. Matt wondered how people in the nineteenth century managed to eat so much, yet still wear such tight-fitting clothes. He was used to having a shower after swimming to wash off the salt, so not being able to have one meant he felt sticky and uncomfortable all over. He was also somewhat unnerved by

Helen, who kept on giving both him and Daniel appraising looks, and he couldn't for the life of him think why. When he had the chance, he asked Daniel if he knew why she was looking at them so oddly.

"No idea," came the reply, "but she did just the same last time we were here. Made me feel like something in a zoo, being stared at all the time."

"I'll never understand women," Matt said, with the air of one who had much experience in the matter.

"Me neither," Daniel agreed. "You want another sandwich?"

◆

The afternoon wore on. Somewhat to Helen's disappointment, Matt turned down her suggestion that he and Daniel might care for another swim. Once was enough, he'd told her. Mrs Debbon and Connor both dozed in their chairs, while Mary-Anne and Bill splashed about in the rock pools. Matt felt much happier now that he and Daniel had more or less sorted things out between them. He sat on one of the rocks and stared out to sea, but there was something niggling away at the back of his mind and he couldn't really settle. He tried to work out what it was that he was uncomfortable about but couldn't latch onto it. He looked at the others, then realised that there was no sign of Charles. He stood and stared around him. Still no sign. He walked over to Bill and asked if he'd seen Charles recently.

"Nah. 'E didn' wan' ter play wiv me an' Mary-Anne."

He wondered if he should wake Mrs Debbon, but decided instead to shake Connor's arm. A rather bleary eye opened and tried to focus on him, but it took some time.

"Uncle Conn," Matt said, when the eye had eventually sorted itself out, "there's no sign of Charles anywhere. Do you think we should go and look for him?"

Connor came wide awake and looked round him.

"Where was the last time you saw him?"

"I haven't seen him for ages. I'm not sure that the others have either."

Connor gently shook Mrs Debbon's arm.

"I'm sorry to wake you," he said, "but Matt tells me that Charles seems to have disappeared. Should we go and look for him?"

"I'll ask James if he has any idea where he is. That boy can be most vexing at times. I have told him that he is not to wander away by himself but he pays very little heed to me. He takes after his father: *he* had a wilful streak in him as well."

She summoned the butler, but was told that he hadn't seen the boy since lunch, nor apparently had any of the other servants. Connor and Helen explored a short way along the path that led away from the cove, while Matt and Daniel clambered around the headland and into the next cove, in case Charles had decided to go for a bathe. There was no sign of him anywhere. By the time they met up again there was a definite look of concern on his mother's face, but she did not permit even a trace of a quiver to affect her speech. She instructed the servants to start to search along the shore and into the woods that backed the coastline. Matt took Connor to one side.

"Is this connected with what's going to happen?"

"I don't know. It may just be a case of an adventurous little boy wandering off, but with what we know about things it would be best to be careful."

"I was thinking about what we overheard, about them just taking the boy if his mother wouldn't go along with their plan, whatever it is. Perhaps they've decided that now would be a good time."

"Possibly," Connor said, "but we can't tell Mrs Debbon that. How about we go back up to where the carriages are stabled? If there's any attempt to abduct Charles, they'll have to go that way."

The two of them made their way as quickly as they could up the steep narrow path through the woods, arriving at the stabling field out of breath and getting more and more concerned. They saw that although the other coaches all had someone in attendance, there was no-one caring for the Belmont carriages.

"Odd," Connor said. "The coachman should be here. Can't

remember his name . . ."

"Edward."

"Yes. He should be here. I know he didn't come down to the cove, because I asked Mrs Debbon about it and she said that he needed to be here to care for the horses."

"So where is he? And come to think of it, where's one of the coaches?"

"What?"

"There's a coach missing, the one that the servants came in. There are only two here."

"So there are. I must have been blind not to see it before."

"What do we do now? Run back down to the beach to tell the others, or what?"

Before Connor could answer Matt suddenly hared across the field to one of the other coaches. Connor could see him talking to a group of coachmen who were gathered together before he came charging back.

"I just had an idea," he said. "I asked the other drivers if they'd seen anything, or knew where Edward had got to. They say he only left a few minutes ago, but if we need to catch him we can take a short cut. Because the lane's so narrow and fairly steep, they have to take it very slowly. If we cut up through the woods we can get to the main road before the coach does."

"You can, Matt, I can't. I'm already knackered from the climb."

"I'll go then."

"Matt, you can't go by yourself, you don't know what you're getting into!"

"No time to argue. I'm off."

With that he ran across the field and entered the woods, oblivious to Connor's shout to him to be careful. He pounded along the narrow path, managing to avoid tripping over the tree roots that seemed hell-bent on getting in his way. He felt his heart thumping and his breathing becoming laboured, but he struggled on, eventually coming out of the woods just where the lane down to the cove started. He stopped to recover his breath, but wasn't certain what to do next. Should he try running along the main road, or should he take a chance and follow the lane back downhill? He bit the inside of his lip in indecision. Think, Matthew, think, he told himself. Would the coach have made it this far yet? He gambled that it hadn't, and started to run down the lane. He was rewarded by the sight of the coach coming towards him. Deciding that a frontal attack was the best plan he stood in the lane to block the carriage's route. He recognised Edward up in the driver's seat who in turn evidently recognised him.

"Master Harvey?" he said, as the coach halted. "What are you doing here?"

"I should be asking you the same question. What are you doing taking the coach away?"

"Nothing. The horses were getting restless, so I thought I'd take them for some exercise."

This sounded plausible, but Matt wasn't convinced. There was something in Edward's manner, something that suggested he was lying. He took a chance and went around to the carriage door and opened it. Charles was crouched on one of the seats, his hands clasped around his knees. He looked frightened.

"What are you doing with Charles?" Matt demanded. "Where are you taking him?"

"Charles? I don't know what you're talking about."

Edward climbed down from his seat and joined Matt at the door. His eyes opened in surprise when he saw the boy.

"Honest, Master Harvey, I never knew he was there."

Matt said nothing as he climbed into the carriage and put his arm around the frightened child.

"It's all right, Charles, there's nothing to be scared of. You're safe now. Come on, let's get you out."

He helped Charles down from the carriage then turned his attention back to Edward, who was holding the horses' reins in his hands.

"Well?" Matt said.

"Like I said, Master Harvey, I didn't know the boy was there.

I'd never have taken the coach if I'd have known," he said, in some agitation.

"Will I get into trouble?" a small voice piped up.

"Of course you won't get into trouble, Charles. Why should you?"

"I went for a walk and got lost. Then I saw the carriage and was so tired that I thought I'd lie down on the seat. When I woke up and found it was moving I didn't know what to do."

"So you just climbed into the carriage. No-one made you get in?"

"No, I just got in by myself. You're sure I won't get into trouble?"

"I shouldn't think so. Anyway, get back in the carriage again — I need a word with Edward."

Once the boy was back inside and the door closed, Matt turned to Edward.

"He says that he climbed in on his own and then found the coach was moving."

"Like I said, I never knew he was there," Edward repeated.

Matt was still certain that there was something more, something that Edward wasn't saying.

"There's more to this than you're letting on. Charles said he climbed into the coach by himself, so maybe you didn't know he was there, but why would you leave the other coaches unprotected?"

"The horses were getting skittish, so I thought a short trot up the hill and back would calm them down."

"I don't believe you," Matt told him. "However, it's not for me to say anything. I'll leave it to Mrs Debbon."

Matt could see that some sort of inner struggle was going on inside Edward's mind.

"All right, young sir, I'll tell you the truth," Edward sighed, evidently having come to a decision. "You see, I've got this young lady, she lives in Babbacombe. We don't get to see each other very often, what with us both being in service. I thought that while everyone was having an afternoon nap, I'd take the chance and go and see her."

"So why didn't you just say so in the first place?"

"It's not for the likes of me to borrow a carriage and go trotting off by myself. What are you going to do?"

"Me? About what?"

"About me taking the carriage. If Mrs Debbon finds out, I'll lose my position. Me and Agnes, we're hoping to get wed in a year or so, but if I lose my position, then we won't be able to."

Matt said nothing, thinking hard.

"All right," he said eventually, "I'll tell the others that you were just exercising the horses and didn't know that Charles was there. That part's true anyway. She won't hear about your trip to see your girlfriend from me."

"Thank you, young sir, I'm most grateful. I'll not forget this."

"Come on, let's get the coach turned around and back down to the cove before there's any more trouble."

CHAPTER SIXTEEN

Answers from an unlikely source

It was a much subdued party that left Anstey's Cove for the return to Belmont. Mrs Debbon, to Edward's relief, had accepted without comment his explanation of events, backed up by Charles's tearful testimony. Matt kept his word and said nothing about where Edward was really going. Helen tried to lift their spirits and bestowed her smiles equally on Matt and Daniel as the horses clopped along the narrow lanes, between hedges bright in their spring greenery.

"I'm glad you two are friends," Helen told them.

Matt and Daniel glanced at each other, neither of them certain if they were friends or not, but at least they weren't enemies. Rivals perhaps, but not enemies.

"So," she asked brightly, "what are we all doing tomorrow?"

"I'm going down to the office with Father," Daniel said. "There are two ships coming in tomorrow and he's three men short in the office, so I've got to help out."

"And you?" she asked, turning to Matt.

"I'm not sure. It depends on Uncle Conn."

And, he thought, whether we flip back and forth between now and then.

"Do you always travel with your uncle?" Daniel asked him.

"Just sometimes. It depends on where he's going and how much time I can get off college."

"You don't have a private tutor then?" Helen asked.

"No," he said, hoping that the subject would soon be dropped. He was getting more and more concerned about his college work. With exams looming in a couple of months, he could ill afford so much time off, but there wasn't a great deal he could do about it. He'd just have to try and catch up when he got home. When and if they got home, that was.

Luckily, Helen sensed that the topic of college wasn't a popular one with him, so she changed tack and chatted about whatever came into her head for the rest of the journey. After they arrived at Belmont, Mrs Debbon announced that she had a headache, and would be retiring for the evening. She told Connor and Matt that they would be quite welcome if they wished to call the following afternoon, after the family had been to church. Connor took the hint, and thanked her for a lovely day, then propelled Matt towards the door. Matt bade a hasty farewell to Helen and the others, and then James showed them out, to where Edward was waiting with the carriage to take them down to the Belgrave Hotel.

"What's all the rush?" Matt asked when they were in the carriage.

"Mrs Debbon was dropping a very heavy hint that it was time for us to leave."

"I thought she just had a headache."

"I don't know whether she had a headache or not, but that comment that she would be retiring for the evening was a very polite way of saying that she wanted to be on her own."

"Why can't people just say what they mean instead of wrapping everything up in fancy words?"

"It's just the way things are done. By the way, she's very grateful to you for finding Charles for her. You're in her good books at the moment."

"I didn't hear that noise at all, did you?"

"What noise?"

"And you call *me* dim at times. The noise that means we're going to flip, of course."

"Oh, that noise. No, I didn't. I'm not sure what to do about it. Should we stay the night at the hotel, then make our own way up to Belmont and see what happens, or should we go up there tonight. What do you think?"

"You're asking me? That's a first."

"In case you hadn't noticed, you're old enough and ugly enough to make your own decisions."

"Oh. Well, in that case, I vote to stay at the hotel. I need my sleep."

"Suits me. We'll have to be careful when we come up in the morning though, firstly because they haven't invited us until the afternoon, and secondly, I don't want them to see us flip."

"It's only about five o'clock though, so what are we going to do for the evening?"

"No idea. Dinner won't be served until later."

"Good. I'm so stuffed I couldn't eat another thing."

"Well, I'm pooped, so I'm going to get some sleep. If you're going to go wandering off, just be careful."

"I will. I thought I might just go for a stroll along the seafront, see how much it's different to our own time."

"Fine with me."

◆

Once back at the hotel, Connor left Matt to his walk and went up to their suite. Matt sauntered down to the seafront, finding it almost as busy with horses and carriages as it was with cars in his own day, and almost as noisy. He strolled along the promenade, watching the families on the beach and the children playing in the water. As he neared the end of the beach, he glanced over to where the imposing Grand Hotel stood in his own time. In 1898 it was an altogether more humble affair, but there were a number of carriages drawn up outside, so trade was obviously good. The fact that it stood very close to the railway station was obviously in its favour. His heart did a quick jump as he looked at the carriages. One of them bore a familiar coat of arms, marking it out as the one that they had seen when the unknown Marquis had paid his unsuccessful night visit. He was obviously staying in the area, presumably to have another try at persuading Mrs Debbon to go along with his plan, whatever it was. Matt wondered if the other night caller, Major Esterhazy, was also there. He stood for a moment, undecided whether he should go back and tell his uncle, but he felt that it would waste valuable time. Better to grasp an opportunity to learn more about the mysterious comings and goings at Belmont. And about a fire that was steadily and inexorably drawing closer. He slipped into the entrance foyer of the hotel and settled himself on one of the seats behind a conveniently placed potted palm, wondering what to do. He could hardly just sit there. It was only a small hotel, so his presence would soon be noticed and questioned. He didn't want to draw attention to himself by being thrown out. A notice on the wall indicated that high tea was being served from four o'clock to six o'clock. A glance at the clock on the wall told him that it was nearly six, so if the Marquis and his associates were in the dining room, then they would soon be leaving. He picked up a discarded newspaper and pretended to read it, all the time keeping a careful watch.

A quarter of an hour later he was rewarded by the sight of the Marquis, plus three or four others, entering the foyer. Two of them were the henchmen who had accompanied the Marquis on his night visit to Belmont, but he didn't recognise the others. He shrank down behind his paper as they passed close to him, but was disappointed to find that the Marquis was speaking French to one of the others. He wished he'd paid more attention in his French lessons, as he could only pick out one or two words and they didn't help much. Luckily the conversation switched to English when the Marquis addressed his two companions.

"You know what to do?" he asked.

"Of course," came the reply. "Will the Major be taking part?"

"No. He has to leave for Paris tomorrow morning."

"So it will be yourself, the Count and the Countess?"

"Kindly lower your voice. I have told you before not to mention those names in public."

"I mentioned no names."

"You do not have to. The titles are enough to give us away. We are so close we cannot afford any mistakes. The stakes are too high and this will be our last chance. However, there will be two of us calling at the house. The lady will be at her post as usual."

"As you wish. We will be ready on Tuesday evening. However," one of the men said, glancing at his partner, "we feel it only fair to say that we both think that it will be a waste of time.

She will not agree."

"With two of us there, she may well yet see sense. If not, then she has only herself to blame. The boy will come with us. He must be in Paris before the fifth of May."

"As you wish. We will be ready with the coaches on Tuesday."

"See that you are."

With that, the two henchmen left the hotel, while the others made their way to the stairs. Matt let them get out of sight before dropping his paper and racing back to the Belgrave Hotel. He found Connor fast asleep and had considerable difficulty waking him up. Once he was sure that his uncle was paying attention, he told him what he'd found out.

"Brilliant, Matt. That's the first bit of luck we've had. At least we know they're going to try something on Tuesday night. Presumably the other man speaking French was this Major Ester-whatever."

"Esterhazy."

"Quite. Anyway, they're going to have another go at persuading Mrs Debbon to go along with them. I think I agree with whoever it was who said they didn't stand a chance. She isn't going to play ball with them and that's that. You'd have thought they'd have sussed that out by now."

"So would I, but they're obviously not too bright."

"Or maybe just too desperate. From what you've said, if she says no again, as she will, then they're going to try to kidnap Charles straight away?"

"That's the impression I got."

"But the fire isn't until Thursday night."

"I know. I don't understand it. Perhaps they try to take Charles on Tuesday and fail, so they have to have another go on Thursday."

"I'd be a whole lot happier if I knew why that boy is so damned vital to their plans," Connor said. "I don't suppose you've got any idea?"

"Not a clue. At least we know that nothing's going to happen until Tuesday. That means that we don't have to worry about whether or not we should be keeping watch on Belmont tonight. We can sleep in peace."

"I feel I should point out I was already sleeping peacefully until you woke me up."

"You can be very crabby at times. Anyway, isn't it dinnertime yet? I'm starved."

"It's seven o'clock, and you're the one who said he couldn't eat another thing after that whopping picnic you had."

"That was hours ago. Come on, let's eat."

◆

Morning mist was rising gently from the sea just across the promenade. Connor opened his hotel room window and leaned out, breathing in the air of the new day. He liked mornings, in fact preferred them to any other time of day. Mornings were full of promise, a blank page on which nothing had as yet been written. By noon, the day's course would be set, but here and now, with the sun's rays just starting to lift the shroud of mist that obscured the view across Torbay with Brixham in the distance, anything and everything was possible. He left his bedroom and entered the sitting room. A copy of the local paper had been placed there, the headline indignantly demanding that something should be done about the antisocial behaviour of some of the younger elements of the local population. Connor decided that it was gratifying to note that some things were just the same in 1898 as they were in his own time. He wondered whether to wake Matt up, but decided to let him sleep.

◆

Later that morning, after Matt had worked his way through a substantial breakfast and Connor had eaten two slices of toast, they took a cab to the end of the lane leading past Belmont.

"It must be getting time for us to flip," Matt remarked. "We've been here for ages."

"We'd better walk slowly so we've got time to sort ourselves out if we're about to flip."

Neither of them was looking forward to the experience, especially now that Matt had identified the noise they always heard as the sound of the Debbon family screaming in terror. They neared the bend in the road that concealed the house from their sight and, as they approached, they both glanced at each other nervously. The noise had started again.

"I passed out last time, Matt, so I probably will again."

"I know. If it's any worse, I expect I'll join you."

"I think we should get well off the road. We don't want to be found lying unconscious in the middle of the road in our own time. Plus there's a chance we could be hit by a car."

Matt nodded his agreement, so they climbed the bank and scrambled through the hedge into the field that butted up against the Belmont grounds. The nearer they got, the worse the noise became.

"I think we're close enough," Connor said. "I think we should wait here."

They waited for the pain to overwhelm them. The noise grew louder, and, now that they knew what it was, they both found they could hear a number of separate voices, each crying out in agony and despair. Before darkness washed over him and he sank into unconsciousness, Connor found that the tears were pouring down his face. He managed to glance at Matt before he lost his hold on awareness. The look on his nephew's face told him that he could hear the same things.

◆

Matt recovered first and crawled over to where Connor was curled up in the long grass. He checked his breathing and pulse, found them to be steady, and settled down to wait for him to recover consciousness. He'd managed to stay conscious himself, but it had been a very close call. He doubted he'd manage it the next time. He heard several cars pass by in the lane and knew they were home. Connor groaned, and tried to sit up, but found it was very painful.

"How are you feeling?" Matt asked.

"Lousy. It gets worse each time. I think you're right about the noise, it certainly sounds like people screaming."

"I'm sure that's what it is. I don't know if I can take much more of this."

"I don't know if I can either. Let's get back to your place. It must have been raining here overnight. The grass is wet."

He tried to stand but found that his legs didn't want to support him.

"Give me your arm, Matt. I think I'll fall over otherwise."

Leaning heavily on Matt, Connor managed to stagger to the hedge, and clamber through it into the lane. As they emerged, a small group of walkers passing by looked at them with distaste.

"Bit early in the morning to be drunk, isn't it?" one of them shouted.

Connor was too weak to reply, but Matt started to laugh.

"What's so damned funny?"

"That's got to be the first time you've ever been accused of being drunk."

"If this is what being drunk feels like, I'm glad I never have been."

He then also saw the funny side, and laughing like a pair of idiots, they reached Matt's house and let themselves in. After a strong cup of coffee, Connor's spirits had risen to just about normal.

"I don't know how long we're going to be here for, so we'd best be prepared. First thing to do is to phone your parents. They've no doubt been trying to contact you and are probably wondering where the hell you've got to."

"I'll do it now."

He got his phone out of his pocket and tapped in a number.

"Hi Dad, how are you? . . . yes, I know, we've been out a lot in the evenings . . . er, to the cinema and things . . . I've tried to phone when we got back each evening, but your phone's either been switched off, or there's no signal . . . Yes, I know we've got a landline, but I think there's something wrong with it. There's no dial tone when you pick it up . . . yes, we're back at our place again.

Uncle Conn's finished what he needed to do, so we've moved back here again. How's everyone? . . . yes, we're both fine . . . sorry, I think the battery's about to go, it's started to bleep at me . . . yes, I'll phone as soon as I can . . . yes, I love you too. Bye Dad, see you soon."

He put the phone down with a sense of relief that he'd got away so lightly. He showered and changed, then trotted back downstairs to find Connor had made himself another coffee and had raided the biscuit tin.

"I think I'm starting to get used to my 1898 clothes," Matt said as he entered the room. "These jeans feel very funny after what I've been wearing. Dad says 'Hi' by the way. I think he more or less accepted that we've been out every night, so couldn't phone."

There was no response.

"Uncle Conn?"

Still no answer.

"Uncle Conn!"

"Huh?"

"I wish you'd hang out a notice or something when you're not in, it'd make life a lot easier. What are you thinking about anyway?"

"This biscuit."

"Why?"

"Because it's just told me the answer to what this whole affair is all about."

"A biscuit? You're kidding me."

"I wish I was."

He then swore softly, much to Matt's amazement.

"I've only ever heard you swear a couple of times in my life. What brought that on?"

"The answer to the riddle of the French connection. It's been staring me in the face all along, quite literally, but I've been too blind and stupid to see it."

"Well I *still* can't see it, so give!"

"I don't think the Debbons have a *connection* to France. I think they *are* French, or at least descended from a French family."

"And a biscuit told you that? How?"

"Try putting young Charles' name into French."

"Sorry, don't follow you."

"I think that their name — Debbon — is an anglicised form of their original French name. Shortened a bit as well."

"Go on."

"I think it's not plain Lewis Charles Debbon. I think it's Louis-Charles de Bourbon."

"So?"

"The last Louis-Charles de Bourbon known to history was also known as His Majesty Louis XVII, King of France. He's said to have died as a child in the Temple Prison in Paris. His father, Louis XVI, was executed during the French Revolution. Ever since, there have been rumours that the child King didn't die in prison, but was smuggled out somehow. Assuming that to be true, then I believe that young Charles is his direct descendant."

"You mean Charles is the King of France?"

"Yes. Or at least someone thinks he is."

"This sounds heavy."

"I rather think it is. And a lot more serious than I'd ever imagined."

"Do you think he knows?" Matt asked eventually, having taken some time for his uncle's idea to sink in. "Charles, I mean. Does he know he's the King?"

"No, I don't think so."

"What made you suddenly get the answer?"

"I told you, a biscuit. I was hunting for something other than a plain digestive. All I could find," he said, showing Matt the biscuit tin, "was one of these. A chocolate bourbon. I looked at the biscuit, realised what it was called, and it suddenly clicked. Not Debbon, but De Bourbon. We need more information. I think this means another trek to the library."

"Why?"

"To find out about the French Royal Family after the Revolution."

"No need to drag down there. I'll go online and look it up.

There's bound to be tons of stuff on there about it."

"Go to it then."

A few minutes later, Matt had found several sites that seemed worthwhile.

"How about that one?" Connor said, looking at the list that Matt had brought up on the screen.

The site was linked to the research department of an American university and had a whole section on the subject.

"It says here," Matt said, pointing to the relevant paragraph on the screen, "that King Louis XVI was executed on January 21st, 1793, but Queen Marie Antoinette and their two children were kept alive for some months afterwards."

"Does it say what happened to the Dauphin?"

"Who?"

"The Dauphin. The heir to the throne."

"Oh. Yes, it says that he was forcibly removed from his mother in July of that year and incarcerated, whatever that means, in the Temple Prison. It doesn't call him King though, just the Dauphin."

"He would automatically have become King the moment his father died, but as the monarchy had by then been abolished, they never referred to him as King."

"Anyway, it goes on to say," Matt said, returning to the screen, "that the boy was kept in prison for another two years, until June 10th, 1795, when he died of tuberculosis. Poor little sod."

"Only he didn't."

"Didn't what?"

"Die. Not if my theory is true. Does it say anything there about the rumours of him escaping?"

"Yes. The stories started up almost as soon as it was announced that he'd died. Some said that he'd escaped and some that he'd been smuggled out. There seem to have been quite a few people claiming to be the Dauphin, or rather the King. Most of them were just out to see what they could get out of it."

Connor leaned back in his chair and tried to make sense of it all.

"Let's assume, just for the sake of argument," he said, "that the boy *was* somehow smuggled out of prison. Let's also assume that he managed to flee abroad, maybe even here to England. He grew up, married and had children. They in their turn had children, and so on, down to young Charles."

"Yes, I'm with you so far."

"France is currently, and by that I mean currently in 1898, in a bit of a political mess. The right-wing parties are losing ground fast, partly because there's nothing for them to focus on."

"So you're saying that if Mrs Debbon can be persuaded to agree, she takes Charles back to France. Then what?"

"He's proclaimed King. He's the rightful heir: all the other claimants to the French crown will fall by the wayside. There'll be something to unite the parties."

"But Mrs Debbon won't play ball."

"No. She's far too sensible. An announcement like that will create chaos. It also explains what the rush is all about. There are elections coming up in France, or at least there are back in 1898. That's why those who are planning this must get him to Paris before the elections start. Have a look to see if you can find anything about the elections, will you?"

Matt soon found the information he was looking for.

"Here we are. The left-wing parties won a landslide. There's nothing here about anyone being proclaimed King, or anything like it. So they didn't get Charles to France. He died in the fire along with all the others."

"I don't know what to say to you, Matt. I agree that it looks hopeless, especially as I firmly believe that history can't be changed. But I believe, just as firmly, that there's a purpose to all this. I don't accept, *can't* accept, that we're flipping back and forth purely at random. We've a job to do, and we haven't done it yet."

"Will we know when we have?"

"Yes, I'm sure of it."

"OK. As long as I think there's a chance, I can carry on. Anyway, I'll see if there's any more info about it all."

He returned his attention to the screen, bringing up page after page. All of them seemed to have much the same story, even though told in different words. Eventually he found an article that made him sit up in his chair.

"There's a problem," he told Connor.

"There's always a problem. What's this particular one?"

"I think your whole theory's just been blown out of the water."

"Why?"

"It's about Charles being the King of France. He can't be."

"Why not?"

"Look here," Matt said, indicating the screen. "In early 2000, a French author and historian, Philippe Delorme, arranged for DNA tests to be carried out on the heart of the boy who died in the Temple Prison in 1795. The scientists then compared the sample taken from the heart with a sample from a lock of hair known to have come from Queen Marie Antoinette. The tests matched their DNA, proving without any doubt that the child was the Dauphin, or more accurately King Louis XVII. The stories about him being spirited away, or smuggled out, are all false. He died in prison. Charles can't be his descendant, it's not possible."

"Can you print this off?"

"Sure, I'll just go and turn dad's printer on and then I'll send this across to it."

Connor read through the six or seven printed sheets in silence. They confirmed beyond all doubt that the child who died of tuberculosis in the Temple Prison in June of 1795 was King Louis XVII.

"So young Charles is just another pretender to the throne?" asked Matt.

"It makes no sense, Matt, none at all. Mrs Debbon obviously believes he's the exiled King, as do those who want to take him back to France. But Mrs Debbon doesn't *want* him to be who she thinks he is. It's others who are trying to use him, not her."

"So next time we flip back, we prove to her that he isn't who she thinks he is. Then this whole business will fizzle out."

"But we can't prove it, Matt. She won't believe a word of it. Reports on computers, DNA testing and so on. We can prove it here and now, but not back in 1898."

"But we've got to try. Perhaps that's our job, what we've got to do. Prove that Charles isn't the long-lost heir to the throne."

"Maybe. Any idea how we do it?"

"No, but you'll think of something."

"Thanks."

"You're welcome."

◆

Those who watched the house day and night exchanged nods as one came to relieve the other. Their time was getting closer. If the fates had dealt a different hand, if there had been no Revolution in France, then those who watched the house would not be there. They would not need to be outside in the cold and the rain. They were both the descendants of émigrés, French aristocrats who had fled the country of their birth to escape the guillotine. They had escaped with their lives but little else.

They felt a burning anger that others now occupied their ancestral homes. They should be cosseted in luxury in vast chateaux, their every whim pampered to by an army of servants. Real servants, not these modern, grasping, above-themselves people who went by the name of servants.

They watched and they waited. The time for them to act was now very close and when it arrived, they would find the old order returned to France. They would be able to go home to a country that had long since ceased to trouble itself about them.

◆

Matt, still busily searching for information on his computer, glimpsed something out of the corner of his eye and glanced out of the window.

"I think we're about to flip again," he shouted downstairs, "I've just seen Mary-Anne in the garden."

Connor came to the bottom of the stairs to answer him.

"We've only been back a few hours. The time between flips is getting shorter and shorter."

"What if we don't go outside? What if we just stay inside and ignore it?"

"I don't know. Is that what you want to do?"

"No, not really," Matt said, sighing heavily.

"So get your 1890s gear back on and let's get on with it."

"Slave driver."

Once Matt had changed his clothes, they walked out of the front door and along the drive until they reached the gate. When they turned back, Belmont was standing there in all its glory.

Grand Hotel, Torquay,

CHAPTER SEVENTEEN

Attempting a warning

"What time do you think it is?" Connor asked.

"Just gone quarter past two," Matt said, glancing at his watch.

"Matt!"

"What?"

"Take your watch off, dimwit. How are you going to explain a digital watch if someone sees it?"

"Sorry, forgot," he said, taking the watch off and slipping it in his pocket. "I'll keep it out of sight with my music player and my phone."

"You've brought them as well?"

"Sure. If I can't get to sleep then I just listen to my music for a bit. That always makes me nod off. Anyway, nobody's going to see them. The music player's only the size of a ball point pen and I can keep it and the headphones tucked away in a drawer."

"Well, make sure you do. And why do you need your phone anyway? No-one's going to call you here."

"Because when I didn't have my phone before I kept on checking my pocket for it. I just don't feel comfortable without it. And I've bought one of dad's lighters with me as well. Might come in handy."

"I thought Steve had given up smoking."

"He has, but there are still a few lighters kicking about the place. Stop being such an old fusspot. Everything's cool."

"I'm not a fusspot. Anyway, what time did you say it was?"

"A fusspot with a bad memory as well," Matt answered. "It's just gone quarter past two, or it was before you started being niggly."

"We're all right to call then," Connor said, ignoring the jibes. "Mrs Debbon said after lunch, so they should have finished eating by now."

"Do you think they'll have anything left? I'm starved."

"You had a huge breakfast," Connor reminded him.

"That was hours ago."

"No doubt if you turn those puppy dog eyes on Helen she'll get you something."

"I hope so. By the way, did you notice there was no mist this time, we just sort of blinked and here we are."

"Yes, I noticed. The mist has been getting thinner and thinner each time we've flipped."

"Are you going to tell Mrs Debbon about what we know?"

"Yes. I'll need you to back me up though, so whatever story I come out with, you'll have to go along with it."

"Any ideas at all?"

"Just one, but it sounds very far-fetched. I thought I'd try to make out that I work for the government."

"What as?"

"Some sort of agent."

Matt almost collapsed with mirth. It took him a few moments to get his breath back enough to speak.

"You? A secret agent? Oh, come on — she'll never fall for that."

"I didn't mean a secret agent, or at least not the sort you mean. I just meant that I worked for one of the government agencies, perhaps dealing with foreign affairs."

"My uncle, Secret Agent Double-O-Nine-and-threequarters," said Matt, still struggling to curb his merriment.

Connor ignored him. They walked to the front door and rang the bell, James opening the door to them shortly after.

"Madam is expecting you," he said. "Please follow me."

Instead of taking them into the drawing room, as they'd expected, he ushered them out into the garden, where the family was relaxing on the top terrace.

"Mr Harvey, Matthew, how pleasant to see you," Mrs Debbon said, standing to greet them. "It's another wonderful day, is it not?"

"It certainly is," Connor said, "and made all the brighter by your presence."

"Mr Harvey, you'll make me blush. Please sit down here," she said, indicating the seat next to her. "No doubt you would prefer to join my daughter, Matthew?"

"Thank you," Matt replied. "I would."

Matt strolled along the terrace to where Helen was waiting for him. Within two minutes, as Connor had predicted, she was arranging for a cold meat platter to be brought for him from the kitchens.

"That nephew of mine is always hungry," Connor observed. "With the amount he eats you'd think he'd be grossly overweight, but there's not a spare ounce on him. I don't know how he does it."

"He is a most athletic young man. Helen is quite taken with him."

"He is very popular with young ladies."

"You have no children of your own, Mr Harvey?"

"No," he said, deciding not to mention Laura's pregnancy. "Sadly, my wife died young. We had only been married for five years. We had always planned to have children, but we decided to wait a little after we were married. If we had known that she was seriously ill, we might have decided not to wait, but as it was, by the time the illness was diagnosed, it was too late."

"I'm so very sorry. When Robert, my husband, died I was distraught. It had never occurred to either of us that one of us would go, leaving the other behind. It took me some considerable time to gather myself together enough to carry on. I was, however, most fortunate in that I had my children with me. Something of Robert lives on in them. I do not know what I would have done if I had been left on my own. You have my deepest sympathies, Mr Harvey."

"Thank you. It has been nearly fifteen years since Laura died, but I still think of her every day."

Without conscious intent, they took each other's hands.

Meanwhile, Matt had finished eating his way through the substantial amount of food on his plate.

"Thanks," he told Helen. "I needed that."

"You are most welcome," she replied. "Have you any preference for what you would like to do this afternoon?"

"No, not really. I'll leave it to you to decide."

"Very well. Do you think that, if we were to walk to Barton Hall, Mr Brown would give us another ride in his motor car?"

"I should think so. He seems to like to show it off."

"Wonderful. I'll tell Mama that we're going to call on Mr Brown. I don't think I'll mention the motor car though. When I told her about the ride we had last time, she was not pleased. She thinks that motor cars will be the ruin of the country."

Helen and Matt left Mrs Debbon and Connor sitting on the terrace, the two younger children playing nearby. Connor decided that he would have to try to explain to Mrs Debbon as soon as possible about their discoveries, but wasn't sure how to start. He also wasn't at all sure if she'd believe him.

"Mrs Debbon," he said, eventually.

"Yes, Mr Harvey?"

"I need to try to explain something to you, but it will not be easy. I hope that you will not take offence, or feel that I have in some way misled you."

"Is there something wrong?"

"Yes, I believe there is. My name is genuinely Connor Harvey, and I *am* employed by the Great Western Railway, as I've told you. I do, however, have another task, one that I have not told you about."

"Pray continue."

"From time to time, I am called on to undertake certain jobs. My work for the railway means that I can move around the country without it seeming unusual. This means that my presence in sometimes remote areas is not found to be noteworthy."

"I have always thought that there was more to you than meets the eye, Mr Harvey, much more."

"What I am about to tell you, you may find difficult to believe, but I assure you that it is all true. Although I am indeed interested in local history, that is not my main purpose in being here. I am sometimes asked by the government, specifically the foreign office, to do some work for them, in an unofficial capacity."

"Unofficial?"

"Yes. It means if I make a mistake, the government can say it's never heard of me and disclaim all knowledge. On the other hand, if I get it right, they don't have to acknowledge it."

"How very convenient for the government," she said dryly. "And Matthew?"

"He really is my nephew. He comes with me to help with my cover story sometimes."

"And he knows the truth?"

"Yes."

"And you have been asked by the government to investigate me?"

"No ma'am, not you nor any member of your family. But there are those that mean you great harm, those who will stop at nothing to further their own ends, even if it were to mean murder. You, all of you, are in grave danger."

Mrs Debbon did not betray, by even the slightest flicker of an eyelid, any surprise or emotion at this statement.

"You don't believe me?" he said.

"I most certainly believe you, Mr Harvey, but it is nothing new. My family and I have been in danger for as long as I can remember. That is one of the reasons my late husband chose this property to lease. As you will undoubtedly have noticed, it is built more like a fortress than a country house."

"I understand. However, there is a particular danger at the moment. It is concerned with your belief that your son, Charles, is the rightful King of France."

For the first time, there was a slight flicker of surprise on her face.

"You are extremely well informed, Mr Harvey. I did not know that the government was aware of this. Does this mean that you also know of what others are trying to persuade me to do?"

"I believe so. There are those, including a number of exiled French noblemen, who want to take your son back to France, and proclaim him King. I know that Major Esterhazy is among them, but I do not know the names of the others."

"I see. And what have you been instructed to do about it?"

"As regards the plan itself, nothing. Her Majesty's Government cannot be seen to be interfering in the affairs of another European power. Whether you decide to go along with this scheme or not is up to you. I am here to try to ensure that you and your family do not come to harm. I have been given information which may just enable me to do that."

"Go on."

"You believe quite firmly, that Charles is the rightful heir to the throne?"

"Of course."

"It is your belief, and presumably that of a number of others, that the Dauphin, or rather Louis XVII, escaped from the Temple Prison?"

"No, Mr Harvey, he did not escape. He was never there. The boy who died in prison had been substituted for the Dauphin before the revolutionary troops came to take the Royal Family into custody."

"I see. Suppose I could prove to you that this was not the case? Suppose that it could be shown, beyond any doubt, that this was not so? That would mean that the plan to take Charles and proclaim him King would never work, would it not."

"That is correct, but he *is* the rightful heir, much as I would wish it otherwise. He became so as soon as my husband died. The French Government is in chaos, and the old monarchist and conservative parties are split into factions. Several substantial groups are advocating the return of the monarchy, but there are two rival claimants to the crown, each with their own army of supporters. If a candidate could be found that both parties could unite behind, then there are those who believe that the Republican parties could be defeated. As it is now, it is likely that those on the left wing of politics will win the forthcoming election handsomely. There are those who would try anything to stop that happening. That is why these people are so anxious that my son and I should travel to France. As the direct successor to Louis XVI, he would be the undisputed King."

"But suppose it could be *proved* that all of these plans are based on a false assumption. Proved beyond doubt. Would that not put an end to the plans and the plotting and mean that you and your family could lead a normal life, without fear?"

"Yes, it would."

"Then I ask that you listen to what I have to say. You will find it hard to accept, but please believe me when I say I only have your best interests at heart."

"Very well, Mr Harvey, you have my undivided attention."

"There are tests, new scientific tests, which can be done to determine without any doubt the parentage of a child."

"I see."

"Tests have been carried out, and please do not ask me how I know as I cannot tell you, on the heart of the child who died in the Temple Prison in 1795. The tests confirmed, without any doubt, that the child was the Dauphin. That means that neither your late husband, nor your son, can be descended from him."

"That is not possible."

"I regret there is no possible doubt."

"Even if you are unable to tell me how you know this, can you explain a little more?" Mrs Debbon asked him.

"Everyone in the world is unique: no two people are the same in every single respect. When two people have a child, what makes his or her parents unique is carried on into the child. The two identities are joined together to form a new identity. It is, however, possible to test the child, or even the smallest part of that child, even a flake of skin, to determine who the parents are. Tests have also been carried out on some of the remains of Queen Marie Antoinette. Her 'identity' is in that of the heart that was tested. The child in the Temple Prison was her son."

"I do not dispute that."

"But, forgive me, I thought that . . . "

"These tests," she interrupted. "Were they carried out on any remains of the King?"

"Not as far as I am aware."

"Then I repeat that my son is the direct descendant of his late Majesty, Louis XVI. You look puzzled, Mr Harvey. Perhaps it is my turn to do some explaining?"

CHAPTER EIGHTEEN

Proof in the vault

"This is wonderful, Mr Brown. It's really very kind of you," Helen said, as they chugged along the lanes, smoke belching from the exhaust behind them.

"A pleasure, m'dear," he shouted back. "Only too glad to show her off. Mrs Brown's not to keen, to tell you the truth."

"Is this the first car you've had?" Matt asked.

"Lord, no," he replied. "This is my third, but she's the best yet. Goes like the wind, wouldn't you say?"

Both Matt and Helen nodded their agreement. Matt was squashed up very tightly against Helen. The car was officially a two-seater, and although it was a generous seat for two, Mr Brown was a portly gentleman, and didn't leave a great deal of room for Matt and Helen. Not that Matt was complaining. He could feel her warmth through his clothes, and in spite of the smell from the exhaust, he could also detect the perfume she was wearing. He was very happy. He'd decided that, for now at any rate, he would put his knowledge of the forthcoming fire to the back of his mind. He had his arm around her waist, and, while Mr Brown's attention was taken up with a sharp corner in the road, he leaned over and kissed her. The resulting smile she gave him almost dazzled him.

"How about trying to see how fast she'll go," Mr Brown boomed at them. "What do you think?"

"Fine with me," shouted Matt.

"And with me, Mr Brown," Helen called into his ear.

"Excellent," came the reply.

He turned the car onto the main road and built up the speed. Matt was used to being driven along the road at forty or fifty miles an hour, or at least he was when the heavy traffic allowed it. But this seemed different. For one thing, they were in the open, and for another, there didn't seem much between themselves and the countryside that was flashing past. He couldn't tell how fast they were going, but guessed it wasn't far short of twenty miles an hour. It seemed, however, very much faster, and much more exciting. Helen had her arms around him and was clinging on tightly, which Matt didn't object to in the least. They bowled along merrily as far as the nearby town of Newton Abbot, when they were forced to slow down by the amount of traffic that was building up, several of the owners of the horses and carriages glaring at them as the car belched past.

"I never thought that it would be possible to get from Torquay to Newton Abbot so quickly, Mr Brown," Helen shouted. "It's wonderful. Even the train doesn't do the journey in such a short time."

"Cars are the future, m'dear," he shouted back. "I predict that soon they'll be so common that almost everyone will have one. What do you think of that, young man?"

"I think you're right, Mr Brown," Matt yelled back. "The problem will be that there'll be so many, the roads will be overcrowded with them."

"Then they'll just have to build more roads."

With that, he turned the car and headed back to Torquay.

◆

The afternoon sun was warm in the garden at Belmont. Mrs Debbon made a steeple of her fingers and stared at her son, happily playing with Mary-Anne in a game of hide and seek.

"Charles knows nothing of this, Mr Harvey," she eventually said. "Nor do my other children. Their father and I decided when Charles was born that we would say nothing until he was old enough to understand and to make his own decisions. Now that Robert is no longer here, I have to decide when to tell him. When, and if."

"You may decide not to tell him at all?"

"Perhaps. My husband was a wonderful man, but given to very romantic notions of what being a King was all about. When a number of ex-aristocrats approached him with a view to him

returning to France and claiming the throne, I regret that he saw
only what he wanted to see. He envisaged a vast crowd cheering
him on his return, a splendid coronation, and then spending his
time hosting receptions and dinner parties, with the occasional
state visit thrown in. He could not see, did not *want* to see, the
trouble that would be caused. Some, undoubtedly, would
welcome him, but many would not. There would be the real
possibility of civil war. Even if by some chance his return as
reigning monarch could have been achieved peaceably, then it still
would not have worked. Those who were trying to persuade him
were not interested in restoring the monarchy because they
believed in it for its own sake, but only for what they could get
out of it. They wanted the titles, land and money back that their
families had lost at the Revolution. They wanted the real power
for themselves, to try to return France to a feudal system."

"And your husband was in agreement?"

"Yes. I tried to persuade him of the folly of the idea, but he
could see only the glory. He was a King without his throne and
here was his chance to regain it. He was never a strong man
physically, and all the schemes, plans, and secret assignations wore
him out. He died of a heart attack ten years ago, only two months
after Charles was born."

She fell silent again, and stared out across the gardens and the
rich Devon countryside. Looking at the view, Connor tried to
imagine the inner turmoil that Mr Debbon must have gone
through. A happily married man with two wonderful children,
another child on the way, a very comfortable lifestyle and in a
beautiful part of the country. Then along comes a group of people
to tell him that he can become a King, a real King, not one living
in exile, where no one knew who he was. He would have a palace,
a vast retinue of servants, and people waving and cheering
wherever he went. It must have seemed too good to be true. That
was the problem, of course. It *was* too good to be true, but Mr
Debbon couldn't see that. In the end, the stress probably proved
too much for him and brought on the heart attack.

"I'm so sorry, Mrs Debbon," he said, "this must be very

painful for you."

"Yes, but in a way it's a relief to be able to talk to someone about it. I have had to cope with it all on my own for a long time."

"You were going to explain about Charles."

"Yes, I was. Two years before Louis-Charles was born to King Louis and Queen Marie Antoinette, the Queen bore a son by her lover, the Swedish diplomat Count Axel Fersen."

"There is no record of that in any of the archives."

"Of course there isn't," she snorted. "Things were done differently then. As soon as his wife's delicate condition became apparent, the King let it be known that she was to make an extended visit to the south of the country. In reality she went to a remote chateau in the Midi region. There the child, a boy, was delivered."

"The King arranged this?"

"Certainly. Such liaisons were not uncommon. Kings had their mistresses, Queens had their lovers."

"Would it not have been easier just to have the pregnancy ended?"

"Such operations are very dangerous. The King could not risk making the Queen unable to bear more children. They already had a son, the Dauphin Louis-Joseph. However, he was a sickly child, and it was believed that he would not survive into adulthood. In this they were proved correct, because Louis-Joseph died at the age of eight in 1789. The King therefore needed another son, which meant that the child the Queen was carrying would have to be carried to term."

"But the risk in allowing the child to be born must have been great. What if someone had let it be known that the Queen had borne a son to someone other than the King?"

"There was little chance of that. As I said, things were done differently then. The child was taken away as soon as he was born and placed with the family of the local Count and Countess. To everyone else, he was their son. They named him Jean-Paul."

"But they must have known?"

"No. They thought he was the child of a minor member of the

Royal family. That would explain the secrecy, without making them too worried about the future. There was a large number of, how shall I say this, inconvenient children born to high-ranking members of the nobility. Farming them out to lesser aristocrats was quite common."

"But someone knew."

"Yes. Some of the Queen's closest and most trusted supporters were aware of the situation and kept a distant eye on the boy over the years. Even then there were rumblings of discontent about the monarchy."

"You said that Kings had their mistresses and Queens had their lovers. Did King Louis XVI have a mistress?"

"No. He had no mistresses before his marriage, and none after."

"So it was only Marie Antoinette who fell from grace."

"Yes, but it was not entirely her fault. For the first few years of her marriage, it was unconsummated. The King had a very delicate problem and was unable to please her. Marie Antoinette was a young and beautiful lady. If the King was unable to gratify her, then she perforce had to look elsewhere for her pleasures."

"I have read some of the stories about her."

"Do not believe most of them. The public blamed her for not producing children. They could not believe that it was the King who had the problem. As a woman, and moreover as a foreigner, she got the blame. Other stories followed. Some, no doubt, were true, but most were not."

"But she was hated by the general population?"

"Yes. When the Revolution swept across France, neither the King nor the Queen stood very much chance of survival. There were those close to the family who were well aware of what was to come. Before the revolutionary troops came to Versailles, Jean-Paul was brought there from his home in the Midi and Louis-Charles was smuggled out of the palace and out of the country. Although Jean-Paul was two years older than Louis-Charles, they both had their mother's looks, and, once he was dressed as a prince, only those who knew him very well would realise what had happened. It was Jean-Paul who died in the Temple Prison."

"I see," Connor said.

"You do not approve?"

"It was a long time ago, Mrs Debbon, and no doubt everyone thought that they were making the right decision."

"But you do not?"

"It is not for me to judge, Mrs Debbon, but to take the child, Jean-Paul, from his home, knowing that he would probably die, seems very callous."

"I agree, Mr Harvey, I agree entirely. To try to save the life of Louis-Charles was one thing, but simply to sacrifice another child in his place? No, that was very wrong. I have tried to convince myself that those who made the exchange did not know what would happen, that they believed that the child would simply be kept under close supervision. I have tried, and failed. They would have known only too well what was to come. Even though it was a hundred years ago, and there is nothing I can do about it, I look at Charles and find myself thinking about Jean-Paul. What that poor child must have gone through, what he must have suffered, without ever knowing why."

"Is that why you are so opposed to returning to France with Charles and proclaiming him King? Because you feel guilty about Jean-Paul?"

"I do feel a sense of guilt, it is true, but that is not my reason. The scheme simply will not work. Some years ago, on the fall of Napoleon III, there were many who suggested that the time was right for the restoration of the monarchy. Henri, Count de Chambord, was believed to be the legitimate heir to the throne. He was living in England at the time and he was approached by representatives from the National Assembly with a view to establishing a constitutional monarchy, such as exists here in England. This was a wonderful chance and Robert and I watched the proceedings with great interest. We decided that, if the plan succeeded, we would say nothing, but let the crown pass to Henri. We were happy and content as we were. Sadly, Henri was a man set in his ways and opposed to change. His teachers, and later his advisors, had stressed to him how important he was and that he should, by rights, be an absolute monarch. He refused to allow any concessions. He insisted that he would only return as King if everything were restored as it was in the time of Louis XVI. Even those close to him knew that the country would never accept this. Eventually the offer to Henri to become King was withdrawn and the chance was lost. This present plan has no more chance of succeeding than the previous one. I will not allow it."

"I do not doubt your sincerity, Mrs Debbon," Connor said, choosing his words carefully, "but there have been many stories about the young King escaping from the Temple Prison. What you have told me is very plausible, but will the authorities not require proof?"

"Doubtless they would."

"And without that proof, then young Charles could be passed off as yet another pretender to the throne?"

"He could."

"Then why not just tell everyone involved that he is *not* the long-lost heir, that he is, in reality, just another pretender."

"Because it would not be true. There is proof, ample proof, that he is who I say he is. There are papers and documents, signed and witnessed by those in a position to know, that Charles is the rightful King."

"Papers and documents can be forged."

"They can indeed."

Their conversation was interrupted by the return of a flushed and very excited Helen and Matt from their outing. Mrs Debbon noted Helen's rather windswept appearance.

"I trust that the two of you enjoyed your outing in Mr Brown's motor car?" she asked dryly.

Matt and Helen glanced at each other, before Helen burst into a fit of giggles.

"I'm sorry Mama, I thought that you wouldn't approve so we hoped to keep it a secret."

"You look as if you have just spent the last week on the deck of a fast sailing ship. As you have not had the time for that, it was fairly obvious where you have been. I hope that you did not annoy Mr Brown too much."

"I'm sorry, Mrs Debbon," Matt said. "It's my fault. I suggested the ride."

"It is very generous of you to try to protect my daughter," she said, "but I know full well whose idea it would have been. However, as it such a glorious day, I do not wish it spoiled, so we will say no more on the subject."

"Thank you, Mama," Helen said.

"Now I suggest that you go upstairs and change."

"Yes, Mama," she said, and left to do as she had been instructed.

"Matthew?" Mrs Debbon said, once Helen was out of earshot.

"Yes, ma'am?"

"Your uncle has been telling me about his work for the government. I understand that you know about this?"

"Yes, I do."

"And you also know about my family, about who Charles is?"

"Yes."

"I see. Then it seems only fair that you should accompany us on a short walk. Mr Harvey is of the opinion that the papers and documents that exist concerning my son's lineage could be dismissed as forgeries. I intend to show him something that will prove beyond doubt that my story is genuine. I would like you to join us, but I need your promise that you will never divulge a word concerning what you are about to see to anyone, least of all my children."

"I promise."

"As do I," Connor added.

"Thank you," she said. "Now I must first ensure that Charles and Mary-Anne are both otherwise engaged."

She called the two children to her side from where they had been playing with a hoop on one of the lawns.

"I think it is time that the two of you went for a nap. I will get Susan to take you inside."

"But Mama . . ." Charles began, but was cut off by his mother raising her hand for silence.

"There will be no arguments, thank you," she told him, walking to the door leading from the terrace into the drawing room and pulling the bell cord that was hanging by it. The maid appeared and took the two disgruntled children inside the house, Charles obviously wanting to protest loudly at being forced inside on such an afternoon but deciding that the look on his mother's face was such that he dare not risk it.

"Now the children are out of the way for a while I am free to show you the proof of my story. Please wait here for a moment as I need to retrieve some keys from my boudoir."

She returned a few minutes later and led them along the terrace, down the broad steps to the next terrace, and then stopped at the green door let into the supporting wall. Matt had seen it several times and assumed that it was a gardener's store, or some such. Mrs Debbon glanced around to ensure that she was unobserved and then unlocked and opened the door, revealing the passage beyond. She ushered them in, closing the door behind her.

"If you would be so kind as to take the lantern that you will find hanging above you," she said to Matt.

"Sure. Here it is."

"Thank you. You will find a tinderbox on the shelf by your side. If you would care to light the lantern, please."

Matt found the tinderbox without any trouble, but didn't have a clue how to use it. He glanced at Connor, who just shrugged his shoulders. He evidently didn't know how it worked either. Matt tried an experimental tug on the handle and was relieved to find a shower of sparks emerge. Glancing back on the shelf he saw several half-burnt tapers, so grabbed one and after a few failures managed to light the taper from the tinderbox. He was then easily able to light the lantern.

"If you would care to hold the lantern up high, Matthew, then we will follow you along the passage. You will see a door on the right-hand side shortly."

When they reached the door, Matt stood aside to let Mrs

Debbon open it and then to lead them into the small room. She carefully removed a number of loose bricks in the wall and then asked Matt to reach in and bring out the large tin box that was in the recess behind. He handed the lantern to Connor and moved to do what Mrs Debbon had asked.

"Be careful, Matthew, the box is much heavier than it appears."

"It certainly is," he said, struggling with the box.

Eventually he managed it and placed the box on the room's sole piece of furniture, a small table against the wall. Mrs Debbon took another key from her pocket and unlocked the box, standing back so that the others could see what was in it. Connor held the lantern aloft and then nearly dropped it in surprise. Both he and Matt stared at the contents as if transfixed. The illumination from the lantern was returned tenfold from the box, as a rainbow of light flashed around the chamber.

"Here is your proof, gentlemen," Mrs Debbon said. "As you say, papers and documents can be forged. This cannot. It is the Crown of France. After the Revolution, most of the Crown Jewels were either looted or seized by the state and eventually sold off. It was traditional that each new monarch would have a crown made for them, although often using historic gemstones. This is the crown of Louis XVI. It has always been believed that it was broken up and the gems dispersed, but that, as you can see, was not so. It was brought to England at the same time as young King Louis XVII was smuggled across the Channel. It has been in the family's possession ever since. Matthew, would you be kind enough to lift it out of the box the box, please?"

Matt did as he was asked. The light became even stronger as it reflected off the diamonds, emeralds and rubies that encrusted the crown. It was magnificent.

◆

Matt recalled a college trip to London, when they'd been taken to the Tower of London to see the British Crown Jewels which were protected behind bulletproof glass and, superb as they were, they seemed somehow remote, like most things do that live in museum cases. This was different. To hold the crown, to see the fire locked in the gems released as the crown was tilted one way and then the other in the lamplight was beyond anything that he'd ever seen. It seemed alive somehow, not just an inanimate object. Matt was almost afraid of it, as if it were something not quite of this world. Which, in a way, he supposed it wasn't.

Neither of them knew what to say and it was left to Mrs Debbon to break the silence.

"I take it that you agree this proves my son's claim?"

Connor nodded his assent, his eyes still glued to the glittering spectacle before him. Matt stared at the bejewelled splendour in his hands for a while longer, then slowly, carefully and not without a small sigh of relief, he replaced it in its box and closed the lid. The tiny room seemed to go suddenly dark.

"Has anyone ever put a value on it?" Matt asked, when he finally managed to get his vocal cords working. The words came out as a hoarse whisper.

"If you mean its monetary value, then no. Such a thing is beyond mere money. Yet it has a price and many have paid it through the centuries — far too many in fact."

"They have?"

"Yes. A price in blood, Matthew. There are those who have wallowed in blood in order to wear the crown. Murder, greed, corruption and torture have all played their part. Many of those who started out with good intentions have been corrupted by its weight. Not all of course, for that would be to debase the memory of many fine men who have held the kingship, but even some who started their reigns with high ideals and noble aims have found that the power that went with the crown turned them to evil."

"And is that the main reason that you don't want Charles to be King?" Connor asked.

"It is one of the reasons. He is only a child, but already I see much of his father in him. A man who knew the difference between right and wrong, and wanted badly to follow the correct path, but was all too easily led astray by others. That is what worries me about Charles. As King he would be surrounded by those who would seek to use him for their own ends."

She locked the box and Matt returned it to its hiding place. None of them spoke again until they were back in the warmth of the spring sunshine. Connor decided to gamble.

"I assume Major Esterhazy doesn't know the crown is here?" he asked.

If she was surprised by his question, she didn't show it.

"No, Mr Harvey, he doesn't. Nor do any of those involved in this mad scheme. In fact, no one alive knows except me — and now the two of you, of course. I would prefer it to stay that way."

"No-one will ever learn of it from either of us, Mrs Debbon. You have my word."

"Thank you, Mr Harvey. It is something of a relief to be able to discuss the matter with someone else. So, now that you are fully aware of Charles' true lineage, what do you believe Her Majesty's Government will do about it?"

"I don't believe it will make any difference to the government's position. You have made it clear that you will not go along with the scheme to try to restore the monarchy to France, or at least not at this time. If that is your decision, and incidentally I think it's the right one, then they will not attempt to change your mind. They will still take the view that the political machinations of a foreign sovereign state are no concern of theirs. But the fact still remains that those who are in favour are dangerous people who must realise that their time is running out."

"They are certainly very foolish people if they think this ludicrous scheme will stand any chance of succeeding. However, I do not wish to further spoil such a beautiful day so I suggest we say no more on the matter for the time being."

Connor decided that a "suggestion" from Mrs Debbon was more in the way of a royal command, which, he suddenly realised for the first time, it actually was. Whilst her husband was alive, she would have been the rightful Queen of France. Now that was something to think about. All the time that he'd been considering how regal her bearing was, he had been right. He almost laughed out loud, but managed to turn it into a cough.

"You will stay for dinner, of course," she said.

Another royal command, Connor thought.

"We'd be delighted," he answered, suppressing a sudden urge to bow but succumbing to another cough, earning him an odd look from his nephew.

"Excellent. Then if you will forgive me, I think I will retire for a while. I believe Helen will be down shortly, Matthew. Mr Harvey, do you wish to take some rest?"

Connor assured her that he would be fine sitting in the garden.

"In which case I will see you both later," she said, leaving them to digest what they had just witnessed.

"That has to be the most amazing sight I've ever seen," Matt told his uncle. "That crown's got to be worth millions."

"Many millions I would guess, but it's the sort of thing that you can't really put a financial value on. If all the gemstones were removed and the gold melted down, they would still fetch a colossal fortune. But all together in a royal crown dating back centuries, at least in part, then the value would be incalculable."

"Plus," Matt reminded him, "it means our best plan to scupper this whole affair is now dust."

"Yes, it is. Quite where we go from here I don't know. You got any bright ideas?"

"I wish I had. We've only got four days left to stop the fire."

"I know, but I don't know what to do next. We really do need to try and persuade Mrs Debbon how serious this whole affair is."

"And we're staying for dinner again this evening?"

"Why, don't you want to? I can always make up some excuse why we need to get back to the hotel or something."

"No, it's fine," Matt told him. "It's just that I miss sprawling out on the sofa with a takeaway watching the TV sometimes. Everything's so formal here. I have to watch what I'm doing and saying all the time. It gets a bit tiring."

"Tiring or tiresome?"

"Both, actually," Matt replied with a grin. "Don't you feel the same sometimes?"

"Of course I do. But needs must, etc. Anyway, there's something that's about to cheer you up."

"What?"

"Helen. She's just coming out onto the terrace."

"I'll see you later," Matt told him as he scrambled to his feet.

◆

Try as he might, Connor couldn't think what to do next. Dinner came and went in a whirl of courses and glittering silverware, but he was hardly aware of what he had eaten. He was now seriously worried. In four days' time Belmont was due to burn to the ground, taking all the Debbons with it and he didn't have a clue how to prevent it happening. He glanced across the drawing room at Matt and Helen enjoying some private joke. He wished with all his heart that he hadn't involved his nephew in this increasingly dangerous situation.

Later, as they were travelling back to the hotel, Matt was deep inside his own thoughts.

"Penny for them," Connor said.

"Huh?"

"You were miles away. What were you thinking about?"

"Everything. The fire, the family, you, me. And Helen. Mostly Helen. It's all so complicated," Matt grumbled.

"At your age everything's complicated. It goes with being sixteen."

"But things are different for me than they would have been for you when you were sixteen. You wouldn't understand."

"You think so?"

"Yes. I'm not being mean, but things were probably easier when you were my age."

"Life was certainly less frantic when I was sixteen than they are in our time, but some things don't change. At sixteen you're not a boy anymore but you're not quite a man either. You still get drawn to look in toy shop windows and sometimes wish you were young enough to play with some of the toy cars that you can see on display. But you feel embarrassed at thinking like that and hope that none of your mates see you looking in the window. At the same time you want to have enough money to buy the latest fashions in clothes so you can show off, which is something you wouldn't worry about as a kid. You feel mature enough to expect other people to respect your opinions and you don't like it if people ignore you because you're not a child anymore. But if something goes horribly wrong you wish that there was someone else there to take over and say, 'Don't worry — I'll take care of it for you.' Sometimes you feel you can take on the world single-handed whilst at other times you just want to curl up in a corner and everything to go away."

Matt gave him a startled look which made Connor laugh.

"As I said: some things don't change. So I do understand something of what you're going through."

"Why is life so complicated?"

"That's a question that's been asked ever since Adam and Eve got thrown out of the Garden of Eden."

CHAPTER NINETEEN

Taking photographs

Edward came to collect them in the Belmont coach at ten the next morning and by half past they were enjoying the view from the terrace and sipping freshly made lemonade. Daniel had arrived at about the same time, much to Matt's annoyance, and the two of them were busily vying for Helen's attention on the middle terrace. Mary-Anne, Charles and Bill were playing at hoop-and-stick further along the terrace. It was another beautiful spring day, the sun shining down out of a sky of cloudless blue. The lush green of the Devonshire countryside was picture perfect and Connor found it hard to equate the scene in front of him with the knowledge that not far away others were plotting murder and in the most callous way possible. He shivered involuntarily, causing their hostess to look at him in concern.

"Are you cold, Mr Harvey? We could always retire inside if you wish."

"No, I'm not cold. Just worried."

"About us?"

"Yes. I had a communication early this morning by messenger from London," he lied. "The government is of the belief that an attempt will be made very shortly to remove Charles by force and take him to France if you refuse to co-operate."

"I think the government is a little over-anxious," she replied. "Even if by some evil mischance Charles were to fall into the hands of the schemers, it would avail them little. I would simply let it be known that he was forcibly removed from his mother and without consent. That would weaken their case so much that it would be bound to fail."

"You are assuming that you would be able to pass that information on."

"And why would I not be able to?"

"Because these are ruthless people you are dealing with. They see a glittering prize almost in their grasp and only one stubborn lady in their way. It is my belief, and that of Her Majesty's Government, that they would not hesitate to remove that barrier — permanently."

"You are suggesting that they would stoop to murder a woman?"

"Yes."

"I am sorry, Mr Harvey. I know that you mean well, but this is all very far-fetched."

"My information is very reliable."

She sighed deeply and gazed out over the lower terraces towards the distant heights of Dartmoor.

"Please do not think me ungrateful for your concern," she said at last. "I appreciate all the trouble that you have gone to on my behalf, but I cannot bring myself to accept that they would try to murder me. Such a thing is unheard of."

It may be unheard of in your world, Connor thought, but it sure as hell isn't in mine. He decided not to press the matter, nor to further complicate things by trying to convince her that it wasn't only her own life that was in danger, but that of her two daughters. He decided to try a different approach.

"Could you at least arrange for some extra security? Explain to the local police that you have heard rumours of a possible attempt to burgle the house and see if they will agree to post a guard."

She thought it over for a while, before shaking her head.

"No, that would only frighten the children and I do not want them involved. However, there is one thing that can be done — something I really should have suggested before."

"And that is?"

"To invite yourself and Matthew to stay here at Belmont, of course. There are a number of guest rooms that are unused and it seems pointless the two of you having to travel down to the Belgrave Hotel each evening. I've no doubt that some of our friends will be scandalised at me inviting an unmarried gentleman to stay, but I am really beyond caring what others think. With the two of you here I feel we will be quite safe."

Connor cursed himself for not having foreseen this, but he could hardly refuse. Now that he'd built up a cover story about being a government agent, albeit an unofficial one, he couldn't come straight out and tell her that he considered that he'd be about as much use as a fried egg if it came to a fight. He tried to find some other reason to get out of staying at Belmont, but failed and ended up agreeing.

"Excellent," she said, "I will send Edward down to the hotel to collect your belongings."

Connor was about to thank her, then had a moment's panic when he realised that there were things in Matt's luggage that should remain hidden. What an inhabitant of the late nineteenth century would make of them he didn't know and would rather not find out.

"It's very kind of you, but I think it would be best if I go down with him to sort our things out. Matt has a habit of turning wherever he sleeps into something resembling a rubbish tip within a matter of minutes."

"As you wish. Would you like to go at once?"

"Yes, thank you. I'll just go and tell Matt the news. I suspect he'll be pleased."

Matt was more than pleased — he was delighted.

"Brilliant!" he said, making sure Daniel was out of earshot. "It means I get to spend more time with Helen without Daniel hanging around watching my every move."

"What do you expect him to do? He's obviously been friends with Helen for years, then you come along, out of nowhere as far as he's concerned, and elbow him out of the way. Anyhow, I'm off down to the hotel to collect our clobber. Do you want to come, or do you want to stay here?"

"I'm fine here, thanks. Just be careful with my music player and don't drop my clobber."

"Would I do a thing like that?"

"Yes."

"You know, when I first held you when you were only a few

hours old, and your dad asked Laura and me to be godparents, I just knew you were going to be trouble."

"Trouble? Me?"

"Yes, you. Anyway, I'll see you later."

◆

After he'd seen his uncle off, Matt returned to where Helen was lying flat on her back on the lawn.

"This is another of those days that I would like to last forever," she announced.

"If I had my camera with me, I could take some photos. Then you'd be able to look at them whenever you wanted."

"Mama has a camera," Charles piped up, collecting his hoop from where it had fallen at Helen's feet. "She doesn't use it very often, but I know where it is."

"Of course!" Helen said, sitting up. "That's just the thing. I'll go and ask if we can use it."

Both Matt and Daniel watched her as she ran up the broad terrace steps to where her mother was sitting.

"The way that dress clings to Helen's body doesn't leave a great deal to the imagination," Matt said.

Daniel stared at him in surprise for a few moments before bursting out laughing.

"What?" Matt asked.

"You say the oddest things sometimes. However, I agree. I'm just not sure if it's the done thing to say so, that's all."

"I don't see why not."

"Well, now that you mention it, nor do I."

They both returned to the task of admiring Helen's figure, until she disappeared into the house. She returned a few minutes later carrying the camera and a large box. When she reached them, she handed it straight to Matt.

"As you have a camera of your own I expect you'll know how to use it," she told him.

Matt stared at the huge lump of equipment in his hand. He hadn't the faintest idea how it worked, and in fact wasn't even sure which end was the lens and which was the viewfinder.

"Sorry Helen, but I haven't got a clue how to operate it," he admitted. "I can't even tell where the film goes. It's nothing like the one I've got at home."

"I do," Daniel said, getting to his feet. "It's like the one father uses to take photographs of some of the special cargoes that he's sometimes asked to ship abroad. You put a photographic plate in the back and then you look through here. You have to remember that the picture will be upside-down, but it's easy enough. Then you just click this lever. Have you got any photographic plates?"

"I think there are some in here," Helen replied, indicating a large leather-bound box.

"Yes," Daniel told her after he'd investigated. "There are about twenty in here. How many can we use?"

"All of them. Mama says that they need using up before they spoil. If we use them now, I'll get one of the servants to take them down to a photographer's in Torquay. Now, who's going to be first?"

"Me," Charles stated. "It was my idea, so take one of me."

"You are most certainly not a gentleman," sniffed Mary-Anne, "otherwise you would let the ladies go first."

"Since when have you been a lady?" he replied, before hightailing it along the terrace, out of reach of Mary-Anne's undoubted revenge.

"I think you should be first," Matt told Helen.

"Agreed," added Daniel.

In the end they all had two or three pictures taken, sometimes singly, sometimes in groups, even though Bill took some persuading before he allowed his own photograph to be taken. In the end he gave in to Mary-Anne's pleading.

"All right, but I still fink it ain't natchural."

There was just one plate left and Matt asked if he could use it to take another of Helen.

"Very well. Where would you like me to stand?"

"Over there, by that arch of flowers."

"What a good idea. They're always among the first things to

bloom in the garden."

"What are they?" Matt asked.

"Clematis," he was told. "Clematis montana to be exact."

"You know about flowers and plants and stuff?"

"No," she laughed. "Not in the least. I only know because I asked one of the gardeners what they were a couple of years ago."

He managed to position her so that the arch of deep pink flowers framed her face. He knew that the photograph wouldn't be in colour, but it made such a fine picture that he thought it would look good anyway.

"Excellent," Helen said when the last plate had been removed from the camera. "I'll go and ask James to send someone with them right away. I don't know how long it takes to have them developed — is that the right word?"

Daniel assured her it was.

"It will take a few days, but we should get them back by next weekend."

Matt had to turn quickly away so that the others couldn't see his face. Before the following weekend, when the photographs had been developed, Belmont would have been reduced to a smoking ruin and all of the Debbon family would have burned to death. It was a grim thought and one that was slowly but surely growing in his mind.

"Matt?" came Helen's concerned voice from behind him. "Are you ill?"

He forced himself to appear cheerful as he turned back to face her.

"No, I'm fine. Just a bit of a headache, that's all. It's easing off now."

"Are you sure? I can get Hannah to prepare you some powders if you wish. I have always found them most efficacious at relieving headaches."

Matt wasn't at all certain what efficacious meant, but assured a concerned Helen that he didn't need anything.

◆

As Connor gathered their few belongings together in the hotel suite, he made a mental note to tell Matt to keep most of his gear hidden while they were at Belmont. If he left his stuff lying around as he usually did, it could cause some very awkward questions to be asked. He switched on Matt's razor and noticed that the charge was running down and hoped it would last until the next time they flipped and that there would be time to recharge it. He'd never wet-shaved in his life and wouldn't have a clue how to go about it. He was also of the opinion that stubble was almost certainly not fashionable in 1898. As he was leaving, he asked the hotel concierge to pass on his thanks to the staff for looking after them so well, a request that evidently surprised the elderly gentleman.

"On the contrary, sir, thank *you*. It has been a pleasure being of service. I trust that you and the young gentleman will return one day?"

"I'm sure we will," he said, mentally adding that all the current staff would have passed from this world a hundred years or more by the time he and Matt saw the Belgrave Hotel again. It was a sobering thought.

◆

He handed the bags containing his and Matt's belongings to Edward and clambered into the coach.

"Edward?" he called just as the coachman was climbing up to his seat.

"Yes, sir?"

"Could we return to Belmont via the seafront and the harbour please? I haven't managed to see the harbour area since we've been here."

"Of course, sir. Whatever you wish."

"And there's really no need to call me 'sir'. My name's Connor."

"That's very kind of you sir, but Madam would be most annoyed with me if I did. She'd say I was being familiar."

"Madam wouldn't know about it," Connor told him.

"Maybe not sir, but I might forget myself and call you 'Connor' in her hearing and that wouldn't do. It wouldn't do at all."

"As you wish," Connor laughed. "I must admit that I wouldn't like to get on the wrong side of Mrs Debbon. I have a feeling she would be a fearsome opponent."

"On that, sir, you have my full agreement."

As the coach clattered its way along the seafront towards the harbour, Connor tried to think of some way that he could impress on Mrs Debbon the seriousness of the current situation and on what a slender thread her life, and the lives of all of those she loved, was hanging. They also needed help, but he couldn't think where to get it from. The coach slowed when the traffic became heavier as they neared the harbour. In his own time, it was an attractive area, with pedestrianised areas, flowerbeds and large numbers of seats. The harbour itself was also almost exclusively the domain of pleasure craft, only a very few fishing vessels using its facilities, and cargo boats almost unheard of.

In 1898, Connor noted, it was a very different scene. The outer harbour boasted a few sleek private steam yachts, presumably owned by some of the wealthier visitors to the resort, but they were heavily outnumbered by commercial craft. A cargo vessel, its funnel belching black smoke, was being gently nudged by a steam tug to a berth against one of the quays. Its decks were laden with timber and Connor had a vague memory of reading somewhere that Torquay once had a flourishing trade in timber brought in from the Baltic. While the coach waited for a clear path to ease its way through the crowds of other coaches, wagons, drays and a rare motor car, Connor watched the cargo ship tying up. He noted her name of *Petrel* and underneath the words "Hardwick Line, Torquay". She was evidently one of Daniel's father's fleet. Edward eventually found a clearing in the jam of traffic large enough to get the coach through and they turned away from the harbour and into the only slightly less crowded town centre.

The sight of the *Petrel* berthing had given Connor an idea and he pondered on it during the rest of the trip. By the time they were trotting along the lane towards Belmont he'd come to a decision.

Moving in

The coach crunched along the gravel drive towards the front door, and Connor was startled to find a crowd of people assembled outside, with Mrs Debbon at its centre. He could see Matt standing to one side but no sign of the rest of the family. What now, he thought?

Edward jumped down and opened the carriage door for him as he clambered out, Matt joining him as he did so. Connor raised his eyebrows in a question and got a shrug of the shoulders in response.

"All I know is that Mrs Debbon said I had to meet you here when you got back, so here I am. No idea what the reception committee is all about."

"Mr Harvey, Matthew," Mrs Debbon said, coming to greet them. "It is correct practice for those coming to stay to be formally introduced to all the staff and I see no reason why the formalities should be dispensed with just because you are both frequent visitors. So if you would both care to come this way I will introduce you properly."

Connor and Matt glanced nervously at each other as they followed their hostess towards the line of servants.

"James, our butler, you know quite well, of course."

After a brief bow from James, they continued by being introduced to Mrs Gregson, the housekeeper, whose frosty greeting seemed to indicate that their arrival to stay was a serious affront to her sensibilities. The line-up continued with Frederick, the first footman; Geoffrey, the second footman; Edward, the coachman and third footman, who had settled the horses and then run round to get in line; Sarah, the lady's maid; Miss Pearson, the younger children's nurse; Ben, the head gardener; and finally Betsy, Dora, Bella, Mary and Sophie, the housemaids. All either gave a short bow or a curtsey to the visitors, making Matt in particular feel very uncomfortable.

"Of course there are also the members of the kitchen staff and the gardeners, grooms and stable boys and so on, but you are not likely to meet them very often," Mrs Debbon told them.

"Of course," Connor replied, somewhat bewildered by the turn of events.

Managing, not without considerable difficulty, to persuade their host that they didn't need Frederick and Geoffrey to act as their personal valets for the duration of their stay, they followed the housekeeper up the stairs, the two footmen coming behind with the bags.

"This will be your room, Mr Harvey," Mrs Gregson told him, indicating a door halfway along the first-floor corridor. "Master Harvey will be opposite. If you wish for anything, just pull the bell cord."

"Thank you, Mrs Gregson," Connor said, trying to conceal his amusement. He was reminded of one of his grandmother's sayings, when she said that someone's expression could sour milk whilst it was still in the cow.

"It is my duty, sir," she replied, seeming to indicate that she wasn't doing it by choice.

The guest rooms at Belmont were even more lavishly appointed than the suite at the hotel. When he saw the room that he'd been given Matt felt that it wasn't really a room that should be used — it was more like a room in a museum or in one of the National Trust houses that his parents dragged him to sometimes. He decided he'd best keep his stuff in the drawers and wardrobes rather than left on any convenient flat surface, such as the floor, which was where his clothes usually ended up at home. He tested the bed, bouncing up and down on it a few times and then lying full length with his hands pillowing his head. The room was big enough to swallow not only his own room back home, but most of the other rooms as well. He started guiltily as he realised that he'd scarcely given his family a thought in the past few days. The realisation washed over him that they were all an impossible distance away from him, separated by a gulf of well over a century. He suddenly felt very lonely and went to look for his uncle. Connor's room was more or less a mirror image of his own, on the opposite side of the corridor.

"Hi," Connor said, when he noticed Matt standing in the doorway. "I've stayed in some fine hotels over the years but I've never had a room like this one before."

"Nor me."

Something in the way he spoke made Connor look more closely at him.

"You OK?"

"I was just thinking about mum and dad and the others and wondering what they're all doing. I suppose it's only just registered with me that even my great-grandparents haven't been born yet."

"You'll see them all again, Matt."

"Sure?"

"As sure as I can be. I think that as soon as this business is over, we'll flip back for good and that'll be that."

"But then I won't see Helen again."

"No."

"Heads I lose, tails I lose."

"Life can be desperately unfair sometimes, but there's nothing either of us can do about it, so the best thing is just to accept it."

"I know. Bloody hard though!"

"It's certainly that. You unpacked yet?"

"Yes. And before you ask, I've made sure all my non-1898 stuff is well hidden. What do we do now?"

"Get changed for dinner and then wait for the gong I would guess."

"Do we have to wear all that clobber?"

"'Fraid so. You don't want Helen thinking that you're not a gentleman, do you?"

"I suppose not."

Matt returned rather gloomily to his room to change. He felt miserable and confused but had no idea how to get himself out of the mood. Even the thought of sitting next to Helen at dinner wasn't really helping matters. He decided that it must be because he couldn't see how they were going to change things. He'd run it through his mind over and over again, and every time the result was the same. Belmont went up in flames and the whole family died in the fire. It was a deeply depressing thought.

◆

Dinner that night was not, in Matt's opinion at any rate, an unqualified success. He felt hot and uncomfortable in his borrowed evening suit and the food, though plentiful, was not to his taste. Something that looked vaguely disgusting was on his plate at that moment, which Helen said was cold poached egg in aspic. A glance across the table told him that he wasn't alone. Connor was trying hard to look as if he was eating, whereas in fact he was just reducing the contents of his plate to a mush. At least at the hotel they'd had a choice about what they ate.

"You're not eating, Matthew," Helen said, glancing at his plate. "Is the dish not to your taste?"

"I guess I'm just not very hungry," he told her.

"If there's something that you would like, you have only to have a message passed to Cook and she will undoubtedly prepare it for you."

"Really?"

"Certainly. Although Mama didn't really approve, I spent quite some time in the kitchen when I was younger."

"You are quite correct, young lady, I did not approve," her mother said, although not without a smile. "However, as it seemed that there was no way to keep you out of the kitchen other than by locking you in your room I had perforce to accept the situation."

"Hannah — that's Cook — has a wonderful fund of stories," Helen continued. "She was always able to cheer me up when I felt miserable, especially after Papa died. Mary-Anne and Charles still often go down there, even though Mama tries to dissuade them. Hannah has a very large range of recipes and enjoys trying them out."

Matt made a mental note to go and see Hannah at the earliest available opportunity. He doubted that she'd have a recipe for what he wanted, but he was determined to give it a go.

"Do you smoke, Mr Harvey?" Mrs Debbon asked, as the servants were clearing away the remains of the last course.

"No, I've never indulged."

"My late husband used to enjoy a cigar in the evening, but the smoking room has seen little or no use since he passed away. Matthew?"

"No, ma'am, I don't smoke either."

"In which case perhaps you would both care to accompany Helen and myself on a short turn in the garden before we retire?"

"Can I come?" Charles piped up.

"You most certainly may not. You know perfectly well that you and Mary-Anne will go to bed now. James," she added, addressing the butler, "please ask Nurse if she could see the children up to the night nursery."

"Certainly, madam."

◆

Gas lanterns hissed and flared along the terraces and steps in the garden, giving it a completely different feel to that which it had in daylight. Matt found himself alone with Helen, Mrs Debbon and Connor having taken a different path, whether by design or accident he didn't know.

"A most romantic evening, is it not?" Helen asked him.

In the soft light from the nearest lantern, Matt thought she looked beautiful beyond compare. Her skin took on a translucent quality and her hair sparkled as if there were strands of pure gold woven into it. He finally admitted to himself what he'd really known all along. He was deeply in love with her. The thought that she had only a few short days to live unless they could find a way to alter history almost choked him and he tried and failed to stifle a shiver.

"Matt? Are you cold? We could go in if you prefer."

"No, I'm not cold, it was just a shiver, that's all."

Submitting to an impulse he couldn't control, her took her in his arms and kissed her. He wanted her so badly that it was almost physically painful. His kisses became more passionate, his embrace earthier and it was only a slight look of alarm in her eyes that warned him he was running too fast. He released her and they stood silently, neither knowing what to say.

"I'm sorry," Matt said at last. "I got carried away. I went too far."

"No, really, there's no call to apologise. It's just that it was so . . . I don't know how to explain it. It was just so different to when we kissed in the primrose meadow."

"I know. I'm really sorry."

"I've never been kissed like that before," she told him, giving him an appraising look. "Daniel treats me as if I was made of glass and will break if he isn't very careful. And before, in the meadow, you seemed almost shy, but this time, well, I don't fully understand, but you made me feel like a woman instead of a girl."

"You don't mind? You're not angry with me?"

"No. Hold me again. Please?"

He held her tightly and only the sound of approaching voices caused them to break apart.

"*There* you are," Mrs Debbon said, as she and Connor joined them. "I was starting to wonder where you were. I'm not certain it's quite proper for a young lady to be alone with a young gentleman in the dark."

"I'm sorry, Mama, we got talking and I wasn't sure where you and Mr Harvey were."

"Very well, there's no harm done. Now, I suggest we all return to the house. James will have arranged for drinks to be served in the drawing room before we retire for the night.

Matt couldn't trust himself to speak, so he said nothing. He just took Helen's hand and the four of them walked up the broad terrace steps and into the house. Connor also said nothing. The flushed look on Matt's face had spoken volumes and he worried how deeply his nephew was getting involved.

◆

The sound of a gong reverberated around the house, waking Connor from a deep but not particularly satisfying slumber. He had too much on his mind to sleep well and the nearer the day of fire approached, the more he worried. He still had no idea at all what, if anything, he and Matt were supposed to do to try and alter events. If nothing *could* be changed, if events were already mapped out, then he would be genuinely distraught. He had come to care a great deal for Mrs Debbon and her family and badly wanted to be of some help, but in spite of his own feelings, it was Matt he was worried about. He'd seen the way he looked at Helen and knew exactly what it meant. It was the same way he himself had looked at Laura when he finally realised that he loved her and that he wanted to spend the rest of his life with her. He'd asked her to marry him the next day. If anything happened to Helen, then Matt would be devastated and he didn't want him to go through the pain and suffering that he'd gone through when Laura had died. He managed to get his thoughts in enough order for him to wash and dress, then to go and see if Matt was ready. As he'd expected, Matt was still fast asleep. Nothing short of a radio alarm clock set on full volume could wake Matt in the mornings, so a gong stood no chance at all. He looked at Matt sleeping soundly and wondered how different his own life would have been had Laura lived and had his own son been born.

"Matt."

No answer.

"Matt!"

Still nothing.

"MATTHEW!"

The lump in the bed moved, an eye blearily opened, and, with some difficulty, focused on him.

"G'nuhng."

"Assuming that grunt meant 'good morning', then good morning to you too. Get yourself sorted, the gong's sounded. I guess that means we're expected downstairs for breakfast."

"Wassertime?"

"How should I know? Breakfast time, I assume."

The lump moved some more and a pair of feet and legs emerged from under the covers and slowly made contact with the floor.

"I miss my morning shower."

"So do I, but you'll have to make do. There's a jug and basin over there with cold water in, so splash some on your face and get dressed. Where's your razor?"

"Second drawer down, under my shorts. Uncle Conn?"

"Yes?"

"What we're trying to do, it is all going to be all right in the end, isn't it?"

"I believe so," Connor answered, not knowing whether it was or not.

◆

Breakfast was, by Belmont standards, almost casual. Silver heated servers were ranged along a sideboard in the dining room, bearing dishes containing scrambled eggs, bacon, sausages, kippers, mushrooms, tomatoes and something that Matt discovered were called devilled kidneys. He decided to give those a very wide berth, but tucked in heartily to everything else. Although James and Geoffrey were standing to attention in the dining room ready to help when needed, breakfast was very much a self-service affair, which Matt greatly appreciated. He took his heaped plate to the table and sat down next to his uncle, who had, Matt noted in some amusement, settled on a slice of toast and two slices of bacon.

"How on earth can you get that amount down you at this time of day without being sick?" Connor asked him.

"No probs," Matt replied, his mouth half-full of scrambled egg.

"In spite of that gong and me having to drag you out of bed, we still seem to be the first down," Connor said.

"I've told you before, one of these days I'm going to report you for cruelty, keeping on getting me up in the early hours."

"It's gone nine," Connor told him, glancing at the longcase clock in the corner of the room.

"Exactly my point. Anyway, where is everyone?"

"I've no idea. James?" he called, the butler walking over see what he required. "What time does everyone come down to breakfast in the morning?"

"The rest of the family have already breakfasted, sir," James told him, "except for madam who rarely partakes of anything in the morning. Miss Helen, Master Charles and Miss Mary-Anne are with their tutors. Madam is in the morning room answering her mail."

"Thank you, James. Now what was that you were saying about having to get up early, Matt? Everyone else has been up for ages, it seems."

"Rats. That means I won't get to see Helen until her tutor lets her out."

"Well, instead you can help me with the cataloguing."

"You still going ahead with that? I'd have thought that . . ." Matt stopped suddenly, keenly aware of the warning look that Connor had given him. "I meant I thought you'd finished it."

"Almost, but not quite. Another few hours should see it completed. So, are you going to give me a hand or do you want to wander off and explore somewhere?"

"No, I'll help out this morning. I haven't got anything else to do."

Once breakfast was over, Connor retrieved his file from his room and continued his cataloguing of the art works in the house. It was, he realised, a total waste of time, as the entire collection would be destroyed in a few days' time. He needed to preserve his cover story though, so continued with his useless task. He'd completed all the more important items and was now working through a large cabinet, the drawers of which were full of engravings and prints, mostly copies of old masters. By late morning Connor decided he'd had more than enough and put his pen and papers down.

"If I see another print of the Madonna and Child with Saints, I think I'll probably scream," he told Matt.

"Suits me," Matt replied, having become almost terminally

bored within half an hour of starting that morning, "but I thought you liked this sort of thing, especially Italian paintings."

"I do, although I'm much less keen on prints and engravings. Apart from anything else, most of them are in black and white, and it's the colour that brings the originals to life. But even the original paintings can become rather tedious if the subject matter never varies. I strongly suspect that most Italian artists before the Renaissance worked on a rota system. I think they would get up in the morning and say to themselves: 'Ah, it's Tuesday. I must paint a Madonna and Child with St Sebastian today.' If it was Wednesday it would probably be a Madonna and Child with St John or something."

"Seriously?"

"No, but that's what it seems like sometimes. Anyway, I've had enough. It must be about time for Helen and the others to be finishing their lessons for the day, wouldn't you think?"

"I hope so."

"Are you sure you're not getting in over your head?" Connor asked, noting the enthusiasm in Matt's voice.

"'Course not. I'm fine. Everything's cool," Matt lied.

◆

Finding that Helen was still ensconced at her studies, Matt ventured down into the cavernous kitchens in search of the cook. Once he'd explained himself and what he wanted he was introduced to a plump, rosy-cheeked woman with an infectious laugh.

"Helen told me that you like trying out new recipes and ideas, ma'am," Matt said.

This ensured another outburst of laughter, which Matt joined in with, even though he didn't have a clue why she was laughing.

"You'm bain't be 'aving to call me 'ma'am', me 'andsome," she eventually managed to say, stifling her laughter with difficulty. "Hannah's me name, so you'm call me that."

"Sorry, Hannah."

"Oh, don' you go apologisin', young zur. I bain't bin called ma'am afore an' I likes it. But it's for real ladies, not for the likes o' us down yer."

Looking around him, Matt could see that the kitchen was large with high ceilings and high-level windows.

"Why are the windows so high up?" he asked. "You can't see anything out of them."

"That's so as they upstairs can't see uz working, and uz can't see they when they'm out walking," Hannah told him. "Now, young zur, what be this new dish you'm wanting uz to try out?"

"Have you got any beef?"

She laughed again, and opened one of the doors leading off the main kitchen. It revealed a meat store, with large joints of beef hanging off hooks from the roof beams.

"'Ow much beef does young zur need?"

"Not as much as that," he answered with a grin. "But it will also need onions, some herbs, tomatoes, cheese and potatoes. Plus some flour and a couple of eggs. Oh, and some bread rolls — large round ones if possible."

Finding that the larders contained copious amounts of everything that was needed, plus being told that they baked their own bread, Matt gave Hannah a detailed description of what he wanted. By the time he'd found his way back upstairs again, still marvelling at the warren of rooms and passages that constituted the 'below stairs' area of Belmont, he discovered that lessons were over.

"It's very warm again, Matt, even though it's somewhat overcast," Helen said when they eventually found each other. "I feel like some fresh air before luncheon. It has been a rather trying morning."

"Some fresh air would suit me fine. Why was your morning trying?"

"Miss Fossett was testing me on my French grammar. I regret that my mind was elsewhere and I believe my answers rather vexed her."

"So where was your mind if not on your lessons?"

"On why Mama seems so preoccupied of late."

"Oh," Matt replied, having hoped that her mind had been on him. "You think your mother is worried about something? She doesn't appear worried to me."

"No-one who didn't know Mama extremely well would notice, but I believe that she is concerned about something."

"Have you asked her about it?"

"I have tried to bring the matter up from time to time, but Mama always tells me there's nothing wrong."

Matt didn't know what to say. He knew that Mrs Debbon had every reason to be worried. From what he'd overheard at the Grand Hotel, he knew that some sort of attempt to spirit Charles away to France was to be made that very night.

"Still, perhaps I am worrying about nothing," Helen told him. "Where do you think we should go for a stroll?"

"Do you think your mother would appreciate another bunch of primroses," Matt asked. "We could go to that field you took me to the other day and collect some more."

"What a splendid idea," she said, "I will just go and collect my coat in case it turns chilly."

◆

Matt, lying on his back in the long grass, decided that he'd never been happier. It was a strange feeling, he thought. Here he was, long before he'd even been born, lying in a field with the most beautiful girl he'd ever seen lying by his side and with whom he'd fallen deeply in love. He'd tried hard not to and he knew his uncle was right to tell him not to get too involved, but it hadn't helped. He was in love and that was that. The future didn't feature in his thoughts. For that day he would live for the here and now and worry about what was going to happen some other time. He felt an insect tickling his ear and he absent-mindedly brushed it away. It tickled him again and he propped himself up on one elbow to find Helen tickling him with a piece of long grass.

"I believe that you had no intention of picking any primroses," she admonished him. "I believe that you brought me here under false pretences. You should be ashamed of yourself."

"As I recall," he answered with a grin, "we didn't collect many primroses the first time either — and coming here was your idea that time."

"I think that perhaps we should collect a few more flowers this time. Mama can detect an indiscretion from at least half a mile away. And I think we should be getting back anyway as it must be getting close to time for luncheon to be served. You don't happen to have a pocket watch, do you?"

"Sure," Matt said, diving into his pocket and producing his watch. "We'll have to hurry though", he told her, glancing at the display, "the gong will be going in about ten minutes or so."

He suddenly realised that Helen was staring at him, or rather at what he held in his hand. He mentally cursed himself for his stupidity, but could hardly put the digital watch back in his pocket and say nothing now Helen had seen it.

"What is that?" she asked. "I've never seen anything like it."

"Um — it's a new type of watch. My dad bought it for me for my birthday."

"May I see it?"

"Of course," he replied, reluctantly handing the watch over.

"But where are the hands? And how do you know what time it is?"

"It doesn't have hands, it has the time in numbers. See here, on the display, it's reading 12.40."

"That's amazing. I've never seen anything like that before."

Nor has anyone else in this age, Matt thought.

"Dad says he thinks they'll replace ordinary watches eventually. But for now we need to get a move on. We don't want to be late."

"We most certainly do not. But I really must collect a few blooms first," she told him, hastily picking some primroses and gathering them together. "There. Now at least it won't be a lie when I tell Mama what we have been doing."

It won't be the truth either, Matt thought. He wondered what her mother would say if she knew just how passionately he had been kissing her daughter — and just how passionately those kisses had been returned. What little knowledge Matt had of the late nineteenth century had come mainly from films and television and they had all seemed to suggest that young people would share a demure peck on the cheek before they were married and not a lot more afterwards. He wondered if Helen was a rare exception, or if Victorians were a lot more adventurous than was often made out. He strongly suspected that it was the latter.

Fleet Street.

CHAPTER TWENTY-ONE

A violent encounter

Lunch came and went. The afternoon was warm but sultry and several times they heard the distant rumble of thunder. Matt and Helen walked along the lane to Barton Hall to check that it was all right for Matt to keep his borrowed evening suit for a few more days. As Helen had hoped, Mr Brown not only agreed with a wave of his hand, he'd also eagerly invited them to another run in his car. This time they'd headed down into Torquay and along into neighbouring Paignton, Matt being somewhat surprised by the sight of a large gasworks belching smoke and fumes halfway between the two towns. In his own time the site was a peaceful park and he hadn't realised the gasworks had ever existed. Mr Brown dropped them back at Belmont and Matt went in search of his uncle.

"As you've been gone for ages, I assume that you haven't just been to Barton Hall and back?" Connor asked.

"Nope. Mr Brown took us for another car ride — to Paignton this time. Did you know that there used to be a gasworks where the gardens are now?"

"Of course. I can remember the gardens being laid out. Those big round beds are the bases of the old gas holders."

"I never knew that."

"The gasworks went long before you were born, that's why. Any idea what you're going to do for the rest of the afternoon?"

"Not really. You?"

"Mrs Debbon likes her afternoon rest. I was thinking of following her example. I'm dead-beat."

"You might want to wait a bit, then."

"Why?"

"Listen."

"Oh, hell!" Connor said, as he realised that the high-pitched whine had started up again. "Of all the times to choose, it decides we should flip now."

"It could be worse, we could be in the middle of dinner."

"I suppose you're right. Go and grab your shaver, then let's get moving."

"My shaver? What do I need that for?"

"You don't, I do. It needs charging."

"A beard might suit you. They say that older people wear them better than younger ones."

"This older person is about to kick you in the rear end. Move!"

They managed to leave the house without any of the servants seeing them and headed for the lane. This time the pain was so intense that they both blacked out. When they eventually recovered enough to get to their feet, they staggered the short distance back to Matt's house. Neither of them felt like mentioning the sounds of screaming that had accompanied their flip forward in time.

"I think we've a couple of hours at best," Connor eventually said, when he'd recovered enough to speak, "so we'd best get busy. You phone your parents, I'll phone your college."

"College? Why?"

"Because you've been missing for several days and will be missing for several more. You don't want someone from the college coming up here to look for you, then contacting your parents when they can't find you."

"I hadn't thought of that."

"Nor had I until just now," Connor admitted. "Anyway, I'll tell them that you've got some bug or other and are likely to be off until next week. You try to think up some excuse why you haven't been in touch with your mum and dad."

"Already have. I'm going to say that I've got so much revision to do that I've turned my phone off so as not to be disturbed."

"You never turn your phone off. You really think they'll go for that?"

"No idea. It's the best I can come up with though. I thought I'd say it was your idea and I went along with it for a quiet life."

"Good luck!"

Connor had no trouble in persuading the college that Matt needed time off, but almost panicked when they said that they would send someone round with revision notes and homework tests so that Matt could keep up with his work. He managed to forestall them by saying that he would go and collect it instead. By the time he'd sorted things out, Matt had come back into the room from phoning his parents.

"How'd it go?" asked Connor.

"All right, I suppose. Mum thinks I must be sickening for something, as I never turn my phone off. She doesn't believe I even know where the off button is."

"She's right. Anyway, that's a good opener she's given you."

"Huh?"

"I've just told your college that you're ill. No problem there, other than I've got to drive over there to pick up some work for you."

"What! Why on earth did you suggest that?"

"I didn't. They were going to send someone over with it. Anyway, your parents are bound to find out that you've missed college while they've been away, so I reckon we'll have to go with the idea of you being ill. We have to say that we didn't tell them as we didn't want them to worry and come rushing back from holiday.'

"They wouldn't have done that."

"Yes they would."

"You're right, they would," Matt agreed after giving it some thought.

"Anyhow, I've got to drive over to the college. While I've gone, you have a think to see if there's anything that we could take back with us when we flip that might be handy."

"Machine-gun?"

"Little bulky to go in your pocket. Give it some thought and I'll see you later."

"Uncle Conn?"

"What?"

"Shouldn't you change clothes first? You've got your 1898 suit on."

"Sod it, so I have. I'd better nip and change," he said, making for the stairs.

Minutes later he left the house and Matt listened as Connor's car coughed and spluttered its way along the lane. Now what on earth, Matt thought, can I find here that will be of any use at all against a group of thugs and murderers, albeit 1898 ones. He rummaged through his drawers and cupboards and came up with precisely nothing. He suddenly thought of something and went into his parent's room. A quick hunt in one of the drawers produced a wicked looking knife that he'd bought his dad as a present the previous year. The blade was still sharp but whether he could bring himself to use it on someone he didn't know.

Three-quarters of an hour later a serious wheezing in the lane told him that Connor's car had returned. Moments later, Connor staggered into the house, his arms loaded down with textbooks.

"If you think I'm carting that lot back to 1898 with me you can think again," Matt told him, taking some of the books off him.

"Wasn't my idea. The college seems to think that you're lying in bed with nothing to do. Besides, as you said yourself, you've got exams coming up. How about just taking the ones in the subjects that you're weakest in?"

"Could do, I suppose," came the reply, Matt's voice ringing with a total lack of enthusiasm.

"What are your weakest subjects anyway?"

"Geography and English."

"Well, just take those."

"OK. What were your weakest subjects at college? If you can remember that far back that is."

"Science," Connor said, ignoring the insult. "As far as I was concerned, my knowledge of science boiled down to the fact that if it wriggled, it was biology, if it smelled rotten then it was chemistry, and if it was meant to work but didn't, then it was physics."

"So no good asking for any help in those subjects?"

"No good at all. However, English was always my best subject so I can perhaps help out there if . . . what on earth is that noise?"

"What noise?"

"*That* noise, the one that sounds like someone yelling."

Matt got up and looked out of the window.

"It's Bill. He's outside chasing Charles round the garden."

"We're off again then. I'd better get changed and grab what we need. Did you find anything, by the way?"

"A knife. Couldn't think of anything else."

"That's one up on me because I couldn't think of anything at all. It might be of some help later when they try and take Charles. You didn't manage to get any idea of what time tonight it was likely to be, did you? "

"No. I just heard them say it would be tonight. At least we'll be back there by then. If we'd have flipped later we might not have been there when they tried. You think this is the last time we'll flip before the fire?"

"I'd guess so."

"Certain?"

"No, just a hunch."

◆

"I'm beginning to feel more at home in my 1898 clobber than I do in my own stuff," Matt told Connor as they walked along the drive a few minutes later.

"Same here. You got your college books with you?"

"No. I decided there's no point. There's no way I'm going to be able to study and even if I did I'd need to take all my coursework as well. I wouldn't be able to keep it all out of sight."

"Sounds suspiciously like an excuse, but I suppose you're right. You got that knife somewhere safe though?"

"Yes, in my side pocket — and before you ask, yes, I've got the shaver and it's fully charged. Happy now?"

"No, but as near as I'm going to get until this whole business is over."

"How come you're so fussy about shaving all of a sudden? I

thought you didn't bother at weekends and suchlike."

"I don't want Mrs Debbon getting the wrong impression."

"If I didn't know better I'd say you'd got the hots for her."

Connor didn't answer, causing Matt to burst out laughing.

"I'm right, aren't I? You go on and on at me about getting involved with Helen and all the time you're going all gooey-eyed over her mother!"

Before Connor could find something cutting to say in reply they both felt the now familiar sensation as if the ground had suddenly lurched under them and they were back in 1898.

"We've only been gone a couple of hours, so if we've been missed we'll just say we fancied a walk."

"Fine with me."

"But where 'ave yer *really* bin?" came a voice from behind the nearest shrub.

"Bill?" Connor asked.

"*Course* it's me, 'oo was yer expectin'?" Bill answered, emerging from the shelter of the greenery.

"Didn't anyone ever tell you it's not good manners to spy on people?" Matt said.

"Course, but I ignores 'em. Anyways, I needs ter know wot's goin' on. I see's you two leave the 'ouse earlier an' walk inter the lane, then, whoosh, yer both gone. Where'd yer go?"

"We just went for a walk. We cut through the hedge at the side of the lane, then across the field."

"No, yer did'n. Yer jus' vanished. Then, two minnits ago, yer jus' comes back. Yer not 'ere, then all of a sudden, yer are 'ere. It ain't right."

Connor had no idea how to answer and mentally kicked himself for not remembering that Bill spent much of his time watching the house and was bound to see them flip sooner or later.

"Bill," he said, coming to a decision. "You know that Mrs Debbon has invited us to stay for a few days?"

"Course I knows. Mary-Anne tol' me."

"Fine. Well, the reason we've been asked to stay is that the family is in a lot of trouble and she's asked us to help."

"Yeah — so?"

"So the fact that Matt and I can both seem to disappear is part of how we're helping. You're right of course, we haven't just been for a walk, we've been trying to find ways to help them, and we'd rather people didn't know too much about where we go and what we do. That's why we just seem to vanish. We've both been trained in how to sort of blend in with the scenery, so that people don't follow us. If you're not expecting it, it must look as if we've suddenly vanished, but that's not possible, is it?"

"No, s'pose not. But wot sort o' trouble is they in?"

"It's very complicated, Bill, we don't know all the answers ourselves yet."

"'Ow can I 'elp?"

"You?"

"Course me! I already tol' yer, I looks out fer the family, seein' as 'ow they ain't got no man abaht the place."

"Yes, so you did. Well, there is one way you can help. Whenever you're watching the house, can you keep a note of any strangers that call, or if anyone that you don't know takes an interest in the house or the family?"

"Yer means like them wot 'ides in the woods ev'ry day?"

Two pairs of eyes turned towards him.

"Like who that hides in the woods every day?"

"The two or free wots bin watchin' the 'ouse for weeks. Sometimes they's together, sometimes they's on their own."

"Have you told anyone about this?"

"Nah."

"Why not?"

"Cos they's so bleedin' obvious, I fort Mrs Debbon must 'ave asked 'em to watch the place."

Connor stared at the boy, and then turned to Matt.

"We should have known this — you remember we saw the Marquis a few nights ago when he left the house late at night. He signalled to someone."

"Yes, he did, but I'd forgotten until now. We should tell Mrs

Debbon about this," Matt said.

"Agreed," Connor said. "You come with us, Bill, this needs sorting out."

As they got near to the front door, Bill's face took on a look of alarm.

"Whatever's the matter, no-one's going to eat you."

"But I ain't never bin in the front door afore. I allus 'as ter go in by the kitchen. I ain't allowed upstairs."

"This time you are," Connor told him, and hauled him, still protesting, through the front door and into the hall.

Bill's jaw dropped as he came face to face with the magnificence of the entrance hall, his eyes flitting from one treasure to another.

"Cor, it mus' be better'n Buckin'ham Palace!"

At the sound of voices in the hall, James emerged from one of the rooms, a slight frown creasing his brow as he saw Bill.

"If you'll pardon the liberty of my saying so, sir, I don't think madam will approve of young Master Stone being in this part of the house. She normally insists that he stay below stairs."

"I understand, James, but Bill has some information that I'm sure Mrs Debbon will want to hear. Is she still resting, or is she in the drawing room?"

"Madam is in the drawing room, sir."

"Thank you. Come on, Bill, it's through here."

If Mrs Debbon was surprised at Bill's appearance in the drawing room, she showed no sign of it.

"It weren't my idea, missus," Bill blurted out, before anyone had a chance to say anything. "I tol' 'em I weren't allowed in 'ere."

"As he says," Connor agreed, "it wasn't his idea. I invited him to come in as he has some news that you ought to hear straight away."

"You make it sound very serious, Mr Harvey."

"I think it is. Apparently the house is being watched, and has been so every day and night for several weeks, if not months."

"Watched? How?"

"Bill has seen people hiding in the woods. Go on, Bill, tell Mrs

Debbon what you've seen."

"Well, it's like 'e says, missus. There's two blokes an' a woman. They climes over the wall an' 'ides in the woods. Sometimes there's jus' one of 'em, sometimes there's two."

"And what do they do?" Mrs Debbon asked.

"Nuffin', they jus' watches the 'ouse and anyone wot calls."

"And this has been going on for some time?"

"Course."

"But why have you never mentioned it before?"

"Not his fault," Connor interrupted. "He thought that as they were, in his opinion at any rate, being so obvious about it, he just assumed that everyone already knew. He thought that perhaps you'd hired them to keep an eye on the place."

"I see."

"I believe that this also confirms what I've been trying to tell you."

"Perhaps. William," she said, turning to the ill-at-ease boy, "I owe you thanks for your help."

"T'wern't nuffin', missus. Only doin' me job — lookin' aht fer yer all."

"I see. Nevertheless, I am most grateful. I will ask James to arrange for you to be taken down to the kitchen so that you can have a decent meal."

"Cor, fanks. I ain't 'ad much ter eat terday."

"I'll take him," Matt said. "No need to send for James."

"As you wish."

Once Matt had left with an excited Bill in tow, Connor returned to his task of trying to persuade Mrs Debbon of the seriousness of her and her family's situation.

"As I said, you must now see that this confirms all my fears — that you are in great danger."

"I'm not sure that I agree. Although I was unaware that we had visitors in the woods, it is not really surprising that we are being watched. Those who wish to proclaim my son King will want to know if we have unexpected visitors. No doubt your own arrival will have caused them some concern. If they realise that you work for the British Government, it may well cause them to stay their hand."

Connor started to wonder if there was anything at all that could shake her Olympian calm. He seriously doubted it.

Those who wait and watch from the shadows of the trees have indeed noted that the man and the youth, whose names they are aware of, are now staying at Belmont. They weigh up whether this will be a problem or not but decide that if that night's visit does not go the way that the Marquis hopes, then the fire that they intend to set later will remove five people as easily as it will three. They will not change their plans. The man and the youth are expendable. As all are who are not vital to their plans. Their goal is in sight and nothing, absolutely nothing, will be permitted to get in the way. In less than a week, France will be a monarchy again.

◆

"Matt has got Hannah to cook something different," Helen informed her mother when they were seated at the dinner table. "He says it's a speciality where he and Mr Harvey come from."

"Really? Then I look forward to trying it. What do you call it?"

"Cheeseburger and chips," Matt said.

"How interesting. And what are the ingredients?"

"Mainly minced beef, onions, cheese and potatoes."

"And this is something that you eat regularly where you come from?" she asked, looking towards Connor.

"It tends to be a dish favoured by the young," he said. "There are cafés that specialise in them."

"You mean that there are restaurants that cater for young people?" asked Charles.

"When you say young people, Mr Harvey, how young do you mean?" added Mary-Anne.

"Any age, young lady," Connor replied.

"Like our age?" asked an incredulous Charles.

"Oh yes."

"I have never seen catering establishments such as those you mention, Mr Harvey? Are they localised in certain areas?" Mrs Debbon asked, her tone of voice indicating that she thought such an idea to be verging on heresy.

"It's an experimental idea in Warwickshire," he told her, cursing himself for not having thought the matter through before opening his mouth and mentally kicking Matt for not telling him they were having cheeseburgers for dinner.

"I am not at all certain I approve of the idea at all. However, I am certain that the experiment will be a failure. The idea of restaurants catering for young people will never become popular, I'm sure. I must admit though that this dish is rather tasty."

Matt, watching Mrs Debbon cutting her cheeseburger into dainty portions with a silver knife and fork, suddenly found himself trying to control an outbreak of giggles. He managed to stifle his laughter and concentrated on trying to eat his meal in a manner that wouldn't offend his host, even though he had to fight the urge to pick up his cheeseburger in his hand and take a large bite out of it. He decided that although it might be acceptable to introduce a modern dish to a Victorian household, it most certainly wouldn't be acceptable to introduce the same era's rather relaxed attitude to eating it. So, fingers were out and silver knives and forks (plus fine linen napkins and crystal finger bowls) were in.

◆

"That was a most interesting dish, Matt," Helen said, as they relaxed in the drawing room, the younger children having been escorted off to bed by their nurse. "Have you eaten it often?"

"Oh yes. It's one of my favourites."

"And in the restaurants that your uncle spoke of?"

"Yes."

"I am beginning to think that one day I should visit Warwickshire. It sounds a most adventurous county."

Matt, who had visited the county on three occasions only, when he was taking part in athletic competitions with his college, decided that a conversation about a place where he was supposed to live but knew little or nothing about was likely to prove difficult. He managed to change the subject without it appearing obvious. He glanced over to where Connor was deep in conversation with Mrs Debbon. He'd only been joking when he'd told his uncle that he thought he'd fallen for Mrs Debbon, but he'd evidently hit the nail on the head. He really couldn't blame him. She was a very beautiful woman and his uncle deserved some happiness in his life. Which, he reminded himself, was going to be destroyed in a couple of days if something didn't start to go their way very soon. A crushing depression settled on him and it was all he could do to appear bright and happy and pay attention to what Helen was saying to him.

◆

Later that evening, after the family had retired for the night, Connor and Matt held a conference in Matt's room.

"We've no idea what time things are going to kick off this evening but I'd guess it won't be too late."

"Why not? Wouldn't late at night suit them better when everyone's asleep?"

"I don't think so. Didn't you say that they were going to make a last attempt to persuade Mrs Debbon to agree?"

"Yes. The Marquis and someone the others called the Count will be here tonight. There's also a Countess but she's going to be doing something else, I think. I don't know what."

"It doesn't matter. What I'm saying is that if they're going to try to make Mrs Debbon change her mind, then they'll need to do so before she goes to bed."

"Hasn't she already gone?"

"She's gone to her room, but she mentioned that she always reads for a while before getting ready for bed. She'll still be up at the moment."

"So we stay awake and listen for trouble?"

"Can't think what else to suggest."

Matt lay down on his bed and was asleep within seconds. Connor settled himself in an armchair. His mind was awhirl with a stream of disconnected thoughts and he found it hard to concentrate on any one thing. There was something nagging him, something that had just been said, but he couldn't quite grasp what it was. He knew it was important, but it still eluded him, dancing around at the corners of his mind without ever quite coming into sight. He envied his nephew's ability to sleep anywhere and anytime. For himself, he often found sleep hard to come by. Even when his body cried out for sleep, his mind wouldn't let it. He would find himself staring at the ceiling, tears coursing down his face, wanting Laura so badly that it was physically painful. He missed her so much. Friends had often suggest he get some tablets from the doctor, but he wasn't about to go down that road again. The temptation to take more than he should would always be there and he might not always be able to resist it. He'd rather have sleepless nights than that.

His thoughts were interrupted by the sound of raised voices. He rose and opened the bedroom door, listening intently. He couldn't quite make out who they belonged to or what they were saying, only that the voices — and there were several of them — were angry. He padded back to the bed and shook Matt awake.

"I think we're on, Matt. Sounds like trouble."

"What sort of trouble," Matt asked, getting up off the bed.

"Not sure. There's shouting coming from the entrance hall."

They made their way along the corridor to the gallery, where Connor put his hand on Matt's shoulder and indicated that they should keep quiet. Matt nodded and they both carefully peered over the gallery railing and looked down. Mrs Debbon and Helen were both there, together with the Marquis and the man that Matt recognised as the one the others called the Count. As they looked down on the unfolding scene, it suddenly came to Connor what had been bothering him, what it was that he'd been trying to latch onto but couldn't. For those who visited at night to know that Mrs Debbon did not go to bed as soon as she had retired for the night, they must have had inside knowledge. Someone inside the house must be working for the kidnappers. And it must have been him, or her, who had opened the front door to let the two men in that night because the door had been locked and bolted earlier. Connor had checked before he went upstairs to his room. Now wasn't the time to be worrying about it but to store it up for later use.

"How dare you enter this house uninvited!" Mrs Debbon stormed. "You have had my answer, now leave at once!"

"You have had your last chance," the Count said. "We can no longer afford the luxury of waiting for you to see sense. The boy comes with us — tonight."

"Never!"

"Who *are* these men, Mama?" Helen asked in a frightened voice. "What do they want?"

"What they cannot have."

"France needs you," the Marquis said. "You have a duty to your country."

"France does not need me. *You* need me, or at least you need my son. What France needs is stability, something that she will not achieve if you and the other lunatics in this plot try to proclaim my son as King."

"The people will rally to the call. There will be a new era in France."

"There will be civil war! I will not permit it."

"You no longer have a choice," the Count snarled.

He stepped forward, put his arm around Helen's neck and with his free hand produced a vicious looking knife.

"Tell us where the boy is. We have no more time for pleasantries. The time has come for action."

"Monsters!" Mrs Debbon gasped, watching as Helen struggled vainly against her captor.

"Where is the boy? I will not ask again."

Up in the gallery Connor tried desperately to think of what to do. He turned to Matt, only to find he was no longer by his side but had positioned himself at the top of the stairs, the backs of the two intruders towards him. Connor wanted to tell him, implore him, to be careful, not to act rashly, but he was too far away and he dare not risk a shout.

"I warn you, I am not a patient man. My colleagues have insisted all along that we should observe the formalities, that in the end you would see the wisdom of our plan. I have always believed they were wrong, that you were a foolish and obstinate woman who cannot see the inevitability of what must happen."

"All I see is the representative of a dead institution, whose only recourse is to threaten the life of an innocent girl."

"I think perhaps you need a lesson to show you I mean what I say. I think perhaps I should put some scars on this girl's beautiful face, so that every time you look at her you will be reminded of your own stupidity."

He raised the knife with the intention of drawing the blade across Helen's face, but he never got the chance. He looked down in some surprise at his left arm, the one around Helen's throat. A knife blade was embedded several inches deep into the flesh. By the time he'd realised what it was, the pain had started to register. Helen screamed and managed to break free; at the same time Matt was charging full-tilt down the stairs, Connor not far behind him. Their plan having suddenly gone sour, the Marquis grabbed his wounded colleague and dragged him towards the door. Matt went straight to Helen, Connor to Mrs Debbon. A door slammed, feet could be heard running along the corridor that led from the servants' wing and James burst into the hall, dressed only in his trousers.

"Stop them, James, if you can," Mrs Debbon shouted.

James didn't waste time answering, just threw himself across the room at the Marquis. The two of them grappled but a right hook from the Marquis knocked the butler to the floor. The two intruders made it to the door and out into the darkness. James picked himself up from the floor and made to go after them but Connor stopped him with a shout.

"No! Don't go out there! There may be more than just the two."

The butler nodded his agreement, closing the front door and bolting it before walking over to where the four of them were huddled together at the foot of the stairs, Matt holding a weeping

Helen and Connor trying to comfort her badly shaken mother.

"I heard a commotion from my room," James said. "I will send for the constabulary immediately, madam. Should I also send for a doctor?"

"No, James, thank you. No doctor and no police."

"You do not wish the constabulary to be called?" he asked, puzzlement apparent in his voice.

"No. Later perhaps, but not yet," Mrs Debbon informed him.

"May I ask what has happened, madam?"

"I will explain later, James. For now, I must think what should be done for the best. My thanks to you, James, for your actions tonight. I trust that you have not been too badly hurt?"

"I believe I will be sporting a black eye in the morning, madam, but that is the limit of my injuries."

"We will pretend not to notice it," she told him, smiling in spite of herself. "Go back to bed, James. We will discuss this further in the morning."

"You are sure that there is nothing more I can do for you? Anything? A glass of brandy perhaps?"

"Nothing, thank you. Good night, James."

"Good night, madam."

Once James had left, a tearful Helen looked at her mother.

"Who were those men, Mama? I've seen one of them before and what is this plan that you won't agree to? And what was that about Charles being proclaimed King?"

"It seems I must tell you something that I had hoped would never have to be revealed, but it is late and I am very tired. It will have to wait until the morning."

"Those men, they won't come back?"

"No, my dear, not tonight. James has bolted the front door. As you are well aware, once all the doors and windows are locked, no-one can enter this house without our permission."

Connor wondered when it was going to occur to Mrs Debbon to ask herself how the two intruders had managed to gain access to the house in the first place, but kept his thoughts to himself. The morning would be soon enough.

"It seems that I am in your debt again, gentlemen," Mrs Debbon told Connor and Matt. "Your arrival on the scene was most fortuitous. I assume that it was one of you who threw the knife at that monster?"

"It was Matt," Connor told her.

"Your aim is excellent."

"Thanks. Dad taught me years ago. He's into that sort of thing."

"I see. Well, his training has certainly paid off tonight." She tapped her fingers slowly on the nearest table before realising what she was doing. She frowned at her hand as if it had committed a serious breach of etiquette and the hand returned, rather guiltily Connor considered, to its accustomed place. Connor decided that this was probably Mrs Debbon's equivalent of having hysterics. "It seems," she continued, "that I have seriously misjudged this entire situation. However, the morning will be soon enough to decide what to do. Come, Helen, let me help you back to your room. Meanwhile, I will bid you two gentlemen goodnight."

She was rapidly regaining her composure and by the time she had her arm around Helen's shoulder and was slowly helping the completely confused young lady upstairs, Mrs Debbon was back to her usual unruffled self.

◆

"She was right about that knife act, Matt," Connor said as they returned to their rooms. "That was some cool shot, getting it right in his arm like that. Absolutely spot on."

"Don't tell anyone, but I was aiming for the middle of his back."

"Well, I won't say anything if you don't," Connor laughed. "Mrs Debbon is well pleased with you. I'd guess you're her favourite young man right now."

"I'd rather be Helen's favourite young man."

"I strongly suspect you're that as well. I take it my advice not too get too much involved has fallen on stone deaf ears?"

"I'm trying, I really am. Every time we're apart I tell myself to cool it, that I'm not here for long, that there's no future in a relationship, and so on. But then, when I'm with her, all my good intentions go out of the window."

They reached the doors to their rooms, but as Matt was opening his, Connor held him back for a moment.

"Something for you to think about, if you're really serious about trying to calm things down between the two of you."

"Yes?"

"If Charles is the King of France, albeit uncrowned and unrecognised, then that makes Helen a genuine, one hundred per cent Princess."

"It does?"

"Of course it does. I'm not absolutely certain what the official title of the eldest daughter of the French Royal Family was, but I think it was something like 'Madame Royale'. The nearest equivalent at home would be 'The Princess Royal'. By rights, you ought to start any conversation with her by calling her 'Your Royal Highness' and bowing."

"I hadn't thought of that."

"Get some sleep, Matt, if you can. It's been quite an evening. With a bit of luck, we may be able to turn this to our advantage."

"How?"

"Because Mrs Debbon must now see how serious this business is and do something about it, instead of sticking her head in the sand."

"I hope you're right."

Matt went into his room and collapsed full-length on the bed. He stared at the ceiling, his mind in turmoil. He tried to imagine Helen as a princess, someone who was way out of his reach, but every time his thoughts settled on how she'd returned his embraces and kisses in the garden earlier that evening. He thought of her smile, of the way the gaslight had glinted in the gold of her hair, of the way that the candlelight reflected off the soft sheen of her skin. Beyond his reach? No, he didn't think so. In fact, he knew that she was well within his reach if he wanted. And there, of course, was the problem. Because he *did* want, very badly indeed. This whole thing, he thought to himself, was getting very very complicated. He eventually drifted off into a troubled sleep.

Connor's sleep was no less troubled. Images of Mrs Debbon became merged with those of his late wife to produce a dream that was dark and disturbing. It was also powerfully erotic. He slept fitfully until the morning sun woke him.

Union Street.

Maria and Connor

Connor and Matt were both up and dressed well before the breakfast gong sounded the next morning, Connor having woken the sleeping teenager half an hour earlier.

"I need to talk to you before we go downstairs," Connor said, in response to Matt's enquiry why he'd been dragged from bed again. "So how did they get in?"

"Huh?"

"The two men last night. Belmont is supposed to be a fortress. Once it's locked up, no-one gets in or out."

"Right."

"So — how did they get in?"

"How should I know? Someone must have let them in, I suppose."

"Exactly. They were let in. That means those people who are keeping watch outside aren't on their own. They get help. Someone here in the house is working for them, letting them know everything that happens."

"Oh, rat farts," Matt groaned. "I think I know who it is. It's Edward, the coachman."

"What on earth makes you think that?"

"You remember that day we all went to Anstey's Cove, the day Charles went missing? Edward gave me a story about how he was going to see his lady friend and didn't know Charles was in his coach. I didn't say anything as he said he'd lose his job and then he wouldn't be able to get married."

"And you believed him?"

"It seemed so plausible at the time, especially when Charles told me that he'd climbed into the coach all by himself. Now I don't know what to think. I'd forgotten about it, but now we're sure someone on the inside is passing on information he's by far the most likely. I'm sorry, I should have said something before."

"Don't beat yourself up over it. Anything else you know about him?"

"No, nothing. He seemed so genuine, though."

"The most clever and devious people usually do. That's how they work. Anyway, we'll know to keep an eye on him."

"Should we tell Mrs Debbon?"

"Eventually, but not just at the moment. I think we need to find out more about him first. Plus we don't want to scare him off."

◆

The breakfast gong eventually sounded, rather later than the previous day, Connor noted. They made their way to the dining room where they found a very embarrassed James trying to apologise to Mrs Debbon, who was calmly refusing to accept that there was anything to apologise for.

"James, I will not say this again. The fact that you overslept a little this morning, and that therefore breakfast is a few minutes late being served, is of not the slightest consequence. I had not even expected you to be on duty today after your exertions of last night. And," she added, glancing at the butler's swollen eye and bruised face, "I repeat my opinion that we should call the doctor to attend to your injuries. I had not realised that you had been so badly hurt."

She allowed a few more spluttered apologies before holding her hand up in an unmistakable gesture.

"Enough! It is my express wish that you go to your room and do not even attempt to return to your duties today. I will get the coachman to go down and collect the doctor. Now, not another word!"

Evidently conceding defeat, he stammered his thanks and, holding his hand to his eye, shuffled out of the room.

"Good morning, Mr Harvey, good morning, Matthew," she said, once the butler had left. "I trust you were able to sleep well in spite of last night's incident?"

The tone of her voice indicated that last night's incident was on a par with a gentle evening of cards, or perhaps a small dinner party. Connor began to wonder if anything short of a full-scale earthquake could shatter her calm.

"As well as possible," he replied, trying to consign the memories of the previous night's somewhat disturbing dream to the dustbin. "We do need to talk, though. You must now see that some sort of action must be taken. You cannot continue as you are."

"I agree. Geoffrey, would you please excuse us for a moment?" she said to the footman who was standing by the breakfast table. Once she was sure the footman had left the room and closed the door behind him, she turned back to Connor. "It seems that I have very seriously underestimated the depths of depravity to which one's fellow man will stoop. I will not make the same mistake again. I composed letters that I have sent by special messenger this morning. One is to His Royal Highness, the Prince of Wales in London; one is to the French Ambassador in London; and one is to President Faure in Paris. However, it will take some time for the messages to arrive and even longer for their recipients to act on them. In the meantime, we are vulnerable."

"I believe that is true."

"Mr Harvey, with your contacts in the government, are you not able to secure some more aid?"

Get yourself out of this one, Connor thought to himself. Having persuaded Mrs Debbon that he was some sort of government agent, he could hardly turn around now and say that he had no contacts whatsoever.

"I'm sorry, but it would take my messages just as long to reach the Foreign Office as yours will," he told her, thinking as quickly as he could. "For the time being, we are on our own."

"Not quite," she said. "James has shown himself to be quite the man of action. Would you be in agreement with asking for his help, without, of course, telling him the truth of what is happening?"

"Certainly. He could be a great help. Would you like us to go and have a word with him?"

"If you would be so kind. But please partake of breakfast first."

Matt had been looking round for Helen, but there was no sign of her, or of the younger children.

"I suppose you are wondering where Helen is, Matthew?" Mrs Debbon asked.

"Yes, ma'am. Is she OK?"

"I have heard you use that phrase before, Matthew, but am not at all certain of its meaning or its etymology. Is it a Warwickshire expression?"

"I believe it has an American origin," Connor interrupted. "If something is OK, then it's well, or good."

"How fascinating. I had not heard it before. Perhaps I should make use of it. However, to answer your question, Matthew: Helen is well. I explained the situation regarding Charles and why those monsters want to take him to Paris. I believe that the news has come as something as a shock and it will take her a little while for to come to terms with it. I have impressed on her that neither Charles nor Mary-Anne are to know of this. They are both aware that a rather distressing incident occurred last night, as the noise in the hall woke them both, so I gave instructions to Nurse to let them sleep in this morning and to inform their tutor that lessons are cancelled for a few days. I believe that the excitement of missing lessons for a while will soon take their minds off last night's events."

"Thank you," Matt said. "Will Helen be down later?"

"I believe she will make an appearance in a short while," she told the worried teenager before he wandered off to help himself to breakfast.

"Mr Harvey," she continued, "there is another matter that I would like to talk to you about. It seems to me, after everything that has happened, a little formal for you to continue calling me Mrs Debbon. I would take it very kindly if you would consent to calling me Maria."

"I would be honoured. And my own name, as you know, is

Connor."

"Thank you, Connor," she said, giving him a warm smile.

◆

James tried hard to appear unsurprised at the appearance of Connor and Matt at the door to his room in the servants' wing, but failed. His habitual deference didn't waver though, and he invited them in, albeit with a somewhat puzzled expression on his face and an apology for the untidy state of his room.

"Mrs Debbon has asked us to come and see if you would be willing to help us, and through us the family, in what is evidently fast becoming a very serious threat."

"My services, as always, are at madam's disposal," he replied, even though he was evidently completely mystified.

"This would be something far outside your normal duties and is not something that you should feel obliged to do."

"If there is anything at all that I can do to assist Mrs Debbon and her family I will do it, no matter what."

Matt glanced at Connor, wondering how his uncle was going to convey the seriousness of the situation without telling him who the night-time callers really were, or what they wanted.

"The family is in serious trouble, James, as you no doubt realise after last night. It seems that the late Mr Debbon entered into some unwise business ventures shortly before his death. One of those ventures failed about two years ago, leaving substantial debts. Some of the creditors are very unscrupulous characters and are really nothing more than thugs. Mrs Debbon's solicitors have looked at the relevant papers and told her that they have no legal claim on any part of the estate. The way the venture was set up as a limited company entailed the business itself being liable for any debts it may incur, so any remaining assets could be sold to help pay the creditors, but the actual investors themselves are not liable. However, some of the creditors are not easily put off. They have formulated a plan to kidnap young Charles and hold him to ransom until Mrs Debbon pays them what they think they are owed."

"I see. May I ask how you and young Mr Harvey come to be involved?"

"Purely by accident. We heard the noise in the hall last night as you did. Mrs Debbon explained to us this morning what it concerned and asked if there was anything we could do to help. She feels that she cannot go to the police for if the story were to get out it would reflect badly on her late husband's memory."

"You will forgive me, sir, if I find this whole business difficult to comprehend. There has never been even the slightest suggestion that the family has financial worries."

"Mrs Debbon has kept the whole matter to herself for some time. No-one else knew of it until last night. She has had to take Helen into her confidence along with Matthew and myself. But she feels that the thugs who were here last night may well try again before she has time to take further action against them and therefore she needs help."

"Any help I can give, I will do so of course. These thugs, you believe they will be back?"

"Yes, and probably quite soon. Certainly within a day or two, I would have thought. Mrs Debbon has sent letters to some very influential friends this morning and as soon as they receive them, then action will be taken which will stop any further trouble."

"Luckily, sir, this house was built to repel would-be intruders. Provided that the doors and windows are kept locked, then none may enter unless invited. There is plenty of food in the kitchens. I believe we can survive a short siege without too many problems."

"I would agree, James, but it would also seem that they have had inside help. I have a habit when at home of checking that all the doors are locked and the windows closed before I go to bed each evening. It is a routine I find hard to break, so before I retired last night I checked the front door myself. It was locked. Yet those two men entered that way."

"Someone opened the door for them?"

"So it would seem. But we believe we may know his identity. What do you know of Edward, the coachman?"

"I don't know that much about him, sir. He keeps himself to himself and tends not to socialise too much with the other servants. I know he came with good references, but I'm not sure that they were ever checked."

"Has he ever been in trouble?"

"Not really, or at least not for anything major. I've caught him a few times trying to sneak into the servants' quarters very late at night, when by rights he should have never been out in the first place."

"Did he say why?"

"He told me he'd been to see a lady friend in service in a house in Babbacombe."

"Same story he told me," Matt interrupted, "but he could have been seeing those people in the woods."

The butler's eyebrows twitched upwards in an unspoken question.

"There are two, or possibly three, people who regularly watch the house at night from the shelter of the woods to the side of the garden."

"Who are they?"

"We don't know for certain, but presumably they are part of the same gang as the two who were here last night. Possibly even the same people."

"How long has this been going on?"

"We're not certain, but we suspect for some time."

"I see. And you think, or at least suspect, that Edward is passing information to them?"

"Someone must be, and he seems the likeliest candidate."

There was silence while James digested this piece of information.

"Then, at the very least, we need to make sure that Edward is dealt with immediately. I assume that none of the other servants knows anything of this?"

"It would be better if they didn't."

"I understand, Mr Harvey. How many people know what has happened and are able to help?"

"Mrs Debbon, Helen, myself and Matthew. And now you."

"If I may be so bold as to say so, sir, it seems a very small number, given the seriousness of the situation. I presume that you do not know how many people this group can command?"

"No. At least four, if you include Edward, but there may well be more of course. In fact, I think that it is very likely that there are more involved."

"Then we must make the best of a very bad situation," James said, shrugging his shoulders slightly. "I regret that, to the best of my knowledge, there are no firearms in the house, but there are some swords that belonged to the late master. I suspect that they will be rather rusty by now, though. However, Cook has a variety of positively lethal looking knives in the kitchen. It might be prudent to arm ourselves with them."

"He's right," Matt agreed.

"How do we explain to the cook that some of her best carving knives have disappeared without telling her the truth?" Connor asked.

"At the moment, I've no idea, sir. I'll think of something. Whatever it is, it will have to be convincing. Cook can have a fearsome temper if anyone interferes in her kitchen," he said, grinning at them. "Leave it to me."

◆

"Well, at least we've got some help," Matt said, as they walked back to their rooms.

"Yes. I think we've been very lucky. It's a pity there aren't a few more like him on the staff."

"So, what are we going to do about Edward?"

"Tell Maria and let her decide. It's not up to us to sort the servants out."

"Maria?"

"Mrs Debbon."

"So you two are on first name terms now?"

"Yes. And before you ask, it was her idea, not mine."

"I never said a word!"

"You didn't need to."

◆

Mrs Debbon was in the drawing room when they returned from their meeting with the butler. Matt was pleased to see that Helen was also there. She gave him a beaming smile as he entered the room.

"James has agreed to help all he can, Maria," Connor told her. "We've told him that your late husband made an unwise investment in a company that has since failed, and some of the creditors are trying to collect what they feel they are owed from you. They want to kidnap Charles and hold him to ransom until you pay what you owe."

"How very inventive of you, Connor. I would never have thought of that."

Helen's eyebrows rose at the use of her mother's and Connor's Christian names. She glanced across at Matt who shrugged his shoulders in return. Helen gave her mother and Connor an appraising look before walking over to join Matt.

"Maria and Connor?" she asked.

"Seems your mother thought that after last night they should be on first name terms."

They both turned to look at the older couple, who were unaware how closely they were being scrutinised.

◆

"But I checked his references myself," Mrs Debbon was saying in response to learning of Edward's involvement. "His last employer, the Honourable Mrs Dawson, spoke most highly of him and only let him go because she was moving to Spain to join her husband, the new British Ambassador."

"Nevertheless, it seems that it is he who has been passing information to those outside and was also responsible for unlocking the front door to admit the Marquis and the Count last night."

"How very vexing. I must write a stiff letter to the Honourable

Mrs Dawson for supplying a reference for such a disreputable character. I'm surprised at her."

Try as he might, Connor couldn't control his laughter. To find that Mrs Debbon was more concerned about an incorrect reference for an employee than the fact that there was a group of thugs and murderers out to do them harm struck him as highly amusing.

"I suppose compared with everything else that has happened, it does seem a trifle petty to be worrying about a reference," she said, joining in his laughter.

"It's good that we can still laugh," he replied. "What are you going to do about Edward?"

"If I were simply to dismiss him, he would presumably go and join the others."

"That would seem to be most likely."

"And his knowledge of the layout of this house would be much to their advantage?"

"Indeed, it would."

"Then I think some direct action is called for."

She rang the bell to summon the butler.

"James," she said, when he appeared in answer to her summons. "I gather that you are prepared to help us?"

"In any way I can, madam."

"Is Edward on duty at the moment?"

"I believe he is in the stables at present, madam."

"Then could you find some excuse to get him back to his room, please?"

"Of course. And then?"

"Lock him in. The doors in the servants' quarters are not quite as thick as those in the main house, but will certainly defeat any attempt on his part to break his own door down. Nor will he be able to exit through the window. We will keep him locked in until the authorities have responded to my messages."

"Certainly, madam. It will be a pleasure."

"However, I do not want him treated roughly. And I shall expect him to be supplied with meals and refreshments regularly.

I will not lower myself to the standards of those outside."

"As you wish, madam."

◆

An hour or so later, James arrived with a selection of knives that he'd borrowed from the kitchen. When asked how he had got them past the cook without having to explain things, his response was to say that it was probably best if they didn't know.

"That way," James continued with a grin, "Hannah won't be asking you any questions that you can't answer."

He opened one of the drawers in a large sideboard and tucked the knives away out of sight.

"I suggest that the knives stay there for the time being, sir," he said to Connor. "Perhaps later they can be spread around the house in convenient locations?"

"Good idea," Connor replied. "I think that we're all going to have a lot to thank you for when this is all over."

"On the contrary, sir, I believe *I* should be thanking *you*. I am happy with my position as butler, but it can get a touch dull at times, if you understand my meaning?"

"I do indeed, James, I do indeed."

CHAPTER TWENTY-THREE

To savour every last moment

Matt's mood matched the day — grey and leaden. A chill wind was blowing in from the Channel and a thin skein of drizzle obscured the view from the drawing room windows. He stared gloomily out, wondering how on earth he'd managed to get himself in such a mess. The warm sunshine and carefree laughter of a few days before now seemed a lifetime away. A movement behind him reflected in the window and his mood lightened as Helen put her hands on his shoulder.

"Miserable morning, isn't it," she said.

"Not any more, it isn't," he said, turning and putting his arms around her.

"You realise, of course, that as a respectable young lady I should complain about how forward you're being, and put you in your place?"

"So are you going to?"

"Only if you stop," she said, returning his embrace with so much fervour that Matt had to fight the desire that rose in him. He wanted her so much and was terrified that by the following evening she would have died in the fire. Something of his inner turmoil must have shown in his expression as Helen backed away slightly.

"What's wrong, Matt? What is it? There's something you're not telling me."

"It's nothing. Just me worrying about anything and everything as usual."

"I don't believe you," she told him. "I haven't known you long, Matt, but I know when you're not being honest with me. I believe you know far more than you have told me. I want to know what's happening, Matt, all of it."

"I don't know what you want to hear, what you want me to

say."

"The truth, Matt. As simple as that. I want the truth."

Matt tried desperately to think his way out of the situation, but all the time his fears and worries were being shown in his expression.

"I can't!" he finally whispered, so softly that Helen had to strain to hear him.

"Why?" she asked.

"Because I don't know all there is to know, only what Uncle Conn's told me."

"Mama told me about your uncle this morning, about how he works for the government and how you go with him sometimes to divert suspicion. I also understand that you may not know everything, only what Mr Harvey has told you, but please tell me what you do know."

"I can't."

"Why not?" she demanded.

"Because."

"Because of what?"

"Just because," Matt countered, trying desperately to find a way of avoiding telling Helen the truth.

"I'm not a child, Matt," she cried. "I'm not going to break down if you tell me something bad. Those men last night, the ones who want to take Charles to France. You know who they are?"

"Not for certain, but I know one is a Marquis and the other's a Count. I don't know their names."

"Their names do not matter. Mama has said that all the outer doors and windows are locked shut. No-one will be admitted for the next few days until help arrives. Yet you are still worried. No," she corrected herself, "it's more than that. You are scared of something."

"Yes," he finally admitted.

"Then tell me what it is! What are you so frightened of? Tell me, I have a right to know!"

Matt looked wildly around him, trying to find some reason, any reason, not to tell her, but in the end he gave in.

"The men who want to kidnap your brother and take him to France. They're mean, vicious scum who don't care how many lives they sacrifice, or whose."

"Lives? You mean they're prepared to kill? Who?"

Matt stayed silent. He didn't need to say anything. Helen's eyes widened as the full implications of what he'd said became apparent.

"You mean they could do more than just put a few scars on my face — they plan to kill me? That's what you don't want to tell me?"

Matt still said nothing, the expression on his face answering her question.

"And when do they plan to do it?"

No answer.

"Matthew! Tell me, I've a right to know!"

"Tomorrow," he said in a voice scarcely more than a whisper, "my uncle believes they plan to try again tomorrow."

"So soon?"

"Your mother has at last realised how serious things are and is calling in help from outside. The French elections are in a few days' time. The kidnappers know that they don't have very long. They have to act fast if they're to act at all. And it's not just you that's in danger. If those scum can't get their own way then they'll have no conscience about killing your mother and sister as well."

"Mary-Anne? But she's just a child. Surely no-one would stoop that low?"

"They'll stop at nothing, Helen, nothing at all. The stakes are too high!"

Helen turned her gaze to the window and stared at the drizzle that was blocking her view. She could see the upper terraces but nothing beyond them. It was as if her world ended a few feet beyond the glass panes. She turned back to face Matt.

"Hold me," she said, simply.

He took her in his arms and tried to comfort her as the tears rolled down her cheeks.

"I'm not the same person I was when I first met you," she said.

"So much has happened. A few days ago, the most serious matter I had to concern myself about was which material to order for my new gown for the summer ball. Now you're telling me I might not even see the ball, I might not even see anything beyond tomorrow?"

"You don't know that, no-one does. With the house secure then those thugs can't get in. Time is on our side."

"Don't say anything else. Just hold me."

◆

Lunch was a difficult time. No-one was very hungry, yet they had to act as if nothing out of the ordinary was happening to avoid frightening the younger children. So the courses came and went, conversation continued and jokes were told. But no matter how hard they tried, or perhaps because of how hard they tried, both Charles and Mary-Anne became more and more concerned as time went on.

"Are you feeling unwell, Mama?" Mary-Anne eventually asked.

"No, my dear. What makes you ask?"

"I don't know. It's just that everyone is acting rather oddly."

"In what way, my dear," her mother asked, glancing at Connor.

"I can't really explain it," she said, "but it's as if everyone is pretending."

"Pretending?"

"Yes. Pretending that everything is normal when it isn't."

"It's nothing to worry about, my dear. It's just that I have a lot on my mind at the moment."

Charles, who had been following the conversation closely, chimed in.

"But when I asked if I could go into the garden, you said that we weren't allowed to go outside at the moment. You usually like it when we go out."

"But the weather today is somewhat inclement. You don't wish to catch a chill, do you?"

"No Mama, but . . ."

"No buts, Charles," his mother interrupted. "If the weather

improves then perhaps you might go outside for a while, but for now you will both stay indoors in the warm."

◆

The afternoon seemed interminable. Connor leafed through some books from Belmont's vast library but nothing could hold his interest. He was desperately worried. The fire was due to take place the following night and he had no idea if what he was doing was the right course of action or not. And he worried about involving his nephew in what was turning out to be a very ugly affair. If anything happened to Matt he didn't know how he'd be able to cope. As his own child had died even before it lived, Matt had become the closest thing to a son that he was ever likely to have. The thought of having to explain things to Steve and Marion if Matt didn't come back filled him with dread. It wasn't so much that he was fearful that they'd blame him, as he knew them well enough to know that they wouldn't. But Connor knew perfectly well who he *would* blame. And he'd carry that blame with him to the grave and beyond.

◆

Charles and Mary-Anne continued to chafe at their mother's order that they confine themselves to the house and looked longingly through the windows at the gardens. Eventually Matt and Helen took pity on them and organised several games of hide and seek, something for which the vast size of Belmont and its maze of corridors and rooms could have been purposely designed. In spite of Helen's admonishments to keep the noise down to an acceptable level, the squeals of delight were enough to wake Mrs Debbon from her afternoon nap. She opened the door of her boudoir to find Matt, Helen and Charles busily opening doors, lifting the lids of chests and peering behind curtains.

"I'm so sorry, Mama," Helen said, on catching sight of her mother standing in the doorway. "Matthew and I are trying to cheer up Charles and Mary-Anne a little by playing hide and seek."

"And succeeding too, by the look of it," she replied, seeing the excited grin on her son's face. "I assume that it is Mary-Anne who is hiding?"

"Yes, Mama," Charles piped up. "We've looked everywhere, but can't find her."

"Then you are obviously not looking hard enough. I will just have to help you in your search."

"You, Mama?" Helen asked in astonishment.

"It may surprise you to learn that when I was young we lived in a house even larger than this one and I became quite an expert in hide and seek."

The idea of the ever-regal and elegantly coiffured Mrs Debbon running full-tilt down corridors and hiding in cupboards was difficult to imagine, but she proved more than equal to the challenge and found Mary-Anne crouching behind a group of potted ferns in the entrance hall without too much trouble. She then insisted that it was her turn to hide and managed it so successfully that she simply couldn't be found. With Charles, Mary-Anne, Helen and Matt all shouting to each other from various parts of the great house, it perhaps wasn't too surprising to find Mrs Gregson standing rigidly at the foot of the main stairs, quivering with disapproval.

"May I enquire what, exactly, is going on?" she asked, her tone a high contender for the "frostiest voice of the century" award.

"I'm sorry, Mrs Gregson," Helen replied, trying hard to look and sound contrite but failing miserably. "We were just trying to cheer up Charles and Mary-Anne."

"Miss Helen, you know perfectly well that madam rests in the afternoon. I would have thought that . . ."

What it was that she might have thought they never discovered as Mrs Debbon chose that moment to surprise them all by emerging from the interior of a very large and grand looking long-case clock that stood close to the front door. Mrs Gregson was evidently too dumbfounded to say anything and just retreated along the corridor towards the servants' wing.

"I'm not sure that Mrs Gregson will ever recover from the shock," Matt said, as Mrs Debbon climbed the stairs to join them.

"The surprise will do her good," was the rather tart reply.

"But how did you fit in the clock case with all the chains and weights," asked an astonished Helen.

"Really, my dear, you must take note of things. That clock has never worked since we moved in for the simple reason that it doesn't have a mechanism. It's there simply because the case is very beautiful. Surely you've noticed that it never shows the correct time?"

"I have to confess that I've never really looked at it," Helen admitted. "It's just always been there."

"Which would explain why you couldn't find me," her mother said. "No doubt Mrs Gregson will now inform all the other servants that I have taken complete leave of my senses."

"Why do you keep her on, Mama?" Mary-Anne asked. "She never seems very happy."

"Because I promised your father that I would let her stay for as long as she wished. Her family has served your father's family for three generations and he wanted to try and repay that debt in some small way."

"Does her husband work here as well?" Matt asked, then wondered why most of the others burst out laughing. "What's funny about that?"

"Nothing, Matthew, and my apologies," Mrs Debbon said. "Mrs Gregson isn't married. It is traditional that housekeepers are called 'Mrs' even when they are still unmarried."

"Sorry, I didn't know."

"It's of no importance. Before Robert died we had a much larger staff and did a large amount of entertaining, albeit on a modest scale. Mrs Gregson made all the arrangements for the various social events that we held and it occupied much of her time. And to be fair, she was exceedingly good at it. All our events always went without a hitch. After my husband's death I decided that I couldn't face the constant round of soirées, balls and dinners, so I curtailed them quite dramatically. Coupled with a reduction in the number of servants it meant that Mrs Gregson had much less to do than previously."

"I'd have thought she would have enjoyed the rest," Matt said.

"I believe that Mrs Gregson thrives on having a lot to do. She manages the house most efficiently, but it isn't enough to keep her fully occupied. The enforced idleness chafes at her, I think. Now — as it will not be long until dinner — I suggest that we all retire to our rooms to change."

"I'll tell my uncle," Matt told her. "I think he's still in the library."

"No, he isn't," Connor said, entering the room. "I heard a lot of shouting and laughing. What was going on?"

"Mama was joining in with a game of hide and seek and was hiding in the clock in the entrance hall. We couldn't find her at all," Charles told him excitedly.

"You were hiding in the clock?" Connor asked in some astonishment.

"A perfectly logical place to hide," she told him, slightly defensively he felt. "However, dinner will not be long and we all need to change."

With that she swept upstairs, her three children following in her wake like a small flotilla.

"Did Maria really hide in the clock?" Connor asked Matt after she had entered her boudoir and closed the door behind her.

"She certainly did. I think that Mrs Debbon isn't quite as straight-laced as she would like us all to believe."

"Interesting."

"Very."

◆

Dinner came and went; a more enjoyable affair than might have been expected under the circumstances. The two younger children were still marvelling at their mother's newly discovered talent for hide and seek, and were trying to persuade her to join in another game.

"Perhaps tomorrow," she eventually told them. "But, for now, kindly remember your manners. What your father would have thought of all this excitement at the dinner table I shudder to think. Now I really feel it's high time that Nurse came and saw you to bed."

"But Mama . . . " Mary-Anne started, but was stopped by the raising of an imperious hand.

"There will be no 'buts', young lady," her mother told her. "James, would you kindly send for Nurse, please. And inform her that the children are rather over-excited and will need a firm hand in order to calm them down."

Within a few minutes Charles and Mary-Anne were being taken off to bed, their expressions indicating that they would very much have liked to stay and argue the point, but they didn't quite dare.

"I'm sorry," Matt told Mrs Debbon, after the door had closed behind the children. "It was my idea to play hide and seek. It sort of got a bit out of hand and they got over-excited."

"No need for apologies, Matthew," she replied with a smile. "They had a wonderful time and it has cheered them up no end. As indeed it did me. I had quite forgotten how much fun a simple children's game could be. I fear that Nurse will have a hard task on her hands persuading the children to go to sleep, but I feel that it will be well worth it. Perhaps you and Helen could organise another game for them tomorrow?"

"I'm sure we could," Matt told her. "It would make having to stay inside the house more bearable for them."

"And for us all, I think. Now I find I am unaccountably tired this evening, so I think I will go straight to my room. I will bid you all goodnight."

"I'll retire as well, Mama. It's been a tiring day," Helen said. "Goodnight, Mr Harvey, goodnight, Matt."

Connor and Matt stood as they left the room, whilst the servants started to bustle about clearing the table.

"It's not a bad idea to have an early night," Connor said. "We don't know what we're going to have to face tomorrow. I think I'll turn in as well. What are you going to do?" he asked Matt.

"I think I'll come up as well. I'm pooped."

◆

Helen was finally forced to confront the fact that this time it wasn't her legs that were leading her astray. She stood motionless outside the door to Matt's room for what seemed like an eternity. After a while she turned away and was about to return along the corridor, but changed her mind. She knocked lightly, but when no answer was forthcoming she opened the door slightly and called Matt's name. A rather sleepy 'hello?' issued from inside the room.

"It's me, Matt, it's Helen."

"Helen?"

"Yes. May I come in?"

"Yes, of course, what's the matter?"

"Nothing. I just wanted to see you," she said as she closed the door behind her and walked over to the bed, where Matt was sleepily trying to sit up. "You don't mind?"

"Of course not. Is there anything I can help with?"

"Yes, I think there is."

"What do you want me to do?" he asked, rubbing the sleep from his eyes.

"You told me that there will be one last attempt to take Charles to France and make him King?"

"That's what my uncle thinks."

"But you agree with him?"

"Yes. Those thugs won't give up that easily. They're bound to try again and tomorrow will be their last chance if they want to get Charles to France in time for it to make a difference to the elections that are coming up."

"And it would be natural to assume that any attempt would be made late in the evening or during the night rather than during the day when there would be too many people about?"

"I'd guess so."

"And you still believe that they would go to any lengths, any at all, to get what they want — even if it means resorting to murder?"

Matt didn't answer.

"Please, Matt; I just need to be sure."

"Yes, both Uncle Conn and I think that there will be one last-ditch attempt, almost certainly tomorrow evening or night."

She said nothing for a while, but just sat on the edge of Matt's bed, staring into the flickering flames of the fire that had been lit earlier to air the room.

"I know I've had a very sheltered life," she told him eventually. "I've been to many receptions and helped to entertain a lot of important people. I've been to dances and balls; I've attended concerts and garden parties. But I've experienced very little of what life has to offer. Even something as simple as having those car rides with Mr Brown has shown me how much more there is out there." She took a deep breath before continuing. "So if tomorrow is perhaps my last day in this world, then I want to experience as much as I can. I want to savour every last moment."

Matt didn't know how to respond. He tried to say something, but the words wouldn't come out as he saw that tears were forming in Helen's eyes. He slipped out of bed and held her in his arms, trying to comfort her. He suddenly realised that he was only wearing a pair of boxer shorts, but he doubted if Helen would know what men's underwear was meant to look like anyway. After a while she stood up and walked over to stand in front of the fire.

"I'm sorry," Matt said, "Are you cold? Do you want a blanket off the bed?"

"No, I'm not cold."

There was something extremely erotic, Matt thought, about the way her skin reflected the flames from the fire. She turned to face him.

"I want to experience everything I can," she said as she undid the ribbons of her negligée, letting it slide from her shoulders and drop to the floor so that she stood naked in front of him.

Matt's subconscious was sending increasingly urgent messages to his brain, telling him of the folly, indeed the total blind stupidity of this, that it was utter madness to be even thinking of it.

"But I haven't . . . I mean, I've never . . . " he said, his voice trailing into an uncertain silence.

"It doesn't matter," she said. "We can both learn."

Matt turned his subconscious off, took her in his arms and carried her to the bed.

◆

Across the corridor, Connor found sleep eluded him. There was something that he hadn't mentioned to Matt, a thought that had come to him several days earlier but hadn't wanted to pass on. The reports in the paper in his own time that told of the fire, the ones that said that the faces of Mrs Debbon and her children could be seen at the first-floor windows screaming for help — what if amongst them were Matt and himself? What if the two of them were the "mysterious strangers" mentioned in the newspaper reports? What if they too were destined to perish in the flames that he was certain would destroy Belmont the following night? How this would equate with his firm belief that the past could not be changed he didn't know. Perhaps when Steve and Marion came back from their holiday they would find that he and Matt were missing and couldn't be found. The thoughts ran round inside his head, so much so that it was the early hours of the morning before sleep finally claimed him.

CHAPTER TWENTY-FOUR

Asking for help

Friday, April 29, 1898.

Connor knew something had happened as soon as he saw Matt's face in the morning. For one thing Matt was up and dressed without having to be dragged from his bed.

"You look happy," he said. "What gives?"

"Don't know what you mean."

"You've got a smile on your face like the Cheshire Cat, and you're wandering about in a dream. Not that that's anything unusual, it's just more apparent this morning."

Before Connor could question him further, Helen walked along the corridor towards them. Connor decided that although her movement would usually be described as walking, it didn't really seem to fit in this case. Helen didn't so much walk as float or glide along the corridor, as if her feet weren't in communication with the floor.

"Good morning, Mr Harvey," she said brightly, "and good morning to you too, Matt."

"Hi," said Matt, grinning at her.

Connor looked from one to the other and back again. Serious doubts started to grow in his mind. No, they couldn't have! Even Matt at his wildest wouldn't have been *that* crazy, surely? As he saw the way the two of them looked at each other, long lingering looks that spoke far more than mere words ever could, the suspicion turned to a cold certainty. He groaned inwardly — this was all he needed. A bad situation had suddenly got very much

333

worse.

"In here, now!" he ordered after Helen had gone, dragging Matt into the nearest available room and shutting the door firmly behind him.

"Have you two done what I think you've done?"

"Don't know what you mean."

"You know full well what I mean. Did you and Helen sleep together last night?"

"Well, what if we did?" Matt countered. "We're old enough."

"Hell's bloody bells, have you gone stark, raving mad?"

"No. She knows that something's badly wrong: she knows that those thugs will probably come back and she knows that they won't hesitate this time to kill. She wanted to experience as much as she could."

"And that meant that you had to take her to bed?"

"She came to *me*, what was I supposed to do? Say to her, 'I'm really sorry, Helen, but I don't do that sort of thing'?"

"And I presume neither of you had any form of protection?"

"Protection?"

"Don't pretend you don't know what I mean."

"Oh. Er, well, no, I suppose not."

"You suppose not. For God's sake, Matt, this is 1898. Young ladies aren't expected to know about that sort of thing, so it was up to you to sort it out."

"How was I supposed to do that? I didn't exactly come prepared!"

"So it's quite possible that you've just made a sixteen-year-old girl pregnant, and that, of course, is besides whatever her mother will say when she finds out."

"She won't find out."

"Oh really? And what makes you so sure about that? It took me about five minutes. She's a very intelligent lady, she'll find out."

"Well, what if she does? We're both sixteen, it's legal. What can she do?"

"What can she do? There are times when I think a bar of

chocolate's got more brain cells than you have. First, this is 1898. I'm not even sure that it *is* legal in this year. Secondly, Maria is the uncrowned Queen of France and you've been at it with her elder daughter, who is, need I remind you, a fully-fledged Princess. She has friends in very high places. And you're asking me what can she do? I would say just about anything she wants. You'll be lucky if you've still got your balls by this evening."

He was about to continue in the same vein, but something in Matt's expression stopped him. He looked close to tears.

"Oh, Matt. I'm sorry. I know how difficult all this has been for you."

"Uncle Conn, I don't want to leave, I don't want to go back. Or at least I do and I don't. It's all so confusing. I want to go back and see Mum and Dad and the others of course, but I don't want to leave Helen. I love her, I really love her, and I believe that she loves me."

"I know you do, Matt. It's what I've been trying to warn you of since we got here, about becoming involved."

"Too late now, I am involved."

"I don't know what to say to you. We had little choice about coming back to 1898 and I've no reason to believe that we'll have any choice about going back to our own time. It'll just happen. What's Helen going to think when you disappear one day and never come back?"

"I won't go!"

"I don't think you'll get a choice. But, just suppose you did have a choice and you stayed here, what would your parents think? You'll have just vanished without trace. They'll be frantic with worry about you and they'll never stop looking for you. And, of course, they'll never find you. It'll destroy them."

"But what can I do? If I stay, I break my parents' hearts — if I go, I break Helen's. What do I do?" Matt said, his voice breaking with emotion.

"Nothing, Matt. We take whatever course is mapped out for us. It's all we can do. I know you love her: I've seen it on your face, in how you behave. And I guess it's nothing like you've felt before, nothing like the feelings you had for your other girlfriends."

"I've never felt like this about anyone else."

"Well, what's done is done and we'll just have to make the best of it. I just hope that Maria has her mind on other things today and doesn't notice the signs." He paused for a few moments before continuing. "Do you mind if I ask you something?"

"No, of course not," Matt answered, making an effort to get his voice back to something approaching normal

"I know it will have been Helen's first time, but was it your first time as well?"

"Yes. I've been close a few times, but something's always held me back."

"Well, they say your first time should be with someone you love, not just lust after, so I suppose I'm glad it was Helen and not just someone you met on a Saturday night."

"Can I ask you something in return?"

"Sure, go ahead."

"Well, have you never wanted to . . . you know . . . ? You don't mind me asking?"

"Of course I don't mind. And to answer your question: no, not since Laura died. I put a lid on my emotions, or at least that sort of emotion. I suppose I felt that if I were to start a relationship with someone it would be disloyal somehow, that I'd be cheating on her."

"Would Laura have thought that?"

"That's the point, Matt: I'm sure she wouldn't. One of things she kept telling me was that afterwards — after she'd gone, I mean — I was to carry on with my life. I wasn't to become a hermit, she didn't want that. She even said that if I met someone else, then I wasn't to hold back on her account."

"But you never have?"

"No. Oh, I had my chances. A number of well-meaning friends would invite me to dinner and there at the table would be another guest, an unattached and attractive lady of roughly my age. I was always polite but never anything more. Gradually the message must have got through that I wasn't interested. I could imagine them all rolling their eyes upwards and wondering what more they would have to do to motivate me."

"So you've never really looked at anyone else."

"Not until now."

"Now? Are you saying that you're in love with Mrs Debbon?"

"Not yet, but I'm becoming increasingly drawn to her, I have to admit. I've never looked at another woman in that way since Laura died, but Maria is opening my eyes to the fact that my life is half-way through and I've spent a fair chunk of that being miserable. Laura wouldn't have wanted that, I know she wouldn't. She'd have wanted me to be happy, until I can see her again."

"So are you going to say anything to Mrs Debbon?"

"No. I think she and I could well have made a go of it if things had been normal, but things are about as far from normal as it's possible to be. For both our sakes I've got to keep things at a friendship level between us and not let it go any further."

"It's gone a lot further than that with Helen and me."

"I know it has and I wish there was something I could say or do that would help make it all better, but there isn't and I can't."

"I know. I got into this mess with my eyes open. I can't claim I was dragged into it. I'll just have to wait and see what happens."

"And if the worst happens?"

"I find the girl I want to spend the rest of my life with and she's either going to die in a fire tonight, or she'll survive and I'll flip back to our own time and never see her again. I can't even think about that at the moment."

"Then let's not think about it all. We've got today to get through. At least we know that nothing is going to happen until tonight, and hopefully not even then. Let's try and get through the day as best we can. And if we're going to try for some level of normality, then we should go and have breakfast."

"Too right. I'm starving."

"Sex makes you hungry. It uses so much energy that you need to eat to replace the energy that you burn off."

"Uncle Conn!" Matt said, sounding extremely shocked.

"What? You no doubt think that any experiences I've had of a sexual nature must predate the building of Noah's Ark, but I was young once."

"Really?"

"Yes, really. Before I met Laura, I was involved with two girls at the same time, so I had to make up two stories so that they wouldn't know. Trying to juggle two stories at the same time proved too difficult, I got in one hell of a mess and ended up telling the wrong story to one of the girls. I'm lucky I'm still alive."

"You never told me that before."

"You weren't old enough before. Anyway, I know what I'm talking about when it comes to sex and food. So let's go and get you some breakfast. And take that dozy grin off your face."

"Sorry," Matt said, looking anything but.

Breakfast proved to be a livelier affair than it might have been under the circumstances. Helen and Matt kept on exchanging knowing glances and Mary-Anne and Charles seemed to follow their mood. Their mother seemed relieved that the younger children were less worried than previously and possibly due to that failed to pick up on the charged atmosphere between Matt and her elder daughter, something for which Connor was extremely grateful. He noted with some amusement the even larger than usual heap of food on Matt's plate and received a wink in return for his raised eyebrows.

A couple of hours later Mrs Debbon was busy in the study and Helen had returned to her room, claiming tiredness. Connor thought it fortunate that her mother hadn't enquired too closely into the cause of her tiredness. Charles and Mary-Anne were in the nursery, leaving Connor and Matt alone in the drawing room.

"Do you think we've done enough?" Matt asked.

"Enough?"

"Enough to change things. To make sure that Belmont doesn't

burn down tonight. I mean we've got Edward under lock and key and James will make sure that all the doors and windows are locked so that no-one can get in."

"I wish I knew. It brings us back to the same old problem. If Belmont doesn't burn down, then our future selves won't learn about it and therefore won't come back to change things. The same paradox that we've discussed before."

"But what else can we do?"

"I'm not sure there's a lot more we can do ourselves, but I've had a sort of idea. But we're going to need help with it."

"Where from? We know we can't go to whatever authorities there are here in 1898 and even if we could they'd just laugh at us. That's assuming that we didn't get arrested as dangerous lunatics, of course."

"No, we can't go to anyone like that. I wasn't thinking of anyone official. When I came back here with our clobber from the Belgrave Hotel, I got Edward to bring me via the harbour so I could see what it looked like. There were two ships of the Hardwick Line in the harbour, which set me thinking. We could ask Daniel to help us."

"Daniel?"

"Why not? We can't tell him what we know, or at least not how we know it, but we can use the same story that we did with James, about the family being in trouble with thugs who are claiming money. James bought it so I'm sure Daniel will."

"You think so?"

"It's worth a try. He knows that there have been some strange goings-on, and he knows that Mrs Debbon is worried. He cares a great deal for Helen and don't look at me like that because you know he does. If he thinks they're in danger then he'll help."

"Even if you can persuade him, what can he do?"

"I'm making this up as I go along, Matt. I don't have a blueprint to work to."

"I know, I'm sorry. I'm scared, really scared. Not so much for me, but for Helen and her family. Time's running out and I don't think we're getting anywhere."

"Don't I know it."

"Couldn't we just get Mrs Debbon to move out of Belmont, just for a day or so? That way, they won't be in the house even if it does catch fire tonight."

"I'd already thought of that one, but I don't think it would do any good. For one thing, Mrs Debbon would never agree to it. She'd see it as cowardice, running away. Secondly, and don't ask me to explain this because I can't, I'm absolutely sure that this is where the final cards in this game will be played."

"Hardly a game."

"I know, but you know what I mean. Just don't ask me to explain."

"I won't. I don't understand half the things you say at the best of times. How are we going to get in touch with Daniel? Will it be safe to walk down to his house?"

"I'm sure it will. We need to make sure that things appear normal so that the ones watching in the woods won't get suspicious."

"Won't they already be suspicious? With Edward locked up in his room he won't have been able to contact them and they'll be wondering why not."

"Possibly, but I think that he'd only get in touch with them if he needed to. I'm hoping that they just assume he's been kept busy."

"So, we just walk down to Daniel's house and hope that he's in?"

"I suppose so. I've no other suggestion anyway."

"What do we do if he's 'not at home' like Mrs Debbon was the first time we tried to see her?"

"I doubt that people of Daniel's age use that expression. Anyway, there's only one way to find out."

They were heading to the front door when Connor suddenly stopped in his tracks.

"You got your music player on you?"

"No, it's in one of the drawers in my room, under my clothes."

"Can you nip and fetch it — it might come in handy."

"I don't see how."

"Fetch it anyway."

After Matt returned downstairs, Geoffrey let them out of the front door. They heard the heavy bolts being drawn across behind them after the door closed and they started to walk along the drive. It was chilly outside and Connor was glad of the warmth of his thick coat.

"Should we have told someone where we're going?" Matt asked.

"Why?"

"In case anyone wonders where we've got to, of course."

"Who did you have in mind?"

"James."

"Oh, yes, I suppose we should have done, but I didn't think of it. You want to run back and tell him?"

"No. Geoffrey would have to go through all the business of unlocking the door again. Anyway, we won't be all that long, will we?"

"Shouldn't think so."

"What do we do if we hear the noise — the one that warns us we're about to flip?"

"I sincerely hope we don't, not at this stage. But if we do, I doubt we'd be back for more than a few minutes if the previous times are anything to go by."

A large shrub close to the gates spoke to them as they passed by.

"Fort you orter know that there's free of 'em this time."

"Bill?"

"'Oo was yer expectin'? Bleedin' Queen Victoria?"

"Sorry, Bill. We should have known you'd be here," Connor said, trying hard not to laugh and also trying not to appear that he was talking to a shrub. "Anyway, what do mean, there's three of them?"

"Wot I says, o' course. There's free of 'em. Two blokes an' a lady. They's in the woods watchin' the 'ouse."

"Thanks, Bill. You're being a really great help. How long have you been there?"

"Since it got light. I ain't goin' ter school or nuffin' untils I knows what's goin' on."

"Have you had anything to eat today?"

"Grabbed some bread an' cheese afore I come."

"We won't be very long, Bill, and we'll bring you something to eat when we get back. Are you sure the people in the woods don't know you're there?"

"Corse they don' know," came the scornful reply.

"OK, Bill. But be careful. Things are starting to get tricky."

The shrub shook its understanding and went back to being a piece of vegetation.

"I know that a lot of people in our own time talk to their plants," Matt said, as they continued along the lane, "but I've never heard of a plant answering back."

"Maybe they're not using the right language."

◆

The maid who answered the door seemed rather taken aback that it was Daniel that they wanted to see and not his father. She asked them to wait and then started to climb the stairs, grumbling to herself about what things were coming to, expecting her to go and announce visitors to a sixteen-year-old. The country was going to rack and ruin, she decided. Daniel himself didn't seem to think that it was anything unusual and clattered down the stairs to greet them, leading Connor to wonder if all sixteen-year-old young men were unable to move without making a noise like a regiment on the march.

"Hello, Mr Harvey. Hello, Matthew," Daniel said, shaking their hands and showing them into a comfortable room to one side of the entrance hall. Although not in the same league as Belmont's drawing room, it was pleasant, with a view across the bay towards Berry Head. "Father bought this house because you can see the whole of the bay," he said, noting his two guests looking out of the broad windows. "It means he can see his ships coming and going even if he's not down at the harbour."

"It's certainly a fine view," Connor agreed.

"But I'm guessing you didn't come to admire the view," Daniel continued. "And from your expressions it's not a social call. How can I help?"

"You are a very astute young man," Connor told him. "And you're perfectly correct. The truth is, Mrs Debbon and her family are in trouble and we're hoping that you can assist."

"Trouble? What sort of trouble?"

Connor briefly outlined his story of the financial problems of the family and of the failed kidnap attempt of a couple of evenings before.

"I know you care for Helen. You're going to have to trust me when I tell you that she, in fact the entire family, is now in grave danger. Unless we can find a way to stop it happening, I believe that another attempt will be made to kidnap Charles, possibly as soon as this evening. If the family resists, they'll resort to violence."

"How do you know all this?"

"We were there when the kidnap attempt was carried out. Matt managed to stop them from seriously hurting Helen."

"But I thought you said that the kidnap attempt happened very late in the evening."

"Yes, that's true. You did know that we're staying at Belmont for a few days?"

"No, I didn't," Daniel replied, a dark frown creasing his forehead. "Now I know why I haven't seen Helen for a while."

"Mrs Debbon thought it would help if we stayed," Matt said, anxious not to get on Daniel's wrong side.

"She didn't ask me though, did she?"

Connor could feel any chance of help from Daniel slipping away from them and decided to risk another story.

"I can understand that you're hurt, but there's something else that you ought to know about us. It may help to explain things."

He gave Daniel the story about working for the government and Matt coming with him to help with his cover.

"You work for the government?" Daniel asked, in obvious

disbelief.

"Yes. I have no papers to prove it of course — that could prove dangerous. But working for the government means that I have access to new ideas and new inventions long before they become available to the general public."

"Such as?

"You like music, Daniel?"

"Yes," came the puzzled reply.

"And how do you listen to it?"

"I don't understand. Listen to it?"

"Yes. If you want to listen to or hear a particular piece of music, how would you go about it?"

"Well, there are band concerts on the seafront from time to time in the summer and then there's . . . "

"Sorry — I meant recorded music," Connor interrupted. "How would you listen to that?"

"My mother has a phonograph that she uses quite often," came the even more puzzled response. "We sometimes have musical evenings when we play a selection of recordings."

Matt began to realise why he'd been asked to bring his music player with him and surreptitiously searched his pockets to find where he'd stuffed it.

"And your phonograph is quite large? It needs a table to support it?"

"Of course."

"And suppose I were to tell you that the latest invention is a music player that will fit in your pocket and can play music as you walk along? Or at least what passes for music," he added as an afterthought.

He nodded to Matt, who dragged his player and headphones out of his pocket. They fitted comfortably into the palm of his hand.

"That's the latest design, Daniel," Connor told him.

"That?" Daniel asked, the scorn apparent in his voice. "That tiny thing can play recordings?"

"Yes. But not the type of recording that your phonograph can play. These recordings are produced by an entirely different method. Show him, Matt."

Matt put the phones in Daniel's ears, selected a tune and pressed play. The effect was instantaneous.

"What the devil is that noise?" Daniel asked, shouting above the sound that he felt was threatening to burst his eardrums.

"Sorry," Matt said. "I forgot to turn the volume down."

He lowered the sound level to what he thought might be acceptable.

"This is music?" Daniel asked in some consternation.

"It's considered so by the young where we come from," Connor told him.

"Pardon?"

"I said . . . oh, never mind. Matt, turn it off for a moment, will you?"

When some semblance of normality had been resumed, Daniel looked at Matt in some concern.

"That's what you listen to in Warwickshire?"

"Yes, most of the time."

"Remind me never to go there."

"I would tend to agree about Matt's musical tastes. However, it's the player that I want you to consider. I don't suppose you've ever seen anything like it before?"

"No," Daniel answered, looking at the player as if it was an alien life form.

"It can record as well," Matt said.

"It can?" Connor asked. "I mean, yes, of course it can. Show him how it works, Matt."

Matt fiddled with the controls on the player until he'd set it to record mode.

"Now say something," he told Daniel.

"What do you what me to say?"

"Anything at all. It doesn't matter."

"I can't think of anything."

"It doesn't matter. That's enough."

He turned the player off, put the phones back in Daniel's ears and pressed play. If anything, Daniel was even more shocked than he had been the first time.

"That's me talking?" he asked in astonishment.

"Yes," Connor told him, relieved that they didn't have to rely on Matt's taste in music. "And in case you were wondering, it's powered by electricity."

"I've seen some electric batteries at an exhibition. But they were huge. You'd never fit one in there."

"It doesn't use batteries. It stores electricity inside it."

"And when will these be on sale to the public?"

"Not for some time," Connor said, thinking to himself that it would be well over a century before anyone saw one again. "It's only government agents who have access to them at present."

"But why would a government agent need a music player?"

"The fact it can play music is only a side issue. It's mainly used for recording messages. Does that convince you that I work for the government?"

"I don't see how you could have got hold of one of those otherwise, so I suppose you must be an agent of some sort."

"That's why Mrs Debbon asked us to stay. She thought that I might be of some use and she could hardly ask me to stay and leave Matt down at the hotel."

"I suppose not," Daniel grudgingly admitted, "but I'm still a bit pissed off that you're staying there and I've only ever been invited for dinner a couple of times."

Connor raised his eyebrows when he heard Daniel using the expression and glanced at Matt, who tried not to look guilty but failed.

"That's an expression I don't think I've heard before," he told Daniel. "Where does it come from?"

"I heard Matt use it to Bill when we went swimming. I've told a few of my friends and they all think it's great. I even heard father using it yesterday when he found that some of his ledgers weren't where he thought they ought to be. I think it's going to catch on."

"Wonderful," Connor said, half to himself, "I'm sure it will."

"But you'll help us — or rather you'll help Helen and her

family?"

"Of course I'll help. What do you want me to do?"

"It could be dangerous. I want you to understand that fully. These are dangerous people we're dealing with, not just some local thugs."

"If I can help in any way, then count me in. A gypsy read my fortune once, said that I was going to run into great danger in a fire, but the danger would be of my own making. Load of old rubbish. As if I'm going to put myself into danger in a fire. But this sort of danger I can cope with, when others are in trouble, especially those I care about," he said, glancing at Matt. "So what can I do?"

"At the moment, nothing," Connor replied, mightily relieved that the young man had agreed to help. "We don't want any more people turning up at Belmont: it might force the kidnappers to act even more quickly than otherwise — and perhaps even more violently. For now, just be aware that we might be calling on you for help at a moment's notice. Is it possible for you to be here for the rest of today and this evening?"

"I'm supposed to be going down to the harbour shortly. We've got another two ships coming in today and Father asked me to help with the paperwork."

"It's important, Daniel."

"I know it is. Yes, of course I'll stay here."

"Thanks. As soon as we know something, we'll get in touch. For now, we have to get back to Belmont. Oh, one more thing. Bill's still keeping watch from the garden and I don't think he's had much to eat today. Have you got something we can take him? I don't want to get anything from the kitchens at Belmont in case someone sees us."

"Of course," Daniel said, "just give me a couple of minutes."

He dived through a door into what was evidently the kitchen and re-appeared a few minutes later with a bulging brown paper bag.

"There's half a loaf in there, plus some ham, cheese, a couple of apples and some cake."

"Brilliant. Bill will really appreciate it."

Daniel saw them to the door, taking Matt to one side as he did so.

"If you do anything that gets Helen hurt, so help me, I'll make you pay for it."

"Look, I know how really angry you must be. I know how I'd feel if someone seemed to be muscling in on my girlfriend, but you've got to believe that I'd never hurt her. I'd do *anything* rather than that. And I've told you before, I'm not here for very long. Probably only another day or so."

"Fine. Let's leave it at that then," Daniel said, closing the door behind them.

Uncle and nephew started the long walk up the hill towards Belmont.

"Well, that went better than it might have done. What that young man would have done if he'd had any suspicions about what you and Helen got up to last night I dread to think. And I gather that you've been responsible for adding yet another questionable expression to the language?"

Matt decided that silence was the best answer to that particular question.

"So what do you think Daniel can do to help?" he asked instead.

"I'm not sure at the moment. It's just an idea floating about in my head."

"Plenty of room for it then."

Connor ignored him.

CHAPTER TWENTY-FIVE

Accepting a dare

They stopped briefly by the gates to Belmont.

"You still there, Bill?" Connor asked, looking in the opposite direction.

"Corse I's still 'ere," the shrub said indignantly.

"Good. I'm going to put this bag down on the ground. Daniel put some food in it for you. Take care, Bill. I've a feeling things are going to get interesting."

◆

"Interesting?" Matt asked, as they neared the front door.

"I didn't want to scare him. No matter what sort of act he puts on, he's still only a child. He should be safe enough if he stays put in that shrub."

Matt yanked at the bell pull at the side of the front door and Geoffrey let them in moments later.

"Your outing was enjoyable, gentlemen?" he asked.

"Yes, thank you, even though it's quite chill out there today. I wish spring would get a move on."

"I believe madam shares your feelings, sir. She was just saying that it must be getting near the time to stop having fires lit every morning."

The mention of having fires lit almost caught Connor off-guard, but he recovered sufficiently to make some polite comment before entering the drawing room.

◆

After lunch Mrs Debbon retired to her room as usual whilst the servants cleared away the dishes. Connor left Matt and Helen in the drawing room whilst he wandered through the various rooms to try and work off his meal. He realised that he'd never been down to the kitchens during his stay and decided to investigate. He knew where the door was to the kitchen area, as Matt had showed him after his foray to ask the cook to rustle up some cheeseburgers. He hadn't realised quite how extensive the kitchens were as all that could be seen from the outside was a row of windows. Standing to one side of the main kitchen, he marvelled at the number of servants bustling about, including a couple of young girls who didn't seem to be very much older than Mary-Anne. The cook was standing in the middle of the seeming chaos issuing a stream of orders. She eventually noticed him standing there and came over to him.

"Beg pardon, zur, didn' see 'e afore. Be 'e wantin' zummat?"

Assuring her that he hadn't come to interfere, but just to have a look, he said he was interested in architecture and always wanted to see the servants' areas as they tended to be very solidly built, mainly because they were usually in the basements and therefore had to carry the weight of the house above them.

"You'm right, zur. Last place as I was at were proper dimpsy all day, bein' as it didn't get no proper light. This kitchen be diff'rent as it b'aint be part of the zervants' wing, but on its own, like."

"So there's no way through to here from the servants' wing?"

"No, zur. I be told that the first owner, 'e didn' want no zervants in the main 'ouse at all at night, but 'e wanted to be able to get to the kitchens in case 'e got 'ungry like, so 'e could fix hisself zummat."

"Sounds a very strange man."

"Would zur like me to find 'e someone to show 'e around?"

When Connor indicated he would like that very much indeed, she summoned a young girl to her side.

"This is Martha, zur. She'll show 'e everything you'm likely to want to zee. Now, I must be busy."

Connor thanked her and she bustled off towards a row of pans, the contents of which were bubbling away on the gas range.

"Hello, Martha," Connor said. "Would you be young Bill's sister?"

"Yes, sir. You must be Mr Harvey. Bill told me you and your nephew were staying here but I don't get to go upstairs so I wasn't sure."

"Yes, Matt and I are staying, but only for a short while."

Martha guided him through a warren of sculleries, drying rooms, larders, creameries and various other rooms that Belmont's builder had evidently decided were vital to the running of a large house.

"Martha, may I ask a personal question?" Connor asked.

"Of course, sir."

"Well, it's only that Bill has a very obvious Cockney accent, but you don't. You don't mind me asking?"

"No sir, I don't mind," she laughed. "When we lived in London, I was in service in a big house in Hampstead. The Mistress seemed to take a liking to me and after six months she asked me if I would like to train for a position of lady's maid. I said that I would, but at the same time as being trained in the house I was sent to a nearby academy that she was the patron of where I had elocution lessons."

"So you lost your accent."

"Not altogether, sir. When I get excited or angry, then it sometimes comes back."

"I see. Why did your family move to Torquay?"

"My father hurt his back in a fall at work. He also broke several ribs and although he recovered he's had trouble with his breathing ever since, so it was suggested that the air might be better for him in Devon. We moved here almost three years ago, but father hasn't been able to find work."

"If you were trained as a lady's maid, couldn't you find work as one here in Torquay? It would be better paid than a kitchen maid, wouldn't it?"

"Oh yes, sir, but as a lady's maid I would have to live in, and mother needs me at home to help her. As a kitchen maid, I get to go home most evenings, unless madam is entertaining, and then I often have to sleep here as there's so much work to do."

"So you applied for this job when it became available?"

"Not exactly, sir. Miss Helen, she does a lot of good work in the village. She often brings baskets of food for the poor and distributes the food to those that need it most. She brought some to us one day, but father refused to accept it, saying he didn't want charity. But Miss Helen isn't the sort to take no for an answer and a little later she enquired if I would be interested in a position here in the kitchens. She said she was sorry she couldn't offer me anything else, but she thought it might help out."

"She's a very kind and generous young lady," Connor told her.

"She is indeed, sir. I only found out much later that there wasn't in fact a vacancy here at all. She had somehow persuaded her mother that the kitchen needed a little extra help and told her that she knew just the person. After I'd been here a few days madam came down to the kitchens to meet me and welcome me to the household. I think she knew perfectly well that they didn't actually need another kitchen maid but madam has a generous heart just like her daughter and didn't say anything. I'll always be grateful to the family for their help."

"Thank you for explaining it to me, Martha, and for showing me around the kitchens. It's been fascinating. But I don't want you getting into trouble by neglecting your work, so I'll wander round on my own for a while. It's been a pleasure meeting you."

"And you too, sir. Bill has spoken a great deal about you and your nephew, sir."

She left him to wander around the maze of rooms. As he did so, a small glimmer of an idea was kindled in his mind. Connor spent a fascinating hour or so in the kitchens, before deciding that he'd better get out of the way and leave the servants to their tasks. He returned to the drawing room expecting to find Matt and Helen there, but there was no sign of them. Finding James in the entrance hall, he enquired if he knew where his nephew and Helen had gone.

"Miss Helen said she was rather fatigued this afternoon, sir, and has gone to her room to rest. I believe Master Harvey went to his own room."

After thanking the butler, Connor climbed the stairs, thinking that he may well follow their lead and have a rest himself. It was likely to be a long night, no matter how things turned out. He knocked gently on Matt's door but when there was no response he quietly opened it and peered into the room. Seeing a lump in the bed and a heap of clothes on the floor he was thinking about picking the clothes up and putting them on the nearest chair when he noted that there were more clothes than there should have been. He looked more closely at the bed and noticed that there were two lumps in it, albeit two lumps closely intertwined. He quietly closed the door, hoping that Matt didn't get his heart broken over all this. When back in his own room he lay on the bed, thinking things over. A couple of hours later he heard Matt's door open and the sound of feet running lightly along the corridor. Ten minutes after that there was a knock at his own door which opened and Matt stuck his head round the edge of the door.

"Just wanted to see if you were alright," Matt said.

"I'm fine. Just resting. And if you're coming in, then get on with it and shut the door. There's a hell of a draught along that corridor at the best of times."

Matt padded into the room, just wearing his boxer shorts, and closed the door behind him. He went over to the fireplace and warmed himself in front of it.

"The fire in my room's just about gone out. It's chilly in there."

"I wouldn't have thought you'd have noticed," Connor said.

"Why not?" Matt asked suspiciously.

"You didn't seem to be cold when I looked in earlier."

"You looked in earlier?"

"Yes."

"Oh. Well, I mean it was . . . "

"Don't worry," Connor interrupted him. "I'm not going to kick up a fuss like last time. I've been thinking about it and you're old enough to make your own decisions."

"It wasn't exactly my decision. I always thought that Victorians were supposed to be prudish and not want to know about sex and that sort of thing," Matt said, a huge grin splitting his face.

"But now you know differently?"

"I sure do. Helen showed me . . ."

"Whoa! Stop right there. I don't want to know the details."

"Sorry. Anyway, I'm starving. What time's dinner?"

"Shortly, I would guess. But I suggest that you put some clothes on before you go down. Helen might appreciate the sight of you in your boxers but I doubt her mother will see it that way."

"I don't know about that. Might cheer things up a bit."

"Let's not risk it."

"OK, OK, I'm going."

◆

The gong sounded soon afterwards, but dinner could not be considered a great success. Matt and Helen seemed to be the only ones with any appetite, even Charles and Mary-Anne just picking at their food. There was little conversation and the various courses came and went untasted.

"Is there anything at all that madam would like to eat? I'm sure Cook would be happy to prepare something light. An omelette perhaps?"

"Thank you, James, but no. I find I have no appetite at all this evening," Mrs Debbon said.

"I confess it is a rather trying time, madam."

"Are there any rumours among the other staff?" she asked.

"There is much speculation about why Edward is locked in his room, but I have dropped some hints that he is suspected of theft and we are awaiting the outcome of an investigation. I think that several of the servants are also aware that something rather odd is going on, but there is nothing definite. Hopefully everything will be resolved shortly."

"I hope so too."

"If it is not too forward of me, madam, I have a little money put by. My wages are quite generous and my needs small, so I have been saving against my eventual retirement from service. If it would help in any way, I would gladly make the sum available if it would help to stave off your creditors."

"Why James, how very kind of you and a most generous offer.

But I couldn't possibly accept: it wouldn't be right. And hopefully when some letters I have written reach their recipients then dramatic action will be taken against those odious men who are trying to extort money from me."

"I understand. But the offer is still available if you feel you have need of it."

"Thank you, I will not forget this," she told him.

◆

After the meal, Connor asked Mrs Debbon if he could have a private word with her.

"Of course you may," she told him, leading him from the dining room into the adjacent but now rarely used smoking room and closing the door behind them.

"My late husband was very fond of his after-dinner cigar," she told him, "and would spend at least an hour in here every evening after the meal. I sometimes think, however, that it was just as much a case of wanting an hour or so on his own as anything else."

"I'm sorry," Connor said, "it must have been very hard for you, trying to bring up a family without him."

"It has been difficult at times," she told him, the sadness evident in her voice. "However, I'm sure you didn't want to speak of the past?"

"No, I didn't. I was down in the kitchens earlier and was shown round by Martha. And that gave me an idea which I would like to suggest to you."

"Please go on."

"You are aware that I believe quite firmly that another attempt to take Charles by force will be made later this evening."

"Of course."

"I had considered suggesting that you all leave Belmont and stay elsewhere, even just for tonight, but I think that the time for that is now past. It would be even more dangerous to expose the family to whoever is waiting outside than it would be to stay here. With the doors and windows all locked, they will find it difficult to force an entry."

"I agree."

"However, I also think that there is much to be said for reducing the risks to all the members of the family. I think that if you or Helen were to attempt to leave, even secretly, then you would be recognised. The house is bound to be under watch both front and rear. I also think that as it's Charles they want, that he ought to stay as close to us as possible."

"Which leaves Mary-Anne?"

"Exactly. I gather that several of the younger female servants live close by and tend to walk home together, both for company and safety?"

"So I understand."

"Then I strongly suggest that Mary-Anne should go with them tonight. If she were to be given a rough coat, and perhaps a servant's bonnet to disguise her hair, I believe she will be quite safe. The watchers will be keeping their eyes open for any sign of the family trying to leave, but a single girl among a group of girls going home as they do every night will not, I believe, attract attention."

"But where would she go on her own?"

"I will go outside in a moment as if I want some fresh air after dinner. I'll walk to the gates where, you will not be surprised to learn, young William is keeping watch from the shelter of a large shrub. I'll tell him what we plan to do and he'll be able to sneak around to the servants' quarters and meet his sister coming out. He's done it many times before and if the watchers do see him, they'll take no notice. He can then also walk home with the girls and he and Martha will take Mary-Anne into their home for tonight. At least you will know that one member of the family will be safe."

"Are you certain of that?" she asked. "Would she not be safer here? You have said yourself that those creatures outside will find it very difficult to break into the house."

"Difficult yes, impossible no. And it will be one less person to worry about. Should something go terribly wrong here, then at the very least, Mary-Anne will escape harm."

She stared into space for a while before evidently coming to a decision.

"Yes, I believe you are correct. She at least should get away from here. However, I am not certain that she will prove easy to persuade. The idea of spending a night away from home, on her own in a strange house with people she barely knows, may well frighten her. I don't think she will take kindly to the idea at all."

◆

"Oh Mama, what a wonderful idea," Mary-Anne cried excitedly when told what was being planned for her. "I'm going to spend the night in Bill's house? How absolutely marvellous!"

"So much for my thought that she would find the idea troublesome," her mother remarked to Connor.

"And I'm to be on my own?"

"Yes, my dear. I do hope that the idea doesn't distress you too much?"

"It's like a dream that's come true," was the reply. "Something that I can do all on my own. Charles will be madly jealous!"

"So you don't object at all? You won't be frightened?"

"Why ever would I be frightened, Mama? Martha and her parents will be there and Bill will look after me. He'd never let anything happen to me," she said confidently. "He likes me."

"I'm sure he does, my dear," was the rather dry response. "I am beginning to wonder if this was such a good idea."

"Of course it's a good idea Mama. It's . . ." she stopped in mid-sentence, frowning as she tried to recall something. "It's something Matthew said — a word he used to describe something he liked."

"I did?" asked a surprised Matt, whilst his uncle groaned and offered up a silent prayer that whatever word Matt had used wouldn't be too out of place.

"Yes. The other day, you said that the view over the valley was . . . awesome! That was the word. That's what the idea is — it's awesome!"

Mrs Debbon looked slightly startled whilst Connor breathed a sigh of relief.

"Awesome?"

"Yes, Mama."

"I see. Well, if you're sure you won't be too worried."

"I won't be worried. It will be fun."

"Very well, my dear, we'll make the arrangements."

◆

The evening sun dipped below the horizon and night enveloped Belmont and its grounds in a cloak of darkness. Lights appeared in windows as servants scuttled about lighting the gas lamps and damping down most of the fires. All the normal signs of a great house settling down for the night, only on this night nothing was even remotely normal. An owl screeched from the darkness of the woods and the night air carried the distant sound of a horse and cart as it rumbled its way along one of the country lanes.

◆

"I think that the fewer people who know where Mary-Anne is going, the better," Connor said.

"But the servants are bound to wonder why she is leaving with them, and in disguise as well," Mrs Debbon replied.

"Why not make out that it's her idea?" Matt suggested.

"Come again?" Connor asked.

"How about if you go down to the kitchen again and explain quietly to Martha that Mary-Anne wants to sneak out for the night, as a sort of dare. You could say that she and Charles have had a squabble and he's told her that she's too scared to spend the night away from here, so she wants to prove him wrong. She's asked you to help, so you can ask Martha if Mary-Anne can stay the night at her place. That way she won't be surprised to see Mary-Anne later on and she can spread the word to the others. If no-one explains anything then the others will obviously wonder what on earth is going on and get all excited about it. And that's the last thing that we want as it may draw attention to her. But if

Martha tells the others that Mary-Anne is sneaking out of her own accord, as a dare, and that they need to act as if nothing unusual is happening then they'll want to help."

"That's brilliant," Connor told him, after digesting the idea.

"Naturally."

"I hate it when he's right," Connor told Mrs Debbon. "He's so smug and irritating."

"Me? Smug?"

Connor didn't bother responding, but left to go down to the kitchen to find Martha.

◆

Fifteen minutes later Connor climbed the stairs from the kitchens, relieved that Martha had been only too willing to help. She told him that her parents wouldn't mind in the least having an unexpected guest for the night. He decided that he ought to tell Bill what was happening as soon as he could, and he also thought that the boy deserved to be told the truth, or at least as much of it as possible without revealing that his hoped-for future girlfriend was of royal blood. He went to find Geoffrey to let him out of the house, explaining to the footman that he needed some air. As he strolled along the drive towards the gates he wondered if it was even in the realms of possibility that a princess of the French royal family would, or could, marry a cockney urchin. He smiled to himself at the thought of Bill courting Mary-Anne in a few years' time and wondered what her mother would make of it. He couldn't see Mrs Debbon even contemplating it, but stranger things had happened. He silently wished the boy well. He'd have a fight on his hands and no mistake.

"Bill?" Connor said when he reached the gates, trying to act as if he wasn't talking to a shrub.

"Yeah?"

"We want to get Mary-Anne out of the house for tonight. We think there's going to be trouble later as some rather nasty thugs are likely to try to break in. We want her to be safe," Connor told him, quickly outlining the plan to get the girl to Bill's house without the watchers being aware of it. "Do you think you and Martha can manage that?"

"Course we c'n manage it," came the indignant reply. "Ain't exackly difficult, is it? But if there's goin' ter be a brew, why don' all of yers come dahn aht the way?"

"I wish I could tell you everything, Bill, but there are reasons why the rest of us have to stay here. But Mary-Anne should be safely out of the way. Leave it about twenty minutes and then get round to the kitchen door. We'll have Mary-Anne ready by then. Thanks, Bill, this will be a great help."

"I tol' yer before, that's me job. Lookin' aht for 'em all."

But especially for Mary-Anne, Connor thought.

"Good luck, Bill, and take care."

There was no reply, but as Connor left to stroll back to the house, he couldn't help getting the feeling that behind him the shrub was quivering with excitement.

◆

Rather to his surprise it was James who let him back into the house. He'd assumed that Geoffrey would still be there.

"Hello, James. I didn't think you were on duty yet."

"I took the liberty of telling Geoffrey he could take the rest of the evening off, sir. I find that I can cope more easily if I have something to occupy myself with."

"I feel the same way myself. That's why I went for a short stroll. I just needed to get out of the house for a while. It's turning rather chill out there now, though."

"It has certainly turned rather cool today, Mr Harvey. Madam is in the drawing room, should you wish to join her."

◆

"Now you understand what you have to do?"

"Yes, Mama," Mary-Anne told her mother. "I'm to explain to the kitchen servants that I'm sneaking out for the night as a dare. Charles told me that I wouldn't be brave enough to spend a night away from the house, so I'm proving him wrong. I'm to borrow a coat and a cap from one of the scullery maids and leave with them when they finish in about ten minutes' time. I'll keep in the middle of the group as we walk down towards Barton and then Martha and Bill will take me into their home."

"And you know that you have to make your own way down to the kitchens and that you mustn't be seen by any of the other servants. Only the kitchen staff must know about it. If the footman or any other above-stairs servants see you they're bound to stop you, or at least report it to me."

"Everything will be fine. There's no need to worry about me. I'll be perfectly safe."

"Very well. Now don't get under Mr and Mrs Stone's feet when you get to their house. Remember you're a guest and they will be doing us a great favour by taking you in for the night."

"Of course, Mama. I understand."

Mrs Debbon opened the drawing room door slightly and peered out.

"There is no-one in the hall, so you should go down to the kitchens now," she said, beckoning Mary-Anne to her side and hugging her tightly. "Goodbye, my darling, we'll see you in the morning."

"Goodbye, Mama," came the reply, as Mary-Anne ran lightly across the hall and opened the door leading down to the kitchens. As the door closed behind her Mrs Debbon turned to Connor, her eyes bright with unshed tears.

"You *are* certain that this is the right thing to do? She is very young for such an adventure."

"She'll be safer there tonight. For the next few hours, Belmont will be a dangerous place. Mary-Anne is better off well away from here."

◆

Mary-Anne's appearance in the kitchen did not, at first, evoke any comment. The servants were used to her running in and out and to begin with they took little heed of her as they prepared to leave and make their way home. Only when the girl announced that she would be coming with them did a certain amount of surprise creep in, but following Martha's lead they joined in enthusiastically. A large mop cap was produced that hid the girl's long hair and a ragged but warm coat that buttoned up at the neck completed her disguise. Keeping in the centre of the gaggle of servants as they left the house, Mary-Anne slipped out into the night. A hand clasped hers as Bill joined the group before they made their way along the lane towards Bill's home. Towards safety.

CHAPTER TWENTY-SIX

Precautions

They are still watching, but now it will only be a few hours before their plan comes into effect. They have seen the servants leave, laughing among themselves, glad that work was finished for the day. They have seen Bill walking with them, but this is not unusual and they ignore him. Likewise, they ignore all the girls and do not notice that there is one more than usual. They are not concerned with servants. They have more important things on their minds. They have noted that their informant has not been in contact for a while, but are not yet unduly concerned by this. Everything is finally in place. They have brought some oil lamps with them. When lit and thrown into a richly furnished room, they will make excellent incendiary devices. Years of hiding in the dark, of concealing their true identities, will soon be at an end and they can return to their homeland in triumph. Everything is ready.

◆

"I know it sounds stupid, but do you think it knows? The house I mean. Do you think it knows it's only got a few hours to live?" Matt asked Connor when they were alone in the drawing room, Mrs Debbon having gone upstairs to collect Charles.

"I believe that buildings can often be more than just brick, stone and mortar. I've been in houses that have had atmospheres so oppressive I haven't wanted to stay in them for more than a few minutes, so I don't see why there shouldn't be something of the sort here."

"It's the waiting I can't stand. It's like when I'm waiting for my turn to race in a swimming gala. I'm fine when I'm ready to go and on the edge of the pool poised for the start, but I hate the hanging about beforehand. This is like that, only a thousand times worse."

"And it's even worse because we don't exactly know what's going to happen. We know what we *think* will happen, but then we may have done something to alter that in the past few days. We can only wait and see."

"I know. And the oddest thoughts keep cropping up in my head."

"Such as?"

"I was just thinking that I could smell Paula's cinnamon cookies."

"Perhaps not as odd as you think."

"How come?"

"Your house stands exactly where Belmont does. If we can flip back and forth in time, maybe other things can as well."

"Like the aroma of cookies from our kitchen?"

"Seems perfectly possible to me. If we can do it, maybe a scent drifting back into the past can as well. Any aroma from your kitchen would drift all through here."

"Would anyone else be able to smell it?"

"Probably not, in the same way that they can't flip in time themselves. But I think it's a good sign."

"How so?"

"Not really sure, but if you're starting to get back in touch with our own time, albeit only via the smell of cooking, then it may mean we're destined to get through this and get back home."

"You could . . ." Matt started to say, but a loud crash from the hall had him flying to the door. He looked out to see one of the housemaids guiltily picking up a tray that she must have dropped whilst trying to negotiate the stairs. Matt felt that if anything else happened he would probably collapse in a heap. He came back into the room and explained it was a false alarm.

"I don't actually think anything will happen whilst the servants are still in the house," Connor told him. "It would be too risky. The live-out servants have already left, so it's only those who live in who are still on duty. When they finally finish for the night, that's when the risk will be at its greatest."

A few minutes later Mrs Debbon joined them, leading a very confused Charles by the hand. Connor noted that she had changed from her elegant evening gown into a sturdy full-length skirt with a blouse and a matching jacket.

"I felt that if something untoward were to occur tonight then an evening gown might prove to be rather unsuitable," she explained.

"Very sensible," Connor told her.

"Mama?" Charles piped up.

"Yes?"

"I don't understand. It's long time past when I usually have to go to bed. I know Nurse has gone to Exeter but shouldn't one of the other servants be helping me to bed? And I can't find Mary-Anne anywhere."

"Your sister was feeling a little unwell and is lying down in my bedroom. As for it being past your usual bedtime you are quite correct. However, I decided that it might be a novel idea for us all to stay up late for once. You are always saying that you don't want to go to bed early so now is your chance not to."

"Oh," Charles said, obviously not at all sure if he really wanted that or not. "How long will I be staying up?"

"Until I decide we should all retire for the night, of course. However, the servants will want to dampen down the fire for the night and close off the room. I think we should all be more comfortable in my boudoir for the rest of the evening. There are ample chairs in there and Sarah will have made up the fire. It will also mean that I will be able to hear Mary-Anne if she calls for me from the bedroom. If you gentlemen would care to join us there in about an hour?"

"A good idea," Connor replied. "A first-floor room would be best."

Matt said nothing until she had left, a still bewildered Charles following in her wake. Only when the door had closed behind her did he say what was on his mind.

"Are you sure the first floor is best?"

"I would think so. If anyone does manage to break in then they'll have further to go to get to us if we're upstairs." When there was no reply Connor looked at his nephew, noting the concerned look on his face. "Or don't you agree?"

"It's the report in the paper. Don't you remember? It said that they could see the family at a first-floor window screaming for help. If we go upstairs, then we could be doing exactly what we *shouldn't* be doing."

"Lord, I hadn't thought of that. I don't see that we can do much about it though. There's no way we can explain to Maria why we don't think it's a good idea after all."

"I know. It's just that no matter what we do, everything still seems to be working out the same way. It's got to the point when I'm thinking that we can't do anything. Everyone's going to die whatever we do to try and stop it happening."

"That's a scenario that I don't even want to consider. However, there is one thing that I've been thinking about."

"What's that?"

"Well in spite of me convincing Maria that Mary-Anne would be a lot safer at Bill's house than here, she's still at risk. One of the watchers may have seen her leave."

"Bit late to be thinking of that now, isn't it?"

"Maybe, but it's not too late to do something about it. I think you should get down there as well. A bit of extra muscle wouldn't hurt if there's trouble. And I know Maria would feel better knowing you were there keeping an eye on Mary-Anne."

"It's a good job you never decided to become an actor."

"What?"

"You don't believe for a minute that Mary-Anne's in danger. You'd never have let her go if you did. You want me safely out of the way just as you did with Mary-Anne."

"Was it that obvious?"

"Probably only to me. And the answer's no — I'm not going anywhere."

"But you know how dangerous Belmont is going to be. I don't want you getting hurt. I really think it may be better if you were to go down to Bill's."

"Not a chance. There's no way that I'm running away and leaving everyone else here. If anything did happen then I wouldn't be able to live with myself. Besides, you've been saying all along that you think there's a reason for all this, a reason that we're here. In which case, I think I'm going to be needed. Whatever it is that we have to do, it's going to take both of us. I'm staying. End of conversation."

"OK, enough said. Let's get up to our rooms and have a rest before things start to kick off."

"No arguments here on that one."

◆

An hour later, Connor took one last look at his room, and then checked his pockets to make sure he had everything he needed. He also checked the windows were locked and left the room, closing the door behind him. After knocking at Matt's door, he went in to find his nephew sprawled full length on his bed.

"Just catching a last rest," he said, in reply to his uncle's unspoken question. "We're not likely to get very much later on."

"I suspect that you're right about that. We need to join the others in Maria's room. Have you got all your clobber with you?"

"What clobber?"

"Anything that you don't want to be destroyed in the fire if it happens."

"Rat farts — I hadn't thought of that," Matt replied, diving into the chest of drawers and digging out his music player, watch and phone, plus his dad's lighter and knife. He stood for a moment undecided and then pulled out a couple of pairs of boxer shorts and stuffed them in his jacket pocket.

"I brought every pair I've got with me," he said, by way of explanation. "If we flip back I'll have nothing to wear."

"*When* we get back, not if. Anything else you need?"

"No. The rest is all the 1898 stuff. If there's no fire it'll still be there, and if there is and we flip back then I won't need it anyway."

"OK, let's go. They'll be wondering where we are."

◆

Helen had already joined her mother and brother in the boudoir by the time Connor and Matt arrived. She had followed her

367

mother's example and was wearing daytime clothing.

Last to arrive was James, who had also discarded his formal wear in favour of a thick outdoor suit.

"I took the liberty of changing my clothing, madam. I should have asked first of course, but felt that . . . "

"A very sensible idea," Mrs Debbon interrupted him. "As you can see, I and my daughter had similar thoughts. The doors and the windows are all secured?"

"Yes, madam. As soon as the last of the servants had left, I checked them all myself. I have also taken the liberty of locking the door into the servants' wing, so no-one can enter the house from that direction."

"Thank you. It seems that we shall be in your debt when this is all over. I will not forget what you have done for us."

"Not at all, madam. May I ask where Miss Mary-Anne is?" he asked, looking round for the missing girl.

"She was feeling unwell and is lying down on my bed," she told him, lying so convincingly that even Connor thought it sounded plausible. He felt bad about not telling James where Mary-Anne had gone, but he'd agreed with her mother that they didn't want Charles to find out and so the less people who knew the better. He hoped she wasn't having too miserable a time of it at Bill's house.

◆

In fact Mary-Anne was having the time of her life. In spite of his ailments, Jem Stone could still produce a nifty tune on his accordion and he was in full flow. His wife was busy producing a hearty late evening supper, whilst Martha and Bill were trying to teach Mary-Anne the steps of a country polka, a task not made any easier by the fact that all three kept on collapsing with fits of giggles.

"If you don't mind me saying so, Miss, I don't think you're ever going to be a great dancer," Martha told her, as Mary-Anne had once again fluffed her steps and landed in a heap on the floor. Mary-Anne was far too busy laughing to even attempt a reply. Bill helped her to her feet, trying hard to control his own mirth. He had the feeling that as Mary-Anne's intended future husband it wasn't perhaps the done thing to be laughing so much at her failure to complete even one set of dance steps, but as she herself was almost crying with laughter then he felt that maybe it didn't matter. He alone out of his family knew the real reason for the girl's arrival in his house. He wondered if he ought to get back to keeping watch on Belmont, but decided that, for the time being at any rate, his place was with her. Martha and their parents had all accepted the story that it was a dare on Mary-Anne's part — to see if she could spend a night away from home without anyone noticing.

Bill wondered how the others had been so easily deceived as he knew perfectly well that if the girl had indeed sneaked out of Belmont, then she would have been missed within half an hour, when her nurse would have gone to check on her.

Although she had far more freedom than most children of her age and station in life, Mary-Anne still chafed against the rigid routine of meals, lessons and having to behave as a lady at all times. She had a rebellious streak in her that rarely had a chance to show itself, but this taste of what life could be like beyond the sometimes stifling atmosphere of Belmont had already convinced her, young as she was, that she had no intention of playing the part that her mother would undoubtedly map out for her.

After eating her way through a supper that seemed to her to have consisted of the most delicious food that she had ever tasted (with the possible exception of the cheeseburger and chips that Matt had introduced her to) she was shown upstairs in the tiny cottage to a small bedroom under the thatch. She frowned as she looked around the room, noting the single bed.

"What is it, Miss Mary-Anne?" Martha asked, having shown the girl to the room. "Is there something wrong?"

"Is this your room?" she asked.

"Why yes, Miss, but the bed's quite comfortable really. Mother filled the mattress with fresh straw only a week ago."

"But if this is your room, then where will you sleep tonight?"

"Oh, don't you worry about that, Miss. Mother has made up another mattress downstairs and I'll sleep there."

"No, that simply will not do at all. I will have the mattress downstairs. I cannot have you giving up your own bed."

In spite of loud protests from all the family, except Bill who had been expecting her response all along, Mary-Anne refused to even consider taking Martha's bed from her.

"But what will madam think when she finds out?" Martha asked her, trying a last-ditch attempt to get her to change her mind.

"Mama won't find out, but even if she does, I will just say that it was all of my doing and then there won't be any trouble."

Finally admitting defeat, the family settled down for the night. In spite of her insistence that she would be perfectly comfortable sleeping on the straw mattress downstairs, Mary-Anne privately considered that she wouldn't be able to get a wink of sleep. In fact she was sound asleep within seconds of her head hitting the pillow. Bill, whose own small bed was hidden behind a calico screen in a corner of the downstairs room, waited until he heard Mary-Anne's breathing become regular as she fell into a deep sleep and then quietly rose from his bed. He hadn't bothered to undress, so holding his boots in his hands, he tiptoed past the sleeping girl and carefully opened the front door. He hesitated for a few seconds and then returned to gaze down on Mary-Anne's sleeping form. He bent down and kissed her gently on the cheek before leaving the cottage and starting the walk back up the hill towards Belmont. He'd come to the conclusion that if anyone had seen Mary-Anne leaving the house, then they would already have made their move. As all was quiet, it was safe for him to assume that the watchers thought she was still inside the mansion. His duty was, therefore, to get back to his post as soon as possible. Twenty minutes later he was inside the shrub by the gates and keeping watch on Belmont. Most of the great house was in darkness, the only lights were from two rooms on the first floor and in the servants' wing.

◆

"Stop squirming, Charles. What *is* the matter with you?"

"I need the bathroom, Mama."

"Oh, I see. Well I don't suppose you can come to any harm just going to the bathroom. Mind you come straight back here again afterwards though," she told him.

"Yes, Mama," he said, bolting to the door. They could hear his feet running along the corridor.

"Seems he was getting desperate," Connor told Maria.

"I confess I never even thought about that aspect. We can hardly stay in here all night without needing to use the facilities."

"It could prove a little awkward," Connor agreed. "How did you persuade the children's nurse to leave her post for the evening?"

"We seem to have had a stroke of good fortune there. Quite by chance James had heard that her mother is unwell. She lives in Exeter, so I persuaded Nurse to take the day and the night off to go and see her mother. I gave her the money for the train tickets and told her that I would arrange for one of the maids to look after Charles and Mary-Anne for tonight. I also told Sarah, my personal maid, that I would not need her services this evening. That is not particularly uncommon and so will not be remarked upon."

"So all of the servants, apart from James of course, are either off the premises entirely, or are in the servants' wing which is now locked off from the main house?"

"Yes. We are now on our own here, but with everything locked and bolted I think we are as safe as it is possible to be."

Connor didn't answer. Unless he and Matt had somehow already altered history, then they weren't in any way safe.

When it happened, it happened fast. One moment everything was quiet, the next a high-pitched yell broke the silence.

"Charles!" Helen shouted, rushing to the door.

Matt beat her to it, opening the door just in time in time to see a struggling Charles being dragged through a door on the opposite side of the gallery. Two more figures were running up the stairs towards them. Matt shouted for James to help as he was about to launch himself at the intruders, but Connor grabbed him by the shoulder and pulled him back into the room, slamming the door shut and sliding the heavy bolts into place.

"What the hell are you doing!" Matt yelled at him. "We need to get Charles back now! Why did you stop me!"

"The two running up the stairs — one had a gun. You wouldn't have got anywhere near them!"

Matt glared at his uncle for a few seconds before nodding his agreement.

"But how the hell did they get in? Everything was locked and barred, I checked myself. It doesn't make any sense," Matt fumed.

"No, it doesn't. Did you see who they were?" Connor asked him.

"No, not really. It's quite dark with only the night lamps lit. It was a man holding Charles. I'm not certain but I think one of the others was a woman."

"I think you're right," Connor told him. "I also think the other one may have a problem with his arm. He seemed to be holding it as he ran up the stairs. There wasn't time to see more."

"His left arm?" Matt asked.

"I think so."

"Could it be the same man that was here the other night, the one I threw the knife at?"

"That would make sense," Connor told him. "Do you know who he is?" he asked Mrs Debbon.

"That monster styles himself the Marquis de Chambourg. Claims to be the rightful heir to the title and is probably the leader of that nest of vipers."

"Something to worry about later. For now we need to get Charles back. Any ideas anyone?" Connor asked.

"If one of us could get to Barton Hall we could get help from there," Helen said. "Mr Brown and his sons go shooting regularly and will have guns."

"I'll go," Matt offered. "I'll go along the corridor to my room, open the window and shin down the drainpipe."

"But the window will be locked and there's no way you'll be able to break it open," Connor said, unhappy about Matt taking such a risk, but realising that it may be their only hope. His own days of climbing up or down drainpipes were long past.

"I'll take the window key with me. James will have it on him."

"For God's sake be careful, Matt. You know the sort of people we're dealing with!"

"I know. I'll be careful."

"Then God grant you safety, Matthew," Mrs Debbon said, kissing him lightly on the cheek before turning to James. "James, could you kindly give Matthew the key to the window in his room, please?"

"I regret that will not be possible, madam."

"Why ever not?"

"Because I cannot allow anyone to leave this room."

Everyone turned to stare at him. And at the small twin-barrelled pistol that he held in his hand, a pistol pointing directly at Mrs Debbon. She looked at him as if he had suddenly grown horns.

"What is the meaning of this? Have you taken leave of your senses?"

"No, but it is necessary that you all remain here. And I also need to know where Mary-Anne is. I looked into your bedroom a few minutes ago and she isn't there."

She remained silent, staring at him as if she hadn't seen him before until realisation finally dawned.

"So *you* are the traitor. You are the one who has been working for those fools outside. Indeed, I take it you are part of this sordid and utterly ridiculous scheme to kidnap my son and take him to Paris?"

James didn't answer, just kept the firearm pointing at her.

"And am I to assume that your name is not James Miller?" she continued.

"I am Jean-Paul Mentier, Duc de Drasbourg."

"Another lunatic with a title that is dead and buried and of no consequence to anyone."

"When our plan succeeds, then my lands will be restored to me, and my title will, once again, be acknowledged. France needs me."

"France needs stability."

"If there were any justice in the world then I would not need to be holding you all prisoner in this unseemly manner."

"If there were any justice in the world you would have been smothered at birth! And poor Edward has been made to suffer for your crimes. I shall have to ensure that he is adequately recompensed afterwards."

"I greatly regret that it is unlikely you will be able to do so. You have had many chances to accompany the King to Paris and have spurned them all. It is now too late and you are seen as a hindrance. Steps have already been taken to ensure that you and, I regret, the other members of your family and your guests, are no longer able to interfere."

Even as he spoke, thin grey tendrils of smoke slithered under the door and entered the room.

"What have you done, you monster!"

"Tomorrow's newspapers will carry the tragic story of a fire that destroyed this house and how most of the family died as they were overcome by the smoke. Only Charles escaped owing to the heroic efforts of the butler, who managed to fight his way through the flames to save him. It seems the King will have to manage without you, but it doesn't matter. He will have advisors. Loyal advisors."

"Loyal leeches," she said scornfully. "I, too, am descended from kings. Do you really believe you can intimidate me?"

"That was never our intention."

"The last Duc de Drasbourg was a loyal servant to King Louis XVI, was he not?"

"He was."

"And I presume that you claim that you, like him, are a loyal servant of the crown?"

"Of course."

"Then how dare you speak to me in this manner!" she stormed. "I am the Dowager Queen of France. My son, the King, is not yet of age. I am therefore by ancient right the Queen Regent. Why are you not on your knees in front of me, you miserable wretch?"

"You have always refused to use your title, or to acknowledge your rightful position."

"Then I choose to do so now! As Queen Regent of France, I command you lay down your gun!" she thundered.

A slight look of doubt crossed his face and for a moment his hold on the pistol wavered and it pointed at the floor. It was the moment that Matt had been waiting for. He'd never taken his eyes off James since he'd produced the weapon and at the first sign of hesitation he launched himself across the room and rugby tackled him to the floor. Connor also flung himself across the room, but Helen was even quicker. She grabbed a heavy poker from the fireplace and struck James as hard as she could, but it wasn't enough to stop him grappling with Matt for possession of the gun. Connor didn't dare to try anything else, not while James still had the weapon in his hand. The two protagonists rolled on the floor, each seeking a weakness in the other's defence. Matt was young and his love of sports made him fit and strong, but his opponent was fighting with a desperation born of panic that their long-held plans were in danger. Suddenly there was a loud report as the gun went off and both fighters lay motionless on the floor, the others unable to see if either of them was wounded. But as they stared, momentarily transfixed, they could all see a bright red stain spreading across Matt's shirt.

"No!" cried Connor, as he rushed to kneel by the side of his nephew.

CHAPTER TWENTY-SEVEN

Faces at the window

Smoke had started to seep into the servants' wing and within seconds most were awake and hastily throwing on some clothes. They tried the door into the main house but finding it locked, raced to find the housekeeper to unlock it. Hastily throwing a coat over her nightgown, Mrs Gregson snatched up her keys and ran to the dividing door and unlocked it. It still refused to open.

"It must be bolted from the other side," she said in a shocked voice to Sarah, who had joined her in trying to open the door. "There's no way in."

The smoke was by now billowing under the door and, coughing and spluttering, the servants were forced to leave the wing and evacuate the house. Assembling on the front lawn, Mrs Gregson hunted for James, but finding no sign of him, shouted to Geoffrey instead.

"Get a horse from the stables and ride down into Torquay. Get the fire engine here as quickly as you can!"

Geoffrey didn't waste time in answering but rushed to the stables, threw a saddle on the nearest horse and galloped off along the lane as fast as he could.

"Mrs Gregson," Sarah shouted, above the noise of the fire which was fast taking hold in the main house, "has anyone let Edward out of his room?"

"Dear God in heaven, I completely forgot. I'll go now."

The housekeeper ran back into the smoke-filled servants' wing. She could hear Edward hammering at his door along the corridor.

"I thought I'd been forgotten," he said, sighing with relief as she unlocked the door.

"I'm so sorry," she gasped, out of breath from running along the corridor, "it was Sarah who reminded me that you were still in here."

"What the hell's happening?"

"The main house is on fire and we can't get in. All the doors and windows are locked and the servants' door is bolted from the other side."

"But that door's never even locked, let alone bolted."

"Well, it is now. And we need to get out of here before we both choke."

Without further words they stumbled their way out into the fresh night air. Running around to the front of the house to join the other servants, they could see flames in several parts of the house.

"This can't be right," Edward shouted to Sarah. "Fires don't start in different places all at the same time. This is all wrong. Where's Geoffrey?"

"Mrs Gregson sent him to get help."

"Do you think you can help me carry a ladder? There's one behind the gardener's bothy."

◆

They raced around the house to the small stone hut where the gardeners kept their tools and found a long ladder propped against the rear wall. Grabbing it, they ran panting with it back to the front lawn.

"I don't think it's long enough to reach the first floor," Sarah told him.

"I know. I don't want to use it as a ladder. I want to use it to try and break one of the windows!"

"I'll 'elp yer," came a small voice, as Bill grabbed hold of the middle of the ladder.

Edward didn't waste time arguing, but took hold of the front end of the ladder, with Sarah at the rear. They ran as fast as they could at the nearest window and hit it full tilt, the shock knocking all three of them to the ground. A few of the small diamond-shaped panes cracked, but nothing more. They tried over and over again, getting more and more frantic as the flames spread through the house, but it was a useless attempt. Several of the small panes had shattered, but the metal glazing bars did no more than bend slightly and the mullions didn't even move. Belmont had been designed to keep unwanted visitors out and the triple glazing of the window was proving more than a match for the improvised battering ram. The ladder finally gave up and broke into pieces. After that Edward was forced to hold on tightly to a struggling Bill who was desperately trying to use parts of the broken ladder to continue trying to break into the house.

◆

Ernest Hardwick was feeling every day of his fifty-one years and was not in the best of moods as he walked the last few hundred yards to his house in Barton. Two of his ships had docked that afternoon, and there had been a lot of work involved in seeing the cargoes landed, sorting out the paperwork and giving his captains their orders for their next trips. His temper was not improved by the fact that Daniel, who was supposed to have helped him, had absented himself with a rather feeble excuse. He intended to have a serious word with him in the morning. If the boy was ever going to run the business for him when he got older he needed to show some sort of commitment. Ernest reached into his pocket for the house key, muttering to himself that a lot of the trouble was due to the lad's infatuation with the Debbon girl. Not that he could blame him for that, the girl was without doubt a stunning beauty, but there was a time and a place for everything. Thinking of this he glanced further up the hill towards Belmont. The house couldn't be seen as the brow of the hill was in the way, but he could sometimes see the silhouette of the trees against the skyline. They stood out clearly that evening against the orange glow behind them. His eyes widened as he realised what the glow meant. Even as he watched, it became brighter and was streaked with flecks of red and yellow. His tiredness forgotten, he let himself into the house and ran up the stairs.

"Daniel," he shouted as he flung open the door to his son's room. "Get your coat quick, there's trouble."

"Whatever's wrong?" Daniel asked, seeing his father's flushed face and worried expression.

"It's Belmont, it's on fire."

"What?" he yelled, pulling the heavy curtains back from the window. Cold talons gripped his heart as he saw the flames leaping up behind the brow of the hill.

"You go on ahead, I'll get the neighbours up and see what we can do to help. We'll be there as soon as we can."

Daniel didn't hear him. He was already charging downstairs and out of the house. His heart pounding, he ran as fast as he could up the steep hill and along the lane. He hoped and prayed that there was a mistake, that it was the woods that were aflame and not the house, but in his heart he knew what it was. He reached the gates and stopped dead as he saw a sight that haunted his sleep for years afterwards. Belmont was burning from end to end, great sheets of flame rising monstrously into the night sky. The noise was appalling: a deep roaring sound that assaulted his ears. There was a crowd of people on the front lawn, some he recognised as servants and others he didn't. He searched desperately for the faces that he wanted to see, one in particular, but they weren't there. A small figure appeared at his side.

"Mary-Anne ain't there, but the rest are inside. They can't get aht!"

He looked down at Bill's tear-streaked face. He looked again at the house and raced to the front door, Bill right behind him. He tugged wildly at the handle, until Edward dragged him away.

"The door's locked and we think barred as well on the inside. We've tried breaking through a window but no luck. We've found something that might help with the door though, so grab one of these," he yelled, thrusting a heavy axe into Daniel's hands.

Together they set to work on the door, Bill right behind them, desperate to help. They were making little or no headway when they heard a shriek from behind them. Sarah was pointing to an upstairs window.

"It's them!" she screamed. "It's madam and the children. They can't get out!"

They looked up to where there was a frantic hammering at a window, but it was defying all efforts to break the glass. Terrified faces could just be seen behind the panes. The clanging of bells sounded in the lane and the fire engine, its team of horses blown from the steep hill, arrived in the grounds. Knowing immediately that there was nothing to be done to save the house, the firemen, seeing what the onlookers were pointing at, seized their ladder and tried to put it up to the first floor window. The ladder hit the window ledge and one of the firemen was racing up as fast as he could when there was a great explosion from inside the house and the room erupted in flames, blowing the window out and forcing the fireman to slide back down the ladder away from the flames now roaring into the night. Edward shouted at Daniel to get away from the house as the gas lines blew and more explosions rocked the building. Daniel ignored him as Edward dropped his axe and ran to get clear, Bill grabbing the fallen axe and joining Daniel in the futile attempt to break down the door, each of them knowing in his heart that that task was hopeless. One last explosion finally defeated the front door which was blown out onto the gravel drive, flinging both Daniel and Bill back with it. Flames belched from the open doorway, revealing the raging inferno inside. Daniel's father, who had arrived with team of local men, had to restrain his son from trying to run into the flames.

"There's nothing you can do, Daniel," he shouted, "there's no way anyone can get in there."

"Helen's still inside," he yelled, his eyes wild, "I've got to get to her, I've got to!"

"I'm sorry, son. It's impossible. No-one could survive that heat, no-one."

Daniel slowly sank to his knees, the tears streaming down his face, as he gazed at the blazing house. A great crashing roar reverberated across the lawn as one of the huge chimneys collapsed into the fire, a shower of sparks and burning debris shooting skywards. The servants, the firemen, the helpers and the onlookers were all slowly driven back by the intense heat. Belmont had gone, taking all those still inside with it.

CHAPTER TWENTY-EIGHT

Forty-five minutes earlier

Connor knelt by the blood-soaked body of his nephew, desperately feeling for a pulse — anything to show that he was alive. Mrs Debbon was holding her weeping daughter tightly, both looking with frightened eyes at the scene before them. To Connor's everlasting relief Matt opened his eyes, blinked and tried to sit up but lay back down again.

"What hit me?" he asked, before realising that everyone was staring at him. "What?" he asked. "What are you all looking at?"

"You, you great dummy. You're covered in blood. We thought . . . I thought . . ."

"Oh, that," Matt said, finally sitting up and looking down at himself. "The blood isn't mine, it must be James's, or whatever his real name is. The gun went off."

"I know it went off, you stupid great idiot. I thought you'd been shot!"

"Not me. He must be badly hurt though — I think he fired both barrels."

Once she had seen that Matt was alive and well, Mrs Debbon went to where James lay on the floor, the blood now pooling by his side and staining the carpet a deep red. She felt for a pulse, then knelt by his side and put her cheek against his mouth.

"He's dead," she told them. "Poor misguided fool. He dreamed of returning in triumph to a new order in France and all it gained him was death in a foreign land. You are sure you are not hurt, Matthew?"

"No, I'm fine," he said, glancing at the smoke now gaining in strength as it seeped under the door, "but we have to get out of here as fast as we can. They've torched the house."

"So I see," she replied "I gather that was the aim, that we all die in the fire and they escape to France with Charles. However, if we can get down to the front door we should be able to escape that way."

"The door will be locked, Mama," Helen said, her arm around Matt, heedless of the blood staining her clothes.

"James will have the keys on him. Kindly do not give in to panic, Helen. We need to remain cool and calm."

She knelt by James's body and felt in his pockets, retrieving a large bunch of keys.

"Regrettably I have no idea which key opens which door, so it may take some time finding the right one."

"Time is something we don't have, Maria," Connor said. "Stand well back," he told the others as he unbolted the door, "the fire may be just the other side."

He waited for them all to get as far away from the door as they could, before inching it open, making sure that he himself was protected as far as possible by the door. He peered round the edge of the door to see that the vast entrance hall was a writhing mass of flames, the great tongues of fire licking greedily at the ornately carved woodwork of the first-floor gallery, and some already reaching for the roof timbers. Even a quick glance told him that the house was beyond saving. That part of history couldn't be changed. It remained to be seen, he thought to himself, whether it was possible to change anything else. He risked another look before shutting the door against the roar of the flames.

"No go," he said to the others. "The route to the front door is completely blocked. The fire's between us and the door. I couldn't see over the gallery to check if the corridor to the side door is passable or not but, judging where the seat of the fire is, I doubt it very much."

"Can we can reach the door down to the kitchens?" Mrs Debbon asked.

Connor opened the door again and stuck his head briefly around the edge.

"If we're quick," he said, turning back to the others, "but we'll have to go now."

"Those monsters still have my son. I cannot leave him here."

"But they'll have got him out of the house by now, won't they?"

"I do not think so. They will be waiting for James to return to say that we have been dealt with."

"She's right, they won't know we're free," Matt said.

"No, they won't," Connor agreed, "but we have very little time. They've set the fire going assuming that James would be with them almost straight away. If he's not there within a couple of minutes they'll have to leave without him or get caught in the fire themselves. We don't know which room they'll be in."

"I do," Matt said. "I saw the first man dragging Charles through the door on the opposite side of the gallery. I think it's the nursery."

"Then we're going to have to be bloody quick, the fire's directly under the gallery!" Connor shouted, opening the door again, coughing as the smoke billowed into the room. He bent to retrieve James's pistol from the floor, but Matt stopped him.

"No use, Uncle Conn. It's a two shot pistol and he fired both barrels. Even if he's got more bullets on him, I've no idea how to reload it."

"I'll take it anyway," Connor said, picking the weapon up from the floor. "They won't know that it's empty and it might give me the edge I need."

"But there are three of them over there," Matt argued, "and they're probably all armed. And all you'll have is an empty pistol!"

"Best I can do, Matt. I'll just have to trust to luck and hope they're taken by surprise. They'll be expecting James, so maybe it'll shake them when they see it's not him at the door." He turned to where Mrs Debbon was still comforting her daughter. "Maria, take Helen and Matt and get out. I'll get Charles and join you in the kitchen."

"He's my son, Connor. I should try and save him myself," she insisted.

"There isn't time to argue, Maria. You're needed here. You know your way around Belmont, I don't. Get the others down to the kitchens. If I'm not there in five minutes, then get everyone out."

She looked at him for a moment, as for probably the first time in her life, she stood undecided.

"Save my son, Connor," she simply said.

"I will, or die trying."

He ran around the gallery towards the door to the nursery, suddenly realising that Matt was by his side and hadn't followed Helen and her mother as they ran down the stairs towards the kitchen door.

"Matt! Get out, follow the others!"

"No chance. You said that whatever we're here for needs us both! And you're certainly going to need help to get Charles away from those thugs."

Connor stopped and stared at him for a few seconds before nodding his agreement.

"OK, no time to argue," he answered as they reached the nursery door, noting that Matt was carrying the heavy poker from the boudoir. "We've got less than two minutes before this gallery goes up in flames as well as the downstairs hall," Connor shouted over the roar of the fire, which was even fiercer now, with tendrils of flame licking at the gallery carpets.

"So what do we do?" Matt shouted back.

"I'll bang on the door. They'll be expecting James so they'll probably open up. Then we'll have to see if we can grab Charles and make a run for it before they recover their senses and start shooting."

"Will that work?"

"How the hell should I know?"

Connor rapped hard on the door and raised the pistol so that it would be pointing directly at anyone opening up. Almost at once the door opened and the scene revealed a youngish man and woman in the middle of the room holding a struggling Charles between them. The man who opened the door was the one that Matt had wounded several days earlier, his arm heavily bandaged.

"Where the hell have you been . . ." he started to say, before realising it wasn't the butler and was taken completely by surprise at the appearance of Connor and Matt and the pistol pointing straight at him. Everyone seemed frozen in position, but the man at the door recovered quickly and swung at Connor with his right hand, knocking the pistol out of his grasp. With the heavy poker he was carrying Matt struck the man's wounded arm before he had time do anything else, and with a cry of pain the man collapsed onto the floor. At the same time Charles took the chance to kick the woman holding him hard on the ankle. She let go of her grip and Charles bolted for the door. Matt grabbed his hand and dragged him out to the gallery. The whole action had taken only a few seconds, but the younger pair were recovering fast from their shock. Connor snatched the key from the inside of the lock and slammed the door shut in their faces, putting the key in the outside of the lock as he did so, intending to lock them in. Before he could, they'd reached the door and were trying to open it. Connor held the door shut with all his strength, but dared not let go to try to turn the key.

"Matt, turn the key."

"But they won't be able to get out, they'll burn to death."

"There's no other way."

"There must be!"

"There's no time, Matt! It's them or all of us. I can't hold this door any longer!"

After one desperate look at his uncle, Matt turned the key in the lock. Connor picked up Charles in his arms and he and Matt ran as fast as they could along the gallery and down the stairs. Reaching the door to the kitchen stairs, Matt wrenched it open just as one of the columns supporting the gallery came crashing down in a blaze of sparks. The gallery sagged perilously for a few seconds, then gave up the unequal challenge and collapsed into the inferno below.

"Inside, quick," Connor shouted.

Matt slammed the door shut behind them. The glow from the burning house coming through the windows gave them enough light to find their way down the steep stairs into the cavernous kitchen. The fire itself had not yet reached that area, but judging by the smoke billowing round the edges of the shutter of the dumb waiter it wouldn't be long before it did.

Connor put Charles down and the boy ran across the kitchen into his mother's arms.

"Mama," he cried, the tears streaming down his face, "I don't understand what's happening. And where's Mary-Anne?" he asked, looking around him frantically.

"Your sister is quite safe, Charles. She left the house some time ago. She is at young William's house, no doubt fast asleep. As for those men, there is no time to explain it all to you now, but suffice it to say that they were trying to kidnap you and force me to pay them a great deal of money. Now dry your tears, you're going to have to be very brave and help look after your sister and me."

The thought that he was being given responsibility forced Charles to make an obviously huge effort to appear as calm as his mother wanted.

Helen ran across the kitchen to the back door.

"It's locked, Mama," she said, tugging frantically at the huge door. "Have you got the key?"

"No, my dear, James wouldn't have had the keys to the below stairs areas on him, so all of the outside doors will be locked."

"So we can't get out," Helen said, a note of panic creeping into her voice, "we're all going to die!"

"Nonsense, Helen," Mrs Debbon retorted, "I have absolutely no intention of departing from this life by such a vulgar method as dying in a house fire. And *please* try to control yourself. Kindly remember that you're a lady!"

"She's magnificent," Matt whispered in Connor's ear. "You'd think we were at a garden party instead of stuck in a burning house with no way out."

"Magnificent indeed," agreed Connor.

"Now," said Mrs Debbon, totally unaware of her own magnificence, "hopefully the door over there will not be locked, just bolted."

She indicated a white painted door in one corner of the kitchen.

"But, Mama," said Charles, his voice quivering, "that door doesn't lead to the outside, just into the cold scullery."

"I am perfectly well aware of where the door leads, thank you Charles. I trust that you are not also going to panic at the least little thing?"

"No, Mama, of course not," he replied, his voice seeming to indicate that he wasn't certain about the truth of his answer.

When they reached the door, they found that it was, as hoped, bolted but not locked. Once the heavy bolts had been drawn back, the door swung open easily, revealing a long, narrow scullery, one side lined with shelves and cupboards, the other bare save for two small, heavily barred windows. Although small, the room seemed much lighter than the main kitchen, and looking up through the windows it wasn't hard to see why. Flames were roaring from several of the first-floor windows, and it wouldn't be long before the great house was entirely engulfed by fire.

"Where now, Mrs Debbon?" Matt asked.

"The door at the far end of the scullery, see if it will open, will you, please, Matthew?"

He tried the door, almost panicked when he thought it was locked, then realising it was bolted, slid the bolts back and tried again. To his immense relief the heavy door swung open. Beyond was not another larder or pantry as he'd been expecting, but instead there was a long, dark flight of steps. The bottom of the steps couldn't be seen, even with the glow from the fire behind them.

"We will need candles or lanterns," Mrs Debbon called to him once she'd seen that the door was open. "There are no windows on the stairs or along the passage."

"There are two oil lamps on the shelf, Mama," Helen told her.

"Very good. Now if you could light them, Matthew, we can be on our way."

Matt looked round him for something to light the lamps with but couldn't see anything. The lack of a naked flame in a house that was burning down around their ears almost caused him to laugh out loud but he managed to control himself in time. He doubted if anyone else would find it funny. In the end he just said 'sod it' under his breath and dived into his pocket, producing the cigarette lighter. He clicked the flame on and lit the two lamps, ignoring the puzzled stares from Helen, Charles and their mother. With the lamps lit and Mrs Debbon leading the way, they started down the steps, Matt bringing up the rear with the second lantern and closing the door firmly behind them.

"The fire will eventually burn through the door," Mrs Debbon said, as she walked along the passage, holding a scared Charles by the hand, "but the passage itself is brick lined and cannot burn. The closed door will hold the smoke back long enough for our needs."

The steps ended after what seemed an eternity to Connor and in front of them stretched a level passage, receding into total darkness. Matt couldn't even guess its length, or where it would lead, even though, as he realised with a jolt, they were underneath what would, in over a century, be his own house.

"In a few moments we will need to proceed with great caution," Mrs Debbon told them. "In front of us is a very deep, unprotected drop."

Matt looked questioningly at his uncle, who shrugged his shoulders in return. Neither of them had a clue where they were going. After a few more moments, Mrs Debbon stopped, holding her lamp high above her head. In front of them yawned a huge, circular brick-lined pit. Connor peered over the edge, staring down into the gloom.

"Of course," he said, "I should have known. It's an icehouse."

"What?" Matt asked.

"An icehouse. It's where ice would be brought in during the winter and stored here until it was needed in the summer."

"That's one hell of a lot of ice," Matt observed, staring at the massive chamber.

"The former tenants entertained a great deal," Mrs Debbon explained, "but we never entertained on a scale sufficient to warrant such a large amount of ice. The icehouse hasn't been used since we moved in."

"But what do we do now, Mama," Helen asked. "Wait here for the fire to die down and then try to get back?"

"No. As the plan was to see us all dead, I believe we should let everyone think that is what has happened, at least for the time being. When all danger has passed, and the authorities have tracked down those involved in this unseemly and sordid exercise, then it should be safe for us, seemingly miraculously, to re-appear. The passage that we have just walked along was used by the servants to collect the ice for use in the house, but you may notice a door on the other side? That leads to another passage which was used by the delivery men bringing the ice."

As soon as she had pointed it out to them, they could all see another door almost opposite, reached by what Connor thought was a dangerously narrow ledge running halfway around the pit.

"Matthew, if you could take your lamp and go first please and open the door, then we will have enough light to make our way safely around the ledge. Be careful, as it is a little narrow."

Understatement of the year, Matt thought, as he edged his way along the ledge, keeping his back pressed firmly against the brick lining. Even then, the front of his feet stuck out over the edge. Luckily, the door opened easily when he reached it and he was able to enter another corridor without any trouble.

"Now," Mrs Debbon said, handing her lamp to Connor, "I will go next and Charles, you will hold my hand as we go. Do not attempt to hurry."

Inching along the ledge, Charles clutching her hand as tightly as he could, they reached the other door, Matt ushering them into the safety of the passage behind him.

"You next, Helen," Connor told her.

"I don't think I can," she whispered to him.

"I know it's narrow, but it's perfectly safe," Connor said. "Take it slowly and you'll be fine."

"I'm scared of heights," she said, trying to keep her voice calm, but not quite succeeding.

"We're not that high up, "he reassured her.

"High enough. One of the servants took me out on the roof

once, and I fainted. I had to be carried back into the house. Mama doesn't know. I made the servants promise not to tell her."

"Wonderful," Connor muttered under his breath. "Don't worry," he told her, "we'll get you round there. You'll be fine."

"Is there a problem, Connor?" Mrs Debbon asked, seeing Helen hesitating.

"It seems Helen is scared of heights," he called back. "She's kept it secret until now."

"I would say her timing is not of the best," was the dry response. "Helen, my dear, you really must try to defeat your fears."

"It's alright, Mama. You all go on and leave me here. If you leave me one of the lanterns I'll be quite safe until after the fire has burned out. You can then come and get me."

"I'm afraid that simply won't do at all, my dear. We must keep together."

"I'll get her," Matt said, handing Mrs Debbon his lantern, then inching his way back around the ledge.

"OK," he said, when he was standing by Helen's side. "This is what we're going to do. I'm going to take hold of one of your hands and Uncle Conn will hold the other. I'll creep along the ledge, you come in the middle and my uncle will come last. If you keep your back pressed tightly against the wall, we'll make sure that you can't possibly fall."

"I don't think I'll be able to," she said, trembling on the brink of tears.

"Then the best thing to do is to keep your eyes firmly shut. Provided that you keep your heels against the wall and shuffle slowly sideways, then you'll be around in less than a couple of minutes."

Matt took her hand and started along the ledge. With Helen keeping her eyes firmly closed, the three of them slowly made their way around the ledge and into the corridor.

"We're here Helen, you can open your eyes now," Matt told her.

She slowly opened her eyes, blinking at the light from the

lanterns. She and Matt glanced at each other, before reluctantly letting go of each other's hands.

"Well," Mrs Debbon said, "I suggest that you give each other a kiss now that we're all safe."

"Mama?" Helen said, the puzzlement evident in her voice.

"Really, my dear, do you think I'm blind? It was perfectly obvious what has been going on. No," she said, raising her hand as Matt was about to speak. "This is neither the time nor the place for discussions."

After a nervous glance at her mother, Matt threw caution to the wind, took Helen in his arms and kissed her.

"Now," Mrs Debbon said, once Matt had, somewhat reluctantly, released Helen from his embrace, "let us continue along the passage. I wish to get as far away from here as is possible."

"I told you she'd find out," Connor whispered in his nephew's ear.

Matt didn't reply, just took Helen's hand and helped her along the corridor, Connor bringing up the rear and grinning at the sight. After a short time they passed a door let into the left-hand side of the passage and Connor realised with a shock that they had been there before. The door gave access to the small room where the crown of France was secreted behind the brickwork. Mrs Debbon didn't even glance at it but continued along the passage until they reached the door at the end. She reached above the door and felt along the ledge until her fingers found a key.

"I always made sure there was a spare key positioned here in case it was ever needed," she explained.

"You anticipated all this happening?" Connor asked her in some surprise.

"No, not at all, but I did anticipate that it may be necessary to leave Belmont at some time without being seen."

She unlocked the door and led them out onto the garden terrace and into the fresh night air.

They looked behind them as great pillars of fire shot up from the blazing house and made the night sky as light as day. A huge crash shook the ground beneath them

"The chimneys are starting to collapse," Connor said, staring at the death throes of the great house. "I'm sorry, Maria. The fire spread so fast there was no way it could be stopped."

"It's of no real consequence. We are all safe, that is all that matters."

"But all your belongings, all your treasures."

"Things, Connor, just things. Things do not matter. People matter. Things can be replaced, people cannot. I and my children are safe, and for that you, both of you, have my eternal gratitude."

She kissed both Connor and Matt warmly on the cheek.

"But what about the papers and stuff," Matt asked, glancing round to make sure Charles couldn't hear him, "the ones that you say prove that Charles is the true heir to the throne."

"They were never in the house in the first place," she told him. "They are with our solicitors in London. As for the house, it is, of course, a great loss, but from a personal point of view it was only leased, as indeed were most of the contents. Money is not a problem. We will lease another property in the area once I have matters sorted out, and I am sure we are safe from further meddling. We have friends in Exeter. We will stay with them for a while. They can be trusted to keep our presence a secret whilst I write another note to President Faure to explain what has happened. Once the elections are over in a few days' time then I am sure action will be taken to erase this mad scheme once and for all. The only pressing need is for shelter for the rest of the night."

"Now there I believe I can help," Connor said.

"But how? It would not be safe to try and book into a hotel: we are too well known in the area."

"I agree. Matt," he said, turning to his nephew. "Make your way round to the front of the house. Try to keep as low a profile as you can and try not to let any of the servants see you. If they do, then just tell them that you and I had gone to visit friends or something and only knew about the fire when we heard the fire engine climbing the hill."

"Alright, but what do I do when I get there?"

"Daniel will be there. He'll be trying to help, trying to get into the house to rescue the family. Find him, tell him everyone's safe, and bring him round here."

"That's why we went to see him earlier, isn't it?" Matt said, realisation dawning on him. "You want everyone to stay at his place for tonight."

"Yes. It's not far away and he already knows that the family are in danger. He'll get his parents to take us all in," he said, turning to Mrs Debbon, "and he'll make sure no-one knows about it."

"But it would be a great inconvenience for them," she protested. "I have never actually called on them but their house is not large."

"Large enough for tonight. Tomorrow you'll be able to travel to Exeter to stay with your friends. Go on Matt, quick as you can. We need to get away from here before we're seen."

◆

Matt wasted no time in answering but dashed off up the nearest steps onto the upper terrace. There were quite a few people there staring at the flames from a safe distance, but Matt didn't recognise any of them. He assumed they were strangers attracted by the fire. Just like those who had suddenly appeared when his own house had caught fire, Matt realised. What on earth there was to see in someone else's misfortune he had no idea. He ran around to the front of the house, keeping as far from the blazing building as he could. Even at that distance the heat was almost intolerable. A great crash told him that another chimney had given up the fight. He stopped on the front drive, alarmed at the size of the crowd that had gathered there. He wondered how he was going to stay unrecognised, until he noticed that the servants all seemed to be grouped together at the far side of the lawn.

Pulling his collar up to try and hide his face as much as he could, his eyes darted keenly among the crowd, trying to find Daniel. He knew his uncle was right: Daniel would be bound to be there. There was no way he'd have stayed away. Besides, the newspaper reported that he'd tried desperately to get into the burning building. He *had* to be there. Suddenly he saw a small figure lying face down on the ground and realised it was Bill. Daniel was kneeling by his side, trying to comfort him. Keeping as low a profile as he could, Matt edged his way across to them. Luckily everyone else was busy staring at the flames and had no time to even glance at him. He reached Daniel's side and crouched down beside him.

"Daniel," he said in his ear, "it's me, Matt."

He was shocked at the look on Daniel's tear-streaked face as he turned towards him: a look of utter horror and despair.

"Matt?"

"Listen, I've no time to explain, but Helen, Charles and their mother are safe and well. They've sent me to fetch you."

Daniel didn't answer, just stared uncomprehendingly at him.

"Daniel," Matt said again, more urgently, "I promise you, they're all fine, but we need to go now, before anyone sees me. It's important!"

"She's safe? Helen's safe?"

"Yes. All of them, they're fine. They escaped through the kitchens and out into the garden."

"But why aren't they here, why . . ."

"No time for explanations," Matt interrupted him. "My uncle told you earlier that they were all in danger. The fire is the result. Now they need your help. Come with me. And Bill, of course."

Bill was still lying on the ground, weeping inconsolably, unaware that Matt was there. Daniel gently shook him by the shoulder until the boy finally turned to look up at him.

"Bill," Daniel said, "Matthew's here. He says they're all safe. Helen and all of them. They're all safe!"

"Safe? But the fire? They was all at the winder — we seen 'em all."

"Later, Bill. They'll explain later. But we've got to go."

Daniel helped the boy gently to his feet, Bill wincing from the pain in his arm where a chunk of wood from the front door had hit it. Scarcely daring to believe what they'd heard, Daniel and Bill followed Matt back around the house and into the near darkness of the lower terraces. When he saw Helen standing with her mother, Daniel let out a shout of joy and ran to her, gathering her in his arms and holding her tightly to him.

"I thought you were dead," he told her, his voice choking with emotion, "I thought I'd lost you."

"I'm fine Daniel, really," she told him, rather taken aback at the fierceness of his embrace. "We escaped along a passage that leads from the kitchen to one of the terraces."

Mrs Debbon, who at first was almost as surprised as her daughter by how tight Daniel was holding her, glanced behind him and saw Bill hovering on the edge of the group.

"William," she said, "come here, young man."

Bill did as he was instructed. She crouched down in front of him, noting that his face was as tear-streaked as Daniel's.

"We are all safe and well, William. There is no need to be concerned. I trust that Mary-Anne is well?"

"I fink so. She were fast asleep when I left 'er. I come back ter try an' 'elp. Didn' do a very good job, though."

"Nonsense, William. You have done a most remarkable job."

"But the 'ouse, it's all gone!"

"I know, but that is something to worry about another time. For now, we have other priorities. Including tending to your injuries," she added, seeing that the boy was holding his arm.

"Nah, aint nuffin. Just got caught wiv some wood when the front door blew aht."

"Nevertheless, I will arrange for it to be looked at as soon as possible."

"Now, Daniel," she said, getting to her feet, "Mr Harvey has suggested that you may be able to help us. We have nowhere to stay for the rest of the night and I need to get Charles and Helen inside as soon as possible. He has suggested that you and your family may be kind enough to take us in for tonight? Of course I understand that it may prove difficult and if so, then please say. We can always make other arrangements."

"No, of course you must stay with us," Daniel said, slowly regaining his wits. "My father was here earlier with the neighbours to try and help, but once he realised that there was nothing he and the others could do he thought it better to get out of the way. He didn't like all the strangers here just staring at the fire. Ghoulish, he called it. I'll run down and tell him and mother that you're on your way."

"Thank you, Daniel, that's most generous of you. And I see that you also have received injuries," she said in some consternation, noticing his trousers were torn and bloodstained. "I hope they are not severe?"

"No. Honestly Mrs Debbon, they're not as bad as they look. When the front door blew out, both Bill and I got thrown across the drive. My trousers took most of the impact from the gravel — my legs just got grazed a bit. Now, I'll head down home and let my parents know what's happened."

"One thing before you go, Daniel," Connor said. "We told you about the thugs who tried to kidnap Charles the other night. This fire is all part of the same plot, it isn't an accident. It's vital that no-one knows that the family are staying with you. Everyone has to believe that they all died in the fire until things can be sorted out."

"I understand. I'll explain to my parents. There won't be any trouble on that score."

"You go back to your house by the quickest way you can," Connor told him. "We'll have to find a slightly longer way to avoid being seen, so we may be a little while, but don't worry. We'll be there as soon as we can."

"On my way," Daniel replied.

He was about to leave when he stopped suddenly. Instead, he hugged Helen tightly to him again and kissed her, before racing off around the house.

"It would seem to be your night for kisses," Mrs Debbon said, somewhat startled by the attention her daughter had been receiving. "Still, these are hardly usual circumstances, so perhaps it shouldn't be so surprising."

"Wot abaht me? Wot should I do?" Bill asked.

"Come with us, of course, William. You can help look after us on the walk down to the Hardwick residence. Would you be able to do that?"

"'Course I can do that! Bin doin' that fer years!"

Mrs Debbon couldn't help smiling at the small figure in front of her.

"So you have. When we get to Daniel's house, I will see that your arm is tended and then I would like you to go back home to make sure that Mary-Anne isn't too distressed when she learns what has happened. Could you also kindly explain to your mother and father, and your sister of course, that they must keep it a complete secret that we are safe and well. When you feel it is safe to do so, could you then please bring Mary-Anne to us?"

"'Course. Anyfink yer wants."

"Thank you, William. Now, I think we need to go down to the lowest terrace and out into the lane, but after that I confess that I am not sure which direction we should proceed in."

"I know, Mama," Helen said. "If we walk along the lane towards Daccombe, there is another lane on the right that climbs the hill only a short distance along. From there we just need to walk down to Daniel's house."

"Excellent. Then it is high time we were on our way. Helen my dear, if you wouldn't mind leading the way and perhaps Matthew could join you with one of the lanterns?"

"Yes, Mama."

"Good. Then if William doesn't mind accompanying Charles and myself, Connor can bring up the rear with the other lantern and we can proceed."

And so they pressed on down the terraces and into the darkened lane, the air thick with ash from the dying house.

CHAPTER TWENTY-NINE

Partings

Connor was carrying an exhausted Charles by the time they arrived. Daniel's parents were looking out for them, and ushered the tired and emotional group into the warmth of their sitting room, where Mrs Hardwick bustled around, providing hot drinks for them all.

"Now young man," Mrs Debbon said, looking at Bill. "Let us take a closer look at your arm."

"Nah, no need. It ain't that bad."

"Nervertheless, I insist. Mrs Hardwick, perhaps you could help me? William was hurt when he was hit by part of the Belmont front door when it blew out. I wish to ensure that there is no serious injury."

"Of course," Mrs Hardwick replied.

Bill was very unhappy about being fussed over, but eventually agreed to taking his shirt off so that the two ladies could look at his arm.

"Doesn't seem to be any major damage," Mrs Hardwick said after a while, "but there are going to be some very large bruises there in a while."

"Tole yer it weren't nuffin," Bill said, somewhat disgruntled as he put his shirt back on.

"Very well," Mrs Debbon said, smiling at the boy's expression. "Now if you would be kind enough to go and ensure that Mary-Anne is still well, we will see you in the morning. Good night to you William, and my thanks for all you have done."

Much to his embarrassment, she kissed the boy warmly on the cheek. Bill then left to run down to his own house, promising that he would see Mary-Anne safely returned to them in the morning.

"I'm sorry we don't have enough bedrooms for everyone," Mrs Hardwick told them apologetically, once Bill had left, "but we've done the best we can."

Having been assured by Mrs Debbon that they would be grateful for whatever they could provide, they were shown to their rooms. Mrs Debbon and Helen shared the guest bedroom, Charles had a bed made up in Daniel's room and Connor and Matt found themselves on the couches in the sitting room.

"I don't care where it is, Mrs Hardwick," Connor told her, in response to her worried apologies that they didn't have any more beds. "I could sleep on the bare floor at the moment."

Connor fell asleep the moment he lay down, but Matt found it hard to shake off the day's events. He tossed and turned for what seemed like an eternity, but even when he did finally fall into an exhausted sleep, his dreams were invaded by a burning house and screaming figures.

◆

A damp morning witnessed Mary-Anne's tearful re-union with her family. Bill had let her sleep until the last possible moment before waking her with the grim tidings of Belmont's destruction. Donning her disguise of a mop cap and a cheap coat she had managed to escape being recognised on the walk through Barton village, throwing herself into her mother's arms as soon as she arrived. Helen then took charge of her younger siblings, trying to keep them occupied to take their minds off things. Mrs Hardwick, clucking round them like a mother hen with her chicks, herded them to the bathroom, where she and Helen did their best to get as much of the previous night's dirt off their clothes as possible.

Daniel walked over to Matt, holding a shirt in his hand. "Helen told me that you saved her life last night by tackling the man who was pointing a gun at you all. The least I can do is give you a clean shirt."

"Thanks," Matt said, taking his own blood-stained shirt off, "but I didn't do anything that you or anyone else wouldn't have done."

"Maybe, maybe not, but Helen and her family are all here, and that's down to you and your Uncle," he said, holding out his hand for Matt to shake.

◆

"I've told our coachman that he's to say nothing to anyone about last night's events, or about you all still being alive," Mr Hardwick told Mrs Debbon. "He's been with us for years and can be trusted completely. He'll not breathe a word. He'll drive you all to Exeter as soon as you're ready. The best route will be up the hill and along the ridge to Milber and down to Newton Abbot. You should get to Exeter in about three hours. That will avoid going through the town and also avoid having to go past Belmont, where there is bound to be a crowd of onlookers, plus your servants, of course."

"That would be most kind of you. I will make sure you are recompensed for your trouble as soon as I have put our affairs in order."

"There'll be no talk of recompense, Mrs Debbon. That is what friends and neighbours are for."

"Thank you. There is another task that I would ask if you are able to perform, if it is not imposing on your generosity too much. It will require a certain amount of ingenuity on your part as I confess I cannot think myself how to go about it."

"Name it."

"It's the servants from Belmont. As they think we all died in the fire, they will naturally assume they are all out of work and will be distressed and wondering what to do. I would like to take them all on again once I have found another property in the area, but they will need assurances that they have not been forgotten, or to think that they will immediately have to seek other employment."

"I understand. I will tell them that you had made previous arrangements for them in the event that anything untoward should happen to you, and that you had asked me if I could employ them all for a period of, shall we say six months? I could say that you had left a sum of money with me to cover the costs and that I could use them for any task that seemed appropriate in the short term."

"That is a splendid idea, but how would you employ them?

This house is not big enough to warrant such a large staff and . . ."

"That won't be a problem," he interrupted. "We could use two or three here, plus I can genuinely use some extra hands in the harbour office, even if only to run errands. I would also use a number of them to see if anything at all could be salvaged from the ruins of Belmont. Although the fire was fierce almost beyond belief it's still possible that something may be recovered. I did notice that the servants' wing was still relatively intact, so it may even be possible to use that as sleeping quarters in the short term. Perhaps your butler could take charge of that part of the operation?"

"If James is agreeable then I have no objection," came the smooth response. "However, it is possible that he may have absented himself and left the area."

"Why would he have done that? I only met him a few times but he struck me as a very capable sort of fellow."

"It is possible that James wasn't all he seemed to be. We have been suffering a few minor thefts in recent weeks and although James tried hard to suggest that one of the footmen was to blame, it would seem likely that he was responsible himself."

"And you think that he may have taken the chance to flee the area in the confusion."

"Perhaps. Of course, if James is still on the scene then it may well be that my suspicions are unfounded. Only time will tell."

Connor marvelled at her composure, as she calmly discussed the man who had tried to murder her less than twelve hours earlier. And she had evidently thought of a very plausible reason why the butler wouldn't be found. Calling to Daniel to help the coachman get the horses attached to the family carriage, Ernest Hardwick left to start getting things ready for the family's journey to Exeter.

"I'll give them a hand," Matt said, leaving Connor and Mrs Debbon alone in the sitting room.

"You're sure that you want to return to Torquay once things have calmed down?" Connor asked. "Wouldn't it perhaps be better to start again somewhere fresh, where no-one knows you?"

"It may well be the wiser course, but I couldn't possibly go and live elsewhere. Robert is buried here and I would feel that I was deserting him if I were to set up house somewhere else. I have left instructions that when my time comes, I am to be interred with him."

"I understand. How long do you think it will be before things are safe for you to return?"

"I believe that we will be quite safe within a few days. Once the elections have been held in France then it would be a pointless exercise to try to get Charles to France. If the left-wing parties win a substantial majority, as I believe will happen, then the old order will have gone forever. However, to make completely certain that no other madman tries to use Charles, or any of us, in any form of plot again, I will wait until my letters have reached France and for President Faure to take action against any surviving members of this scheme. I think two or three months will be ample time. In the meantime, I will ask Mr Hardwick to search for a suitable property that we could lease or purchase in the area."

"You will find nothing even remotely as grand as Belmont," Connor told her gently.

"I know. However, much as I enjoyed our time there, it was really far too large for us. When Robert was alive and we did some entertaining it suited our purpose, but I have no desire to return to those days again. Somewhere smaller and less formal would be much more suitable. I also want the children to have a somewhat less rigid life than they have so far had. I was, I have to confess, rather surprised at how much Mary-Anne enjoyed her stay at William's house. I think that perhaps I should encourage the children to have a wider circle of friends than they currently have."

"I think that would be an excellent idea. Things are changing fast in the world and your children will live through the most amazing times."

"It would seem you were right all along to be so worried," she told him. "I have been guilty of the most terrible complacency."

"You are all alive and well. I'm sorry about the house, but as you said yourself that isn't in the least important, not compared to your lives."

"I am not concerned about the house. Or rather, I am sorry at its loss and that of the treasures it contained, but I am frankly terrified at the thought of how close we all came to dying."

Connor tried hard to imagine the imperturbable Maria Debbon being anything even remotely approaching terrified but found he couldn't.

"I believe that some things are meant to be, whilst others are not," he told her instead. "None of you were meant to die in the fire, and hopefully you and your children will have long and happy lives in front of you."

"I hope so."

"And Charles?"

"Will never know that he is the rightful King of France. As far as history is concerned, King Louis XVII died as a child in the Temple Prison in 1795. It is better that way."

"I think you're right. He needs to be able to find his own way in life without the burden of knowing what he cannot have. What will you do with the papers that prove who he is?"

"I will collect them from the solicitors as soon as it is safe to do so. I will then destroy them."

"And the crown?"

"Can stay where it is. I have no wish ever to set eyes on it again. It has brought us nothing but trouble. Let it stay sealed up."

"But what will you do if someone finds it?"

"I think that most unlikely. If it survived the fire, which it may well not have done, then no doubt the passage that leads to the icehouse from the terrace will be explored when the owners are deciding what to do with the ruins and the land, but even if they were to explore the small storeroom where the crown is hidden, the chances of them removing the bricks from the wall to reveal its hiding place are remote. No, it can stay there. As far as I am concerned, it no longer exists." She sighed deeply before speaking again. "And what of you, Connor? I assume that you and Matthew will be saying goodbye soon and returning home?"

"I doubt there will be time for good-byes, Maria. One day we will be here, the next we will be gone, and you will probably not see us again. It is the nature of my work."

"I will miss you. Both of you. Helen, I am sure, will be distraught when Matthew leaves. I believe they have formed an attachment."

"Yes, they have."

"She is too young, they are both too young."

"Love does not respect age, Maria."

"No, it does not."

"There is another who cares for her deeply."

"Daniel?"

"Of course. His actions last night, and Bill's for that matter, show that both of them care deeply for your daughters."

"William? But he is far too young to understand about such things."

"He's not too young to know those that he is prepared to risk his own life for."

"You are right, of course. I think I will have to make some arrangements to ensure he has a more formal education than he presently receives. I must also find a way to help his family. I know that Helen has assisted them as much as she can, and I also know that William's father would not take kindly to anything that he would consider to be charity, but I will find a means that will satisfy them all."

Connor decided that it wasn't perhaps the most appropriate time to tell her that Bill was starting out on the road to hopefully becoming her son-in-law. He wasn't at all sure that her gratitude would extend quite that far.

"I will have to adapt to the fact that both of my daughters have acquired admirers," she said with a sigh.

"Matthew, Daniel and Bill love your daughters. And I love their mother," he told her, finally admitting it himself.

"I know," she replied, smiling at him. "And, as I am certain you are aware, the feeling is returned."

Connor didn't say anything, but took her in his arms and kissed her.

"Were all right with the world, I would be down on one knee asking you to marry me," he said, his voice choking with emotion.

"And if all were right with the world, I would be saying yes. But we inhabit different worlds, you and I. I believe that there is much that you have not told me. Both you and Matthew are sometimes . . ." she broke off, trying to find the right words. "Both of you seem at times so confused by simple, everyday events yet can take for granted things that seem outlandish to me. When we were escaping from Belmont, I asked Matthew to light the two lanterns. The tinderbox was right there on the shelf but he didn't notice it, instead taking a small metal object from his pocket and lighting the lanterns with it. I noted when I showed you both the crown last week that he struggled with the tinderbox then: it was as if he'd never seen one before. I put it down to being nervous, but now I am not so sure. That object he had in his pocket produced a brilliant flame with a single touch. I have never seen anything even remotely like it before, yet neither of you so much as blinked. You are both accustomed to it, yet not to a tinderbox. There have been other things as well. Matthew's surprise at learning that Mrs Gregson isn't married, the strange clothes you both wore when you first arrived, your extreme reluctance to have footmen to wait on you, the way you both had to leave so suddenly at times."

"There is a great deal about both of us that I haven't explained, but I'm afraid that if I were to try to tell you the full truth you simply wouldn't believe me."

"I think I would prefer not to know," she said, smiling warmly at him. "An air of mystery can be a most alluring asset at times."

They embraced again, only reluctantly parting when Matt returned to tell them the carriage was ready. It was perhaps fortunate for both of them that there was a flurry of activity to get everyone ready for the journey to Exeter so that they were too busy to dwell on their feelings.

"Mrs Hardwick has done her best, Mama, but I still smell like the gardener's bonfire," Helen complained to her mother. "And Charles flatly refused to have a bath with any of us in the room with him."

"It doesn't matter, my dear. When we get to Exeter, one of the first things we will do is to send out for some fresh clothes. Then I will visit the bank and arrange for a line of credit to be drawn up so that we can purchase whatever we need."

"But I look such a fright. I haven't even been able to arrange my hair properly."

"You look beautiful, young lady," Connor assured her. "Besides, having a slightly dishevelled look often helps. You'll no doubt have a string of young men in Exeter all wanting desperately to help you."

At this, both Matt and Daniel glared at him, but he ignored them both. Even though he was talking about Helen, his eyes were firmly fixed on her mother. Her clothes were not as elegantly arranged as usual and bore dirt marks and soot stains, her hair was unpinned and falling around her shoulders and she was obviously tired. She was also, Connor thought, stunningly beautiful. The knowledge that they were soon to be parted forever was like a lead weight inside him. He glanced at his nephew and saw him smiling broadly at something that Helen had said. It obviously hadn't yet registered with him that he almost certainly wouldn't see her again.

"You'd best be off, Mrs Debbon," Daniel's father said. "You'd best be away before too many people are about."

"Of course. Helen, will you please get Charles and Mary-Anne settled in the carriage?"

"Yes, Mama. Matt, Daniel, could you both please help me? Charles and Mary-Anne are somewhat excitable at present and may need a firm hand."

"Sure," Matt told her, taking Charles by the hand and leading him, not without an effort, out of the house. Bill had to be forcibly prevented from getting in the coach with Mary-Anne.

"But ow' am I supposed ter look after yers all if I ain't there ter do it?" he asked plaintively.

Mrs Debbon assured him that she would send word as soon as they were settled, and that he could resume his duties once they were able to return to the area. When Charles and Mary-Anne were inside the coach, Helen turned to Matt and Daniel.

"I don't know how long we'll be with Mama's friends in Exeter, but it may be some time. However," she said, handing them each a sheet of paper, "I have written the address down here and I trust that you will both visit us as often as you can?"

"Try and stop me," Daniel said, grinning at her.

Matt read the address on the paper and said that he'd be there as soon as he could. Maybe the next day if he could manage it. Daniel gave him a hard look but said nothing. Before anything else could be said, Mrs Debbon arrived with Connor, whilst Mrs Hardwick fussed about behind them.

"Will I see you again, Connor?" Mrs Debbon asked quietly.

"I honestly don't know. I wish I could say otherwise, but I can't."

"I understand. I hope that I may see you again, but in case I do not . . ." she broke off and embraced him, almost knocking him off his feet. The others all stared at the two of them in amazement.

"Mama!" said a shocked Helen.

"Yes, my dear?" came the reply, when she and Connor had finally separated.

"I, I mean, I . . ."

"Yes?"

"Nothing, Mama, nothing at all."

"Excellent. Now, if you could say goodbye to Daniel and Matthew, my dear, we must be on our way."

"Yes, Mama."

Helen kissed both Matt and Daniel and went to climb into the coach. At the last minute she changed her mind and came over to where Connor was standing, and hugged him, placing a demure kiss on his cheek.

"Thank you, young lady."

"My pleasure, Mr Harvey."

She clambered into the coach, and immediately became embroiled in a row that had broken out between her younger siblings. Their mother was about to climb in after them when

Connor stopped her.

"Connor?" she asked.

"Just one more thing, Maria," he said quietly, so that the others couldn't hear. "You may have decided to renounce any and all claims to royalty, but you are nevertheless still the Queen Regent of France. And so, for what may well be the last ever time, I would like to acknowledge that."

He bowed low before her.

"A long life to Your Majesty," he said. "God go with you, my love."

"And with you, my dearest," she replied, a single tear coursing down her cheek as she turned and climbed into the coach.

As soon as she was seated, the coachman clambered up into the driver's seat and set the coach rattling off up the hill.

◆

"What do you and your nephew want to do now?" Mrs Hardwick asked Connor, once they had watched the coach until it went from sight. "You're both welcome to stay here as long as you wish."

"That's very kind of you. To be honest, I don't know what we're going to do at the moment. I think maybe we should take a walk to see what's happening at Belmont."

"I'll come with you," Daniel said. "There may be something that I can do."

"I'd best come as well," his father said. "I've got to let the servants know that they're to be taken care of."

"You ain't leavin' me 'ere," Bill stated, making them all laugh.

The five of them walked up the hill and along the lane to the gates of the house, where they all stood and stared in a shocked silence. Instead of a pristine and beautiful house there stood a gaunt and blackened ruin. What was left of the building was testimony to the ferocity of the flames that had destroyed Belmont. The roof and all the floors had fallen in, the metal windows had melted and all that was left of the main house were the outer walls and some of the chimneystacks.

"It's a miracle that anyone got out of that alive," Daniel said hoarsely.

"A miracle indeed," Connor quietly agreed.

"I was wrong about the servants' wing," Mr Hardwick said. "I thought it was still intact but the fire must have burned through the connecting door eventually."

They looked in the direction of the wing and saw he was right. The wing was now just a still smouldering shell, but they could also see several heaps of furniture and other items piled up on the lawn in front of the ruins, with a number of people wandering rather aimlessly about.

"It's the servants," Matt said. "The poor sods must have been outside all night. They wouldn't have had anywhere to go."

"I should have thought of that myself," Mr Hardwick berated himself. "They'll be cold and hungry and worried sick. Come on, we need to let them know that everything's going to be fine."

"You can't tell them that the family survived, you know," Connor reminded him. "They've got to think that they all died."

"I know. I'll be careful what I say."

"What about us, Uncle Conn? Should we let them see us?" Matt asked.

"Too late, they already 'ave," Bill told him.

"We'll just have to say that I was called away late last night on business and you came with me. We only got back this morning and didn't know about the fire until we got here."

By this time most of the servants had crowded around them, with a very distressed Mrs Gregson in their midst. The fire seemed to have taken all the spirit from her and she was only a shadow of her former self.

"Mr Harvey, Master Harvey," she said, her voice weak and rather querulous. "We didn't know you had escaped. Are madam and the children with you? Are they safe?"

"I'm sorry, Mrs Gregson," Connor told her gently, "Matthew and I had to leave late yesterday evening. We only learned of the fire this morning. The family were all here when we left."

She slumped and would have fallen if Geoffrey hadn't managed to catch her in time.

"So it's true?" he asked. "The whole family gone?"

"We don't know that for certain, Geoffrey," Connor replied, choosing his words carefully. "All I can tell you is that they were in the house when we left, but that was some time before the fire started."

"There doesn't seem much doubt," he said, turning to stare at the ruins. "No-one could have survived that."

"James is also missing," Sarah told him. "But we think he may well have run away."

Connor and Matt glanced at each other before Connor spoke. "What makes you think that?"

"Because of me," Edward spoke up. "I gather it was him who spread all the lies about me, about me stealing from the family and so on. I never did any such thing. I reckon if there was any stealing going on it was him what done it and he tried to put the blame on me. He had me locked in my room so I couldn't say anything. When I was let out yesterday because of the fire I think he got scared that I'd prove I hadn't done anything, so he scarpered."

"Well, that's possible, of course," Connor said, thankful that an explanation for the butler's absence had come so easily to hand. "I see you managed to save most of the contents of the servants' wing."

"Yes, sir," Frederick said. "When we realised there was nothing more we could do either to save the house or to rescue the family, we decided that we could at least empty the wing before the fire burnt through the door."

"But what's to become of us all?" Sarah asked, her voice showing her to be close to tears. "There are precious few jobs around here these days and most of the big houses are laying off servants, not taking them on."

Mr Hardwick stepped forward to reassure them, explaining that Mrs Debbon had left a considerable sum of money in his care so that he could employ them all for at least six months, giving them time to try to arrange alternative places for themselves.

"But did madam foresee this happening?" Mrs Gregson asked.

"No, of course not, but she was aware that she may have an

accident or an illness and wanted to ensure that you were all taken care of."

The servants looked at each other, not daring to hope that this was genuine.

"How many of us are you to take on, then?" Geoffrey asked.

"All of you, or at least all those who want, of course. If anyone here has another opportunity that they would like to take up then they are, naturally, free to take it."

"May I ask what our duties would be, sir?" Mrs Gregson asked.

As Mr Hardwick launched into a description of some of the tasks that he hoped they would be able to undertake, Connor nudged Matt and indicated that they should move away from the group of highly relieved servants.

"I'd rather they didn't start asking us too many questions about where we went last night and what was it that was so important that we had to leave late at night," he said, once they were out of sight of the knot of people on the front lawn. "They might start to get suspicious."

"OK. So what now? Are we going to stay at Daniel's place, or are we going to book into a hotel? And how do we go about getting train times?

"That's a lot of questions in one go. And what's with the train times?"

"So I can go and see Helen in Exeter tomorrow, of course. I can hardly get Mr Brown to drive me there, can I?"

Connor didn't answer for a while, trying to find a way of telling his nephew that he doubted very much if they would still be there the next day. Before he could say anything he noticed that Matt had suddenly shivered.

"What's up?" he asked. "Cold?"

"Yes, it's suddenly turned a lot colder all of a sudden. Hadn't you noticed?"

"Can't say that I . . . Wait, you're right. It's freezing all of a sudden. And there's a fog blown in from somewhere."

They looked around them as a dense, freezing fog obscured everything from sight. Even the nearby ruins had vanished. There was just a wall of grey.

"No!" Matt shouted, suddenly realising what the fog meant and what was happening. "No, not now! I don't want to go, it's too soon, I want to stay here, I want to stay with Helen! Uncle Conn, make it stop!"

"I'm sorry, Matt, there's nothing either of us can do."

"There must be! I'm not going back — I'm not!"

Before Connor could stop him, Matt had started to run blindly through the fog, not caring where he was going. Connor lost sight of him almost at once.

"Matt, where are you? You can't see where you're going. Matt!"

There was a sudden cry of pain from somewhere inside the greyness.

"Matt! What is it? MATT!"

Connor stumbled in the direction where the cry had come from, his arms held out in front of him. Groping blindly, he moved slowly forward, eventually hearing a soft crying not far away. As quickly as it had appeared, the fog blew away, revealing a bright, sunny day. Matt was sitting on the ground, nursing a nasty looking cut on his forehead. Connor knelt by his nephew and tried to stem the blood flowing down his face with his handkerchief. He looked around, realising that Matt must have run full-tilt into a brick wall that was right in front of him. It was the garden wall of Matt's house. They were home.

CHAPTER THIRTY

Picking up the pieces

"I've lost her, haven't I?" Matt asked, raising a tear-streaked face to his uncle.

"I'm so sorry, Matt. There was nothing either of us could have done."

"You knew this would happen?"

"I thought it might. We've done what we were meant to do. The family is safe. They didn't die in the fire. So it was time to leave."

"I didn't want to. I still don't want to. I want to go back. I want to be with Helen. I love her so much!"

"I know you do. And if there was any way I could arrange it, any way at all, I'd do it. But there isn't. We're home and somehow we've got to pick up the pieces and get on with our lives."

"How am I supposed to do that? It's alright for you — you didn't leave anyone behind that you'd fallen in love with!"

"You think so?"

"Well, did you?"

"Yes, I did. We both did. You the daughter, me the mother."

"But, I thought . . ."

"You thought that because I'm a middle-aged man with thinning hair and the start of a paunch, I can't fall in love, or feel lost and bereft at parting from her?"

Matt was silent for a long time, just sitting on the ground, hugging his knees.

"I'm sorry," he eventually said. "That was a mean thing to say. I knew that you'd fallen for Mrs Debbon. It was obvious."

"It's OK, Matt. We've both lost someone we love. But remember that you've got a loving family to support you and a bright future ahead of you. I've just got an empty house and memories. Anyway, we'd best get inside and start to sort out what we're going to do."

"About what?"

"We've been away for days. Your parents are going to be worried sick that they haven't heard from you. We need to come up with a really plausible story why we've been out of touch for so long. You're usually glued to your phone."

"I don't think I can even start to think about things yet," Matt said, getting slowly and unsteadily to his feet.

"Well, the first thing is to do something about that cut. What happened anyway?"

"I ran straight into the wall. I thought I was still at Belmont."

"Come on, let's go and find a plaster. If we can find one big enough that is. That's a hell of a cut you've got there."

◆

Once Matt's cut was cleaned it proved to be not as bad as Connor had feared and he was able to stick a plaster over it. An hour later they were showered, shaved and changed into clean clothes.

"This seems so unreal," Matt complained. "I know I'm at home, all my stuff is in my room and all my clothes are either in the wardrobe or on the floor where they usually are, but I don't feel I belong."

"I know what you mean. I keep expecting the gong to sound to let us know that lunch is ready or something."

"I want to go down to the library."

"The library? What for?"

"I want to see the paper. I want to be sure that things have changed."

"But we know that they're all safe, Matt. They all survived the fire."

"I know. I just need to see it in print."

"When do you want to go?"

"Now."

"Now? You mean right this minute?"

"Yes."

Matt looked at the newspaper report when they were settled in the library, his dismay self-evident.

"But it hasn't changed — it's just the same as it was. It says they all died."

"But we know they didn't, Matt. They all made it out of the house with us. They just assumed they'd all died as they couldn't find any trace of them. Don't forget that Maria was anxious that everyone should assume that they'd died until she felt it was safe."

"Yes, but it still says about the family being seen at the window, screaming for help. How could that be if they all got out safely?"

Connor was silent, wondering how to tell Matt what he now knew to be the truth. He opened his mouth to speak, but Matt cut him off.

"No, you don't have to tell me," he said, his face ashen and with a haunted look in his eyes. "I've just realised. Those faces behind the glass, they weren't the family, were they? They were the people we locked in the room. Or rather the people I locked in the room. That's who burned to death — that's who we could hear screaming every time we flipped back!"

Connor nodded, not knowing what to say.

"I locked those people in that room, knowing full well there was no way out and they were going to die. I committed murder back there."

"No, you didn't."

"What would you call it then, locking three people in a room knowing that there was no way out for them and they were going to burn to death?"

"Self-defence, retribution, justice. Any or all of them. There was no choice, Matt. It was them, or Maria and her family, as well as the two of us. And never forget that it was their intention to watch us all burn to death."

"It doesn't make it right."

"Right and wrong don't come into it. There was no other choice. There'll be other times in your life when you find you have to do things that you don't want to do, things that you think aren't right, but you still have to do them."

"But not things that get people killed."

"Really? How many people who have been called up when there's been a war have actually wanted to hurt someone, let alone kill them? But that's what countless thousands have had to do down the centuries. They didn't have a choice. Nor did you. If there had been any way that I could have held that door shut and locked it myself, then I'd have done it and spared you this, but there wasn't. You did what you had to do."

"But I can't get it out of my mind. It's like a waking nightmare."

"And it will stay with you for some time, I don't doubt. But eventually, as you come to terms with what's happened, the memory will fade. And in the end there'll be an acceptance that it was something that you had no choice about. And I mean that quite literally. You didn't have a choice because it had already happened. This paper proves it — it's part of history. I was right all along: the past can't be changed. You *had* to lock that door. There was no other way."

"Doesn't mean I have to like it, though."

"No, it doesn't. And I'd think a good deal less of you if you did. The fact that you feel so bad about doing something over which you had no choice, something that saved not only our own lives but those of Maria, Helen, Mary-Anne and Charles as well, proves that you have a heart and a conscience. It also makes you a fine young man and one that I will always be proud to call my nephew and my godson."

"Thanks," Matt said, his voice trembling on the brink of tears.

"No need. It's the truth. Now I suggest we look through some more papers for any more news."

"But we looked last time, and you've just said that nothing has changed — nothing *could* change. If we didn't find anything last time, then we won't this time."

"Don't be so sure of that. I think that maybe we didn't look far enough ahead. Let's skip a couple of months and then start to search again."

"OK, if you think it'll help."

It took less than ten minutes to find what Connor was looking for. An article dated nine weeks after the date of the fire was headlined:

MIRACULOUS RE-APPEARANCE
OF LOCAL FAMILY!

"There," Connor announced, "just what I was expecting."

Four members of a local family who were believed to have died in the fire that destroyed the noted local mansion of Belmont in late April, have arrived in Torquay to take up residence at another property in the town. Mrs Maria Debbon and her three children were all feared dead in the blaze, but it now appears that they had in fact left the house earlier that day to stay with friends in Exeter. They did not learn of the fire for some days, and when they did so, Mrs Debbon was too upset to return to Torquay and she and her children stayed on in Exeter.

When contacted by a reporter from this office, Mrs Debbon said that she was sorry if any distress had been caused, but added that she was unaware of the reports of the family's demise. She has assured everyone that she and her children (Helen, Mary-Anne and Charles) are all perfectly well. Most of the former servants at Belmont will be joining the family in their new premises. They continued to receive their wages during the period the family was absent. Only two of the former servants will not be taking up their positions again: Mr James Miller, the former butler, who is believed to have left the area, and Mrs Anna Gregson, the former housekeeper, who has found alternative employment as the manageress of the main office of the Hardwick Steamship Company.

When asked if she was aware of suggestions that the fire had been started deliberately, Mrs Debbon immediately poured scorn on the idea, calling it utter nonsense. Our reporter also asked if she had any comment about the fact that several of the servants, plus members of the public, had stated that they had seen the family members screaming for help from an upstairs room. Mrs Debbon stated that it was self-evident that they were in error. As no-one else would have been in the main house at the time, it must have been a trick of the light, and the screaming was probably something as simple as the gas jets for the lighting.

Mrs Debbon has asked if friends and acquaintances would kindly allow the family two weeks to become settled in their new abode before calling.

"But why didn't we see that last time we came down?" Matt asked.

"Two reasons, I think," Connor replied. "First, we weren't looking far enough ahead because we didn't think we needed to."

"And second?"

"That we weren't *meant* to see it."

"I don't understand."

"Neither do I, not really. I can only say that if we had seen this article, then we maybe wouldn't have been so bothered about going back and helping out, because we'd have known that they all survived. But because we were meant to go back, then we didn't see it. Don't ask me to try to explain it any better because I can't."

"You don't need to. I know what you're trying to say. We had to go back. If we hadn't, they'd have all died. And so we weren't allowed to see this article."

"That's about it. At least no-one found anything suspicious about James disappearing. And no doubt Maria's letter to the French President sorted out any outstanding problems that might have still been hanging around."

"And Mrs Gregson stayed on in Mr Hardwick's office. That must have been a comedown for her."

"Not on your life. A whole office full of people to boss about and a large and flourishing company to run? She'd be in her element. She'd be a changed woman."

"You could be right. Can't see Daniel's dad taking too kindly to her trying to boss him about, though."

"It would have been fun to see. Anyway, we now need to get back to your place as we've got to work out how we're going to explain to Steve and Marion why we've been out of touch for another three days, and that is not going to be easy. I doubt they'd go for the same excuse as last time, about having to study so not having your phone switched on."

"You'll think of something."

"It's not going to be me phoning them. That's your job."

◆

It had taken all of Connor and Matt's combined acting talents to persuade Matt's parents that all was well. Matt claimed that his phone had died and he'd had to take it in for repair. His phone insurance covered the repair, but not the hire of a replacement phone in the meantime, he told them. And by a very unlucky coincidence, the landline to the house had developed a fault and had only just been repaired. Questions why neither of them had thought to borrow another phone, or nip down to Connor's house and use his landline were eventually fended off, but it was obvious that neither Steve nor Marion were totally happy with the answers.

"I think that went about as well as possible," Connor said. "Did they say when they were coming home?"

"Yes, tomorrow evening."

"Which means we've got the rest of today and most of tomorrow to get this place cleaned and everything as it should be for when they get home."

"Cleaned? Why?"

"Because we've been away a couple of weeks, more or less, and Marion won't be too happy if she comes home to a house that needs vacuuming and cleaning. Plus the grass needs cutting. If we don't sort it all out they're going to wonder what we've been doing."

"Suppose you're right," came the less than enthusiastic reply.

"Anyway, I need something to do to try and take my mind off things rather than just sitting and staring into space."

"You and me both. How about we sort the grass today and do the rest tomorrow?"

"Suits me."

◆

Neither of them woke much before noon the following day, Matt claiming that he found himself lying in bed waiting for the gong to summon him to breakfast. Cleaning the house and getting rid of any trace of their travels to and from 1898 didn't take as long as Connor had feared and everything was sorted to his — and he hoped to Marion's — satisfaction by early afternoon.

"Did they say what time this evening they were getting back?" Connor asked.

"'Bout six or thereabouts."

"Great. Gives me time for a nap first. I'm whacked."

◆

The sound of excited barking outside warned them that Matt's family had arrived home. Barney was first in and was racing wildly around the house.

"Hi, Matt, hi, Uncle Conn," chorused Ben and Paula, as they followed the collie in. "We've had a great time," Paula enthused. "You should have been there, they've got a swimming pool and everything. You must have had a boring time here by yourselves."

"It had its moments," Connor said, trying to stop Barney from ruining their cleaning efforts by peeing on the carpet in his excitement at being home. "Matt, can you cope with Barney whilst I go and help with the cases?"

"Sure," Matt said, and was then almost knocked flat when Barney leapt on him. "Get off, you stupid dog. Anyone would think you'd not seen me for six months!"

"Hello, you two," Connor said as Marion and Steve struggled into the house with some of the luggage. "Here, let me take some of those."

CHAPTER THIRTY-ONE

Past and present

Connor's phone woke him early the following Saturday.

"Yes?" he answered groggily.

"It's me."

"Matt?"

"Yes. What are you doing today?"

"I'm supposed to be going in to work to try and catch up on the backlog that built up whilst we were away, but I assume that you want me to do something that involves me not doing that?"

"Yes. Can you pick me up in half an hour?"

"I suppose so. What are we doing?"

"I want to know where they're buried. Helen and everyone. I want to know how long they lived, what they did, if they married."

"Are you sure about this? Everything's still very raw — you might just be making more misery for yourself."

"Maybe, but I just need to know."

"What are you going to tell your parents?"

"I'll just tell them that I want to spend the day with you. They won't mind."

"OK, I'll pick you up in half an hour."

◆

The young lady in the office was very helpful and looked through all the registers, but drew a blank. No-one named Debbon was buried anywhere in the rolling acres that made up the grounds of the Torquay cemetery.

"Maybe they just upped sticks and moved away after the fire," Matt said.

"I don't understand it. Maria was most emphatic that she was going to be buried next to her husband, who must have been buried locally. Even if they did all move away in later years, she would have made arrangements to have been brought back after she died."

"You don't think that instead they would have made arrangements to be buried in France? In the Royal Vaults for example? She was the Queen of France after all."

"I wouldn't have thought so. But we've now tried every cemetery and graveyard in Torquay and not a sign of any of them. And if they did all move away then I don't know how to go about finding out where they went. Let's get back to your place. Something may occur to me."

"I'd really like to know what happened to them. I can't sleep properly for worrying about them. I mean, I know that they survived the fire, but I want to know what they did with the rest of their lives. I need to know."

"We both need to know."

◆

They were both silent and subdued as Connor drove them back to Matt's house. When Matt had gone upstairs to his room, Marion took Connor to one side.

"Have you noticed anything different about Matt lately?" she asked him, keeping her voice low.

"In what way?" Connor asked.

"I don't really know how to explain it. He just seems so much more grown-up, so much more an adult than he did before we went away. It's as if he's had another two or three years added to him."

"Young people mature very quickly at his age. Maybe you just forgot how much he was growing when you went away."

"No, that's not it. It's like he's experienced a whole chunk of life in two weeks. And there's something else. He still laughs a lot, still plays the fool with Paula and Ben and still drives Barney insane, but underneath all that there seems to be a deep sadness in him somehow. I can see it in his eyes. I'm sure I've heard him crying late at night as well, although he always denies it when I ask him about it."

"Well, you know he split up with Karen?"

"Oh yes, but he's always splitting up with his girlfriends, as you well know. I don't think that Karen was any more special than any of the others. When we went away, he was still more boy than man, but now he isn't."

"It happens."

"In a fortnight?"

"Maybe he's just realised that he needs to buckle down and get on with his college work."

"Maybe," was the doubtful reply.

◆

It was a warm day, and Connor was sitting in the back garden nursing the coffee his brother had given him. He could hear shouts and laughs coming from deep inside the hedge at the bottom of the garden and after a few minutes saw Ben struggling free from the undergrowth to come racing up the lawn.

"Hi, Uncle Conn."

"Hi, Ben. What are you and Paula up to?"

"We've made a really neat den inside the hedge. Come and look!"

Connor followed the excited boy down the sloping lawn to the hedge that separated his brother's property from the neighbouring field. He'd never looked at the hedge too closely before. It was wild and unkempt, and it was only with a considerable effort that he was able to part some of the branches and follow his young nephew into the green dimness.

"It's just over here," Ben told him as Connor struggled his way after him. "There's some big stones that we've been able to use."

Connor's eyes slowly adjusted to the gloom and he could see that Ben had joined Paula at the bottom of a steep slope. He hauled himself over a couple of thick tree roots and hunkered down by their side.

"Whaddya think? Isn't it great?" Ben asked excitedly.

The hedge was far wider than Connor had imagined. He'd always assumed it was just a normal type of hedge, but could now see that it stretched a fair way down the hillside and would make a brilliant playground for his brother's children.

"It sure is," Connor agreed. "How long did it take the two of you to get it how you wanted it?"

"Ben and me have been working on it for ages," Paula told him proudly. "We couldn't get all the stones we wanted to, though. They're too heavy."

Connor looked around him and saw lumps of broken stonework lying everywhere. He looked closer and realised that there were also sections of fallen balustrade, evidently the remains of some of the Belmont terracing. A thought struck him and he peered back up the slope that he'd just clambered down and then in the opposite direction, to where another steep drop opened up.

"Mum says we're not allowed any further than here," Paula told him, seeing where Connor was looking. "She says it's too dangerous."

"She's probably right," Connor said, although his mind was elsewhere by then. A memory had struck him, a memory of something Mrs Debbon had said to him the day they parted. He scrambled back up the slope, out of the hedge and up the lawn to the house. Looking back, he tried to picture in his mind where the various garden terraces of Belmont would have stood. He eventually worked out that the hedge had to be on the site of the middle terrace. He sat back down on the bench again and picked up his now cold coffee. He was still deep in thought when Matt joined him a few minutes later, bursting into laughter as he looked at his uncle.

"What?" Connor asked.

"How did you get in such a mess?"

"Ben and Paula showed me the den they've made."

"That explains why you're currently sporting the 'hedge backwards' look then." Matt looked at Connor more closely. "But there's something else isn't there? I recognise the look."

"Yes. Did you ever play in the hedge when you were younger?"

"A bit. I was never as keen on it as Ben and Paula are though. Why?"

"Not totally sure yet. I'm still working it out. Do you know where your land stops?"

"What?"

"The land that goes with your property. How far does it stretch? Does it include the hedge?"

"Yes. The boundary is the other side of the hedge."

"You're sure? It includes all of the hedge? It stretches for some way, that hedge — it's a lot thicker than I realised."

"Sure I'm sure. Dad always told me to make certain I stayed inside the hedge if I ever went in there as if I came out on the other side then I'd be trespassing on the farmer's field. Not that I think Farmer Billy would have cared one way or the other, but I always stuck to the hedge."

"Have you been in there recently?"

"No, not for years now. Why?"

"Come on — let's go and look at the den your brother and sister have made."

"What on earth for?"

"You'll see when we get there."

◆

Ben and Paula, evidently tired of their den for the time being, passed them as they made their way down the lawn to the hedge.

"I'm going to show Matt your den," Connor told them.

"Just make sure he doesn't trash it," Paula told him. "He's very clumsy sometimes."

Matt ignored her as he also ignored his uncle's laughter. They forced their way into the hedge and down into the den.

"I'd forgotten how wild it is in here," Matt told him, looking round in some surprise.

"Look at the stones that they've dragged around. Do you recognise them?"

"Don't think so . . . Why?" He paused as it dawned on him what he was looking at. "Of course. It's some of the stones from the terraces of the Belmont gardens."

"Yes. In particular, the middle terrace."

"Yes, I suppose it would be," Matt replied, thinking things through.

"That slope we just scrambled down must be the remains of the supporting wall between the top and the middle terraces. And there's another steep drop just over there," Connor told him, pointing to the other side of the den. "That must be where the land falls down to the site of the lower terrace."

"Farmer Billy must graze his sheep where the lower terrace was. I hadn't realised."

"Nor had I, not until Ben dragged me down here. But there's more to it than just looking at broken stonework."

"You sound serious."

"Maybe. It's something that we need to decide. Or rather you do."

"What?"

"When I was talking with Maria, just before they left for Exeter, I asked her what she was going to do about the crown. She said she wasn't going to do anything. She never wanted to see it again. As far as she was concerned it could stay in its hiding place and rot."

"Are you trying to tell me that the crown is still here?"

"Almost certainly. As far as I know, there's never been any story about the crown of France ever being found. That means that either Maria came back for it at some point and hid it somewhere else — which I think is highly unlikely — or it's still here, buried underneath the rubble."

"But we'd never find it — not under all that lot."

"Don't be so sure of that. The tunnel that led to the icehouse was very solidly built and may well have survived. We could work out more or less where the door would have been. In fact, I'd say it was probably just about there," Connor told him, pointing to a spot further along the hedge. "I reckon that would be about right. It wouldn't be easy to dig through to it, I'll grant you, but not impossible. The question is — do you want to?"

"But even if we found it, would it belong to us?"

"Now that I'm not sure about. I know that things can be

declared to be treasure, what used to be called treasure trove, but that applies when the owners can't be found. In the case of the crown, I assume it would belong to the French Royal Family, or whichever branch of the family was claiming to be the rightful heirs, or possibly the French government."

"But not the Debbon family?"

"No. Even if there were descendants, then I doubt they'd know of their claim. If neither Maria nor Helen passed on the information to the next generation then they wouldn't know anything about it."

"So even if we found it, then we wouldn't get anything out of it. It would go to the rightful owners."

"Yes and no. I strongly suspect that you'd get a percentage of its value as the finders."

"How much would that be?"

"Almost certainly into the millions."

"Wow. I wouldn't need to worry about my exam results with that sort of money!"

"You really worried about them?"

"Yes. I missed a lot of revision time whilst we were away and I'm struggling to catch up. What would you do with your share?"

"My share?"

"Of course. You don't think that dad would keep it all to himself, do you?"

"I wouldn't want any of it. If there was a share for me, then you'd be welcome to it."

"But that's stupid!"

"Maybe. But it would feel wrong somehow."

"Not to me."

"That's why I said you'd got to decide what you wanted to do. If you want to dig it up, then we could say that we've been doing research on the history of Belmont, discovered a plan showing the tunnel to the icehouse, went looking for it and found the crown by accident."

"And you really wouldn't want a share?"

"No."

"But would you still help me with looking for it?"

"Of course. I don't have a problem with that. When would you want to start?"

"Now?"

"Let's make it tomorrow. We've spent most of the today traipsing round cemeteries and I'm bushed."

"Tomorrow it is then. I can't wait to see the look on mum and dad's face when they see the crown!"

◆

Leaving the hedge, they toiled back up the lawn to the house, Connor collapsing on the bench just outside the back door.

"Do me a favour and get me another coffee, will you?" Connor asked. "I left most of the last one and it's gone stone cold."

"Sure," Matt replied, heading indoors.

Whilst waiting for Matt to return with his coffee, Connor gazed at the view across the Daccombe valley, the same view that had obviously attracted the builders of Belmont. The distant tower of Coffinswell church thrust upwards from behind a belt of trees. Connor stared at the grey tower for some time before suddenly sitting bolt upright. He jumped to his feet and dashed through to the kitchen.

"Whatever's the matter?" Matt asked, noting his uncle's flushed face.

"Nothing, but I've just realised something. Your house — it's the wrong side of the road!"

"What are you gibbering about? It's always been this side of the road."

"I mean it's the wrong side of the road for Torquay."

"But all of this area is in Torquay," Matt said, wondering what on earth had got his uncle so excited.

"Your house may officially be in Torquay, but not for church purposes. Everything this side of the road is in the parish of Coffinswell. That means that the Debbons would have been buried in the churchyard at Coffinswell, not in any of the churchyards in Torquay. We've been looking in the wrong place!"

"You sure?"

"I'm certain. I should have realised straight away."

"Well, don't beat yourself up about it. I live here and I didn't know."

"Grab a coat. I'll get the car started."

◆

The churchyard in early May was not the bleak place that might have been expected. A sea of wild flowers carpeted the area between the old grey headstones, and shafts of late afternoon sunshine warmed them as they hunted through the rows of lichen-covered headstones.

"Over here," Connor called softly, indicating a row of headstones beneath the branches of a moss-covered tree. They read the simple inscriptions in silence.

LEWIS ROBERT DEBBON 1851–1888
AND MARIA DEBBON 1855–1941

DANIEL HARDWICK, 1882–1957
AND HELEN HARDWICK
NÉE DEBBON 1880–1965

MARY-ANNE DEBBON 1886–1972

"So Mary-Anne didn't marry Bill after all," Connor said after a time. "Perhaps Maria felt that the differences between their positions were just too great."

"But Helen married Daniel," Matt said.

"You weren't there anymore," Connor said quietly. "Daniel was."

"I know, but it still hurts," he said, and buried his face against Connor's shoulder, who said nothing, just held him.

"I'm sorry, I know I'm being stupid, but I can't help it. I'm in love with someone who died before I was born," Matt said after a while. "She grew older, married, had a long life and then died. If she remembered me at all, it would have been as a distant and hazy memory. Yet as far as I'm concerned we only parted a week ago. It's so unfair."

"No-one ever said life was fair. But I don't believe for a moment that she'd have forgotten you. Not ever. Even though she married Daniel, you'd still have been there in her mind. You were her first love. You don't forget something like that, no matter what life throws your way."

"Do you think she was happy?" Matt asked after a while.

"We can probably find out, if you really want to."

"How?"

"Look underneath the names on the inscription."

Beneath the names of Daniel and Helen was added the following:

IN LOVING MEMORY OF OUR PARENTS
AND GRANDPARENTS
FROM THEIR GRIEVING CHILDREN
AND GRANDCHILDREN

Matt looked enquiringly at Connor.

"It means that Daniel and Helen had children and grand-children. Some of the grandchildren may well still be alive, and could be living in this area. If we could trace them, we could ask them about their grandparents."

"But we could never tell them what really happened. They'd never believe us."

"We'll think of something. Perhaps we could say we're doing research for a local history project or something."

"Where would we start?"

"We could start just by looking in the phone book. If any of the children and grandchildren were boys, they'll have the same surname, so we could check to see if there are any Hardwicks listed."

"Then what?"

"We phone them with this local history story, to see if they're descendants of Helen and Daniel. Incidentally, did you notice something about the graves?"

"Yes. There's one missing. Charles isn't there."

"So he at least flew the coop. If we find any descendants locally they might be able to tell us what happened to him."

"OK, seems a good idea."

They were leaving the churchyard when Connor suddenly stopped in his tracks.

"What's up?" Matt asked.

"Just a thought. And not a very pleasant one."

"I don't understand."

"I just hope I'm wrong."

Connor walked back into the churchyard, opened the heavy oak door of the church itself and entered the simple and airy interior. Connor searched the walls followed by a mystified Matt. He eventually halted in front of a stone tablet on the south wall, engraved with a list of names. There were very few of them, so it was a matter of seconds before Connor found what he was looking for.

"Oh, dear God, no. What a waste! What a sheer, bloody, useless waste!"

"What is it, what's the matter?" Matt asked in alarm.

"Look there, on the memorial."

Matt looked where his uncle was pointing. And then he could see what had so upset him. And he understood why Charles wasn't in the cemetery.

TO THE GLORY OF GOD AND IN HONOURED
REMEMBRANCE OF THOSE WHO GAVE THEIR LIVES
IN THE GREAT WAR, 1914–1918
CAPTAIN LEWIS CHARLES DEBBON
9TH BATTALION THE DEVONSHIRE REGIMENT
FELL AT MAMETZ JULY 1916.

"I should have thought of that," Connor said, making no effort to stem his tears. "He'd have been in his twenties when the

First World War broke out."

"So he'd have been called up?"

"I doubt they'd have needed to call him up. He'd have enlisted. It was the thing to do. Daniel and Bill would have gone as well, but Daniel evidently survived. It makes me wonder if Bill wasn't killed as well. It would explain why Mary-Anne never married."

"How would we find that out?"

"If he'd been killed then he'd be on the war memorial either in Torquay or St Marychurch. We need to check."

Matt wasn't able to answer, his throat closed up with emotion. The two of them just stared at the memorial, each remembering Charles as a boy, chasing round Belmont and laughing at the top of his voice. They walked to the door in silence. As they were about to leave, an elderly man entered the church, greeted them and then walked towards the vestry.

"Excuse me," Connor called after him.

"Yes? Can I help you?"

"Would you know anything about the war memorial over on the wall?" Connor asked.

"I'm one of the churchwardens, but I'm afraid that there are no records of who sculpted the memorial, if that's what you wished to know."

Connor explained that it was one of the names they were interested in, not the actual memorial.

"In that case, I could be able to help. I've been undertaking research on those from the parish who fell in both world wars."

"We were looking at the name here, Lewis Charles Debbon," Connor said. "He died at Mametz and may be an ancestor of ours."

"Ah, I can certainly help you there. It was a well-known story at the time, although sadly it's all but forgotten these days. It seems that three local men all joined up shortly after the outbreak of the war."

"Three men?"

"Yes. There was Lewis Charles Debbon, Daniel Hardwick and William Stone. All three were great friends and they all joined the

Devonshire Regiment on the same day. They stuck to each other like glue, each of them looking out for the other two. And then they got involved in the sheer hell that was the Battle of the Somme. Both Captain Debbon and Lieutenant Hardwick were wounded in the first attack on the German lines at Mametz and were in a very exposed position. Second Lieutenant Stone left the safety of the trenches and crawled out to where they were both lying.

"He could see that Captain Debbon was the more badly hurt, so he single-handedly pulled him back through the mud to the British trenches, even though he was under constant fire. Once he'd seen Captain Debbon down to the first aid post, he went out again to get Lieutenant Hardwick. He was then wounded himself in the leg but crawled on to where Lieutenant Hardwick was lying. He managed to drag him most of the way back but was then hit again. Lieutenant Hardwick told him to leave him there, to save himself, but Lieutenant Stone was having none of it. He slowly, inch by inch, hauled his friend to safety. They both fell into the trench and were immediately helped by the medical orderlies. Sadly, Lieutenant Stone's injuries proved fatal. They couldn't stop the bleeding and he died a few hours later. Captain Debbon also succumbed to his injuries later that day. Happily, Lieutenant Hardwick made a full recovery. They awarded Second Lieutenant Stone a posthumous Victoria Cross. He and Captain Debbon were buried side by side in the Devonshire Cemetery at Mametz."

"Thank you," Connor said.

"You're most welcome," was the reply. "I hope that I've answered your question?"

"You've answered several questions," Connor assured him.

"In which case I'll bid you both good-day," the man said, lifting his hat to them.

"Good-day to you as well," Connor said as they left the church.

"Now we know why Mary-Anne didn't marry," Matt said, once they were outside. "She couldn't have Bill so she wouldn't have anyone."

"And he ended up a hero. No doubt he'd have said that it weren't nuffink. 'E were jus' doin' 'is job — lookin' aht for 'em all," Connor said, in a fair imitation of Bill's slang.

"But it cost him his life."

"He wouldn't have wanted it any other way," Connor told him. "And Charles made it to France after all. And so a King of France and a cockney urchin lie side by side in a foreign field."

"Mrs Debbon must have been devastated."

"No doubt. As Bill's family would have been. And Mary-Anne. And countless others who lost loved ones at the time. And all for a few yards of stinking mud. Well, we said we wanted to know what happened to them. Now we do. So why don't I feel any better?"

"Because we remember them as children and not as the men they would have been when they went to war?"

"Maybe."

"Uncle Conn, I've changed my mind."

"What, about wanting to know about Helen?"

"No. About the crown. I'll take my chances with my exam results and hope they're good enough to let me take the A-Level courses I need to get me into uni. Let the crown stay hidden. I don't want anything to do with it. It wouldn't be right."

"Sure?"

"Positive."

"You can always change your mind later if you wanted to."

"I won't."

"Come on then, let's see if there's a happier story about Helen and Daniel."

"I really hope so."

◆

A trawl through the local directory caught a number of Hardwicks. Working his way through them, Connor found that most were incomers to the area, and had no local connections.

"Of course, if most or all the children were girls, then they'd have changed names when they married," Connor said, after another fruitless call. "Still, there are another three to go."

The last but one Hardwick in the list produced results.

"I think we're on to something," Connor said, his hand cupped over the mouthpiece of the phone. "This Mrs Hardwick says her husband's grandmother was called Helen, and his family have lived in this area for several generations."

He returned to the call, making arrangements to visit her and her husband the following Saturday afternoon.

◆

Connor picked up Matt in his car shortly after lunchtime on the Saturday and drove to the address Mrs Hardwick had given him. It was only a mile or so from Matt's house and they were there in minutes.

"Nervous?" Connor asked as they knocked at the door.

"Very. Stupid, isn't it."

"No, it isn't, not after what we've been through."

The door opened, and they were invited in. The Hardwicks were an elderly couple and after the preliminary introductions, Mr Hardwick produced a large photograph album.

"My grandma Helen were a barrel o' laughs," he told them as he leafed through the pages. "She and grandpa Daniel were always laughing and joking. When I went to stay with them when I were a kid, it were a real treat and I were never bored. Ah, here are the ones I were looking for. Seems that most of the family photographs were destroyed when Belmont burned down, but there were just one set that by chance were still at the local photographers being developed. Grandma managed to collect them later."

He handed the book over to Connor who looked at the pictures neatly stuck in the pages. There were the faces of Helen, Mary-Anne, Charles, Bill and Daniel smiling out at them. Something ran delicate fingers up and down Connor's spine as he looked at the pictures and recognised Matt in some of them.

"Would you know who's who in the photos?" he asked Mr Hardwick.

"Yes," he said. "Grandma often showed me these photos when I were staying." He named all the characters, except Matt. "It seems that fella there," he said, pointing to a photo of Matt in a group with some of the others, "was some young man that she'd taken a real shine to, but I don't know his name.'"

It was fortunate, Connor thought to himself, that with the photos being in black and white and with Matt wearing his 1898 clothes, it would take someone using a magnifying glass to pick Matt out. Otherwise that could prove to be a problem that they wouldn't be able to explain.

"That photo there," Mr Hardwick continued, indicating a particular shot, "she were always talking about. She said it were taken by the lad she had a liking for."

Connor took the album from him and showed it to Matt. The picture was the one that Matt had taken of Helen in the garden, her face framed by flowers.

"She were quite taken with him, it seems," Mr Hardwick continued, "but he left suddenly after the fire. She tried hard to find out where he'd gone, but he'd seemingly disappeared off the face of the earth. Grandma used to get quite upset whenever she talked about it."

Matt said nothing as he stared at the smiling face in the photograph, but Connor could see the glitter of tears in his eyes.

"Grandpa Daniel told me once that he thought grandma had settled for him as second best. They were happy together, as I said, but he always thought that if this other young man hadn't suddenly gone off like he did, then grandma would've married him."

"And what did your grandpa do for a living?"

"He were quite well-to-do at one time. His pa owned several cargo ships and grandpa Daniel inherited them when his own pa died. Over half of them were sunk in the Second World War and things were always a bit tighter after that, but they lived well enough, even so."

"And how many children did they have?"

"Two — my pa and his older brother. My uncle took over the

company when grandpa retired but he weren't no businessman like grandpa Daniel were. It weren't long before trade started to fall off and most of the ships were laid up. After a while most of them went for scrap. Grandpa Daniel weren't pleased and nor were my pa neither. My uncle emigrated to Australia a few years after that."

"And your grandma Helen? Did she help in the company when your grandpa still ran it?"

"She certainly did. Real go-getter, my grandma. Grandpa Daniel told me that his own pa had a woman as a manager. She'd been the housekeeper at Belmont, but after the fire she went to work for great-grandpa. Took to it like a duck to water, even though it were frowned on — a woman helping to run a business. Anyway, after she retired, my grandma took over as manager. That really caused eyebrows to be raised!"

"I bet it did," Matt said.

"Oh yes! Seems that some of the other shipping firms suggested that grandpa should persuade her that it wasn't a job for a real lady."

"Did he try?" Matt asked.

"Not him — he had more sense than to try! Grandma Helen wouldn't have taken kindly to that at all. Grandpa tended to go along with whatever she suggested. He told me it were easier that way. One of the first things she made him do after they got married was to buy a motor-car."

"What was unusual about that? They'd have been quite common by then, wouldn't they?" Connor asked.

"Oh yes, but grandma were the first woman in Torquay to learn to drive one. She used to take it out regular, like. Grandpa rarely got the chance to drive it himself!"

"That figures," Matt muttered under his breath.

"Your great-grandmother, Maria Debbon, she was really wealthy, wasn't she? It must have taken a fortune to maintain a property the size of Belmont," Connor said.

"Oh yes. Even when they moved to a smaller property, grandma said that they still had a large staff and money were never a problem. But when great-uncle Charles were killed in the Great War, great-grandma set up a charity to help look after the wounded who weren't able to find work after the war were over. Most of the family money were put into a trust to run the charity. It's still going strong today, helping ex-servicemen who can't find work."

"Good for her," Connor smiled.

"Not everyone agreed, of course. Some said she were mad to give away most of her fortune, but she took no notice. Great-aunt Mary-Anne became the Chairman of the Board of Trustees. She'd lost someone in the Great War, a young local lad called William Stone. He saved grandpa's life in the war."

"Yes, we heard that story, about the three friends all joining up at the same time."

"That's right. Anyway, this William Stone, he came from a very poor family who moved down from London. Great-aunt Mary-Anne took a real liking to him even when they were still children. Great-grandma must have taken a shine to him as well because she paid for him to go to a private school and get a proper education. It were hard for him at first as some of the other pupils made fun of him, but it seems he soon won most of them round."

"So your great-aunt lost her intended in the war, your great-grandma lost her son in the war, and your grandma lost her mysterious admirer some years earlier?"

"That's right, but it weren't only grandma that lost an admirer."

"Really?" Connor said, rather startled at the information.

"Seems that the young man that grandma had taken a shine to were staying at Belmont with his uncle. Grandma told me that her ma had fallen for him in the same way that she'd fallen for his nephew. She was just as upset as grandma were when they both disappeared."

Matt glanced at his uncle, who seemed to be stumped for what to say in response.

"I wonder if I could ask a favour of you," Connor said eventually. "Would it be possible to have copies of these photographs for the project that we're doing? I'd pay all the costs of course."

"Don't see why not. You're welcome to borrow them to have copies made, but I'd appreciate them back safe and sound."

"I will take very great care of them, I promise," Connor told him. "I can have them copied and back to you in a couple of days."

As they were speaking there was a thump from above them.

"Sorry about that," Mrs Hardwick told them. "That'll be our granddaughter sorting her stuff out. My daughter and son-in-law have been living up country for the last twenty years, but they've decided to come back here to live. The three of them are staying here for a few weeks while they're buying their own place."

She went to the door and called up the stairs.

"Come down a minute, can you, dear? We've guests I'd like you to meet. They're doing some research into local families."

Footsteps descended the stairs and a teenage girl entered the room. Matt jumped out of his chair when he saw her.

"Helen!"

"No, my name's Rachel," she said, looking rather taken aback at Matt's reaction.

Connor stood up and put his hand on Matt's shoulder.

"I'm sorry," he said, "we've just been looking at the photographs that your grandparents kindly showed us. You're the exact likeness of your great-great-grandmother. It was almost as if she'd just walked into the room. I'm Connor by the way, and this lump is my nephew, Matt."

Rachel looked over at the photos.

"Oh, the one with the flowers. I've heard the story of that one many times. It's a lovely picture. Such a shame it's in black and white. I've always wanted to know what colour those flowers were."

"A very deep pink," Matt told her.

"Really? How can you tell?"

"Oh, well, it's clematis montana. We had one like it at home so I recognised it," Matt said, mentally kicking himself.

443

"I recognised it as well," Mrs Hardwick said, "but that strain of clematis comes in lots of different colours."

"I'm quite into photography," Connor said, trying to lift his nephew out of the hole he'd dug for himself. "You can often tell what colour something should be in a black and white photograph by the shade of grey. I'd say Matt was right — definitely a deep pink."

"That's great," Rachel said. "That makes the picture so much better. It means I can imagine the scene a lot more easily if I know what colour everything was. What about the dress?"

"I'd say a very pale yellow with deeper yellow trimmings," Connor told her, trying to visualise it in his mind.

"Thank you, that's brilliant. Do you live locally," she asked, turning to Matt.

He had to swallow hard before he was able to answer.

"Yes, only a mile up the road."

"Mum and Dad are out trying to sort out a college for me at the moment. They're looking at somewhere called Winterbourne. Do you know it?"

"Yes, it's where I go."

"That's lucky. What's it like?"

"OK, I suppose. Better than most round here, anyway."

He paused, not knowing quite what to say.

"It's only about three miles from here," Connor interrupted. "Why don't you come with us and I'll drive over that way and you can have a look. Matt can show you round if you want. That way at least you'd know your bearings before you got there. Might make it easier for you."

"Would they be open at weekends?"

"Oh, sure," Matt said. "They take boarders as well as day pupils so the place is always open. And the sports facilities are used all the time, anyway. Are you interested in sports?"

"I enjoy watching most sports, but as for taking part, then it's mainly swimming. Are there many good swimmers there?"

Matt wasn't at all sure how to answer that one, but Connor just grinned.

"My nephew is wondering how to tell you that he's a champion swimmer without it making it sound as if he's boasting," he told her.

"Really?" she replied. "You wouldn't be Matthew Harvey by any chance?"

"Yes," was the startled response. "But how on earth did you know that?"

"I did some research to see who had won the local competitions and galas. Your name was usually there somewhere. I was going to see if I could find a way to meet you. Now I don't have to."

"You two should get along fine," Connor told them. "Let's get you in the car and I'll run you over to the college."

Connor noted that Matt, who usually insisted on sitting in the front passenger seat no matter who else was in the car, sat in the back with Rachel on the ride to Winterbourne College. He drove into the car park and said he'd wait for them, before driving them both back to their respective homes. Seeing the way the two of them were walking closely side by side as they strolled towards the entrance, Connor settled himself more comfortably in his seat and turned the radio on. It was likely, he thought, that he was in for a very long wait.

Collinswell Church

AFTERWORD

This is a work of fiction. As far as I am aware, there was no fire in which an entire family died at any time in Torquay in 1898. The setting, though, is as accurate as I am able to make it. Torquay in 1898 was just starting its gradual transformation from a winter resort for the wealthy into a summer resort for families. There are accurate weather reports for the period, so if in the book it was fine and sunny on a particular day, then it was so in fact. Torquay Reference Library does indeed hold full sets of all the local newspapers and the members of staff there are invariably helpful and knowledgeable on matters of local history. The description of the Belgrave Hotel and its owners is accurate, and Monsieur Lerida did come over from Paris to manage it. The Union Hotel stood towards the bottom of Union Street and had been greatly enlarged only three years before Connor and Matt booked in for three days in 1898. It was a favourite with commercial travellers and the charges per room were much less than the larger hotels that catered for the wealthier visitors. It was demolished in the 1960s and replaced with shops. The Grand Hotel did have humble beginnings, opening in 1881 as the Great Western Hotel and with just twelve letting rooms. It was renamed the Grand Hotel in 1887 and enlarged following its purchase by J. B. Gilley, but by 1898 it still had only twenty-two letting rooms. Barton Hall (which still stands) was in the ownership of the Brown family at the time of the book, but I have no information whether the master of the house in 1898 was a lover of automobiles or not.

The great mansion of Belmont did not exist, save in my imagination, although its site is real enough and is located to the north of the Kingskerswell Road, a few hundred yards west of Barton Cross. If you stand there and look north-west, there is a magnificent view across the valley and towards the tors of Dartmoor. The land does slope steeply down to the lane that leads to Daccombe, meaning any gardens on the site would have had to be terraced. The woods to the west, where the watchers hid themselves, are as described. I have, however, taken a slight liberty

447

with the geography as there isn't enough level land at the top of the slope to support even a modest dwelling, let alone a mansion the size of Belmont. Its site would have placed it in Coffinswell parish, the tower of whose church can easily be seen from there. The church does contain a war memorial on its south wall to those who fell in the Great War, but anyone who visits will search it in vain for the name "Debbon".

As for the historical basis for the story, the information concerning the French elections in May 1898 is accurate, as is the story of the Dreyfus Affair and the open letter, known as "J'accuse", written by Emile Zola. Philippe Delorme did carry out DNA testing on some of the remains of the child King Louis XVII and that of Queen Marie Antoinette as I have described. It is true that the marriage of Louis XVI and Marie Antoinette remained unconsummated for a number of years, probably due to the King suffering from a sexual dysfunction (possibly phimosis) and it was even longer before the couple were able to have children. It is, therefore, widely accepted that the Queen did take the Swedish diplomat Count Axel Fersen as her lover, a liaison that continued even after the birth of the royal couple's first two children.

It is also true that there have been many stories of the boy-king Louis XVII being smuggled out of the Temple Prison, but all have been proved false. So far!